Dear Reader,

I'm thrilled to present my brand-new paranormal trilogy, Lords of the Underworld, which began with *The Darkest Night* and continues with *The Darkest Kiss*. In a remote fortress in Budapest, six immortal warriors—each more dangerously seductive than the last—are bound by an ancient curse none has been able to break. When a powerful enemy returns, they will travel the world in search of a sacred relic of the gods—one that threatens to destroy them all.

Join me on a journey through this darkly sensual world, where the line between good and evil blurs and true love is put to the ultimate test.

Wishing you all the best,

Gena Showalter

Gena Showalter

THE
DARKEST KISS

HQN™

ISBN 13: 978-0-373-77232-2
ISBN-10:   0-373-77232-7

THE DARKEST KISS

To Karen Marie Moning. Thank you!
Your talent constantly amazes me,
and your generosity blesses me.

To Kresley Cole. You would let me
wear your skin if at all possible—and I won't
mention what you'd let me do to your eyeballs,
though I will thank you for it—and for that, I will
always be in your debt. Also, sorry I stole your
bike pump and blamed it on Slurpie!

To Marjorie Liu. Because you spank on
and there's nothing cooler!

To Jill Monroe. You are a sister of my heart—
hearter? sisart?—and even though you stole my
gnome, I can't imagine a life without you.
For realsies.

And to Tracy Farrell, Margo Lipschultz and all the
wonderful people at Harlequin Books who have
blessed me in countless ways. You're making all my
dreams come true! Art director Kathleen Oudit and
designer Juliana Kolesova—I owe you big-time!
The lips on this cover…Shiver! And you didn't
blink twice when I mentioned one brown eye and
one blue eye.

Thank you, Low Down members, for your support! And thank you to Kerensa Wilson and Elaine Spencer for all you do! You are both amazing women.

PROLOGUE

HE WAS KNOWN AS THE Dark One. Malach ha-Maet. Yama. Azreal. Shadow Walker. Mairya. King of the Dead. He was all of those things and more, for he was a Lord of the Underworld.

Long ago he had opened *dimOuniak*, a powerful box made from the bones of a goddess, unleashing a horde of demons upon the earth. As punishment, he and the warriors who aided him were forced to house those demons inside themselves, melding light and darkness, order and chaos, until they were barely able to retain any tether on the disciplined warriors they'd once been.

Because he was the one to open the box, he had been given the demon of Death. A fair exchange, he supposed, for his action had nearly caused the demise of the world.

Now he was charged with the responsibility of collecting human souls and escorting them to their final resting place. Even if he opposed the idea. He did not like taking innocents from their families, found no joy in delivering the wicked to their damnation, but he did both without question or hesitation. Resistance, he'd soon learned, brought something far worse than death to his door. Resistance brought an agony so complete, so inexorable, even the gods trembled at the thought.

Did his obedience mean he was gentle? Caring? Nurturing? No. Oh, no. He could not afford softer emotion. Love, compassion and mercy were enemies to his plight.

Anger, though? Rage? *Those* he sometimes embraced.

Woe to anyone who pushed him too far, for man would become fully demon. A beast. A sinister entity who would not hesitate to curl his fingers around a human heart and squeeze. Squeeze so tightly that human would lose his breath and beg for the sweet kiss of eternal sleep only he could offer.

Oh, yes. Man had a very short leash on demon. And if you weren't careful, they would come for you....

CHAPTER ONE

ANYA, GODDESS OF ANARCHY, daughter of Lawlessness, and dealer of disorder, stood on the edge of a crowded dance floor. All of the dancers were human females, beautiful and nearly naked, chosen specifically by the Lords of the Underworld to provide the night's entertainment. Both vertical and horizontal.

Wisps of smoke cast a dream-fog around them, and pinpricks of starlight rained from the swirling strobe, illuminating everything inside the darkened nightclub in slow, sweeping circles. From the corner of her eye, she caught a scintillating glimpse of a taut immortal ass pounding forward, back, forward, into an ecstatic female.

My kind of party, she thought with a wicked grin. Not that she'd been invited.

Like anything could have stopped me from coming, though.

The Lords of the Underworld were delectable immortal warriors who were possessed by the demon spirits that had once resided inside Pandora's box. And now, with a few rounds of hard liquor and even harder sex, they were saying goodbye to Budapest, the city they'd called home for hundreds of years.

Anya wanted in on the action. With one warrior in particular.

"Part," she whispered, fighting her intrinsic compulsion to

shout "Fire" instead and watch as the humans raced away in a panic, screaming hysterically. *Let the good times roll.*

An erratic pulse of rock music that matched the erratic beat of her heart blasted from the speakers, making it impossible for anyone to hear her. They obeyed, anyway, compelled on a level they probably didn't understand.

A path cleared, slowly…so slowly….

Finally the object of her fascination came into view. Heated breath caught in her lungs, and she shivered. Lucien. Deliciously scarred, irresistibly stoic and possessed by the spirit of Death. Right now he sat at a table in back, expression blank as he stared up at Reyes, his friend and fellow immortal.

What were they saying? If Lucien wanted the keeper of Pain to procure one of those mortal women for him, a false declaration of "fire" would be the least of their worries. Teeth grinding together, Anya tilted her head to the side, zoned in on them while discarding all surrounding noise, and listened.

"—she was right. I checked the satellite photos on Torin's computer. Those temples *are* rising from the sea." Reyes knocked back the contents of the silver flask he held. "One is in Greece and one is in Rome, and if they continue to rise at such a swift rate, they'll be high enough to explore sometime tomorrow."

"Why do humans not know about them?" Lucien scrubbed his jaw with two strong fingers, a habit of his. "Paris has watched the news stations and there has been nothing. Not even speculation."

Silly boy, she thought, relieved sex was not the night's topic. *You know about them only because I wanted you to know.* No one else would—or could—see them. She had made sure of that with a sweet little thing called chaos, her strongest source of power, hiding the temples with storms to keep humans away, while at the same time feeding the Lords enough information to draw them the hell out of Buda.

She wanted Lucien out of Buda and off his game. Just for a little while. A disconcerted man was easier to control.

Reyes sighed. "Perhaps the new gods are responsible. Most days I am sure they hate us and long to destroy us, simply for being half-demon."

Lucien's expression remained blank. "Does not matter who is responsible. We will travel in the morning as planned. My hands itch to search one of those temples."

Reyes tossed the now-empty flask onto the table. His fingers curled around the top of one of the chairs, his knuckles slowly bleaching of color. "If we're lucky, we'll find that damned box while we're there."

Anya ran her tongue over her teeth. Damned box, aka *dim-Ouniak*, aka Pandora's box. Constructed from the bones of the goddess of Oppression, the box was powerful enough to contain demons so vile even hell had not been able to hold them. It was also powerful enough to suck those same demons out of the Lords, their once unwilling hosts. Now these wonderfully aggressive warriors were dependent on the beasts for their survival, and needless to say, they wanted the box for themselves.

Again, Lucien nodded. "Do not think about that now; there'll be time enough for that tomorrow. Go and enjoy the rest of your evening. Do not waste another moment in my boring presence."

Boring? Ha! Anya had never met anyone who excited her more.

Reyes hesitated before ambling off, leaving Lucien alone. None of the human women approached him. Looked at him, yes. Cringed when they saw his scars, sure. But none of them wanted anything to do with him—and that saved their lives.

He's taken, biyatches.

"Notice me," Anya commanded softly.

A moment passed. He didn't obey.

Several humans glanced in her direction, heeding her demand, but Lucien's gaze latched on to the empty flask in front of him and remained, becoming a wee bit wistful. Much to her consternation, immortals were immune to her commands. A *courtesy* of the gods.

"Bastards," she muttered. Any restrictions they could place on her, they did. "Anything to screw with lowly Anarchy."

Anya hadn't been favored during her days on Mount Olympus. The goddesses had never liked her because they assumed she was a replica of her "whore of a mother" and would jump their husbands. Likewise, the gods had never respected her, again because of her mother. The guys *had* wanted her, though. Well, until she'd killed their precious Captain of the Guard and they'd deemed her too feral.

Idiots. The captain had deserved what she'd done to him. Hell, he'd deserved worse. The little shit had tried to rape her. If he had left her alone, she would have left *him* alone. But *noooo*. She didn't regret cutting the black heart out of his chest, didn't regret placing said heart on a pike in front of Aphrodite's temple. Not even a tiny bit. Freedom of choice was precious, and anyone who tried to take hers away would feel the sting of her daggers.

Choice. The word rang inside her mind, bringing her back to the present. What the hell would it take to convince Lucien to choose her?

"Notice me, Lucien. Please."

Once again, he ignored her.

She stomped her foot. For weeks she'd cloaked herself in invisibility, following Lucien, watching, studying. And yes, lusting. He'd had no idea she lurked nearby, even as she willed

him to do all sorts of naughty things: strip, pleasure himself…
smile. Okay, so the last wasn't naughty. But she'd wanted to
see his beautifully flawed face light in humor just as much as
she'd wanted to see his naked body glisten with arousal.

Had he granted even that benign request, though? No!

A part of her wished she'd never seen him, that she hadn't
allowed Cronus, the new king of the gods, to intrigue her with
stories about the Lords a few months ago. *Maybe* I'm *the
idiot.*

Cronus had just escaped Tartarus, a prison for immortals
and a place she knew intimately. He'd imprisoned Zeus and
his cohorts there, as well as Anya's parents. When Anya
returned for them, Cronus had been waiting for her. He had
demanded Anya's greatest treasure. She'd declined—duh—
so he'd tried to scare her.

*Give me what I want or I'll send the Lords of the Under-
world after you. They are demon-possessed, as blood-hungry
as starving animals, and they will not hesitate to peel the
lovely flesh from your bones.* Blah, blah, blah. Whatever.

Far from frightening her, his words had caused excitement
to bloom. She'd ended up seeking out the warriors on her own.
She'd thought to defeat them and laugh in Cronus's face, a
sort of look-what-I-did-to-your-big-scary-demons kind of
thing.

One glance at Lucien, though, and she'd become instantly
obsessed. She'd forgotten her reasons for being there and had
even *aided* the supposedly malevolent warriors.

It was just that contradictions tantalized her, and Lucien had
so very many. He was scarred but not broken, kind but unbend-
ing. He was a calm, by-the-book immortal, not blood-hungry
as Cronus had claimed. He was possessed by an evil spirit, yet
he never deviated from his own personal code of honor. He
dealt with death every day, every night, yet he fought to live.

Fascinating.

As if that wasn't enough to prick her interest, his flowery fragrance filled her with decadent, wicked thoughts every time she neared him. Why? Any other man who smelled like roses would have made her laugh. With Lucien, her mouth watered for a taste of him and her skin prickled with white-hot awareness, desperate for his touch.

Even now, simply looking at him and imagining that scent wafting to her nose, she had to rub her arms to rid herself of goose bumps. But then she thought about *him* rubbing her, and the delicious shivers refused to go away.

Gods, he was sexy. He had the freakiest eyes she'd ever seen. One was blue, the other brown, and both swirled with the essence of man and demon. And his scars… All she could think of, dream about, *crave,* was licking them. They were beautiful, a testament to all the pain and suffering he'd survived.

"Hey, gorgeous. Dance with me," one of the warriors suddenly said at her side.

Paris, she realized, recognizing the promise of sensuality in his voice. He must have finished screwing that human against the wall and was now looking for another bimbo to sate himself on. He'd just have to keep looking. "Go away."

Unaffected by her lack of interest, he grabbed her waist. "You'll like it, I swear."

She brushed him aside with a flick of her wrist. Possessed by Promiscuity, Paris was blessed with pale, almost glittery skin, electric-blue eyes, and a face the angels probably sang hallelujahs over, but he wasn't Lucien and he did nothing for her.

"Keep your hands to yourself," she muttered, "before I cut them off."

He laughed as if she were joking, unaware she'd do that

and more. She might deal in petty disorder, but she never uttered a threat she didn't plan to see through. To do so smacked of weakness, and Anya had vowed long ago never to show a single hint of weakness.

Her enemies would love nothing more than to exploit it.

Thankfully, Paris didn't reach for her again. "For a kiss," he said huskily, "I'll let you do anything you want to my hands."

"In that case, I'll cut off your cock, too." She didn't like having her ogling interrupted, especially since she rarely had time to indulge. Nowadays, she spent most of her waking hours dodging Cronus. "How's that?"

Paris's laughter intensified and managed to snag Lucien's attention. Lucien's gaze lifted, first landing on Paris, then locking on Anya. Her knees almost buckled. Oh, sweet heaven. Paris was forgotten as she fought to breathe. Did she imagine the fire that suddenly sparked in Lucien's mismatched eyes? Did she imagine the way his nostrils flared in awareness?

Now or never. Licking her lips, never removing her gaze from him, she eased into a sensual bump and grind and made her way toward his table. Halfway, she stopped and motioned for him to join her with a crook of her finger. He stood in front of her a moment later, as if he'd been pulled by an invisible chain, unable to resist.

Up close, he was six-feet-six of muscle and danger. Pure temptation.

Her lips edged into a slow smile. "We meet at last, Flowers."

Anya didn't give him time to respond. She ground her left hipbone against the hard juncture between his legs, turning erotically and presenting him with a view of her back. Her ice-blue corset was held together by nothing more than thin ribbons, and she knew her skirt hung so low on her waist that it failed to cover the bands of her thong. Oopsie.

Men, mortal or otherwise, usually melted when they caught a glimpse of something they shouldn't.

Lucien hissed in a breath.

Her smile widened. Ah, sweet progress.

Her unhurried movements were completely at odds with the fast-pounding rock, but she never ceased the slow gyrations of her body as she raised her hands over her head then leisurely ran them through the thick mass of her snow-white hair, down her arms, stroking her own skin but imagining his hands instead. Her nipples hardened.

"Why did you summon me, woman?" His voice was low, yet as disciplined as the warrior himself.

Listening to him speak was more arousing than being touched by another man, and her stomach clenched. "I wanted to dance with you," she said over her shoulder. Bump, bump, slllooow grind. "Is that a crime?"

He didn't hesitate with his answer. "Yes."

"Good. I've always enjoyed breaking the law."

A confused pause. Then, "How much did Paris pay you to do this?"

"I get paid? Oh, goodie!" Stepping back, grinning, she brushed her ass against him, arching and swinging as sensually as she was able. Hello, erection. The heat of him nearly liquefied her bones. "What's the currency? Orgasms?"

In her dreams, he always grabbed her and meshed the hard length of his cock into her at this point. In reality, he jumped backward as if she were a bomb about to detonate, creating more hated distance between them.

A sense of loss immediately blanketed her.

"No touching," he said. He'd probably done his best to sound calm, but he had sounded on edge. Strained. More tense than arousing.

Her eyes narrowed. All around, people watched their interaction and his rejection of her. *This isn't prime time,* she projected at them with a scowl. *Turn the fuck around.*

One by one, the humans obeyed. However, the rest of the Lords closed in on her, staring intently, no doubt curious as to who she was and what she was doing here.

They had to be careful, and she understood that. They were still pursued by Hunters, humans who foolishly believed they could create a utopia of peace and harmony by ridding the world of the Lords and the demons they carried inside them.

Ignore them. You're running out of time, chica. She returned her attention to Lucien by twisting her head to face him without actually turning all the way around. "Where were we?" she asked huskily. She ran a fingertip over the top band of her thong, not stopping until she drew the hot focus of his gaze to the glittery angel wings in the center.

"I was just about to walk away," he choked out.

At his words, her nails elongated into little claws. He still thought to deny her? Seriously?

She'd shown herself to him, even knowing that the gods would be able to pinpoint her exact location—something it was best to avoid since they planned to snuff her out like a mangy animal. She would *not* leave this club without a reward.

Determination intensifying, she swung around with another roll of her hips, the length of her pale hair caressing his chest. As she nibbled on her bottom lip, she plumped her breasts. "But I don't want you to leave," she said with a practiced pout.

He backed up another step.

"What's wrong, sweetness?" Merciless, she moved forward. "Afraid of a little girl?"

His lips thinned, but he didn't reply. Thankfully, he didn't move farther away, either.

"Are you?"

"You have no idea at what game you play, woman."

"Oh, but I think I do." Her gaze swept over him, and she stilled in renewed amazement. He was utterly magnificent. Rainbow-colored strobe lights rained down his face and body, a body so finely sculpted it could have been chiseled from stone. He wore a black tee and stone-washed jeans, and both hugged rope after rope of hand-over-your-panties muscle. *Mine.*

"I said no touching," he barked.

Her gaze snapped back to his and she held up her hands, palms out. "I'm not touching you, sweetcakes." *But I want to...I plan to...I will.*

"Your gaze suggests otherwise," he said tightly.

"That's because—"

"I'll dance with you," another warrior said, cutting her off. Paris again.

"No." Anya didn't switch her attention. She wanted Lucien and only Lucien. No one else would do.

"Could be Bait," a different Lord piped in, probably eyeing her with suspicion. She recognized the deep timbre of his voice. Sabin, keeper of Doubt.

Please. Bait? As if she would try to lure anyone anywhere for reasons that weren't completely selfish. Bait, stupid girls that they were, were all about self-sacrifice; their job was to seduce a Lord to distraction so Hunters could sneak in and slay him. And really, what kind of moron wanted to kill the Lords rather than make out with them a little?

"I doubt Hunters were able to assemble so quickly after the plague," Reyes said.

Oh, yes. The plague. One of the Lords was possessed by the demon of Disease. If he touched any mortal skin-to-skin, he infected that person with a terrible sickness that spread and killed with amazing swiftness.

Knowing this, Torin always wore gloves and rarely left the fortress, willingly keeping to himself to protect humans from his curse. Not his fault a group of Hunters had sneaked inside the fortress a few weeks ago and cut his throat.

Torin had survived; the Hunters had not.

Unfortunately, there were many, many more Hunters out there. Seriously, they were like flies. Swat one away, and two more soon took its place. Even now, they were out there somewhere, waiting for a chance to strike. The Lords had to remain cautious.

"Besides, there's no way they could have figured out a way to bypass our security," Reyes added, his harsh voice drawing Anya from her thoughts.

"Just like there's no way they could get into the fortress and nearly behead Torin?" Sabin replied.

"Damn this! Paris, stay here and watch her while I check the perimeter." Footsteps, muttered curses.

Well, shit. If the warriors found any trace of Hunters out there, there'd be no convincing them of her innocence. Of that crime, at least. Lucien would never trust her, never relax around her. Never touch her except in anger.

She didn't allow her trepidation to play over her face. "Maybe I saw the crowd and snuck in," she told Paris and another Lord who was studying her, adding tightly, "And maybe the big guy and I can go the next few minutes without an interruption. In private."

They might have gotten the hint, but they didn't leave.

Fine. She'd work around them.

As she began to once again rock softly to the beat, she kept her gaze on Lucien and caressed her fingers down the planes of her stomach. *Replace my hands with yours,* she projected.

Of course, he didn't. But his nostrils did that delicious flare as his eyes followed every movement of her palms. He swallowed.

"Dance with me." This time, she said the words aloud, hoping he would not so easily ignore her. She licked her lips, moistening them.

"No." Hoarse, barely audible.

"Pretty please, with a cherry on top of me."

His eyes flickered with fiery provocation. Not her imagination, she realized. Hope flooded her. But when several seconds ticked by and he failed to reach out for her, that hope turned to frustration. Time really was her enemy. The longer she stayed here, the greater her chance of being caught.

"Do you not find me desirable, Flowers?"

A muscle ticked below his eye. "That is not my name."

"Fine, then. Do you not find me desirable, muffin?"

The ticking spread to his jaw. "What I find you matters little."

"That doesn't really answer my question," she said, close to pouting again.

"Nor was it meant to."

Grrr! What an infuriating man. *Try something else. Something blatant.*

As if I haven't been blatant already.

Alrightie, then. She turned and bent down to the floor. Her skirt rode up her thighs and gave him another, better, glimpse of her blue thong and the wings stretching from the center. As she pushed to a stand, mimicking the motions of sex as she did so, she slowly circled, offering a lingering full-body shot.

He sucked in a breath, every muscle in his powerful body tense. "You smell like strawberries and cream." As he spoke, he looked like a predator about to pounce.

Please, please, please, she thought. "Bet I taste like it, too," she said, batting her lashes despite the fact that he'd made the fragrance seem like a horrendous affront.

He growled low in his throat and took a menacing step toward her. He raised his hand to—grab her? Hit her? Whoa, what was *that* about?—before stopping himself and fisting his fingers. Before remarking on her scent, he'd been distant but maybe-kinda-sorta interested. Now he only seemed interested in throttling her.

"You're lucky I do not strike you down here and now," he said, proving her thoughts. Still, his hand lowered to his side.

Anya ceased moving, staring up at him in openmouthed astonishment. Because she smelled like fruit, he wanted to hurt her? That was—that was supremely…disappointing. Her mind had tried to supply the word *devastating,* but she'd cut it off. She barely knew the man; he couldn't devastate her.

Wasn't like she'd expected him to fall at her feet, but she *had* expected him to respond favorably. At least a little.

Men liked women who threw themselves at them. Right? She'd observed mortals for too many years to count, and that had always seemed to be the case. *Key word, chica—mortals.* Lucien wasn't, and had never been, mortal.

Why doesn't he want me?

In all the days she'd watched him, he hadn't favored a single woman. Ashlyn, his friend's lover, he treated with kindness and respect. Cameo, the only female warrior in residence here, he treated with gentleness and almost parental concern. Not desire.

He didn't prefer men. His gaze didn't linger on males with hunger or any hint of softer emotion. Was he in love with a specific woman, then, and no other would do? If so, the bitch was going down!

Anya ran her tongue over her teeth, and her hands clenched at her sides. Smoke continued to billow through the building, hazy, dreamlike. The human females began to crowd the dance floor again, trying to lure the Lords back to their sides. But the warriors continued to observe Anya, waiting for the final verdict of just who and what she was.

Lucien hadn't moved an inch; it was as if his entire body were rooted in place. She should give up, walk away, cut her losses before Cronus found her. *Only the weak give up.* True. Determined, she raised her chin. With only a thought, she changed the song blasting through the speakers. The beat instantly slowed, softened.

Forcing her expression to follow suit, she sauntered the rest of the way to him, closing that hated distance between them. She trekked her fingers up his strong, hard chest and shivered. No touching—ha! He would learn. Anarchy was hardly an obedient lapdog.

He didn't pull away, at least.

"You're going to dance with me," she purred. "That's the only way to get rid of me." Just to taunt him further, she stood on her tiptoes and gently bit his earlobe.

There was a rumble in his throat as his arms finally wrapped around her. At first she thought he meant to push her away. Then he jerked her deeper into the curve of his body, flattening her breasts against his torso and forcing her legs to straddle his left thigh. That quickly, she was wet.

"You want to dance, then we will dance." Slowly, decadently, he swayed her side to side, their bodies staying meshed together, her core rubbing just above his knee. Spears of pleasure ignited, traveling through her bloodstream and leaving no part of her unaffected.

Gods in heaven, this was better than she'd imagined. Her eyes closed in surrender. He was big. Everywhere. His shoulders were so wide they dwarfed her; his upper body so muscled it enveloped her. And all the while, his warm exhalations caressed her cheek like an attentive lover. Trembling, she moved her hands up his back and tangled them in his dark, silky hair. *Yes. More.*

Slow down, girlie. Even if he wanted her the way she wanted him, she couldn't have him. Not fully. In that respect, she was as cursed as he. But she could still enjoy the moment. Oh, could she enjoy it. Finally, he was responding to her!

His nose nuzzled her jawline. "Every man in this building wants you," he said softly, yet his words were so sharp they could have cut like a knife. "Why me?"

"Just because," she said, inhaling his heady rose perfume.

"That answers nothing."

"Nor was it meant to," she said, parroting his earlier words. Her nipples were still hard, so hard, and rubbing against her corset, enhancing her desire. Her skin was wonderfully sensitive, her mind hyperaware of Lucien's every move. Had anything ever felt so erotic? So…right?

Lucien gripped her hair tightly, almost pulling some of the strands from her scalp. "Do you find it amusing to tease the ugliest man here?"

"Ugliest?" When he appealed to her as no one else ever had? "But I'm nowhere near Paris, sugarpop."

That gave him pause. He frowned and released her. Then he shook his head, as if trying to clear it. "I know what I am," he growled with the faintest trace of bitterness. "Ugly is being kind."

She stilled, peering into his seductive bi-colored eyes. Did he truly have no idea of his attractiveness? He radiated strength and vitality. He exuded savage masculinity. Everything about him enthralled her.

"If you know what you are, sweetness, then you know you're sexy and deliciously menacing." And she needed more of him. Another of those shivers raked her spine, vibrating into her limbs. *Touch me again.*

He glared down at her. "Menacing? Does that mean you want me to hurt you?"

Slowly she grinned. "Only if it involves spanking."

His nostrils flared again. "I suppose my scars do not bother you," he said, completely devoid of emotion now.

"Bother me?" Those scars didn't ruin him. They made him irresistible.

Closer…closer… Yes, contact. Oh, great gods! She glided her hands over his chest, luxuriating in the feel of his nipples as they reached for her, savoring the ropes of strength that greeted her. "They turn me on."

"Liar," he said.

"Sometimes," she admitted, "but not about this." She studied his face. However he'd gotten the scars could not have been pleasant. He'd suffered. A lot. The knowledge suddenly angered her as much as it entranced her. Who had hurt him and why? A jealous lover?

Looked like someone had taken a blade and carved Lucien up like a melon, then tried to put him back together with the pieces out of order. Still, most immortals healed quickly, leaving no evidence of their injuries. So even if he had been carved up, Lucien should have healed.

Did he have similar scars on the rest of his body? Her knees weakened as a new tide of arousal flooded her. She'd watched him for weeks, but she hadn't gotten a single peek at his delectable form. Somehow, he'd always managed to bathe and change after she left.

Had he sensed her and kept himself hidden?

"If I didn't know better, I would think you were Bait, as my men do," he said tightly.

"And what makes you know better?"

He arched a brow. "Are you?"

Had to venture down that road, did you? If she assured him she wasn't Bait, she would seem to be admitting that she knew what Bait was. She thought she knew him well enough to know that, in his eyes, the acknowledgment would negate the claim that she wasn't. He would then feel obligated to kill her. If she claimed that she *was* Bait, well, he would still feel obligated to kill her.

Total lose-lose.

"Do you want me to be?" she said in her most seductive tone. "'Cause I'll be anything you want, lover."

"Stop," he growled, that ever-calm mask loosening its hold on his features for the briefest of moments and revealing a stunningly intense fire. Oh, to be burned. "I do not like this game you are playing."

"No game, Flowers. I promise you."

"What do you want from me? And do not dare lie."

Now, there was a loaded question. She wanted all of his masculinity focused on her. She wanted hours to strip and explore him. She wanted him to strip and explore her. She wanted him to smile at her. She wanted his tongue in her mouth.

At this point, only the last seemed achievable. And only by playing unfairly. Good thing Devious was her middle name.

"I'll take a kiss," she said, gazing at his soft, pink mouth. "Actually, I insist on a kiss."

"I didn't find any Hunters nearby," Reyes said, suddenly standing beside Lucien.

"That doesn't mean anything," Sabin replied.

"She's not a Hunter and she is not working with them." Lucien's attention never wavered from her as he waved his friends back. "I need a moment alone with her."

His assurance stunned her. And he wanted to be alone with her? Yes! Except his friends stayed put. Jerks.

"We are strangers," Lucien told her, continuing their conversation as if it had never ceased.

"So? Strangers hook up all the time." She arched her back, pressing the core of her into his erection. Mmm, erection. He hadn't lost it, was still aroused. "There's no harm in a little bittie kiss, is there?"

His fingers sank into the curve of her waist, holding her still. "You will leave? After?"

His words should have offended her, but she was too caught up in the tide of pleasure that simple embrace elicited to care. All of her pulse points began a wild dance. A strange, luscious warmth fluttered inside her stomach.

"Yes." That's all she could have from him, anyway, no matter how much she desired more. And she'd take it any way she could get it: coercion, force, trickery. She was tired of imagining his kiss and craved the reality of it. *Had* to have the reality of it. Finally. Surely he would not taste as amazing as she dreamed.

"I do not understand this," he muttered, eyes closing to half-mast. Dark lashes cast shadows over his jagged cheeks, making him appear more dangerous than ever.

"That's okay. I don't, either."

He leaned into her, hot, floral-scented breath scorching her skin. "What will a single kiss accomplish?"

Everything. Anticipation beating through her, she traced the tip of her tongue along the seam of her lips. "Are you always this talkative?"

"No."

"Kiss her, Lucien, before I do. Bait or not," Paris called with a laugh. Good-natured as the laugh was, it was still edged with steel.

Lucien continued to resist. She could feel his heart beating against his ribs. Was he embarrassed by their audience? Too bad. She'd risked everything for this, and she wasn't about to let him back out now.

"This is futile," he said.

"So what. Futile can be fun. Now, no more stalling. Only doing." Anya jerked his head down to hers and smashed her lips against his. His mouth instantly opened, and their tongues met in a deep, wet thrust. There was an intense rush of heat through her as the addictive flavor of roses and mint bombarded her.

She pressed deeper, needing more of him. All of him. Plumes of fire infused her entire body. She rubbed against his cock, unable to stop herself. He fisted her hair, taking complete control of her mouth. Just like that, she was caught in a whirlwind of passion and thirst only Lucien could quench. She'd entered the gates of heaven without taking a single step.

Someone cheered. Someone whistled.

For a moment, she felt as if her feet were swept off the ground and she was without any kind of anchor. A moment later, her back was shoved against a cold wall. The cheers had somehow suddenly died. Frigid air nipped at her skin.

Outside? she wondered. Then she was moaning, unconcerned, and winding her legs around Lucien's waist as his tongue conquered hers. One of his hands crushed her hip in a bruising grip—gods, she loved it—and the other tunneled through her hair, fingers once again curling tightly around the thick mass and angling her head to the side for deeper contact.

"You are—you are—" he whispered fiercely.

"Desperate. No talking. More kissing."

His control vanished. His tongue thrust back inside her mouth, their teeth banging together. Passion and arousal were a hot blaze between them, a raging inferno. Truly, she was on fire. Frantic. Achy. He was all over her, already a part of her.

She never wanted it to end.

"More," he said roughly, palming her breast.

"Yes." Her nipples tightened, throbbing for his touch. "More, more, more."

"So good."

"Amazing."

"Touch me," he growled.

"Am."

"No. *Me*."

Understanding dawned, and with it an intensification of her desire. Maybe he did want her. After all, he yearned to have her hands on his skin, which meant he longed for more than just a kiss.

"My pleasure." With one hand, she gripped the hem of his shirt and lifted. With the other, she caressed the ropes of his stomach. Scars. She felt scars and shivered, the jagged tissue wonderfully hot.

His muscles clenched against each stroke, and he bit her bottom lip. "Yes, like that."

She almost came, his reaction like fuel to an already blazing fire. She did moan.

Her fingers traced the circle of his nipples before dabbling at the tips. Each time she grazed them, her clitoris throbbed as if she were touching herself. "I love the feel of you."

Lucien licked his way down the column of her throat, his tongue leaving a trail of sensual lightning. Her eyelids cracked open, and she nearly gasped when she realized they were indeed outside, leaning against the club's exterior in a shadowed corner. He must have flashed them there, the naughty boy.

He was the only Lord capable of transporting himself from

one location to another with only a thought. A skill she possessed, as well. She only wished he'd flashed them to a bedroom.

No, she forced herself to add, fighting a wave of despair. Bedroom bad. Bad, bad, bad. Bad Anya for thinking otherwise, even for a second. Other women could enjoy the electric press of skin against skin and naked bodies straining for release, but not Anya. Never Anya.

"I want you," he bit out roughly.

"About time," she whispered.

He raised his darkly haloed head, blue and brown irises intense, before pinning her with another scorching kiss. On and on it continued, until she was willingly, blissfully drowning in him. Branded to her very soul, where she was no longer Anya but Lucien's woman. Lucien's slave. She might never get enough of him, would have allowed him to penetrate her then and there if she'd been able. Gods, reality was so much better than fantasy.

"I need to feel more of you. I need your hands on me." She dropped her legs from him, standing, and was just reaching for his fly, wanting to free his cock and wrap her fingers around its swollen thickness, when she heard a nearby echo of footsteps.

Lucien must have heard them, too. He stiffened and jerked away from her.

He was panting. So was she. Her knees almost buckled as their gazes locked together, time momentarily suspended. Passion-lightning still sparked between them; never would she have guessed a kiss could be that combustible.

"Right your clothing," he commanded.

"But…but…" She wasn't ready to stop, audience or not. If he'd just give her a moment, she could flash them someplace else.

"Do it. Now."

No, there would be no flashing, she realized with disappointment. His hard expression proclaimed he was done. With the kiss, with her.

Tearing her gaze from him, she looked down at herself. Her top had been anchored underneath her breasts. She wasn't wearing a bra, so the hardened pink tips of her nipples were visible, two little beacons in the night. Her skirt was around her waist, showing off the front of that barely-there thong.

She smoothed her outfit, blushing for the first time in hundreds of years. *Why now? Does it matter?* Her hands were shaking, an embarrassing weakness. She tried to will them to stop, but the only command her body wanted to hear was to jump back into Lucien's arms.

Several of the Lords rounded the corner, each glaring and sullen.

"I love it when you disappear like that," the one called Gideon said, his irritated tone making it clear he didn't love it at all. He was possessed by the spirit of Lies, Anya knew, so he wasn't capable of uttering a single truth.

"Shut up," Reyes snapped. Poor, tortured Reyes, keeper of Pain. He liked to cut himself. Once, she'd even seen him jump from the top of the warriors' fortress and luxuriate in the feel of his broken bones. "She might appear innocent, Lucien, but you failed to check her for weapons before you swallowed her tongue."

"I'm practically naked," she pointed out, exasperated. Not that anyone paid her any heed. "What weapon could I possibly be hiding?" Okay, so she *was* hiding a few. Big deal. A girl had to protect herself.

"I had everything under control," Lucien said in that unaffected voice of his. "I think I can handle one lone female, armed or not."

Anya had always been fascinated by his calmness. Until now. Where was his lingering passion? Wasn't fair that he'd recovered so quickly while she still struggled for breath. Her limbs hadn't even stopped trembling. Worse, her heart pounded like a war drum in her chest.

"So who is she?" Reyes asked.

"She might not be Bait, but she's something," Paris said. "You flashed her, but she isn't screaming."

That's when all of their narrowed gazes finally shifted to Anya. She'd never felt more raw, more vulnerable, in all the centuries of her life. Kissing Lucien had been worth the risk of capture, but that didn't mean she had to endure an interrogation. "All of you can just shut it. I'm not telling you a damn thing."

"I didn't invite you, and Reyes told me no one here claims you as a friend," Paris said. "Why did you attempt to seduce Lucien?"

Because no one would *freely* consort with the scarred warrior, his tone proclaimed. That irritated her, even though she knew he hadn't meant it to be rude or hurtful, was probably just stating what all of them considered fact.

"What's up with the third degree?" One by one, she glared at them. Everyone but Lucien. Him, she avoided. She might crumble if his features were still cold and emotionless. "I saw him, he appealed to me, so I went after him. Big deal. End of story."

Each of the Lords crossed their arms over their chests, a yeah-right action. They'd formed a semicircle around her, she realized then, though she'd never seen them move. She barely managed to stop herself from rolling her eyes.

"You don't really want him," Reyes said. "We all know that. So tell us what you do want before we *force* you to tell us."

Force her? Please. She, too, crossed her arms. A short

while ago, they'd cheered for Lucien to kiss her. Hadn't they? Maybe she had cheered for herself. But now they wanted a play-by-play of her thought process? Now they acted as if Lucien could not tempt a blind woman? "I wanted his cock inside me. You get it now, asshole?"

There was a shocked pause.

· Lucien stepped in front of her, blocking her from the men. Was he…protecting her? How utterly sweet. Unnecessary, but sweet. Some of her anger evaporated. She wanted to hug him.

"Leave her alone," Lucien said. "She doesn't matter. She's unimportant."

Anya's happy buzz evaporated, too. Doesn't matter? Unimportant? He'd just held her breast in his hand and rubbed his erection between her legs. How dare he say something like that?

A red haze winked over her vision. *This must be how my mother always felt.* Nearly all the men Dysnomia had taken to bed had hurled insults at the woman when their pleasure had been sated. *Easy,* they'd said. *Not good for anything else.*

Anya knew her mother well, knew Dysnomia had been slave to her lawless nature, as well as simply looking for love. Mated gods, single gods, it hadn't mattered. If they had desired her, she had given herself to them. Probably because for those few hours in her lovers' arms, she had been accepted, cherished, her darker urges sated.

Which made the betrayal afterward all the more painful, Anya thought, eyeing Lucien. Of all the things she'd expected and yearned for him to say, *unimportant* hadn't been close. *She's mine,* maybe. *I need her,* perhaps. *Don't touch my property,* definitely.

She hadn't wanted the same life as her mother, much as she loved her, and had vowed long ago never to let herself be used. *But look at me now. I begged and pleaded for Lucien's kiss, and he never saw me as anything more than* unimportant.

Growling, channeling all of her considerable strength, fury and hurt, she shoved him. He propelled forward like a bullet from a gun and slammed into Paris. Both men *hmphed* before ricocheting apart.

When Lucien righted himself, he whipped around to face her. "There will be none of that."

"Actually, there's going to be a lot more of that." She stalked toward him, fist raised. Soon he would be swallowing his perfect white teeth.

"Anya," he said, her name a husky entreaty. "Stop."

She froze, shock thickening every drop of blood in her veins. "You know who I am." A statement, not a question. "How?" They'd spoken once, weeks ago, but he'd never seen her before today. She'd made sure of it.

"You have been following me. I recognized your scent."

Strawberries and cream, he'd said earlier, accusation in his voice. Her eyes widened. Pleasure and mortification blended, spearing her all the way to the bone. All along, he'd known she was watching him.

"Why did I get the third degree if you knew who I was? And why, if you knew I was following you, didn't you ask me to show myself?" The questions lashed from her with stinging force.

"One," he said, "I did not realize who you were until after the discussion about Hunters had taken place. Two, I did not wish to scare you away until I learned your purpose." He paused, waited for her to speak. When she didn't, he added, "What is your purpose?"

"I—you—" Damn it! What should she tell him? "You owe me a favor! I saved your friend, freed you from his curse." There. Rational and true and hopefully would move the conversation away from her motives.

"Ah." He nodded, his shoulders stiffening. "Everything makes sense now. You've come for payment."

"Well, no." Much as it would have saved her pride, she suddenly realized she didn't want him thinking she gave her kisses away so easily. "Not yet."

His brow furrowed. "But you just said—"

"I know what I said."

"Why have you come, then? Why stalk my every waking moment?"

She pressed her tongue to the roof of her mouth, her frustration renewed. There was no time to reply, however, as Reyes, Paris and Gideon closed in on her. All three were scowling. Did they think to grab her and keep her still?

Rather than answer Lucien, she snapped at the men, "What? I don't recall inviting you into the conversation."

"You are Anya?" Reyes eyed her up and down, his revulsion clear.

Revulsion? He should be grateful! Hadn't she liberated him from the curse that had forced him to stab his BFF every night? Yes, damn it. She had. But his look was one she knew well, and one that never failed to raise her hackles. Because of her mother's amorous past and the widespread expectation that she, with her free-spirited ways, would follow suit, every Greek god in Olympus had projected that same sort of revulsion at her at one time or another.

At first, Anya had been hurt by their smug disdain. And for several hundred years, she'd tried the good-girl thing: dressing like a freaking nun, speaking only when spoken to, keeping her gaze downcast. Somehow she'd even squelched her desperate need for disaster. All to earn the respect of beings who would never see her as anything more than a whore.

One fateful day, when she'd come home from stupid

goddess training, crying because she'd smiled at Ares and that bitch Artemis had called her *ta ma de*, Dysnomia had pulled her aside. *Whatever you do, however you act, they are going to judge you harshly,* the goddess had said. *But we all must be true to our own nature. Acting as anyone other than yourself merely brings* you *pain and makes you appear ashamed of who and what you are. Others will feed off that shame, and soon it will be all that you are. You are a wonderful being, Anya. Be proud of who you are. I am.*

From then on, Anya had dressed as sexily as she pleased, talked whenever and however she wanted and refused to look at her feet for any reason other than admiring her strappy stilettos. No longer had she denied her need for disorder. An offhand way of saying "fuck you" to the ones who rejected her, yes, but more importantly, she *liked* who she was.

She would never be ashamed again.

"It is…interesting to see you in the flesh after all the research I've done on you lately. You are the daughter of Dysnomia," Reyes continued. "You are the minor goddess of Anarchy."

"There's nothing minor about me." Minor meant unimportant, and she was just as important as the other, "higher" beings, damn it. But because no one knew who her father was—well, she did, *now*—she had been relegated as such. "But yeah. I am a goddess." She raised her chin, showing him no emotion.

"The night you made yourself known to us and saved Ashlyn's life, you told us that you were not," Lucien said. "You told us you were merely an immortal."

She shrugged. She hated gods so much she rarely used that title. "I lied. I often do. It's part of my charm, don't you think?"

No one replied. Figured.

"We were once warriors for the gods and lived in the heavens, as I'm sure you know," Reyes said as if she hadn't spoken. "I do not remember you."

"Maybe I wasn't born yet, smartie."

Irritation flickered in his dark eyes, but he continued calmly. "As I told you, since your appearance weeks ago I have been researching you, learning everything I can. Long ago, you were imprisoned for murdering an innocent man. Then, a hundred years or so after your confinement, the gods finally agreed on the proper punishment for you. Before they could carry out the verdict, however, you did something no other immortal had ever managed to do. You escaped."

She didn't try to deny it. "Your research is correct." For the most part.

"Legend claims you infected the keeper of Tartarus with some kind of disease, for immediately after your escape he weakened and lost his memory. Guards were placed in every corner to fortify security, as the gods feared the strength of the prison depended on the strength of its keeper. Over time the walls *did* begin to crumble and crack, which eventually led to the escape of the Titans."

Gonna blame that on her, was he? Her eyes narrowed. "The thing about legends," she said flatly, "is that the truth is often distorted to explain the things that mortals cannot understand. Funny that you, the subject of so many legends, don't know that."

"You hid here, among humans," Reyes said, ignoring her. Again. "But you weren't content to live in peace even then. You started wars, stole weapons and even ships. You caused major fires and others disasters, which in turn led to mass panic and rioting among the humans, and hundreds of people being imprisoned."

Warmth suffused her face. Yes, she'd done those things.

When she'd first come to earth, she hadn't known how to control her rebellious nature. Gods had been able to protect themselves from it, humans hadn't. Besides that, she'd been almost…feral from her years in prison. A simple comment from her—you aren't going to let your brother talk to you like that, are you?—and bloody feuds erupted between clans. An appearance at court—perhaps laughing at the rulers and their policies—and loyal knights attempted to assassinate their king.

As for the fires, well, something inside her had compelled her to "accidentally" drop torches and watch the flames dance. And the stealing…she'd been unable to fight the voice in her head that whispered, *Take it. No one will know.*

Eventually she'd learned that if she fed her need for disorder with little things—petty theft, white lies and the occasional street fight—huge disasters could be averted.

"I did my homework on you, too," she said softly. "Did you not once destroy cities and kill innocents?"

Now Reyes blushed.

"You are not the same man you used to be, just as I am not—" Before she'd completed the sentence, a sudden wind blustered around them, whistling and harsh. Anya blinked against it, confused for only a moment. "Damn it!" she spat, knowing what would come next.

Sure enough, the warriors froze in place as time ceased to exist for them, a power greater than themselves taking hold of the world around them. Even Lucien, who'd been carefully watching her exchange with Reyes, turned to living stone.

Hell, she did, too.

Oh, no, no, no, she thought, and with the words, the invisible prison bars fell away from her like leaves from a winter tree. Nothing and no one could hold her prisoner. Not anymore. Her father had made sure of that.

Anya walked to Lucien to try to free him—why, she didn't know, after the things he'd said of her—but the wind ceased as suddenly as it had appeared. Her mouth dried, and her heart began an unsteady tango in her chest. Cronus, who had taken over the heavenly throne mere months ago, bringing new rules, new desires and new punishments, was about to arrive.

He'd found her.

Freaking great. As a bright blue light appeared in front of her, chasing away the darkness and humming with unimaginable power, she flashed away. With a sense of regret she had no business feeling, she left Lucien behind—taking the taste and memory of their kiss with her.

CHAPTER TWO

A BLACK FOG HAD DESCENDED over Lucien, locking his mind on a single thought: *Anya.*

He'd been in the middle of a conversation with her, trying to forget how perfectly she had fit against him, how razor-sharp his desire for her had been, and how, in the too-short minutes she'd been in his arms, he would have betrayed everyone he knew for a little more time with her.

Never had a kiss affected him more. His demon had actually purred inside his head. Purred. Like a tamed housecat. Such a thing had never happened before, and he did not understand why it had tonight.

Something must be wrong with him.

Why else would saying Anya meant nothing, *was* nothing, have nearly killed him? But he'd had to say it. For her benefit, and for his own. Such need was dangerous. And to admit to it, lethal to his infamous control.

Control. He would have snorted if he'd been capable of movement. Clearly he'd had no control with that woman.

Why had she pretended to want him? Why had she kissed him as if she'd die without his tongue? Women simply did not crave him like that. Not anymore. He knew that better than anyone. Yet Anya had practically begged him for more.

And now he could not remove her image from his head. She was tall, the perfect height, with a perfect pixie face and perfect sun-kissed-and-cream skin, smooth and shimmering, mouthwateringly erotic. He imagined laving every inch with his tongue.

Her breasts had nearly spilled from the cerulean half corset she'd worn, and mile after mile of delectable thigh had been visible thanks to her black miniskirt and high-heeled black boots.

Her hair was so pale it was like a snowstorm as it tumbled in waves down her back. Her eyes were wide and the same cerulean shade as her top. Uptilted nose. Full and red, made-for-sucking lips. Straight white teeth. She'd radiated wickedness and pleasure, every male fantasy come to glittery life.

Actually, he had not been able to remove her from his head since she'd entered their lives weeks ago and saved Ashlyn. She had not revealed her luscious beauty then, but her strawberry scent had branded him all the way to the bone.

Now, having tasted her, Lucien felt his heart pound in his chest and breath burn in his throat, blistering, sizzling. He experienced the same sensation when he glimpsed his friends Maddox and Ashlyn together, cooing, snuggling close, almost as if they were afraid to let go of each other.

Unexpectedly the fog lifted, at last freeing his mind and body, and he saw that he was still outside. Anya was gone, and his friends were seemingly frozen around him. His eyes narrowed as he reached up and wrapped his fingers around one of the daggers sheathed at his back. What was going on?

"Reyes?" No response. Not even the flicker of an eyelid. "Gideon? Paris?"

Nothing.

There was a movement in the shadows. Lucien withdrew the weapon slowly, waiting…prepared to do what was necessary…even as a thought slid into his mind. Anya could have taken his blades and used them on him, and he wouldn't have known. Wouldn't have cared. He'd been too consumed by her. But she hadn't taken them. Which meant she truly hadn't wanted to harm him.

Why had she approached him? he wondered again.

"Hello, Death," a grave-sounding male said. No one appeared, but the weapon was jerked from Lucien's grip and sent flying to the ground. "Do you know who I am?"

Though Lucien gave no outward reaction, dread slithered through him, devouring everything in its path. He had not heard the voice before, but he knew who it belonged to. Deep down, he knew. "Lord Titan," he said. Not so long ago Lucien would have welcomed acknowledgment from this god. Now he knew better.

Aeron, keeper of Wrath, had received such acknowledgment a month ago. He'd been ordered to kill four human women. Why, the Titans refused to reveal. Aeron had declined the assignment and was now the unwilling guest of the Lords' dungeon, a menace to himself and the world. Bloodlust consumed the warrior every minute of every day.

Lucien hated seeing his friend reduced to such an animal state. Worse, he hated the growing sense of helplessness inside himself, knowing that, as strong as he was, there was nothing he could do. All because of the being materializing before him now.

"To what do I owe this…honor?" he asked.

Fluid as water, Cronus stepped into a beam of amber moonlight. He had thick silver hair and a matching beard. A long linen chimation swathed his tall, thin body, so well-woven it could have been silk. His eyes were dark, fathomless pools.

In his left hand he held the black Scythe of Death, a weapon Lucien would have loved to seize and use on the cruel god, for it could cleave the head from an immortal in only an instant. As Death incarnate, the Scythe should have belonged to him, anyway, but it had disappeared when Cronus was imprisoned. Lucien wondered how Cronus had managed to find it—and if he could find Pandora's box so easily.

"I do not like your tone," the king finally replied, deceptively calm. A timbre Lucien knew well, for he used it himself while trying to keep his emotions under control.

"My apologies." Bastard. Despite the weapon, Cronus did not look powerful enough to have broken free from Tartarus and overthrown the former king, Zeus. But he had. With brutality and cunning, proving beyond any doubt that he was not someone to antagonize.

"You met the wild and elusive Anya." Whisper-soft now, the god's voice drifted through the night, yet it was a lance of power so strong it could have felled an entire army.

Lucien's dread increased a hundredfold. "Yes. I met her."

"You kissed her."

His hands clenched—in headiness at the memory, in fury that the passionate moment had been watched by this hated being. *Calm.* "Yes."

Cronus glided toward him, as silent as the night. "Somehow she's managed to evade me for many weeks. You, however, she seeks out. Why is that, do you think?"

"I honestly do not know." And he didn't. Her attention to him still made no sense. The ardor of her kiss had been faked, surely. And yet, she'd managed to burn him, body, soul and demon.

"No matter." The god reached him, paused to stare deeply into his eyes. Cronus even smelled of power. "Now you will kill her."

At the proclamation, Death rattled the cage of Lucien's mind, but for once Lucien wasn't sure whether the demon did so in eagerness or resentment. "Kill her?"

"You sound surprised." Finally releasing Lucien's gaze, the god brushed past him as though the conversation was over.

Though it was only the barest of touches, Lucien was knocked backward as if he'd been hit by a car, muscles clenching, lungs flattening. When he righted himself, trying to catch his breath, he wheeled around. Cronus was walking into the darkness, soon to disappear.

"If it pleases you," he called, "may I ask why you want her…dead?"

The god did not turn as he said, "She is Anarchy, trouble to all who encounter her. That should be reason enough. You should thank me for this honor."

Thank him? Lucien popped his jaw to quiet the words longing to burst from his lips. Now, more than before, he wanted to cleave the god's head from his body. He remained in place, though, knowing just how brutal the gods' retribution could be. He, Reyes and Maddox had only just been released from an ancient curse where Reyes had been forced to stab Maddox every night and Lucien had been compelled to escort the fallen warrior's soul to hell.

The death-curse had been heaped upon them by the Greeks after Maddox had inadvertently killed Pandora. How much worse would the Titans' punishment be if Lucien assassinated their king?

While Lucien did not care what they would do to him, he did fear for his friends. Already they had endured more torment than anyone should know in a hundred lifetimes.

Still, he found himself saying, "I do not wish to do this deed." *I will not.* Destroying the beautiful Anya would be a curse all its own, he suspected.

He never saw Cronus move, but the god was in his face a heartbeat later. Those bright, otherworldly eyes pierced Lucien like a sword as his arm extended, the Scythe hovering before Reyes's neck. "However long it takes, warrior, whatever you have to do, you *will* bring me her dead body. Fail to heed my command, and you and all those you love will suffer."

The god disappeared in a blinding azure light, gone as quickly as he'd appeared, and the world kicked back into motion as if it had never stopped. Lucien could not catch his breath. One flick of Cronus's wrist and he could have—would have—taken Reyes's head.

"What the hell?" Reyes growled, looking around. "Where did she go?"

"She was just here." Paris spun in a circle, scanning the area and clutching his dagger.

You and all those you love will suffer, the king had said. Not a boast. Absolute truth. Lucien fisted his hands and swallowed a surge of bile. "Let us go back inside and enjoy the rest of the evening," he managed to get out. He needed time to think.

"Hey, wait a sec," Paris began.

"No," Lucien said with a shake of his head. "We will speak of this no longer."

They stared at him for a long, silent moment. Eventually, each of them nodded. He didn't mention the god's visit or Anya's disappearance as he strode past them. He didn't mention Cronus or Anya as they entered the club. Still he didn't mention them as the men scattered in different directions, their gazes lingering on him in puzzlement.

When Reyes tried to move past him, however, he held out a restraining hand.

Reyes stopped short and glanced at him in confusion.

Lucien motioned to the table in back, the one he had previously occupied, with a tilt of his chin. Reyes nodded in understanding, and they strode to it and sat.

"Spill," Reyes said, reclining in his seat and staring out at the dance floor as casually as if they were merely discussing the weather.

"You researched Anya. Who did she kill to earn imprisonment? Why did she kill him?"

The music was a pounding, mocking tempo in the background. Strobe lights played over Reyes's bronze skin and dark-as-night eyes. He shrugged. "The scrolls I read gave no mention of why, only who. Aias."

"I remember him." Lucien had never liked the arrogant bastard. "He probably deserved it."

"When she killed him, he was Captain of the Immortal Guard. My guess is Anya caused some sort of disaster, Aias meant to arrest her, and they fought."

Lucien blinked in surprise. Smug, self-serving Aias had taken his place? Before opening Pandora's box, *Lucien* had been captain, keeper of the peace and protector of the god king. Once the demon had been placed inside him, however, he'd no longer been suitable and the duty had been stripped from him. Then he and the warriors who helped him steal the box had been banished from the heavens altogether.

"I wonder if she means to strike at you next," Reyes said offhandedly.

Perhaps, though she'd had the opportunity to do so tonight and hadn't taken it. *He* would have deserved it, though, no doubt about it. When they'd first come to earth, he and his friends had caused nothing but darkness and destruction, pain and misery. They'd had no control over their demons and had killed indiscriminately, destroyed homes and families, brought famine and disease.

By the time he'd learned to suppress his more menacing half, it had been too late. Hunters had already risen and begun fighting them. At the time, he hadn't blamed them, had even felt deserving of their ire. Then those Hunters killed Baden, keeper of Distrust as well as Lucien's brother-by-circumstance. The loss had devastated him, shaking him to the core.

Understanding the Hunters' reasoning had no longer mattered, and he'd helped decimate those responsible. Afterward, though, he'd wanted peace. Sweet peace. Some of the warriors had not. They'd desired the destruction of *all* Hunters.

So Lucien and five other warriors had moved to Budapest, where they had lived without war for hundreds of years. A few weeks ago, the remaining six Lords had arrived in town, hot on the heels of Hunters who had been determined to wipe Lucien and his men from the world once and for all. Just like that, the blood feud reignited. There would be no escaping it this time. Part of him no longer wanted to escape it. Until the Hunters were eliminated completely, there could be no peace.

"What else did you learn about Anya?" he asked Reyes.

The warrior shrugged. "As I mentioned outside, she is the only daughter of Dysnomia."

"Dysnomia?" He worried two fingers over his jaw. "I do not remember her."

"She is the goddess of Lawlessness and the most reviled immortal among the Greeks. She slept with everything male, no matter if he was wed or not. No one even knows who Anya's father is."

"No suspicions?"

"How could there be when the mother in question had several different lovers each and every day?"

The thought of Anya following her mother's path and taking multiple men to her bed infuriated Lucien. He hadn't wanted to want her, but want her—desperately—he had. *Did.* Truly, he'd tried to resist her. And would have, until he'd realized who she was and rationalized that she was immortal.

He'd thought, *She cannot die. Unlike a mortal, she cannot be taken from me if I indulge in her. I will never have to take her soul.*

What a fool he'd been. He should have known better. He was Death. Anyone could be taken. Himself, his friends. A goddess. He saw more loss in a single day than most endured in a lifetime.

"Surprised me," Reyes said, "that such a woman could produce a daughter who looks so much like an angel. Hard to believe pretty Anya is actually wicked."

Her kiss *had* been sinful. Delightfully so. But the woman he'd held in his arms had not seemed evil. Sweet, yes. Amusing, absolutely. And, shockingly enough, vulnerable and wonderfully needy. Of him.

Why had she kissed him? he wondered yet again. The question and its lack of answer plagued him. Why had she even danced for him? With him? Had she wanted something from him? Or had he merely been a challenge to her? Someone to seduce and enslave, then abandon for someone more attractive, laughing at the ugly man's gullibility all the while?

Lucien's blood chilled at the very idea. *Do not think like that. You'll only torture yourself.* What was he supposed to think about, then? Her death? Gods, he wasn't sure he could do it.

Because she had aided him all those weeks ago, he now owed her a favor. How could he kill a woman he was indebted to? How could he kill a woman he'd tasted? *Again?* He gripped his knees, squeezing, trying to subdue the sudden rush of darkness flowing through him.

"What else do you know of her? Surely there is something more."

Reyes gave another of those negligent shrugs. "Anya is

cursed in some way, but there was no hint as to what kind of curse."

Cursed? The revelation shocked and angered him. Did she suffer because of it? And why did he care? "Any mention of who was responsible for cursing her?"

"Themis, the goddess of Justice. She is a Titan, though she betrayed them to aid the Greeks when they claimed the heavenly throne."

Lucien recalled the goddess, though the image inside his head was fuzzy. Tall, dark-headed and slender. An aristocratic face and fine-boned hands that fluttered as she spoke. Some days she'd been gentle, others unbearably harsh. "What do you remember of Themis?"

"Only that she was wife to Tartarus, the prison guard."

Lucien frowned. "Perhaps she cursed Anya to punish her for hurting Tartarus in order to escape?"

Reyes shook his head. "If the scroll's timeline was correct, the curse came *before* Anya's imprisonment." He clicked his tongue on the roof of his mouth. "Perhaps Anya is exactly like her mother. Perhaps she slept with Tartarus and infuriated the goddess. Isn't that why most women wish ill upon other females?"

The suspicion did not settle well with Lucien. He scrubbed a hand over his face, the scars so puckered they abraded his palm. Had they scratched Anya? he suddenly wondered. Beneath the damaged tissue, his cheeks heated in mortification. She was probably used to smooth perfection from her men, and would remember him as the ugly warrior who had irritated her pretty skin.

Reyes traced a fingertip over one of the empty glasses perched on the tabletop. "I do not like it that we are in her debt. I do not like it that she came to the club. As I said earlier, Anya leaves a trail of destruction and chaos everywhere she goes."

"*We* leave a trail of destruction and chaos everywhere we go."

"We *used* to, but we never enjoyed it. She was smiling as she seduced you." Reyes scowled. "I saw the way you looked at her. Like I looked at Danika."

Danika. One of the humans Aeron had been ordered to slay. Reyes wanted her more than he wanted to take his next breath, Lucien suspected, but had been forced to let her go in hopes of saving her from the gods' brutality. Lucien thought perhaps the warrior had regretted the decision ever since, wishing to protect her up close and personal.

What am I going to do? Lucien knew what he *wanted* to do. Forget Anya, and ignore Cronus as Aeron had. To ignore the king of gods, however, was to invite punishment—just as Aeron had. His friends could endure no more. Of that, he was certain. Already they were poised on the edge between good and evil. Any more and they would fall, just give in to their demons and stop fighting the constant urge to destroy.

He sighed. Damned gods. The heavenly command had come at the worst possible time. Pandora's box was out there, hidden somewhere, a threat to his very existence. If a Hunter found it before he did, the demon could be pulled out of him, killing him, for man and demon were inextricably bonded.

While Lucien did not mind the thought of his own demise, he refused to allow his brethren to be hurt. He felt responsible for them. If he had not opened the box to avenge his stinging pride at not being chosen to guard it, his men would not have been forced to house the demons inside their bodies. He would not have destroyed their lives—lives they had once enjoyed as elite warriors to the Greeks. Blithe, carefree. Happy, even.

He exhaled another sigh. To protect his friends from further pain, he would have to kill Anya as ordered, Lucien decided with a pang of regret. Which meant he would have to hunt the goddess down. Which meant he would have to be near her again.

The thought of being in Anya's presence once more, of smelling her strawberry scent, of caressing her soft skin, both tantalized and tormented him. Even forever ago, when he'd fallen deeply in love with a mortal named Mariah, and she with him, he had not desired like this. A hot ache that infused every inch of his body and refused to leave.

Mariah...sweet, innocent Mariah, the woman he'd given his heart to shortly after learning to control his demon. By then, he'd lived on earth a hundred—two hundred?—years, time seemingly nonexistent, one day the same as any other. Then he'd seen Mariah, and life had begun to matter. He'd craved something good, something pure to wipe away the darkness.

She'd been sunshine to his midnight, a bright candle in merciless gloom, and he'd hoped to spend an eternity worshipping her. But all too soon, disease struck her. Death had known immediately she would not survive. Lucien should have taken her soul that very moment, but he had been unable to force himself to do it.

For weeks, the sickness ravaged her body, destroying her piece by piece. The longer he'd waited, hoping she would heal, the more she'd suffered. Toward the end, she'd begged, sobbed and screamed for death. Heartsick, knowing they would never again be together, he'd finally broken down and done his duty.

That was the night he'd obtained his scars.

Lucien had carved himself to ribbons using a poisoned blade; every time the wounds had tried to heal, he'd prayed for scars and carved himself up again. And again. He'd even burned himself until the skin no longer rejuvenated. In his grief, he'd hoped to ensure that no female would ever again approach him, that he would never again have to suffer the loss of a loved one.

He'd never regretted the action. Until now. He'd ruined any chance of being a man Anya could truly desire. A woman as physically perfect as she deserved a man equally so. He frowned. Why was he thinking like that? She had to die. Desire on either side would only complicate matters. Well, complicate them more.

Once again, Anya's image etched itself into his mind, consuming his thoughts. Her face was a sensual feast and her body a sexual high. As a man, he howled with rage at the thought of destroying that. As an immortal warrior, well, he howled, too.

Perhaps he could convince Cronus to rescind his command. Perhaps... Lucien snorted. No. That would not work. Trying to bargain with Cronus was more foolish than ignoring him. The king of gods would only order him to do something worse.

Damn this! Why did Cronus want her dead? What had she done?

Had she spurned him for another?

Lucien ignored the haze of jealousy and possessiveness that fell over his eyes. Ignored the *mine* ringing in his ears.

"I am waiting," Reyes said, breaking into his thoughts.

He blinked, trying to clear his mind. "For?"

"For you to tell me what happened out there."

"Nothing happened," he lied smoothly, and hated himself for the need.

Reyes shook his head. "Your lips are still bruised and swollen from kissing her. Your hair is in spikes around your head from where she plowed her fingers through. You stepped in front of her when we meant to take her, and then she disappeared altogether. Nothing happened? Try again."

Reyes had enough to worry about without having to carry Lucien's burden, as well. "Tell the others I'll meet them in Greece. I won't be traveling with them as planned."

"What?" Reyes frowned. "Why?"

"I've been commanded to take a soul," was all he said.

"Take a soul? Not just escort it to heaven or hell? I don't understand."

He nodded. "You do not need to understand."

"You know I hate when you turn cryptic. Tell me who and why."

"Does it matter? A soul is a soul, and the outcome is the same no matter the reason. Death." Lucien slapped Reyes's shoulder and pushed to his feet. Before the warrior could utter another word, Lucien strode out of the club, not stopping until he reached the very place he'd kissed—and lost—Anya.

In an unwieldy corner of his mind, he could almost hear her moaning. He could almost feel her nails digging into his back and her hips rocking into his erection. An erection that had not dissipated. Despite everything.

Need still clawed through him, but he shoved it aside and closed his right eye. Surveying the area with his blue eye—his spiritual eye—he saw a rainbow of glowing, ethereal colors. Through those colors he could interpret every deed that had occurred here, every emotion ever felt by visitors. Sometimes he could even determine exactly who had done what.

Having done this infinite times before, he easily sorted through the morass to find signs of the most recent activity. There, against the freshly erected and painted boards of the brand-new building, were sparkling stars of passion.

The kiss.

In this spiritual realm, Anya's passion appeared a blazing pink. Real. Not faked, as a part of him had assumed. That pink trail glittered with a dazzle unlike anything he'd ever seen. Had she truly desired him, then? Had a creature so physically perfect found *him* worthy? That did not seem possible, and yet the proof was shining at him like a pathway to salvation in the middle of a storm.

His stomach tightened, heat shooting through him. His mouth watered for another taste of her. His chest ached, a sharp and hungry throb. Oh, to hold those breasts in his hands again and feel the nipples stiffen against his palms. To sink his fingers into her wet sheath this time and pump in and out, slowly at first, then faster and faster. She would come, maybe even beg for more. He groaned.

She has to die by your hand. Do not forget.

As if he could, he thought, hands fisting. "Where did you go?" he muttered, following the sparks to where she'd stood when she'd pushed him. Blue winked at him. Sadness. She had been sad? Because he'd said she did not matter? The knowledge filled him with guilt.

He studied the colors more closely. Interspersed with the blue was a bright, pulsing red. Fury. He must have hurt her feelings, and that in turn must have angered her. The guilt intensified. In his defense, he had assumed she'd been playing with him, that she hadn't really wanted him. He hadn't thought she would care whether he wanted her or not.

That she had utterly amazed him.

As he continued to sort through the colors, he found the faintest trace of white. Fear. Something had scared her. What? Had she sensed Cronus? Seen him? Known he was about to deliver her death sentence?

Lucien didn't like that she'd been scared.

Every muscle tensed as he followed the muted trail of white. As he moved, he allowed his body to fuse with the demon of Death, becoming nothing more than a spirit, a midnight mist that could flash from one location to another in an instant.

Anya's essence led to his fortress, he was startled to find. His bedroom, more specifically. Clearly she hadn't stayed long, but seemed to have paced from one side of the chamber to another, then had flashed away to—

Maddox and Ashlyn's bedroom. Lucien's brow furrowed in confusion. Why here? The couple was asleep in bed, twined together, cheeks rosy and flushed from a recent sexual marathon, he was sure.

Lucien tried to tamp down a sudden rush of envy before picking up Anya's trail and flashing—

Into an apartment he did not recognize. Moonlight seeped inside through cracks in the black window coverings. Still dark. Was he still in Budapest, then? The furnishings here were sparse: a brown, threadbare couch pushed against the wall, a wicker chair with slats that had come unraveled and would poke the sitter in the back. No TV, no computer or any of the other modern luxuries Lucien had grown accustomed to over the years.

From the next room echoed the clatter of one dagger slapping against another. It was a sound he knew well. He allowed himself to float toward it, knowing whoever was inside would not be able to see him.

He reached the doorway and gaped, waves of shock pummeling through him. Danika, the doomed woman Reyes lusted after, was thrusting two daggers repeatedly into a man-sized dummy hanging from the wall. A dummy that, surprisingly, looked like a cross between Reyes and Aeron.

"Kidnap me, will you?" she muttered. Sweat trickled down her temples and chest, soaking her gray tank to her body. The long length of her blond ponytail was plastered to her neck. To work up such a sweat in so cold an apartment, she must have been at the exercise for hours.

Why had Anya come here? Danika was—or had been—in hiding. Temporarily letting her go had been the only way to give the mortal some semblance of a life before Aeron hunted her down on the wings of Wrath as the gods had ordered. And he would. It was only a matter of time before Aeron escaped the dungeon. Not one of the warriors had been able to bring themselves to take any more of his freedom by binding him with the only thing that could truly hold him: unbreakable links forged by the gods. So yes, Aeron *would* eventually escape.

Lucien was tempted to reveal his presence and talk to Danika, but didn't. She had no good memories of him and would not be willing to help in his search for Anya. He worried two fingers over his jaw. Whatever the goddess of Anarchy's purpose, she had clearly taken an interest in all things Underworld.

He was more baffled than ever.

There were no answers here, only more questions, so he didn't waste another minute. He followed Anya's lighted trail, which was now a bright red—anger was taking root again— and found himself flashing to—

A convenience store. He believed that was what mortals called the small shop.

His eyebrows furrowed together. He was no longer in Budapest, he knew, for sunlight glowed brightly through the store's windows. A multitude of people milled about, paying for fuel and buying snacks.

Unseen, Lucien ventured outside. A horde of yellow cars sped along a nearby street, and mortals rushed along the crowded sidewalks. He found a shadowed alley and materialized without anyone the wiser. Curiosity propelling him, he strode back into the store. A bell tinkled.

A woman gasped when she saw him, then looked away

as quickly as possible. A child pointed at him and was reprimanded by his mother. *Everyone* backed away from him, inching as far from him as they could without seeming blatantly rude. There was a line leading to the cash register, which he bypassed without apology.

No one protested.

The cashier was a teenager, a boy who looked a lot like Gideon. Blue hair, piercings, tattoos. However, he lacked Gideon's savage intensity as he smacked his gum and shuffled the money in his drawer. A quick glance at the tag on the boy's shirt provided his name.

"Dennis, did you notice a pale-haired female in a short black skirt—"

"And ice-blue barely-there top? Hell, yeah, I noticed," Dennis finished for him as he closed the register. Lucien recognized the accent. He was in the States. The boy's gaze lifted, and he stilled. Gulped. "Uh, yeah." His voice shook. "I did. May I ask why?"

Three emotions skidded through Lucien, none of them welcome: jealousy that another man had enjoyed the sight of Anya, eagerness that he was closer to finding her and *dread* that he was closer to finding her. "Did she speak to anyone?"

The boy took a step backward and shook his head. "No."

"Did she buy anything?"

There was a heavy pause, as if he was afraid his answer would send Lucien into a rage. "Kind of."

Kind of? When Dennis failed to elaborate, Lucien gritted his teeth and said, "What did she kind of buy?"

"Wh-why do you want to know? I mean, are you a cop or something? An ex-husband?"

Lucien pressed his tongue to the roof of his mouth. *Calm, stay calm.* He fixed his eyes on the paling human, capturing Dennis's gaze and refusing to release it. The scent of roses began to drift from him, thickening the air.

Dennis gulped again, but his eyes began to glaze over.

"I asked you a question," Lucien said softly, "and now you will answer. What did the woman buy?"

"Three strawberry-and-cream lollipops," was the trance-like reply. "But she didn't buy them. She just grabbed them and walked off. I didn't try to stop her or anything, I swear."

"Show me the lollipops."

With people moaning and muttering in protest at the delay—until Lucien glared at them and they quickly hushed—Dennis left the register and led him to the candy aisle. He pointed to a half-empty box of lollipops.

Lucien pocketed two, not allowing himself to smell them as he so badly wanted, and withdrew several bills. Wrong currency, but giving the boy *something* was better than nothing. "How much do I owe you?"

"They're on me." Dennis held up his hands in a pretend show of friendship.

He wanted to force the boy to take the money, but did not want to cause even more of a scene. In the end, he stuffed the bills back inside his pocket. "Return to your register," he said, then pivoted to slowly survey the rest of the store. On the spiritual plane, there were millions upon millions of colors. Sorting through them proved tedious, but no one dared bother him and he was finally able to locate Anya's unique essence.

His blood heated.

Everything about her, even the minute mist she left behind, called to him, drew him. And, if he wasn't careful, would ensnare him. She was just so…captivating. A beautiful enigma.

Lucien left the store and returned to the abandoned alleyway, where he once again dematerialized into the spirit realm. He flashed to Anya's next location—

And found her in a park. Finally.

Looking at her, the sharp ache returned to his chest and he

suddenly had trouble drawing in a breath. Right now, she appeared serene, not at all like the temptress in the club. She sat on a swing, sunlight bathing her in a golden halo. Back and forth she rocked.

She seemed to be lost in thought, her temple resting against the chain that anchored the swing to the rail. That silky, silvery hair cascaded down her arms, wisping across her pixie face every few seconds as the wind rolled.

He was struck by a nearly inexorable urge to fold her in his arms and simply hold her.

Had a woman ever looked so vulnerable? Had a woman ever looked so alone? She licked one of the lollipops she'd stolen, the pink tip of her tongue flicking out, circling the rosy candy. His cock jumped in response. *No. None of that.* But the command failed to lessen his desire.

However long it takes, whatever you have to do, you will bring her to me, Cronus had said. *Or all those you love will suffer.*

Lucien felt a spark of anger leap through himself, but he quickly tamped it down. No anger. He was Death. Right now he had no other purpose. Emotion would only hinder him; he knew that well.

However longs it takes. Cronus's voice once again echoed in his mind.

For a moment, only a moment, Lucien entertained the possibility of taking forever. An eternity. *You know what happens when you hesitate. The one destined to die suffers a far worse fate than originally intended. Do it! Or your friends, too, will suffer a far worse fate.*

Determined, Lucien materialized and stepped forward. Gravel crunched under his boots, and Anya's head snapped up. Instantly their gazes locked. Her crystalline eyes widened, filling with such intense heat and longing they singed him.

Her mouth fell open in shock as she popped to her feet. "Lucien."

The sweetness of her voice blended with the strawberries-and-cream scent she emitted. As his body tensed erotically, his resolve weakened. Again. *Stay strong, damn you.*

Not realizing the danger she was in, she remained in place, still peering over at him through the thick shield of her lashes. "How did you find me?"

"You are not the only being capable of tracking an immortal," he replied, giving her only half of the answer.

Her gaze traced over him, so hot he thought she might be mentally stripping away his clothing. Women simply did not look at him like that. Not anymore. And that this one did… He was having more and more trouble controlling his reactions. His cock grew harder with every second that passed.

"So you've come to finish what we started, have you, Flowers?" She sounded eager.

"That is not why I've come." He spoke the words precisely. *There is no other way. You must do this deed.*

Her lush red lips edged into a frown. "Then why—" She gasped and anchored one hand on her suddenly cocked hip. "Did you come to insult me some more? Because you should know, I'm not going to tolerate it. I am *not* unimportant!"

Oh, yes, he had hurt her, and the knowledge once again filled him with guilt. Foolish to feel guilt when he'd come here to hurt her irrevocably, but the emotion proved too strong to fight. Still he repeated, "That is not why I've come," this time adding, "I'm sorry, Anya, but I've come to kill you."

CHAPTER THREE

I'VE COME TO KILL YOU.

The words echoed through Anya's mind, a bleak promise she couldn't quiet. Lucien never joked. She knew that well. Had watched him all these weeks without seeing a single smile or hearing a hint of humor pass his exquisite lips. More than that, the spirit of Death radiated from him now, a skeletal mask glowing underneath his skin.

The scent of roses thickened the air, almost mesmerizing, beseeching her to do anything and everything he asked. Even die.

Her heart skipped a beat. She'd seen him take a soul before; it had been a morbidly beautiful sight, yet one she'd never thought to experience firsthand. She was immortal, after all. But she knew better than most that even immortals could be slain.

The night she'd cut the heart from the Captain of the Guard, ending his miserable existence once and for all, the prospect of mortality had become very clear. Of course, it had become even clearer after her arrest and subsequent imprisonment while the gods debated what to do with her.

Every day inside her cell, the bars had seemed to tighten around her and the screams and moans of the other prisoners had seemed to grow louder. Maybe they'd been her screams. Being unable to nourish her need to create disorder had hurt unbearably.

She'd quickly realized life, even for an immortal, could be ruined or ended too soon. And she'd decided to fight for hers, then and always. No matter what. Freedom, whether physical or emotional, would never be taken from her again.

The gods had thought otherwise. Ultimately they'd decided to make her a sex slave to their warriors. *A fitting punishment*, they'd said. She'd taken their captain; now she could comfort the captain's army.

It would have destroyed her—mind, body and soul. Her determination might have withered. But her father had come for her, rescued her, despite the retribution he would heap on himself. Once again, she'd been free. Once again, she'd had a chance at the happiness she'd always craved.

And now Lucien, a man she desired, a man she'd kissed, wanted to end her, take *everything* from her? A thousand different emotions bubbled inside her, and she wasn't sure which to concentrate on first. Fury? Confusion? Hurt?

"Why do you want to hurt me?" she demanded.

"I do not want to hurt you. I must. Apparently, you are too wild to roam free."

Oh, those words rankled! It was one thing for all Olympus to rebuff her—she was used to that. But for some reason, despite everything, Lucien's opinion of her mattered.

"How did you find me?" she repeated.

Not a flicker of feeling touched Lucien's cold expression. "That doesn't matter."

"I could disappear in the blink of an eye."

"Run and I will find you again. No matter where you go, I will always find you."

Both seductive and frightening. "Why don't you attack me, then? Get it over with so there doesn't have to be another chase?"

He raised his chin, his jaw squaring stubbornly. "I will. I want you out of my mind first."

Doing her best to appear casual, she leaned back against the swing's chain. "I don't know whether to be flattered or insulted, honey. Is wild little Anya so bad a kisser the disgust of knowing you've had your tongue in her mouth refuses to leave you?" She sounded as unconcerned as she looked—she hoped—but inside, she trembled.

How did the sight of him still manage to affect her? Worse, now that she knew the taste of him, the feel of his body pressed against hers and the sensation of his hands clutching her, drawing her closer, all of her reactions to him seemed to be intensified.

She craved more. *Perhaps it's time to visit a therapist.*

"I'm sure you know how good your kisses are." There was a trace of bitterness in the words.

"You make that sound like a crime."

"It is."

Anya's eyelids narrowed to tiny slits. She'd been alive a long time; she hadn't lived as a complete innocent, but she hadn't lived promiscuously, either. Why would she, even before her curse, when she knew the pain of being labeled easy?

Like anyone, however, Anya craved admiration and affection. She liked the way men looked at her and had often lain awake in bed, wishing for the sexual relationship she could never allow herself.

"We can do this easily, Anya."

"What, kiss again?"

He gulped forcefully. "See to your death."

Don't give him a reaction. A good warrior always used an adversary's emotions against him, and Lucien was a damn good warrior. But so was she. "Tell me again why you want to kill me, sweetcakes. I've forgotten."

A muscle ticked under his eye. "I told you. I do not want to slay you, but the gods have ordered me to do so."

And no one, not even a Lord of the Underworld, could disobey the gods without severe consequences. Dread curdled her stomach. Still, she had to admit she was glad Lucien had not come eagerly.

"All gods or one?" she asked, though she already knew the answer.

"One. Cronus."

"The bastard king," she said, just for the god's benefit. *I hope you're listening, you greedy coward.*

Lucien cringed, proving he did indeed fear the wrath of the god. He should. Cronus had clearly skipped school the day mercy was explained.

The moment the Titan had broken free of his heavenly prison, he'd quickly and brutally conquered the Greeks and imprisoned the survivors. That's when Anya had returned to the heavens and freed a few. That's also when he'd caught her and locked her back up, demanding her greatest treasure in exchange for her freedom. Before he could punish her for her refusal, she'd escaped. Score one for Team Anya. Shortly after, he'd found her a second time and threatened her with the Lords. Now here she and Lucien were, about to go *Halo 3* on each other. Score one for Team Cronus.

"Sure you want to obey such a meanie?" she asked.

Lucien's gaze met hers, ensnaring her, disrupting her determination. "I must, and nothing you say can sway me from my purpose."

She arched a brow, doing her best to appear confident. "Wanna bet?"

"No. That would only give you false hope." A gentle breeze swirled between them, and strands of his dark hair brushed his face. He hooked them behind his ears, allowing nothing to obstruct the invisible cord between them.

With the action, the dark slashes of his eyebrows, the

strong slope of his nose and the hard cut of his scarred cheeks became more prominent. But it was his eyes she kept returning to. His brown iris seemed to anchor her, while his blue iris swirled, drawing her deeper and deeper into a world where only he existed.

Obey me. Submit.

The words whispered through her mind.

Her jaw clenched, right along with the rest of her. She knew, *knew,* what he was trying to do. Lull her into a sense of calmness and force her to willingly accept his death blow.

Hell, no. Not her. If there was one skill she'd mastered in the centuries since she'd been cursed, it was the art of resisting a man. She shook her head, breaking free of his sensual hold. *Take that.*

Don't give him a reaction, she reminded herself. She moved her gaze to his massive chest and considered what to do next, all the while sucking on her favorite strawberry lollipop. "You owe me a favor, Flowers, and I'm calling it in. You are *not* to kill me."

There was a torturous pause. Then, "You know I must." He stiffened, as if fortifying himself. "Ask me to make it painless. That I can do. Ask me to kiss you before I take your soul. That, too, I can do."

"Sorry, babydoll. I think I'll stick with not killing me. And as a reminder, I told you a few weeks ago that I'd kill you if *you* tried to renege on your favor."

Another pause, this one heavier, longer. He tangled a hand through his hair, his expression one of agony. "Why does Cronus want you dead?"

"You already answered that. I'm too wild." She sat back on the swing, slid one hand slowly, covertly, down her leg and dug into her boot, wrapping her fingers around the hilt of one of her daggers. She might be crazy-aroused by this man despite his mission, but she wasn't going down without a fight.

"I do not believe that is the only reason," Lucien said.

"Maybe he tried to score and I laughed at him." A lie. She refused to admit the truth, however, so the lie would have to do.

Some emotion finally took center stage on Lucien's features; what, she didn't know. All she knew was that it was hard and uncompromising. "Maybe he was your lover and you spurned him. Maybe you chose another over him. Maybe you purposefully aroused him and left him, making him feel like a fool."

Her eyes narrowed once more, focusing on him with razor-sharp intensity. She popped to her feet, hiding the blade behind her back. "That's a very rude thing to say. As if I would lower myself to playing a man I had no interest in."

Lucien uttered something that sounded very much like, "You played me."

Her brows furrowed as her anger spiked. "Believe what you want to believe, but you have no reason to feel hurt."

"You are Anarchy. I doubt you concern yourself with other people's feelings."

"You don't know anything about me," she snapped.

"I know you dance like you're having sex, and I know that you taste like every man's downfall."

Damn him. The words alone would have aroused her. Paired with his husky, wine-rich voice, and she lost her anger, suddenly ready to tumble straight into his arms. Rather than admit that, she said, "I stand corrected. You aren't rude. You're diabolical." What did it say about her that she now found him all the more appealing?

"Nevertheless, it is true." His head tilted to the side as he studied her. Though he'd donned that emotionless mask again, there was a white-hot, dangerous aura to him. "Are you always so free with your affections?"

There had been no condemnation in his tone, but the comment still bothered her. She could recall several gods asking her mother the same question, just as she could recall the flicker of hurt in her mother's eyes each and every time a lover suggested she was not good enough for him. Lucien would pay for that.

Anya ran her tongue over the lollipop's round tip, lingering over the fruity flavor in a pretend show of indifference. Meanwhile, her hidden fingers tightened around the dagger's hilt, her nails reaching skin and cutting deep.

"So what if I am?" she finally said. "Most men are easy with their affections and they're praised, thought of as sexual gods."

He ignored her comment. The Lords were good at that, obviously. "Before I—" He pressed his lips together, shook his head. He must have changed his mind about what to say to her because he didn't finish the sentence. "Explain something to me." As if realizing he would get no answers from her otherwise, he added, "Please."

She batted her lashes at him flirtatiously. "Anything for you, dumpling."

"Tell me the truth. Why did you kiss me? You could have had Paris, Reyes, Gideon or any of the others. They would not have objected. They would have wanted you in return."

First, grrr! *They would have wanted you in return,* she inwardly mocked. Unlike him, who would never want her. She wasn't dog food, damn it. Second, why couldn't he accept that she'd simply desired him and no other?

Maybe it was for the best that he thought her passion faked, she decided. Saved her pride, at least, since she *meant nothing to him* and he *hadn't wanted her.* Jackass.

"Maybe I knew Cronie Wonie was going to tell you to kill me, and I hoped to butter you up like a breakfast muffin so you wouldn't be tempted to obey." There. How'd he like that?

Understanding lit his rough, savage features. "Something makes sense at last," he said with only the barest trace of disappointment.

Or was the disappointment wishful thinking on her part? The man had come to kill her, after all. Softer emotions he couldn't possibly feel.

Submit to me.

Ah, shit. She'd looked at his face and was once again snared. His blue eye still swirled, and the brown one was so rich and deep she could have willingly drowned in it. Her stomach quivered.

No, no, no! She bared her teeth at him and jerked her gaze away. *Hurt him to slow him down, then get out of here.* Now, that was a thought she didn't mind acting on. He was an immortal; he'd heal. But damn it all to the fires of hell, she wasn't ready to leave him. She hadn't talked to anyone in weeks. She'd been too busy following him, watching him. Lusting after him.

Doesn't matter what you want. Strike at him before he strikes at you.

"One last chance to pay up the favor you owe me by protecting me from Cronus," she told him.

"I'm sorry."

"All right, then. Now that we've cleared the air," she said, using her sultriest tone, "let's get this party started." She licked the lollipop and shifted her weight to the left, causing her skirt to ride up on the right and drawing his gaze to her bared skin as she'd hoped.

There was the faintest flicker of desire in his eyes, desire he couldn't hide. *Too late.* She tossed the dagger.

Silver metal flew end over end and embedded in his heart before he even guessed her intentions. His body spasmed and his eyes went wide as saucers.

"You stabbed me," he said, incredulous. Grimacing, he jerked out the now-bloody dagger and rubbed a hand over the wound, then looked down at his drenched, crimson-stained fingers. Anger overrode the incredulity.

"Feel free to keep the dagger as a souvenir." She blew him a kiss and flashed to an icy boulder in Antarctica, knowing he'd follow her and wanting him to suffer for it. Frigid wind instantly slammed into her, cutting through the flimsy clothing she wore. Past skin, past muscle and straight into bone. Her teeth chattered.

Penguins waddled by, scampering to get away from her. Water swirled and churned all around her. Mile after mile of black night greeted her eyes, the only light provided by golden moon rays reflecting off the glaciers.

If she'd been mortal, she would have frozen to death in seconds. Goddess that she was, Anya simply felt miserable. "Worth it, though," she said, breath forming a thick mist in front of her face. If she was miserable, how much worse would it be for the injured Lucien when he—

Materialized right in front of her, so clear to her the sun could have been shining.

He was scowling, his perfect white teeth bared. He'd removed his shirt, and she saw that rope after rope of muscle lined his stomach. He had no chest hair, not even the happy trail that most men possessed. His skin was the shade of pearlized honey, smooth on one side, like velvet over steel, and jagged and scarred on the other. Both sides were so lickable her mouth watered.

His nipples were tiny, brown and hardened like arrowheads. They would feel amazing against her tongue. His chest was smeared in blood, and a long wound marred the skin just over his heart. The tissue had already begun to weave itself back together.

Seeing him like that, bloody from battle, angry and ready for more, turned her on. Her knees did that stupid weakening thing. *You hate weakness.* But damn, it felt good. Would he always have this effect on her?

Silly girl.

When the wind hit him, she knew he experienced a moment of miserable suspension, where blood and oxygen froze inside him. "Anya," he growled.

"Nice to see you again, Flowers." She didn't waste another moment. Using all of her strength, she shoved him into the water.

He could have grabbed hold of her to stop his fall, but he didn't. He allowed himself to tumble backward, rather than risk taking her with him. How…sweet. Bastard! He had no right to be sweet now.

He gasped when he hit, the sound a blend of rage, shock and icy torment. A few droplets splashed onto her thigh, and *she* gasped at the cold.

"Anya!" he shouted when he sputtered to the surface.

"No need to thank me for the bath. I mean, the least I could do after bloodying your chest was to help you clean up the mess. See ya!"

"Don't leave," he rushed out. "Please."

Unable to help herself, she paused. "Why not?"

Rather than flash to the boulder, he treaded water and glared up at her. "You do not want to anger me." A cloud moved and thicker golden beams poured from the silky, inky sky, straight onto him.

"Or what? You'll turn into a hulking green beast? Hate to disappoint you, Flowers, but that kind of revs my engine. Have fun defrosting." Laughing, she gave him a finger wave and flashed to her favorite private beach in Hawaii.

Warmth and sunlight instantly enveloped her, melting the

sheen of ice that had glazed her skin. Usually when she came here, she stripped and lounged on the sand, soaking in the tranquility. Sometimes she barricaded herself inside the house a quarter mile up, surrounded by towering palms, where she vegged out and watched movies.

This time, she stayed on the beach and kept her clothes on, dropped her lollipop and withdrew two more daggers from her boots. She held them at her sides and waited.

A scowling, shivering Lucien entered her line of vision a moment later. His lips were tinted blue and thinned in displeasure. His hair was frosted around his head, his skin glistening with crystallized moisture.

"Thank you. For the beach," he said through chattering teeth.

"How the hell are you following me?" she demanded, raising her chin and returning his murderous glare with one of her own.

Finally, for whatever reason, he deigned to answer. "You leave traces of energy everywhere you go. I simply follow them. Had you not revealed yourself inside the club, I never would have been able to lock on you."

Great. Now she'd never be able to lose him. Stupid urges, prompting her to dance with him. She should've stayed in the shadows. *I must be more like my mother than I realized.* "I won't make this easy for you," she told him.

He lost some of his anger, his lips twitching into the semblance of a smile. "I suspected as much."

How dare he show an irresistible sense of humor *now,* softening his face and adding all kinds of sexy. Where had this amusement been yesterday or the day before?

"I told you once but I will tell you again," he said. "I do not want to hurt you."

"Oh, well." She shook her head, pale hair dancing over her

shoulders. "That makes this okay, then. Go ahead and kill me." Sarcasm dripped from each word.

"Anya."

"Hush it. I've been nothing but nice to you, helped you and your friends, and this is how you thank me?"

A muscle ticked under his eye. Had she, perhaps, hit a nerve?

"I would change the circumstances if I could. I would—"

"You have a choice. You can walk away."

"I can't."

"Whatever, Flowers. Let's just get this over with, 'kay. All this talking is giving me a headache."

His brows arched into his forehead. "You are going to let me take your soul, then?"

"Hell, no. I thought I made it clear I'm going to fight you to the death. Yours, in case you need more clarification. Here and now. I've killed an immortal before. Doing it again should be no hardship."

"Yes, Reyes mentioned Aias." Lucien made no move in her direction. "Why did you slay him?"

She lifted one of her shoulders in a casual shrug. Inside, though, she was anything but serene. The memory of her clash with Aias was not a pretty one. What could have been, what could have happened, still sometimes haunted her. "He wanted to fuck me, and I didn't want him to. He decided to go ahead and do it, anyway, so I decided he'd look good with a hole in his chest."

Lucien popped his jaw. "I hope you inflicted pain."

Her eyes widened. Okay, back up. An immortal—a former Captain of the Guard at that—was *glad* she'd killed an elite warrior? First time that had happened. The knowledge twisted through her, profoundly affecting everything it touched. Finally someone, and a virtual stranger at that, was taking her side.

"No worries there," she managed to work past the sudden lump in her throat.

Lucien's hands curled into fists. Why? Didn't matter, she supposed. She was just proud of herself for noticing because it meant she wasn't staring into those otherworldly eyes like a lovesick puppy.

"It doesn't have to be this way," he said, his tone stiff, flat.

"You said that already. But news flash—yes, it does. I'm not going to bend over and take it just because new gods are running the show and they don't like how I do business. I'm not going to bend over and take it because the big cheese is greedy and wants to steal from me."

Lucien's gaze sharpened. "What does he hope to steal?"

Her lips pursed. Damn her runaway tongue. Of course Lucien had latched on to that last bit of her speech. "Don't listen to me. I spout all kinds of nonsense when I'm scared. Remember when I told you I liked to lie?"

"You are not scared of me or anything, I would bet, and I doubt you were lying this time." He didn't give her a chance to respond. "So you did not spurn Cronus or cheat on him?"

"Does that matter?" She twirled the end of a lock of hair, making sure the point of her dagger glistened in the sun. "Does it make a difference in what you're planning to do to me?"

"No."

"Then I see no reason to answer." If he wouldn't give an inch, neither would she.

He raked a hand down his face, looking utterly exhausted all of a sudden. "I can give you a day, perhaps, to say goodbye to your loved ones."

"Oh, that's so sweet," she said drily. Her sarcasm didn't last long, though. Her short list of loved ones played through her mind, sparking a pang inside her chest. Her mother. Her father. William, her only friend. If Lucien managed to defeat her, they would most likely never know what had happened to her. They might look for her, worry. "Do you extend the same courtesy to all your victims?" *Do not think like that. You aren't and won't be a victim.*

Again, "No."

"So I'm just a lucky girl?"

His lush lips once more thinned in displeasure. No matter how scarred his cheeks were, nothing could detract from the beauty of those lips. Maybe because she knew how soft they actually were. Maybe because they'd branded her all the way to her soul and she'd forever bear their imprint.

"Yes," he finally said.

"I'm going to decline your oh so generous offer, lover. I think I'd just prefer to kill you now rather than wait. See, your presence is really starting to offend me."

He stiffened, and if he'd been anyone other than the (nearly) unemotional warrior she knew him to be, she would have suspected that she'd hurt him. "Now who is rude?" he said flatly.

Did he think she was talking about his scarred appearance? Dummy. Answering him would have opened the topic for discussion, however, so she said, "How shall we do this, hmm?" She gave her blades a little toss, caught the hilts and twirled them in her hands.

He leveled a frown of resignation at her, as if anything else in the world would have been preferable to this inevitable showdown. "Just remember. You chose this. Not me."

"You followed me, sugar. *You* chose it."

She'd barely finished the sentence when he materialized two inches from her face, placing them nose to nose. She gasped, sucking in a deep whiff of his rose scent. He slapped one of the knives out of her grip then quickly moved to take the other.

The first action caught her unaware, but she was prepared for the second. She flashed several feet behind him and knocked his skull with a sharp, upward kick. Why she didn't just stab him in the back, she didn't know.

He stumbled forward, caught himself and whipped around to face her, eyes slitted.

"I've seen you kill," she said, trying not to sound impressed. "I know your moves. Taking me down won't be easy." She flashed behind him again, but he was smarter now, on to her tricks, and spun, banding one of his arms around her waist the second she materialized and finally whacking the other blade from her hand.

She almost moaned at the heady sensation of being back in his embrace, the violence somehow only adding to her arousal. She lingered far longer than she should have, savoring the feel of his…erection? Oh, baby, yes. So he liked their sparring, too? Interesting. Exhilarating. And absolutely delicious.

"So strong my little Lucien is. I'm almost sorry I have to fight dirty," she added, just before kneeing him between the legs.

Howling, he doubled over.

A chuckle escaped her as she flashed a few feet away. "Bad, naughty Anya would have been a lot nicer to that area of your anatomy if you'd come after her for different reasons."

"For the last time, woman, I do not want to hurt you," he gritted out. "I'm being forced."

She gazed down at her nails and yawned. "Are you going to put up a fight or not? This is becoming boring. Or, wait. Are you always this weak?"

Perhaps she shouldn't have taunted him. Light a fire, get burned. He was in front of her a moment later, kicking at her ankles and shoving her to the ground. Her back hit and breath wheezed from her lungs, momentarily cutting off her air supply and leaving her dizzy.

Next his weight pinned her down. Her arms were free, so she balled a fist and slammed it into his nose. His head lashed to the side as cartilage snapped and blood poured. But the cartilage realigned in seconds and the blood ceased flowing.

He glared down at her. "Fight like a girl, for gods' sake," he said between shallow breaths, struggling to grab her wrists. Then, finally, he caught them.

That easily, he had her restrained. Aias had held her down like this, but only for a moment. She'd quickly managed to buck him off. Lucien, she couldn't budge no matter how hard she tried. And yet, she wasn't filled with the same sense of murderous rage. She was excited. "You're hurting me," she lied.

He made the mistake of releasing her wrists. She punched him again, this time in the eye. The bone cracked from the impact, swelling—she laughed; turning black—she laughed harder. Healing—she pouted.

"You are not going to flash," he ground out. His gaze was boring into her and that rose-fresh scent was clouding her mind, urging her to relax, to stay where she was and not fight him any longer.

She softened into the ground and licked her lips. Two could play the seduce-me game. Not because it would be fun, she assured herself. "No, I won't flash. I'm too busy imagining my thighs wrapped around your waist."

His pupils dilated, and he groaned. "Stop that. I command you."

"Stop what?" she asked innocently.

"Stop saying things like that. And stop looking at me like that."

"You mean, like you're going to be my dinner?"

He gave a single jerk of his head.

"Can't," she said with a slow grin.

"Yes, you can. You will."

"When you stop looking so edible, *then* I'll obey." But as she issued the sultry promise, her mind was racing. *You're a fighter, Anarchy. You've battled immortals stronger than Death. Playtime is over.*

Forcing herself from Lucien's erotic pull and drawing on the instincts that had kept her alive through the darkest days of her existence, she flashed behind him. Without her body to hold him up, he smashed facefirst into the sand.

It has to be this way. As he came up sputtering, she kicked him, swiftly sending him back down. Then she leapt on top of him, straddling his hips and wrapping her fingers around his jaw to twist and break his neck.

But he, too, flashed, appearing in front of a palm tree several feet away from her. Her knees hit the dirt before she was able to right herself and stand. He made no move toward her. Panting, she brushed the sand from her legs. The gentle breeze was filled with the mockingly serene aroma of coconuts and salt water. Roses. *I almost killed him,* she thought, shaken.

"At this rate, neither of us will win," he said.

She pasted a cocky grin on her face. "Who are you trying to fool? I'm totally winning."

He slammed a fist into the tree, knocking several pieces of red fruit to the ground. "There must be another way. Surely there is a way around your death."

His vehemence made her tingle; his sudden willingness to try to save her made her ache. She sighed. The man could shove her from one end of the emotional gauntlet to the other in seconds. "If you're thinking of petitioning Cronus, don't. He won't change his mind, and he'll punish you for attempting it."

Lucien splayed his arms wide, the very picture of exasperated male. "Why can't he kill you himself?"

"You'd have to ask him." She shrugged as if she didn't know the answer.

"Anya," Lucien said, a warning. "Tell me."

"No."

"Anya!"

"No!" She could have flashed to her knives, but didn't. She could have flashed to him, but didn't do that, either. Instead she waited, curious as to what the warrior would do or say next.

He expelled a sigh, the perfect mimic of her own, as his arms fell back to his sides. "What are we going to do about this, then?"

"Make out?" she suggested cheekily. She'd meant the words as a taunt, a jest, hating that she would have gone to him in a heartbeat if he'd given her any encouragement. *I'm pathetic.*

He blanched as if she'd struck him.

Irritated, she ran her tongue over her teeth. Was the thought of kissing her again that abhorrent? "Why do you hate me?" she found herself asking before she could stop the words. Damn it. She sounded ashamed, as if the woman she was didn't deserve to be loved. *Sorry, Mom.* Dysnomia had taught her better.

"I do not hate you," Lucien admitted softly.

"Oh, really? You look ready to vomit at the thought of touching me."

A wry smile greeted her words, there one moment, gone the next. Anya nearly fell to the ground in awe. Finally, a true smile from him. She should have known it would be sensually potent, decadent. Addicting. Already she craved another. His grin was as radiant as the sun.

"And yet I have an erection," he said in a tone as wry as his expression.

Okay. Who was this man? First a smile, and now he was teasing her. Her blood heated and her nipples hardened (again). "A man doesn't have to like a woman to want her." He opened his mouth to reply, but she cut him off. "Just hush it, okay. I don't want to hear your response." He would ruin the happy buzz she had going, she just knew it. "Stand there and look pretty while I think."

"You're purposely trying to provoke me, are you not?"

Yes, she was. A foolish move on her part, really. He'd been ordered to render her death blow. Every time she incited him, she probably made the thought of it a little easier for him to bear. But she couldn't help herself. That smile…

"Have you no answer for me?"

"Not one I'm willing to share." Why did he have to look so sexy standing there? The sun was acting like his lover, caressing him, weaving an angelic halo around his dark head. Yes, angelic. He was a fallen angel just then, causing her pulse points to throb and her stomach to quiver.

Why couldn't they have been simply a man and a woman?

Why couldn't he have wanted her the way she wanted him?

Why wouldn't her obsession with him wane, now that he was bound to snuff her out for eternity?

"You are making this difficult."

"You won't break the rules for me?" she asked, batting her lashes. "You won't do me this one teeny-weeny favor? You owe me."

"No. I can't."

He hadn't even hesitated in the delivery of his answer and that pissed her off. The least he could have done was take a few minutes to think about it. Bastard. She scowled. "I'm giving you one more chance to agree. We'd be even, the chalkboard clean."

"I am sorry. I must again decline."

Fine. That meant there was only one way to end the madness.

Finally she *did* flash to her knives. She did flash to him. His eyes widened in surprise as she materialized in front of him. With the hilt facing him, she chop-blocked him in the throat, spun while he struggled to breathe and slammed the other hilt into his temple to render him unconscious.

Contact.

Only, he didn't sink into unconsciousness. He fell to his knees with a groan. Didn't matter. Either way, the outcome was the same. Disappointed that it had come to this, she twirled the daggers in her palms so that the sharp tips pointed directly at him.

Her hands trembled as she stared at the top of his head. Everything inside of her was screaming not to do this, but she swung the blades into a crisscross, anyway. There were only a few ways to kill an immortal permanently and decapitation was one of them. *Do it...no other way...* She'd already placed the blades at his neck, needing only to slam her wrists together. *Do it before he flashes!*

Oh, gods, oh, gods. She did it. Moved to cut him. Instead of flesh, however, her weapons encountered only air.

He'd flashed.

Frustration and elation battled for supremacy. Before she had time to act on either, strong, viselike fingers jammed into her shoulders, spinning her around. Searing lips slammed over her mouth, prying it open and stealing her breath.

Lucien's tongue thrust against hers in a white-hot kiss that would haunt her waking and sleeping for thousands of years to come. Dead or alive. It was bliss and it was agony. It was heaven and it was hell. Having his flavor drown her so perfectly, his strength and heat at the ready, craving more.

"Lucien." She gasped and moaned and reached for him, dropping the weapons in her haste to have his skin under her palms.

"Not another word. Kiss me like before."

His fervency excited her all the more. Apparently, dancing for him and throwing herself at him weren't enough. Apparently, she had to nearly commit murder to arouse him enough to attack her.

His arms snaked around her waist and hauled her snugly into the heat of his body. The action rubbed his swollen penis against the wet, needy juncture between her thighs, and they both groaned in ecstasy.

She wanted to jump into him and devour him whole. She settled for gripping his head, fisting his hair and tilting him to deepen the kiss. A part of her suspected that he was doing this to distract her, but he never went for her throat. He just kept tonguing her as if he couldn't stop himself.

Her nipples were so hard they were probably as sharp as her knives—which she kicked away with the last vestiges of her common sense. "Lucien," she said on another moan, meaning to demand he remove her corset. Skin to skin. She was desperate for it. Dumb, so dumb, to allow skin to skin, but in that moment she wanted it more than she wanted freedom. "Lucien, my shirt."

This time, her voice seemed to snag him from whatever spell he'd been under. He jerked away from her. Without him to hold her up, she almost fell flat on her face as he had done earlier.

"What are you doing?" she demanded as she righted herself.

"I can't think straight right now." Panting, he stepped backward. "I need to get away from you."

There was an angry glint in his eyes, a glint that was dark and violent and utterly menacing. A shiver of fear spread the length of her spine. Fear and even deeper arousal.

What's wrong with me?

He'd told her never to anger him, that bad things would happen if she did. Well, he'd been telling the truth. She'd angered him somehow and he'd stopped kissing her. Nothing was worse than that.

"You're going to leave me like this? Without even giving me an orgasm?" Whoops. She'd meant to sound flippant. She'd sounded needy and whining instead. And breathless.

The glint darkened further. "We will see each other again, Anya. Soon." With that ominous promise, he disappeared.

CHAPTER FOUR

LUCIEN WAS AT A LOSS as he escorted three human souls to the heavens later that night. He was still at a loss as the pearled gates opened wide, revealing golden streets and bejeweled, arched lampposts hanging like diamond-studded clouds. White-clothed angels lined the sides, singing a melodious welcome, their feathered white wings gliding gracefully behind them.

Once the souls crossed the threshold to paradise, the gates closed, blocking him out, and there was only silence.

He was still at a loss.

Usually the beauty and peace he encountered here filled him with twinges of jealousy and resentment, for he would never be allowed inside. Tonight, he did not care. Anya occupied every corridor of his mind; he had no idea what to do about her.

Lucien flashed to his chambers in Buda, his body solidifying at the foot of the bed. He stood unmoving, locked in thought and chaotic emotion he should not have felt. When it came to Death, he knew well the consequences of hesitation. But earlier today he had not only hesitated, he had nearly made love to his intended victim. Tongued her hard, caressed her. He'd had the opportunity to finish her off, so he damn well should have finished her off.

"I am a foolish man," he muttered.

She had come at him with every intention of slaying him. But he'd spun her around, seen the way her glistening red lips parted on a gasp, felt her warm breath on his skin, smelled strawberries and cream, heard his demon purr and had been consumed by the greatest surge of lust he'd ever experienced.

How could he want Anya more than he'd ever wanted Mariah, a woman he'd loved?

How?

Anya had nearly killed him, yet he'd thought, *I cannot die without another kiss from her.* He hadn't cared about anything else. Just her lips. Her body. *Her.*

She was using him to thwart Cronus. She'd admitted as much, which made Lucien's lust all the more foolish. She hadn't seemed to mind his kiss, though. No, she'd seemed to enjoy it, to hunger for more.

"Damn this," he railed, stalking forward and slamming a fist into the wall. Stone instantly cracked and dust plumed around him, clouding his vision. It felt good so he punched again, his knuckles splitting and throbbing. *Relax. Now.*

Nothing good ever came of his anger.

He exhaled slowly as he turned and surveyed his bedroom. Morning had already arrived, he realized with surprise. With all that flashing, he'd lost track of the different time zones. Sunlight streamed through the room's only window. Except for Maddox and Torin, all of the warriors had, most likely, left for their respective destinations in Greece and Rome. *I need to do the same. Anya can be taken care of later, when I'm not reeling from the taste and feel of her.*

He strode to his closet, along the way noticing three vases perched on his vanity. Each overflowed with white, winter flowers and emitted a honey scent. They hadn't been here last night, which meant Ashlyn had been here this morning. Sweet, tenderhearted Ashlyn had probably thought to brighten his day with them, but seeing the blooms caused a pang of regret to tear through his chest.

Mariah used to pick flowers and weave them in her hair.

His door suddenly swung open and Ashlyn rushed inside, concern lighting her pretty face. Maddox, as always, was right behind her, a slash of black menace and lethal grace. He held two blades, poised and ready for attack.

"Everything okay?" Ashlyn asked when she spotted only Lucien. Light brown hair cascaded over her shoulders and down her arms. Arms clutched together in worry. For him? "We were walking down the hall and heard a bang."

"Everything is fine," he assured her. But he kept his attention on Maddox, whose violet eyes were narrowed. *Get her out of here,* he silently willed, not wanting to hurt Ashlyn's feelings. *I am not myself.*

Lucien was dangerously close to losing all semblance of his legendary control. The strain had to show on every line of his face.

Understanding, Maddox gave a nod. "Ashlyn." He curled a hand around her shoulder. "Lucien is preparing for his journey to the temple. Let's leave him to it."

She didn't shrug off the warrior's hold. Rather, she leaned into him. She also refused to budge. Her gaze dipped over Lucien, scrutinizing, gauging. "You don't look fine."

"All is well," he lied. How many would he tell? He bent down, clasped the handles of his bag and threw it onto the bed.

"Your hand is bleeding and your bones are… Dear God." Frowning, she reached out.

Maddox grabbed hold of her wrist, stopping her. He was keeper of Violence, yet he was gentle with his woman, so protective and possessive of her it was almost comical.

"Maddox," she said, exasperated. "I just want to see how bad his injuries are. We might have to reset the bones."

"Lucien will heal, and you need to rest."

"Rest, rest, rest. I'm four weeks pregnant, not sickly."

The proud couple had announced the news mere days ago. Then and now, Lucien was happy for them, but he also wondered what the offspring of a demon-possessed warrior and a mortal female with unusual powers would be. Half-demon? Fully demon? Completely mortal? Once, he'd wondered the same thing about a child of his own. His and Mariah's. But she had been taken from him before they'd even decided to try to conceive.

"Your man is correct," he said. "I am fine."

Determination radiated from Ashlyn, her large brown eyes never leaving Lucien. Tenderhearted she might be, but she was also stubborn to her very core.

She had grown up in a science lab, studied and used for a unique ability she'd only just learned to control. Wherever she stood, Ashlyn could hear every conversation that had taken place there, no matter how many years had passed. She could not, however, hear prior conversations between him and the other immortals, which had to irk her when she desired answers they wouldn't give.

"Word has already spread about you and a woman at the club," she said, blinking innocently. "Who is she?"

"She is no one." Except the new center of his world. *Anya, beautiful Anya.* His hands curled tightly at his sides. Even her name excited him, caused his blood to simmer deliciously and his body to ready for sex. *She's not for you.* "Warriors should not gossip."

He and Anya probably looked silly together. Her, the epitome of lush femininity. Him, an ugly beast of a man. Still, he could not stop himself from imagining his hand fisted in her hair, his body pounding in and out of hers. Hard, fast. Slow, tender.

Pretty, Death suddenly growled.

Lucien blinked in surprise. Usually the demon remained a compulsion rather than a voice; always a part of him, yet always distanced. Why it would speak up now, he didn't know. Still, he found himself replying. *Yes, she is.* Four times he had seen her. Four times he had spoken to her. For these past few weeks, he had scented her. Already she was ingrained in his cells—his thoughts, his desires, his purpose—more than anyone else, even his beloved Mariah, had ever been.

Want her. Death again.

Yes.

Tastes good. Have her before we kill her.

No! Even as he shouted the word inside his head, he felt the demon tugging at him, trying to force him to find Anya.

He planted his feet into the ground. *Not yet.*

"Lucien," Ashlyn prompted, drawing his attention back to her. The pressure inside of him eased. "I'm not a warrior, so I can gossip. You kissed her. Everyone said they saw you—"

"I am fine, and the woman is of no concern," he lied. Gods, another. Usually he abhorred lies. He reached out to tweak Ashlyn's nose, heard Maddox growl and dropped his arm. Maddox did not like for anyone else to touch his female. Ever. And for the first time, Lucien understood that. He despised the thought of other men touching Anya.

Idiot. The woman manipulated with a smile on her perfect face, and he was willing to bet that, like her mother, she had been intimate with legions. Whether she'd used those lovers for pleasure or power, he didn't know. Shouldn't care.

What if she were seducing another right now, trying to secure protection from Lucien?

A roar shoved from his throat and he found himself twisting, moving to confront the wall again, punching, punching, his knuckles throbbing insistently. From the corner of his eye, he saw Maddox whip Ashlyn behind his back.

What are you doing? Anya can well take care of herself. She doesn't need a man to protect her.

Perhaps she was alone on the beach, as needy and confused as he was. The thought softened the edges of his anger, even as it made his body incredibly hard. But as much as he wished to believe it, he knew a woman like her would not crave a scarred man like him. Not truly. No matter how hot her kisses. How many had turned away from him over the centuries? How many had cringed when he neared?

Countless.

And that had been—was—just the way he liked it.

Deep breath in, deep breath out. "How is Torin?" he asked, changing the subject as he stalked to the bed. "I do not like how slowly he is healing."

Ashlyn shoved Maddox aside, and the big warrior scowled, but let her. "I think I figured out why he hasn't bounced back as quickly as the rest of you do. He's Disease, right? Well, I think his cells are affected by that sickness. They have to fight the virus as well as the wound. Anyway, he *is* healing. He's eating on his own now."

"Good. That's good." Lucien still felt guilty about the attack Torin had endured. He should have been here. Should have sensed Torin's pain.

If the Hunters who had sneaked inside hadn't touched Torin's skin, infecting themselves with disease and weakening their forces, Torin *would* have died. Lucien had thought he'd taken the necessary precautions to prevent such an event, for he would rather *his* neck be sliced than one of the others. Yet his necessary precautions had failed.

"And how is Aeron?"

"Well." Ashlyn faltered, sighed. She bit her lip. "He's not so good."

"The bloodlust is so great he's taken to clawing himself," Maddox said, his voice grave. "Nothing I say penetrates his dark thoughts."

Lucien massaged the back of his neck. "Are you two going to be all right on your own?"

"Yes." Maddox wrapped his arm around Ashlyn's waist. "Torin is able to monitor the grounds on his computers and now that my death-curse is broken," he said, hugging his woman close, "I can leave at any time to defend us or procure items we might need."

Lucien nodded. "Good. I'll let you know what we find." He swiped up his bag and said over his shoulder, "Thank you for the flowers, Ashlyn." Without another word, he flashed to the Cyclades Islands in Greece.

Silver stone walls gave way to white stucco. The home he had already purchased and furnished was open and airy, with towering white columns and gauzy white material draping the windows.

He dropped his bag and stepped to the nearest balcony, an airy terrace that looked out onto the clearest water he'd ever seen. Smooth, no waves. Not even a ripple. The sun glowed lovingly—it was already midday—and lush green bushes with bright red blooms framed the edges of the building.

Perhaps he and the other warriors should have stayed in Athens or Crete to be closer to the ancient temple they meant to search, but there was more anonymity on the islands. Fewer tourists and even fewer locals.

"The fewer the better," he muttered.

He did not remember much of his time here, all those thousands of years ago, so he could not compare then with now. Those days had been dark, filled with screams and pain and acts so evil he didn't *want* to remember them.

I am a different man now.

And yet, he felt as if he would soon commit his most evil act yet. Slaying Anya. *Do not think about her death. Not now.*

What *should* he think about, then? he wondered, refocusing on the crystal water. Whether or not she would like the view? He rubbed his jaw with a sigh—and found that he was truly curious. Would she?

Doesn't matter. You can't let it matter. He forced his attention to the left—*do not think about Anya*—and marveled at the newest sight: emerald mountains laced with white and violet. Surely this was the gods' greatest creation.

No, that would be Anya.

His teeth gnashed together. What must he do to wipe her from his mind? He knew what he wanted to do. Strip her right here on the balcony and push her naked body against the iron railing, sunlight caressing her as he meant to do. He would touch her so exquisitely she wouldn't care about his scarred face. He would make her climax, over and over again, shouting his name. Desperate for more of him. So desperate she would forget every other man she'd slept with and think only of Lucien. Crave only Lucien.

The chances of that happening were as slim as those of Lucien's face returning to its former glory. Not that he wanted it to. He'd earned every one of his scars. They were a part of him now, a permanent reminder that loving a woman equaled pain and suffering.

He had never needed the reminder more.

He could not put off thinking of Anya's death, he decided. She would haunt him until he figured this out. *Get it over with.* How should he kill her? He didn't want to hurt her, so it would have to be quick. When should he do it? At night, while she slept? His stomach churned with acid. What exactly would the Titans do if he failed? Like Aeron, would he be driven mad with bloodlust? Would his friends fall, one by one? Fury stabbed at him with the thought.

Lucien withdrew one of the candies he still carried in his pocket, discarded the wrapper and sniffed. Instant arousal obliterated his anger as strawberry fragrance filled his nose. Why had he done such a foolish thing? The anger returned, but now it was directed at himself.

Scowling, he pitched the lollipop over the railing. Heard a splash as it hit the water. Ripples disrupted that smooth tranquility.

Behind him, a door opened. Closed. Male voices and snickering laughter suddenly reverberated. Lucien turned, unconcerned. There was Paris, tall and pale and perfect, radiating sexual contentment. The warrior had just bedded a woman, that much was obvious.

Beside him was Amun, silent, dark and simmering with untold secrets.

Strider, whose ruthlessly handsome face glowed with amusement, was punching Gideon in the shoulder. "You know you're jealous," he was saying.

"Don't hate the player," Paris said, grin widening. "I can't help it if *both* flight attendants wanted to see to my needs midair."

Lucien strode inside the spacious home, warm air replaced by cool. "We paid for a private jet, not a private bedding for Paris."

All four men withdrew a weapon as his voice cut through their good-natured ribbing. As soon as they realized who had spoken, they relaxed. Even smiled.

"Private is the wrong word," Strider said, blue eyes twinkling. "They did it in front of everyone. And I'm not complaining. The movie was crap, so their performance kept me entertained."

Lucien rolled his eyes, doing his best not to appear envious. "Take a look around. Pick a bed." Because he could flash, he was the only one who had been here before. He hadn't yet picked a room because he'd wanted to give the others first choice. He was happy to take whatever was left.

Bags were suddenly thrown aside as the men toured their temporary new "digs," as Paris would say.

"Nice," Paris said after choosing the room in back. "Chicks will certainly love it."

"Sucks," Gideon said, but everyone ignored him as usual. Everything out of his mouth was a lie. He'd taken the room closest to the front door.

"How long have you been here?" Strider asked Lucien as he came back into the living room.

"Only a few minutes."

"How is that even possible?" Strider and Lucien had only been reunited a month ago, Strider part of the group who had remained in Greece to fight the Hunters after Lucien's men had departed for Budapest. Hundreds of years had since passed, and they were only now getting to know each other again. "You didn't fly out before us, and you damn sure didn't fly with us."

Paris swung an arm over the wide expanse of Lucien's shoulders. "My man here did a little something called flashing." He proceeded to explain how Lucien could enter the spirit world and travel from one location to another in the blink of an eye. "Learned it a few years after we arrived in Buda."

Before then, he hadn't had enough control over the demon to master the ability.

Strider nodded, clearly impressed. "Cool skill. But why didn't you just flash all of us?"

Again, Paris answered for him. "Last time he spread the flashing love, Reyes threw up all over his shirt. I never laughed so hard in my life. Lucien, though, has no sense of humor and vowed never to take us again."

"I'm surprised you didn't mention the part where you fainted," Lucien said wryly.

Strider chortled. "Oh, man. You fainted? What a baby! Shit, look at that view," he added with barely a pause, catching sight of the terrace. "Reminds me of Olympus."

"Hey," Paris said, frowning at Lucien. "I told you I hit my head midflash."

"That doesn't make you any less of a baby," Strider tossed over his shoulder. He braced his arms on the balcony frame and leaned forward. "No matter how many times I see this place, it feels like the first time."

Paris wasn't letting the subject drop. "Let's see your reaction to a flash, Defeat. I bet you—"

"Stop," Lucien interjected with a raised hand. Paris knew better than to issue any type of challenge to Strider. Once the man entered into a competition, be it a knife fight, boxing or even the human game he and Paris liked to play, Xbox, he could not lose without suffering intense, debilitating pain. Needless to say, he did anything necessary to win at everything. "We have work to do."

"Work sucks," Gideon said.

Lucien ignored him. "We need to better secure the building in case any Hunters managed to follow us. After that, we'll prepare for our outing tomorrow."

They had the first done in an hour, placing sensors on the windows and around the building. They were sweating when they reentered the living room.

"I had Torin look a few things up before we left," Paris said, digging weapons from his boots and placing them on the nearest tabletop. "He thinks the temple we're going to search is the Temple of the All Gods. Ever heard of it?"

Lucien shook his head. Anya had not mentioned names. *Anya...* He ran his tongue over his teeth, his blood heating. In arousal for the woman, in fury at the god who wanted her dead.

"What do you think we'll find?" Strider asked, his features pensive as he peered at Lucien. "And why the hell do you now look capable of murder? These last few weeks the only expression you've given us was bored. I mention the temples and hello, demon."

The others whipped to face Lucien and were obviously shocked by what they saw. "Hopefully we'll find the box," he said, disregarding the other question. "Or at least a clue as to its whereabouts." Unfortunately, he would have to deal with Anya while looking. *Anya.* Fighting. Dying. Dead.

"Shit. His eyes are red. I've never seen that happen to him before." Paris.

"I remember what he was like back in the demon days, and it wasn't pretty." Strider. "Should we, I don't know, chain him?"

"Yeah, that'll be fun," Gideon said.

"Give me a minute, and I'll be fine." Before they could do anything, Lucien flashed back to Antarctica, right into the frigid water. He gasped, suddenly chilled to the bone. Yet while the icy liquid helped cool the fierceness of his anger, it did little to quench his desire for the woman currently taking up prime real estate inside his head.

He was beginning to think nothing could.

CHAPTER FIVE

ANYA STAYED AWAY FROM Lucien for twenty-four hours. By the end, she seethed with nervous energy, constantly wondering if he'd appear. Every unexplained noise made her jump. Made her gasp. Made her heart kick into overdrive.

She'd paced the floors of her beach home, had tried to watch a movie but couldn't even recall what disc she'd shoved into the DVD player, and then had locked herself in her favorite room. Her treasure room. Usually rifling through the things she'd stolen over the centuries delighted her. Today, not so much.

She'd draped herself in Queen Elizabeth's jewels and played darts with King George V's dagger. She'd sipped strawberry-kiwi juice from an Episcopal chalice and drawn a mustache on the original *Mona Lisa*. Having spent a little time with Leo, she knew he wouldn't have minded.

What would Lucien think of her treasures? she wondered. Would he stumble back, horrified by the glittering sea of contraband? Probably. He was such a downer sometimes. Or maybe he would have understood, she thought, hopeful. Maybe, after battling his demon for so long, he would have realized that theft was her way of protecting humans from the darker side of her own nature. Well, that, and she liked pretty things.

Anya sighed and returned to the glistening sand outside. *He isn't coming,* she thought with disappointment, staring into the pristine ocean waves. The sun had long since set, then risen, then set again. Now violet and amber glowed on the horizon, glinting off the azure water. Sand squished between her bare toes, and coconut and orchids scented the air.

She'd both fought Lucien and kissed him here, the most action she'd seen in hundreds of years, so was loathe to leave. Was it dumb to miss him?

"Probably," she muttered, flinging sand with a flick of her ankle.

A little while ago, she had donned a skimpy sapphire bikini with ties on each side of her waist. If he had returned as she'd anticipated, they would have rumbled hardcore and one of her breasts might have "accidentally" popped out. He would have started sweating, the fighting would have turned to loving and they would have kissed again.

They would have touched again.

She sighed. *Not going to happen.* The gentle breeze whisked a strand of pale hair over her eyes. She hooked it behind her ear and frowned. What was he doing? Did he miss her? Even a little?

Was he plotting the best way to kill her, even now?

The bastard was probably happy to be away from her. "And that just won't do."

Her eyes narrowed as her hands tightened into fists. If he wouldn't come to her, she'd just have to go to him.

HUNTERS HAD BEATEN THEM to the Temple of the All Gods.

The tiny island had only begun to rise from the sea a few weeks before, and so far, the rest of the world did not seem to know about it. Not even with their satellites and other technology. Therefore, Hunters *should* not have known about it.

Who, then, had told them?

What Lucien knew, he knew because of Anya. When she had helped Maddox, she had helped them all by revealing the location of the ruins and explaining the new gods' intention for them: to bring the world back to the old ways of worship and blood sacrifice. Had she told the Hunters, as well?

Perhaps she'd done so to spite him, he thought. He'd tried to kill her, after all.

And a worse attempt I've never seen. Disgraceful!

His jaw locked in irritation. *Now is not the time to think of her.*

When is *a good time?*

Later.

He could almost hear Death clapping happily in his mind, and he didn't think it was because the demon was eager to take Anya's soul. He didn't understand why the demon cared to see her, but he had no time to reason it out.

The Hunters were camped in the surrounding foliage and they had to be disposed of quickly, surely. Once, he had turned away from this war. Once, but not again. Everything the Hunters did, every move they made, was meant to harm and destroy his friends.

Lucien hadn't noticed them this morning when he flashed to the island to look around before bringing the others here. But then he'd only been here a few minutes. Death had begun to pull at him, a spiritual pull that often became a physical tearing if he resisted for long.

He'd ended up spending the day ushering one human after another to their final destination, only returning at twilight, at last able to search as he'd hoped and make sure all was safe for the others.

That was when he'd caught a glimpse of the Hunters. He'd been shocked. Was still shocked. Not only because they'd beaten him to the temple, but also because they had rallied their forces so soon after the plague. Their determination was greater than he'd realized.

Only a little while ago, they had walked away from the

ruins and headed back to their camp. A camp they had hidden extremely well, using leaves as roofs and tunnels they'd either dug or found as shelter.

How long had they been here? Whatever the answer, he already knew what they had planned.

"We'll kill them all," he'd heard one of them say as they'd walked. Lucien had been in the spirit world, so they hadn't seen him.

"Make sure they suffer first," another had cackled.

"When those demons are locked up, I think I'll wear one of their keeper's teeth as a necklace. Every time they take a breath, exhaling their evil onto the world, it seems like someone I know or love is struck with sickness or misfortune, and I'm tired of it. If they'd been disposed of years ago, my Marilyn wouldn't have died of cancer. She'd still be here. I know it."

"World won't be right until they're gone. They might have fooled the people of Buda into thinking they're angels, but history has proven otherwise. You guys see the portrait of Death in ancient Athens?" Shudder. "Not a single survivor."

Block his words. Obviously they were searching for the box. For all he knew, they might already have found a trace of its location. He hated that they wanted it, but knew why they did. After they had killed Baden, the demon of Distrust had sprung from the lifeless body and even now wandered the earth, more crazed and destructive than ever before.

That was when the Hunters realized they could not kill the Lords *and* their spirits. And so, to rid the world of both, they had to capture and subdue the Lords, then secure the demons back inside the box. If they found it.

Time was more of an enemy than ever. Lucien flashed to the warriors, who were watching a movie inside the rented house, waiting for him.

"Finally," Strider said, spotting him. "Was getting worried."

"Hunters," he said, and they instantly sat up.

Paris jumped to his feet, whipping up his weapons in a blink. "How many?"

"I counted thirteen above ground. There could be more in their tunnels, coming and going. Since I can't watch more than one location at a time, my count could be off."

Amun withdrew a semiautomatic from the waist of his pants and checked the magazine.

"There is *not* going to be a bloodbath tonight," Gideon said with a grin.

Rather than take a boat as originally planned, Lucien flashed them all to the island, one at a time. He would rather prance around Anya in a dress than wait. To everyone's amusement, Paris passed out during their journey and it took several minutes to revive him. Strider handled his first flash with ease, grinning the entire split second required to move from one location to another. Amun didn't show any reaction at all. As Reyes had once done, Gideon vomited but quickly pulled himself together.

All the while, Lucien could feel Anya's eyes on him. The soul-deep burn had returned, stripping him bare. Death even started purring again.

Knowing she was there caused Lucien's muscles to tighten with strain. Not because he thought she'd attack—he expected that, but didn't fear it—but because he could not forget how she felt in his arms. He could not forget the way she moaned when the hot tip of his tongue ran over her throat. The way her nipples hardened, begging for his mouth. The way her legs parted, welcoming him as close to heaven as a man like him could ever hope to get.

Right then, he wanted off the island. He wanted her naked and in his bed. He wanted his hands on her body, and *her* hands on *his* body. Wanted his mouth between her thighs, and her mouth on his cock. He just…wanted.

And he could not have.

Concentrate! Crouching in moonlight and dewy foliage, water rushing all around, he muttered, "Do not interfere."

"What?" Strider asked, confused as he crouched beside him.

"Never mind." The moon was high and laced with golden ribbons, caressing the sand and greenery. Insects sang happily. He could have taken the Hunters down on his own. Simply flashed inside their tunnels and attacked, but he did not want to risk one getting away.

"Are you sure they're Hunters?" Paris asked, squatting in the leaves on Lucien's other side.

"Yes. I saw their marks." Every Hunter sect branded themselves with a symbol of Infinity on their wrists. "Infinity without evil" was their credo.

Lucien did not consider himself completely evil. At one time, yes, he had been. His demon had constantly compelled him to take lives, not just souls, and he had. Gladly. But no longer. The desire to kill had thankfully been tamed. Now, he fought only for peace and protection.

Regret struck him that he could not have more, and he squeezed his eyes shut for a moment. Were he merely a mortal, he would have married long ago. He and Mariah would have had a dozen children. He would have spent his days caring for his family and his nights loving his wife. And when he died he would have been welcomed into paradise.

But he had not been created to enjoy life. He had been created to guard the god king and to defend the heavens. And then, once he and the demon had joined, even that had been taken from him. *You deserved it, you know you did.*

"This could be a trap," Strider said, drawing his attention.

"They did not know I was here, nor did they seem to be preparing for any type of battle."

Paris gripped the hilt of a dagger. "How should we do this?"

"We'll encircle their camp. On my signal, we'll rush the tunnels silently, locking them inside with no chance of escape. There are four entrances. I looked earlier. Paris, double with Strider and take the west. Gideon, the east. Amun, north. I'll take south."

Each man nodded and silently obeyed.

"Oh, goodie. A battle." Anya laughed softly, suddenly materializing at Lucien's side. She, too, crouched, every bit the warrior.

He was instantly enveloped by that strawberries-and-cream scent. His blood heated—sizzling, blistering. "Quiet," he growled, refusing to look at her. That might prove to be his undoing.

"Aren't you going to attack me?" she asked, and he would swear he heard a pout.

"I have not the time for you right now." He meant the words as an insult, but they emerged dripping with disappointment rather than rancor. "We can fight later."

"You've been neglecting me, and I don't like it."

"You should be grateful for my neglect."

"Don't flatter yourself." She didn't leave in a huff as he'd half expected. Instead, she shifted closer to him. "Can I help you fight the Hunters? Please, please, please, can I?"

"No. Be silent." If the warriors heard him from their positions, they gave no indication. He could just make them out in the bushes, only the tips of their heads visible as they waited for his signal.

"But I'm an expert fighter."

"I know," he replied drily. His chest still ached where she'd stabbed him. Should have been illegal for a woman who looked like her to be so sexily bloodthirsty. And he should not have found that bloodthirstiness so attractive. "Did you tell these Hunters about the temple?"

"Ugh. Why would I help the Hunters?"

"So that they would kill me, and you would no longer have to worry about being killed by me."

"I don't worry about that now," she said matter-of-factly.

Gods save him. Had women always been this way? "What are you doing here, Anya? I left you because I needed space. Time. Is that too much to ask?"

"Yes." She shifted in the grass, angling even closer to him. "I just…I can't get you out of my mind. I missed you."

Hearing that was almost painful. A lie? "Anya."

"No, no. Don't say anything. You'll only make me mad and then bad things will happen. Oh, my gods," she added with a quiet laugh. "I sounded just like you. Look, let me help. I won't get in the way. Swear. Scouts honor. Witches honor. Or whatever kind of promise you want."

A gentle, salt-kissed breeze swept past them, and a lock of her hair brushed his cheek. He experienced an instant and unwanted hard-on as he swatted the silky strands away. "I told you to be silent. I need to study the land." Not that he could concentrate on anything but Anya as her hair continued to stroke him. "And for gods' sake, do something with your hair."

"Cut it?"

"Shave it." Sadly, he doubted even that would lessen her physical appeal. *Concentrate!* he reminded himself. The Hunters had been inside the tunnels for over an hour now. They'd had time to settle, to relax. There was no movement around the entrances, no hint of a watchman.

"Really?" Anya asked with surprise. "You want me to shave it like that sexy warlord Vin Diesel?"

Who was Vin Diesel? And why did Lucien suddenly want to slay him? Lucien popped his jaw. "Yes."

"If I do, will you let me help tonight?"

There was so much eagerness in her voice that he suspected she truly would do it, would shave her head completely bald. Obviously, her hair meant nothing to her. The complete lack of vanity surprised him.

Why did that endear her to him even more?

"No," he finally told her.

"You're such a pain," she grumbled. "Well, guess what? I've already flashed inside those tunnels, and the Hunters have obviously been here a while. They even have prisoners."

Every muscle in his body stiffened. "First, you went inside without my permission, endangering yourself and my purpose?"

"Listen, sweetness." Anger now laced her voice. "Despite what you seem to think, I am a powerful being, and I choose whether or not to endanger myself. Besides, you should be happy I went inside. If I'd gotten caught, they could have saved you the trouble of taking my head."

"Second," Lucien continued as if she hadn't spoken. He could barely get the words out, his throat was so constricted. "They have prisoners?"

"Mmm-hmm. Two of 'em."

Finally, he looked at her—and immediately regretted it. She wore a white gossamer gown with gold threaded throughout, and was even lovelier than he remembered. With the golden glow of moonlight crowning her and emerald plants framing her, she was an ancient queen straight out of a storybook.

The top layers of her pale hair were piled on her head, the rest tumbling down and begging for his touch. Hard fists of desire beat through him. "Who are they?" he forced himself to ask.

"Not a word about my appearance?"

"No." *Looking at you is like finally entering those gates to heaven.* His chest tightened, nearly squeezing his heart to an agonizing stop.

"Seriously, why do I bother?" she grumped. "I could weigh nine hundred pounds, smell like a sewer and wear garbage bags and I'd get the same response from you."

"The prisoners," he prompted grimly.

She shrugged one delicate shoulder and the wispy material of her robe fell to her elbow, revealing inch after inch of creamy skin. Was that...gods in heaven, it was. He could see the plump underside of her breast. He wanted to taste it so badly his teeth actually hurt.

"What about them?" she asked. "They're humans."

He was tempted to offer his own soul to Cronus if the god would spare her and allow Lucien to lick her. A single flick of his tongue. That's all he needed. *Please.* "And?"

Her full lips curled into a slow smile. "They are people who might possess the very knowledge you seek. Don't ask me anything else, though, because I'm not telling. You didn't even comment about my dress and I went to a lot of trouble to steal it."

"Stealing is wrong. But it is...pretty." An understatement. A lie. It was exquisite on her. Would look even more exquisite on his bedroom floor. *Foolish thought.* "Do they know about Pandora's box?"

"I told you, I'm not telling," she huffed. "You weren't supposed to tell me it's pretty. You were supposed to tell me to take it off because I'd look better without it. Lucien, I swear to the gods I'm this close—" she pinched two fingers together "—to giving up on you. This close!"

Do not consider her words. The prisoners knew something about the box, he would bet. Yes, much safer topic. Why else would Hunters have them locked up? His eyes narrowed on the tunnels. He couldn't risk hurting the captives. Not only did he want to protect innocent lives, but whatever knowledge they possessed, *he* wanted to possess.

"You are so frustrating! I'd rather have you try to kill me again than have you ignore me."

With a sigh, he peered at the surrounding foliage. The warriors were still waiting for his signal, most likely wondering about the delay. Without a word to Anya, he flashed to Paris and Strider, told them to be careful of the human prisoners and that he needed a few minutes more. Then he followed suit with Amun and Gideon. Except for the predictably silent Amun, the warriors grumbled.

Then he flashed back to Anya. On top of her, to be exact, trying not to delight in the feel of her warm body pressed to his or the curve of her breasts against his chest when he flipped her over. *You could have landed beside her.* Yes, he could have; he just hadn't wanted to. This ensured she would not run. At least, that was the reason he gave himself.

"Why you little…mmm." Her voice trailed off and she moaned in delight. Her eyes closed to half-mast, the lashes casting spiky shadows over her cheeks. "You want to make out?"

Yes. "No. Wait here." He flashed to his bedroom in Budapest, her exasperated sputtering in his ears. During the seemingly endless span of Maddox's death-curse, they'd had to chain him to his bed every night to keep him from erupting into a fit of unrestrained violence, his control gone, his friends in danger.

Maddox had wanted the metal destroyed once his curse had been lifted, but nothing they tried had melted or broken the godly links. Unable to get rid of them, refusing to use them on Aeron and afraid Hunters would find and use them against a Lord, Lucien had stored them in his bedchamber.

Right now, he swiped them from the closet, pocketed the key and snapped two ends to his bedposts, leaving two ends open and ready. Determined, he flashed back to Anya. She hadn't moved, and he once again settled on top of her.

When she realized he had returned, she wound her legs around his waist and laved her hot tongue up the length of his throat. "Whatever brought about this naughty streak of yours, I heartily approve."

His cock surged, filling and swelling, catching him on fire. Suddenly he was desperate, needier than he'd ever been. The woman he craved and now constantly daydreamed about was writhing against him in truth, running her hands all over him, as eager for more as he was.

One kiss. That's all.

Whether he thought it or the demon spoke it, Lucien didn't know. He only knew that if he kissed Anya, he would not be able to stop. Kissing this woman had proved to be more arousing than making love to another. And even if the time and place were appropriate, he knew better than to indulge with a woman he would soon be forced to kill. *Do not let history repeat itself. End this.*

"Lucien," she gasped. "Kiss me."

"Soon," he vowed, and it was the truth. Depraved as it was, much as he knew better and had just tried to convince himself not to, he would not be able to render that final blow until he'd taken her mouth again.

Remaining on top of her, he flashed them both to his bedroom and onto the bed. When the cool mattress met Anya's back, he swiped up her hands and locked them inside the chains. *Clink.*

She didn't protest as he'd expected.

She glanced around, muttered, "Mmm, your bedroom. I've wanted an invitation real bad." Grinning, she arched her lower body into his—dear gods—and purred straight into his ear. The delicious sound blended with the demon's approving hum. "Is this a kinky new game?" She even bit his earlobe. "What happens in Buda, stays in Buda. Promise."

His erection throbbed as pleasure, so much pleasure, drove into his skin, his muscles. A shiver stole through him, hot and hungry. Again his blood heated; more than burning now, more than blistering. It was lava in his veins, singeing every part of him with desire. His mouth was opening, preparing to ravage her with the kiss he'd promised her, promised them both, but once again he managed to stop himself.

No contact. No kissing. Not yet. There were Hunters to kill.

No falling for her, either. No craving more. Sooner rather than later, she would die. To be her lover, as well as her executioner, would make him as despicable as the demon inside him.

"Aren't you going to play with me?" she asked in that husky voice of hers. "Aren't you going to kiss me? Soon is now."

"Anya." He didn't know what else to say. His heavy weight pinned her down and her legs parted farther, causing him to sink deeper. He was still impossibly hard, and his erection was rubbing at her of its own damn accord, their clothing adding to the electric friction.

She bit the cord of his neck and rocked into him, prolonging the contact. He gripped her hips to still her, and the action cost him dearly. He had to grit his teeth against the wild surge of denied lust.

"I like this game," she said breathlessly. "Any rules?"

"Just one," he forced past a clenched jaw.

"Tell me." Her knees rubbed his sides, beckoning him even deeper.

"The only rule…" He raised his hands and cupped her cheeks, his thumb caressing her velvet-soft skin. Oh, that he could stay here forever. Or that he could bask in her, if only for a little while. "The only rule is that you are to stay here."

"Mmm, I love to break—hey. What?" She frowned up at him. "Stay here with *you,* right?"

"No." He rose from the bed, severing all contact. His body screamed in protest; his demon cursed at him. Of all Lucien's crimes, leaving her like this suddenly seemed the worst.

Her frown deepened. "Lucien? What—" She tried to raise her arms but couldn't. Her narrowed gaze slid to the head-board, lingered for a moment as she gave another jerk, then returned to him. "I don't understand."

"The only pleasure you will receive in that bed is the pleasure you give yourself." *For now.*

Gods, don't think like that.

"I'm down with that. But if you want to watch me pleasure myself, you'll have to remove the chains."

Again not the response he'd expected; he wanted to groan. Anya…hand between her legs…rubbing her clitoris…bringing herself to orgasm… If imagining was wholly erotic and utterly breathtaking and caused his knees to weaken like a human's, what would actually witnessing the event be like?

"Stay here," he choked out, "and stay quiet. I'll come back for you. You have my word."

"Come back for me?" Now her eyes widened. "Where are you going? And you had better say to get a whip and a spiked collar because you want nothing more than to be my bitch or you'll regret it."

"I'm going back to the temple. I'll return as soon as the Hunters have been defeated."

A shocked gasp slipped from her. Perhaps there was hurt mixed in, as well, but he didn't want to acknowledge it. "I can flash with you. Chains can't hold me."

"These can. They were made for immortals."

A second passed. Another.

She stared over at him, mouth drawn tight. He much preferred that mouth soft—and all over his body. Any chance of that had been ruined by his actions today, he would not doubt.

It was better this way, he told himself, but he couldn't halt a surge of bitter regret.

"You're saying I can't flash?" she gritted out.

"That is exactly what I am saying."

"And you're going to leave me like this?"

"Yes. Behave," he said and left her, materializing in the exact spot he'd abandoned.

The moment those lush blades of grass surrounded him, guilt and need flooded him. Guilt because he'd left her helpless. Need because, well, he had the memory of being on top of her inside his mind, fresh, taunting. Wondrous.

And she had seemed to want him. Until he'd ruined it.

What was he going to do with her? The woman was tying him into knots!

She probably hated him now. She would never forgive him. She—appeared right beside him and punched him the eye.

"Bastard," she snarled.

Amazement and pain pounded through him as he gazed at her. Damn, but she was strong. She'd managed to crack the bone, he suspected, the injury swelling. "How did you get free?" Those chains had been unbreakable for centuries.

"I have my ways."

"How?" he insisted.

"I can't be locked up, okay? No matter what restraints you use, *I can't be contained.* And if you ever do something like that again…" Her hands tightened into fists. "Freedom is everything. You know that better than most since you were forced to harbor a demon. You were even bound to take your friend's soul every night for centuries. An obligation I helped free you from. Remember that? For you to try and take *my* freedom… Oh! I could seriously saw you in half with one of my fingernails."

Better this way, remember? "Those chains have been used on gods and have never failed. Only the key can unlock them, and I have that in my pocket."

"Big fucking deal, you son of a bitch. I told you I was powerful—not my fault you failed to listen. I'm helping fight the Hunters now and you'll be lucky if my aim doesn't accidentally-on-purpose veer and kill *you*. In fact, I don't think I'll wait for you." She glanced over at the tunnels and counted with a point of her finger. "See you in the...second one over, sweetcakes. That's where the biggest, baddest Hunter was, last time I checked. I'll just pretend he's you and nail his ass to the wall."

She disappeared a moment later, leaving only a cloud of strawberries, cream and smug fury. Damn this! He gave a whistle and leapt forward. The now impatient warriors sprang forth, as if tethers had been sliced.

Silent, they kicked aside leaves and twigs. When Lucien reached the second tunnel, Gideon's, he tossed the makeshift roof and let himself fall inside, not wanting to flash and startle his men. Gideon frowned but didn't comment as he followed him down. Each of them had weapons raised and ready.

There was a grunt. A shout. Lucien tensed, looking...looking...damn it, he didn't see Anya, nor did he see—

Hunters. There. Two, over in the corner. One was beating an older human male and the other was subduing a middle-aged male. Both prisoners were begging the Hunters to stop.

"Tell me what I need to know," one Hunter said, his reasonable tone at odds with the violence of his actions, "and the pain ends. That's all you have to do."

"I'm sick of coming back empty-handed," the other—the tallest and most muscled—added just as reasonably, kicking the older man in the stomach.

There was a *hmph*. The younger man yelled, "Stop. Just stop. He doesn't know anything else!"

"He does. He has to. Tell us or die. Those are your only options right now."

The kicker stepped forward, leaned down toward the prisoners' faces. "You pick death, and it's not going to be quick and gentle, you get me? You'll die, piece by piece."

"Just leave my father alone." The younger man had thrown his arms around the older one, shielding him with his own body. "I swear to you, we've told you everything we know. Just let us go. Please."

"You haven't. You're protecting those demons, might even be working with them."

As if she'd been waiting for Lucien's arrival, Anya appeared beside the biggest Hunter and simply slit his throat before he knew she was there. His body sagged to the ground, and she flicked Lucien a look-what-I-did grin.

She'd just killed a man, violently, without hesitation, and was covered in blood. Seeing her grin about what she'd done shook Lucien's world on its axis. She was a lush and beautiful angel; she was also a killer. Like him.

Though he was intoxicated by the sight of her still, wanted to bask in her, Lucien still managed to toss two daggers at the second Hunter. One embedded in the man's throat, the other in his thigh. Both were kill spots, and rather than choose, he'd decided two were better than one. Just in case. He didn't like how close Anya was to the action, immortal or not. She could be hurt, and the thought of one of these Hunters touching her sparked a deep rage inside him.

"Behind you!" Anya suddenly shouted.

He turned, but not in time. A Hunter had hidden in the shadows and now silently launched himself at Lucien. They clashed together and tumbled to the ground, a blade inching its way toward Lucien's throat. The man didn't seem worried about killing Lucien and unleashing his demon on the world. Looked like he'd snapped, death his only concern.

"Demon spawn!" his opponent spat. "I've been waiting for this day."

Lucien flashed, causing the Hunter to smash into the ground. Bleeding, he reappeared behind the man, reached down and snapped his neck. At the same time, Anya appeared beside him and stabbed the Hunter in the chest.

Panting, Lucien straightened and asked, "Where are the others?"

"I killed two already, and I haven't seen the rest." She wiped her bloody hands on her gown, the crimson stains stark against the virgin white.

Again, the sight was somehow more erotic than having her splayed out on his bed. A delicate-looking beauty, lethal and courageous. A warrior princess. She seemed impressed by him, as well, her gaze sliding over him with lusty heat.

"Good aim," she told him.

Turning away before she saw the evidence of his arousal, he scanned their surroundings. The Hunters had chosen their hideaway wisely and fortified it well. There were multiple rooms and hallways, the muddy walls supported with timbers. There was a table in back, piled high with cans of food and twigs for fire.

From the corner of his eye, he saw Anya bend down in front of the prisoners, who were cowering on the floor, probably afraid the avenging angel would hurt them, too. "Don't worry," she said soothingly. "I'm all about bad guy destruction. You have nothing to fear from me. We're going to get you out of here."

Such gentleness. Even Lucien was charmed.

From down one of the hallways, he heard a grunt, a thump, followed by a piercing bellow of pain. A split second later, the other hallway erupted with human screams—screams that

were quickly cut off. Lucien jumped in front of Anya, prepared to battle if anyone emerged.

Then Paris stalked from one of the rooms, face cut and
bruised, and Lucien relaxed. "My two are dead," the warrior
said proudly, if a bit weakly.

Amun strode from the other side, blood splattered on his
cheeks. He didn't speak—he never spoke—but he did nod.
His targets were defeated, as well.

Strider and Gideon were behind him and both were
grinning. "I nailed three," Strider said, and Lucien noticed
he was limping. "Took a blade to the thigh, but victory is
ours."

"I failed," Gideon said arrogantly.

"Guess the caves are interconnected," Paris said. Lines of
strain now bracketed his too-perfect face. The fight must have
drained the last of his strength. Usually he'd had one or two
women by this time of day—*needed* one or two women to
sate his demon—but Promiscuity hadn't bedded a woman
since the plane ride yesterday.

Anya stepped from the prisoners to Lucien's side, drawing
every eye to her. All three men sucked in a—reverent?
aroused? surprised?—breath.

"Why the hell is *she* here?" Strider demanded. "And why
would a minor goddess fight Hun—"

"Hey! I'm not minor!" Anya said with a stomp of her foot.

Lucien wasn't given a chance to reply. Death tugged at him
insistently, almost painfully, its need to collect the souls
stronger than usual. Death was also whining inside his head,
conflicted, because it wanted to remain next to pretty Anya
almost as much as it needed to act.

What power did she wield over the being? *How* did she
wield it?

"I'll return," he said. He allowed himself to be pulled completely from the physical world and into the spiritual. He could have left his body behind, but didn't want the warriors to have to worry about guarding it. His friends, and even Anya, faded from his line of vision.

He saw only the Hunters, lying on the ground, each bloody and lifeless. Inside the nearly-dead bodies, their spirits writhed, waiting for him.

"Anya," he called. He did not like leaving her alone with the other warriors. No telling what they would try to do— especially Paris.

She didn't appear. She had followed him to this realm before, he knew she had, for he had felt her. Why not now? *She can take care of herself. You've seen the proof of that.*

Hurry! Lucien wasn't responsible for every soul on earth. Many were actually allowed to remain, roaming the land, invisible. He thought he would go mad if he spent his every waking hour in this realm, doing nothing but traveling from earth to hell or earth to heaven. It was burden enough to be responsible for those whose final resting place had already been determined.

He always felt, deep inside, where he was supposed to escort the souls. Sometimes he even saw the final moments of the person's life, whether those moments were layered with sickening cruelty or unerring kindness.

Lucien sighed, studied his targets. There was a black aura around each of them, revealing the corruptness of their natures. These men would soon burn in the eternal fires. He wasn't surprised. While some Hunters actually made it into heaven, he'd known these would not. They were too fanatical and had indiscriminately tortured innocents for answers.

"Is this the *peace* you always longed for?" Lucien floated his ghostly self to the first body. Opening his hand and stretching his fingers, he reached inside the Hunter's chest. When he felt an ice-cold block, he snapped his fingers closed.

The spirit realized it was captured and began struggling as Lucien tugged it from the corpse. Their eyes met, and Lucien knew his were glowing with blue-brown fire.

"No," it screamed. "No. Let me stay here."

The man's sins suddenly flickered through the demon's awareness and in turn through Lucien's. As the man had already proven, he had considered himself above the law, slaying anyone who got in his way—men, women, children—all in the name of a better world.

Bastard.

Maintaining a strong grip on the protesting spirit, he flashed to the entrance of hell. Not Hades—that gloomy underworld was reserved for those who did not deserve either the tortures of hell or the glories of heaven. This man deserved the flames. Though the gates to the fire pit were closed, Lucien could feel the intense heat radiating, could hear the symphony of tormented screams inside, the demonic laughter. The jeers. The stifling scent of sulfur permeated the entire area, enough to make a man gag.

He'd brought Maddox here every night for thousands of years, hating himself all the while, wishing there were something he could do to ease his friend's anguish but knowing there was nothing. Until Anya. As she liked to remind him, she had saved them.

"Please!" the spirit cried. "I'm sorry for—"

"Save your pleas," he said flatly. Over the centuries, he'd heard every desperate bargain imaginable. Nothing swayed him.

What will you do if Anya begs you? What then?

Suddenly Lucien wanted to vomit, to rail, to kill at the thought of bringing such a lovely creature here. Whatever her crime, he doubted she deserved to burn, the flesh melting and peeling from her luscious body only to regenerate and melt again.

Perhaps when she died, she would be allowed in heaven. He could pray, at least.

"Please," the Hunter's spirit screamed as two thick boulders opened up above the pit. Orange-gold flames shot out, crackling and snapping, the smell of sulfur stronger as it blended with the odors of burned hair and rotting tissue.

The spirit's struggles intensified.

When Lucien saw demonic, scaly arms reach through the flames, when he heard the taunting become eager giggles, he tossed the spirit in. The scaly arms caught it and jerked it downward. There was a scream so filled with pain it was deafening, and then the boulders closed.

He didn't know what kept the demons inside, only that something did. Something that had not been able to hold the demon *he* now housed, which was why it had not been returned to hell after it escaped—*thanks to you*—Pandora's box.

If you hadn't opened the box, you might never have met Anya. And that would have been best, he told himself, despite the sudden flare of rightness that came with knowing her. He wouldn't have been commanded to hurt her.

He repeated the journey with every slain Hunter, and when he was finished, he opened his eyes to find himself back in the physical realm. The cave walls closed in around him, dark and bleak. There was silence, but he wasn't sure the quiet was any better than the screams of the Underworld. His mind wanted to fill every second of it with thoughts of Anya.

She'd obsessed him.

And she was gone, he noticed. Disappointment filled him.

Having realized what was happening, his men had continued about their business and had patched up the innocents. Or maybe Anya had done it before she left. Where had she gone?

"I don't understand," Paris said to one of the beaten humans. "For what?"

"Artifacts," the old man said through swollen lips. "Priceless, godly, powerful. Each will lead the bearer closer to Pandora's box, helping him to finally procure it."

Pandora's box. Words guaranteed to engage his complete attention. Lucien joined the group. "How will the artifacts help us find the box?"

Amun stood off to the side, watching, but turned his head when Lucien spoke. Strider flicked him a glance, muttering, "Nice to have you back."

"The woman?"

"Still here," Gideon replied, which meant she had indeed left.

He moved beside Amun and waited for someone to explain.

"Just up and disappeared, right after you," Strider said. "Why does she keep showing up?"

Lucien didn't answer, for he didn't know what truly drove Anya. *I missed you,* she'd said. Had she really? He just didn't know. She was as mysterious as she was beautiful. "Who are these men and how will those artifacts help us find the box?"

Strider shrugged at the abrupt subject change. "They are mortals who've devoted their lives to the study of mythology. And I don't know."

"Can we go home?" the younger man asked. His brown eyes were watery. "Please."

"Soon," Lucien promised gently. "We just need to know what you told the Hunters."

"Hunters?" both asked in unison.

"The men who imprisoned you."

"Bastards," the younger man gritted out. "You plan to kill us after we tell you?"

"No," Strider said with a laugh. "Please. Look at you, then look at me. I don't do puny targets."

The old man gulped. Opened his mouth.

"Don't," the son said.

"It's okay. I'll tell them." The older human drew a heavy breath past his cut and bleeding lips. "According to ancient lore, there are four artifacts. The All-seeing Eye, the Cloak of Invisibility, the Cage of Compulsion and the Paring Rod."

Two rang a distant bell, delighting him. Two were unfamiliar, puzzling him. Mostly the irony of the situation disgusted him. If these humans were correct, they knew more about the world he'd once inhabited than he, a former soldier to the gods, did. "Tell me about them. Please."

With fear in his eyes, the man continued, "Some legends say that all four belonged to Cronus—some say each belonged to a different Titan. Most accounts agree that when Zeus defeated Cronus, he—Zeus—scattered them throughout the world to prevent the former god king from using them again, if he ever managed to escape his prison. For it had been prophesied that the Titans would ultimately destroy the Greeks forevermore."

Why hadn't Zeus killed Cronus to begin with, then, rather than imprison him? For that matter, why hadn't Cronus killed Zeus after his escape? Why choose imprisonment? Gods. He might never understand them, Lucien thought, even were he to devote years to studying them as these mortals had done. "What else do you know about the four artifacts?"

The younger man shrugged, taking over the story. "The All-seeing Eye provides glimpses into the otherworld, illuminating the right path. The Cloak shields the wearer from prying eyes. The Rod may part the ocean, though that is widely disputed, and the Cage enslaves whoever is locked inside. Like we said earlier, all four are needed to find and win the box, or so the legend goes, but we don't know why."

"And where are these artifacts now?" Paris rushed out. All of the warriors crowded around the men in anticipation of their reply.

The old man sighed even as he inched backward, as if fearing the warriors would erupt with his next words. "Again, we don't know." He laughed, the sound bitter. "We've been looking for them a long time and never found any indication they truly existed."

"That's why those bastards brought us here," the younger one added. "To help them hunt for clues."

"Had they found anything?" Lucien asked.

"No." The younger man shook his head. "And they were more frustrated by the day. They have men everywhere, all over the world, searching. Much as I might wish otherwise, I seriously doubt there's anything to find. If there were, we would have found it by now."

He had known the Hunters were everywhere, but he hadn't been aware of the artifacts. It was his fault, really. For so long, he'd purposely cut himself off from the world, content to live quietly in his fortress, the heavens a distant if bitter memory. Never again.

Cronus had to want the items back. Desperately. Perhaps Lucien could use that to his advantage. He made a mental note to visit Sabin and the warriors in Rome so he could alert them. "That is all you know?" he asked the men.

Both nodded warily.

"We are grateful for this information. Let's get you home now," he said, curling his fingers around each of their wrists.

"Our house is in Athens," the younger man said in a trembling voice dripping with hope. "We live together, and we can find our own way."

Tears of relief streamed down the old man's cheeks.

"Thank you. Are you—one of them? The immortals? You disappeared earlier."

"Give me the address," Lucien said, pretending he hadn't heard the question. "I will take you there."

When the father told him, reverence blooming in his eyes, he flashed them.

Surprisingly, Anya was waiting in their house. She paced back and forth in the sparse but comfortable-looking living room. Not a flicker of emotion played over her features when she spied him.

"I'll wipe their memories," she said, her voice devoid of emotion, as well. "They'll recall nothing of the Hunters, nothing of the Lords."

Despite himself, Lucien was overjoyed to see her and grateful that she still planned to help him. However, he flashed back to the island without uttering a word. One word would have led to another and that word would have led to a plea— *kiss me, touch me, please*—and then he would have challenged Cronus. *I will not kill her. I'll kill you.* Because, at that moment, Lucien did not care about the curses Cronus could heap upon him and his friends. He did not care that the god king could make them suffer for all eternity.

Without Anya, he was going to suffer anyway.

CHAPTER SIX

"SHAVE MY HEAD," ANYA muttered darkly. How would Lucien react if she actually did it? If she next appeared to him bald? Probably call her "ugly" and "gullible" and resist her more fervently. "Jerk."

And yet, foolishly, she missed him.

When he'd slipped into the spirit realm to escort those souls to hell, she had flashed to the humans' home, knowing he would soon arrive. Seeing him again had affected her deeply. She'd almost thrown herself at him, glad that he was healthy and whole, face and neck already healing; she had only managed to suppress the urge by suppressing her emotions, as well.

Afterward, she had returned to her beach in Hawaii, dejected, and had shimmied into her favorite white one-piece. Now she strolled along the water's edge flinging glistening sand in every direction, hair hanging down her back, damp and curling. The sun glowed hotly, stroking her skin. Waves lapped at the pink grains, washing some away, and all the emotions she'd momentarily overridden lapped at *her* just as determinedly.

"All I wanted to do was help him."

And what had she gotten in return for her generosity? He'd pretended to want her, even chained her to his bed—then vanished. That *still* hurt. She'd been desperate for him, and he hadn't been able to get away from her fast enough. "I am such a moron."

Why couldn't she forget him?

No man had ever affected her like this, and despite her curse, she'd dated plenty! All had been mortals, amusing for a little while as they showered her with the compliments she'd always craved from the gods, but most had been as forgettable as she wanted Lucien to be. The more memorable ones had become her friends, even though she had refused to sleep with them.

One by one they had died. Casual though the friendships were, their loss had hurt her, their humanity a weakness she'd come to despise. She no longer hung with humans, hadn't for several years, and some nights she was so lonely she found herself snuggling with the teddy bear she'd stolen from the grand opening of a Toys "R" Us.

With Lucien, she wasn't lonely. She was excited. Every moment with him was a surprise. And he wanted nothing to do with her.

Grrr! From this point on, she would stay away from him. Would make him come to her. He'd have to eventually, if he hoped to obey Cronus. Patience, though, had never been her strongest virtue, and in spite of everything, as the day ticked by she realized she craved another sight of him.

"I'm not a moron. I'm a *fucking* moron." Watching Lucien fight had to be the sexiest thing she'd ever seen. Ev-er. He'd been lethal strength and total Death, fast and fluid as he'd wielded those daggers. His mismatched eyes had glowed with the promise of eternal damnation, and she'd found that irresistible.

Still did.

She liked sparring with him. She enjoyed his company, was bored when parted from him.

Seriously. None of that made sense. As grave as he was, he should have been dull. Yet he amused her, challenged her and made her feel alive. Odd, since he was possessed by Death.

Did he feel anything for her? Anything at all besides disdain and irritation? If so, he hid it well. Except when he kissed her. Then he was another man completely. Passionate and tender, a little wild. He kissed with his entire body, showering her with desire and that rose-scented flavor.

"Who am I trying to fool? I'm going back to him."

Cronus had chosen her executioner well. She couldn't stay away from him, didn't want him to stay away from her, and might even let him try again to kill her, just for another kiss.

"Might be fun," she murmured, flashing.

IT WAS THE STRAWBERRY-SCENTED breeze that first alerted Lucien to Anya's presence when he materialized on the Greek island after escorting a group of souls to heaven. There'd been a bus accident in the States, a carefree troop on their way to a church social. They'd been hit by a drunk driver and every one of them had died.

A waste. Thankfully he'd numbed himself enough that even the children failed to affect him anymore. He couldn't allow them to; as much death as he dealt, he'd be a mess if he did.

You're a mess right now, thinking of Anya.

The thought came from him, but his demon was quick to respond.

Need another kiss.

Lucien wasn't surprised this time. Whenever the woman approached him, Death purred like an excited kitten. A phenomenon he still did not understand. *Why do you want her?* He hated the thought of anyone, even the demon, craving her as he did.

Tastes good.

There was no refuting that.

More and more, Lucien could feel Cronus's anger radiating down at him. It was a burn in his gut, a churning in his soul. The king would not wait much longer, would surely curse him soon if he failed to act. Or curse his friends.

Yet just the thought of seeing Anya again lit an inexorable fire inside him, overshadowing the thought of both her death and his punishment. Since that fight with the Hunters two days ago, he hadn't gone to her and she hadn't appeared to him. He'd missed her as she'd once claimed to miss him.

Lucien searched the Temple of the All Gods for some physical sign of her. He saw moss-covered columns, mounds of crumbled stone and pools of crystal water. No Anya.

So many times he'd pictured her here. In his mind, the pillars were gleaming white with lush emerald ivy and provided the perfect frame for her exotic beauty. In his mind, the puddles were bubbling pools and she liked to frolic. Naked.

"Anya," he said.

She didn't respond.

He waited several minutes, then called her name again.

Again, nothing.

"I know you're here."

Nothing. What game did she play now?

Trying not to frown, he bent over a sand pile and sifted through the grains. If he couldn't coax her out of hiding, at least he could begin looking for evidence of the four artifacts' existence.

Something soft brushed his shoulder blades and the scent of strawberries became stronger, filling his nostrils, tantalizing him; he didn't turn, didn't acknowledge the sensation. Not outwardly, at least. Inside, he shook.

"Whatcha doing?" she asked. Finally she materialized.

Stomach tightening with arousal, Lucien focused on her. Dear gods. Her clothes… He gulped. She leaned against one of the towering white columns. Crumbling rock and Parisian marble walls stretched around her, intricate patterns framing her perfect pixie face. Wisps of hair caressed her, and he experienced a momentary burst of jealousy.

He wanted his *fingers* to caress her, and nothing else.

She wore a transparent white gown—did she have an endless supply?—that draped one shoulder and bared the other's sun-kissed glory. A braided gold belt wrapped around her waist, hugging her curves. A slit rode the entire length of her thigh, revealing inch after inch of smooth, creamy skin, as well as a hint of snow-white panties.

Suddenly Lucien had trouble breathing. With the sun hitting just behind her, he could see the outline of her strawberry nipples.

Strawberry. A word he would forever associate with Anya.

Make her leave. She's a distraction you cannot afford.

Want her to stay! the demon growled.

If only. "Not many more hours of light, so…" His voice was hoarse.

Hurt glimmered in the blue depths of her eyes. "So get lost? Is that what you're saying?"

"Yes." He turned away from her—*for the best, you know it*—and scooped another handful of dirt.

Kiss her. Kisskisskiss.

He clenched his jaw.

A moment passed in silence. Then, "Tsk. Tsk. Tsk. Not wise, giving me your back."

"The other warriors are nearby." They were spread out over the island, close enough to hear but not close enough to kill an immediate threat. "I'll let them worry about my back," he lied. He just, well, he couldn't face her again. She stirred all kinds of emotions inside him. Emotions he was better off without.

"Well, then. Aren't you going to rush me or something? I'm, like, at the top of your destruction list."

"Later. Right now, I'm busy." He heard her shift, heard a rock fall. Wanted to look. Didn't. One more glance at her, and he might never look away. He might rush her as she'd asked, but he wouldn't hurt her. He would kiss her, just as Death craved. Again and again. Until their clothes were shed and he was pumping inside her.

In that instant, his body was so hard he thought he might burst.

"Lucien," Paris called from beyond the far temple wall, his voice tense.

He straightened. Still he did not face Anya. "Yes."

"I smell female. *Your* female."

"Stay where you are." He didn't want the others to see her like this. "All of you. Keep looking for something to point us in the right direction."

Paris grumbled something under his breath. Strider shouted, "You lucky son of a bitch." Amun and Gideon did not reply.

"Guess they won't have your back, after all," Anya said, her tone strangely devoid of emotion.

He didn't like it when she became so unreadable. He was afraid she was doing so to protect herself from pain. Pain he caused.

"So you guys are looking for artifacts, hmm?"

"Do not pretend ignorance. *You* sent us here." He crouched down once more and rolled a large silver stone aside, spotting pebbles and a dead clam underneath. He gritted his teeth, feeling impatient and like a fool. What kind of warrior played in the sand?

"This temple had been buried under the sea for thousands of years," Anya said. "The salt water probably washed all evidence of the past away."

"Perhaps something remains." He had to believe it was so.

"I thought your precious Ashlyn told you the box was guarded by Hydra," Anya said, and this time she spoke with a sneer.

Yes, Ashlyn had heard something about Hydra in her travels with the World Institute of Parapsychology. But why had Anya sneered? She had once aided Ashlyn, had seemed to like her. *Doesn't matter.*

According to numerous sources, Hydra had multiple heads and poisonous breath. Hercules was said to have defeated her at Lake Lerna. But Ashlyn claimed there had been a few sightings over the years. Always in a different location—the Arctic, Egypt, Africa, Scotland and even the States. Humans called her Nessie, Big Foot and all other manner of names. Leave it to mortals not to know what was right under their noses.

Part of Lucien wanted to abandon this temple and search in one of those locations. For if he could find Hydra, maybe he could find the box. Maybe he could destroy it at last and prevent Hunters—and even the gods—from trapping the demons and killing him and the other Lords.

Curiosity, however, held him here. The Titans had resurrected this temple for a reason. Yes, they planned to bring humans back to the days of worship and sacrifice. But there was something here. Had to be. Why else would the Hunters have been looking so diligently?

"I love treasure hunts," Anya said, reclaiming his attention. "They're so exciting."

"You are not helping us."

A pause. Then, suddenly, she was standing beside him,

strands of her hair brushing his bare arm. He'd removed his shirt an hour ago, the sun too bright and too hot. Sweat trickled along the ropes of his stomach, causing that hair to plaster against his skin. He had to grind his molars at the headiness of being connected to her, even in so small a way.

"Why can't I help?" Anya asked, and there was a catch in her raspy voice. A pout. Gods, he loved the sound of that pout. "I've proven myself invaluable so far."

Foolish him, he finally dared a glance up at her. He saw her panties first and had to swallow a wave of need. He forced his gaze to continue its upward slide, not stopping until their eyes locked. So pretty. He pushed to his feet, damned legs shaking.

Her gaze immediately dropped to his chest. To the black butterfly tattooed over his torso and shoulder. He gulped, had to look away again. Stark desire radiated from her. She even reached out to touch him, caught herself, and lowered her arm.

Do it. Touch me. Too many days had passed since he'd felt the fire of her fingertips.

She didn't, though. "It's lovely," she said, motioning to the butterfly.

"Thank you." Disappointment slammed into him when she didn't reach out again, but he knew it was better this way. "I hate it," he admitted.

"Really? Why?"

"It is the mark of the demon. After Death was thrust inside my body, the tattoo simply appeared."

"Well, FYI. It's a babe magnet. Maybe I'll get one. A dagger or maybe even angel wings. Oh, oh. I know. I'll get a matching butterfly. We'll be twinkies!"

Anya, tattooed. A design for his tongue to trace. He gulped. *Touch me. Please touch me.* "To answer your earlier question, you cannot help us because you will distract us from our purpose," he said a little more forcefully than he'd intended. He was barely able to concentrate on anything but her scent and her beauty every time she neared him. "I'm sorry."

Her gaze snapped to his. "You're not sorry, but whatever," she said tightly, crossing her arms over her chest. "Now I won't tell you where the box is."

He was gripping her arms in the next instant. "You know where it is?"

She grabbed his wrists and squeezed. Not to push him away, but to hold him in place. "Would you stop trying to kill me if I did?"

"No."

Scowling, she stomped her foot. The action caused her breasts to bounce gently against his arms. "I don't even know why I'm bothering with you."

"You said that before."

"Well, it's important enough to be mentioned twice."

He sighed. "Why *are* you here, Anya?"

Her expression became mulish. "None of your business, Flowers."

"Trying to butter me up some more?"

Her eyes closed off like blinds drawn over a window, but he could see the blue fire banked there through tiny slats of inextinguishable emotion. "You're a real pain in the ass, you know that?"

Unable to stop himself—would it always be so?—he jerked her up and into him, body to body, placing them nose to nose. He had not felt this out of control since those early days with the demon. Anya's nipples poked at his chest deliciously. "So are you. You are driving me insane."

"Boo fucking hoo. *You're* driving *me* insane."

He shook her and she suddenly gasped, losing all hint of

anger. She moaned. Moaned! "Mmm. Must be my lucky day. You have another erection."

His nostrils flared, potent desire heating his blood. Well, *more* desire. *Concentrate.* "What do you know about the box, Anya?" She had mentioned it, yes? He couldn't recall. Could only remember the way she tasted, hot and wild.

Her luscious little tongue flicked out and traced the seam of her lips. "Confession. I don't know where it is, but I do know you'll never find it."

No emotion. No damn emotion. "Why not?"

"Even the gods don't know where it is. If they did, it would have been found and put to use by now."

Yes. That made sense. "What else do you know?"

She arched her hips, brushing against him softly, and groaned. "After the Titans defeated the Greeks...well, defeated *most* of the Greeks—some got away. Anyhoo, there was a nasty game of torture and interrogation. Cronus and his crew want those artifacts back. Zeus told him what had been done to them, and Cronus got his search on, but didn't have any luck."

Lucien ground his teeth against the pleasure-sensations she was sparking inside of him. "Why does Cronus want them?"

"Better question—who wouldn't want them? They're a great source of power. If they fell into the hands of his enemies, little Cronie could very well be defeated again. But if Cronus has them, he's pretty much assured of eternal success."

"But how do the artifacts lead to the box? Why would the gods even want the box? It houses demons, nothing more."

"Uh, wrong. Think about it. That box is made from the bones of the goddess of oppression. It can suck the spirit out of *anything.* With Tartarus falling to pieces and Cronus having to use his soldiers to keep the Greeks locked inside, the box would be the perfect solution, a home for his enemies *and* your demons. What better revenge? The gods that caused him trouble locked away with the demons that caused *them* trouble."

For a moment, a red haze fell over Lucien's vision. Death had endured a thousand years of confinement in that damned box, an existence that hadn't truly been an existence. There'd been screams, so many screams. Darkness, so much darkness. The demon would not be placed back inside willingly. Death would destroy Lucien first, of that he was certain.

"You look ready for a battle, Flowers. Want to fight me? Huh, huh, please?"

Calm down. He released her arms and tried to back away. Fighting her…pinning her…tonguing her… *Calm down!* She retained a grip on his wrists, not letting him get very far.

"Why doesn't Cronus simply kill the Greeks?"

"You've spent some time with the gods, right?"

"Long ago."

Unexpectedly she released him. Neither of them moved farther away. No, they stepped closer. "They're obsessed with their amusements, you could say. That, and they live by a code of revenge. Zeus will not suffer as Cronus has suffered if he's dead. And Cronus would have no one to brag about his victories to, no one to taunt, no one to challenge him, without Zeus. Eternity would be boring, no surprises on the horizon."

"Why isn't Cronus here, searching?"

Anya grinned. "Why should he? You're doing all the work for him."

Which meant the god would not want Lucien and the other warriors dead. Which in turn meant Lucien had a little time to figure out what to do about Anya. Suddenly he wanted to grin as Anya was doing. The only thing ruining the spark of happiness inside his chest was the fact that Cronus would snatch whichever artifacts Lucien found. Unless, of course, he figured out a way to hide them.

"How do the Cage and Rod, Eye and Cloak lead to the box?" he asked.

"Now that, I don't know." She shrugged, brushing her shoulder against him.

He bit the inside of his cheek, Death purring wildly. The pleasure of her touch, even one so innocent, rocked him to the core.

"Maybe they're like a key or a map, and point a person in the right direction," she said breathlessly. "So what are we going to do, you and I?"

The touch must have affected her, as well.

"I do not know."

Her features softened, her eyes glowing. "What do you *want* to do?"

He forced himself to say, "Continue my search of the temple," when he wanted to beg her for a kiss. How he suddenly envied Gideon, who spun a web of lies with such ease. No guilt.

Eyes narrowing, Anya stepped away from him. He felt bereft without her nearby, and heard the demon growl inside his head.

"You were using me for information, huh? Leading me on, looking at me as if you wanted me, but it was only to get me to spill my knowledge."

"Yes," he lied.

Her features fell.

He experienced another wave of shame. He had to stop being cruel to her. She might be as promiscuous as Paris, might be—was probably—using Lucien for her own gain even as she accused him of doing the same. But she was sweet and funny and challenging.

"You rebuff me, fine," she said, tossing her hair over her shoulder. "You think you're better than me, whatever. But you know what? You're not. You're sitting back, doing nothing as the gods pull your strings. I, at least, am trying to fight them."

"Anya—"

She wasn't finished. "What are you going to do when your little friend Aeron escapes that dungeon and slaughters the human girl Danika and her family? Still nothing? When he comes to his senses, his life will be forever ruined because of his actions. And you'll have helped him. You'll have taken their souls to heaven even though their lives were cut short."

She was right, he realized, and he hated himself for it. What kind of man was he? All this time, he had been Cronus's puppet. He had not fought the god as a warrior should have, hadn't tried to cut those damned strings in any way.

"Perhaps the women are not innocent," he said, knowing the words were a lie. He simply didn't know what else to say. "Perhaps there is a good reason Danika and her family were chosen for extermination."

"You're right about that. There *is* a reason they were chosen."

"Tell me." Thinking about the mortals was easier than thinking about himself and his failure.

"Figure it out on your own, asshole. I think I've told you enough."

He turned away from her. He'd seen the lie in her eyes— she didn't know. But she was clearly hurting, and he wanted to comfort her and had no right to do so. "At least tell me if I'm wasting my time looking for direction here." She owed him nothing, but he couldn't stop himself from asking.

For a long while she didn't speak. He doubted she

moved, either, for she made no noise. "You're not wasting your time here."

"Thank you for that. What—"

"Nope. No more questions; I'm not telling you what to look for and I'm not telling you how to find it. Even though that *thank you* was pretty damn awesome." Sarcasm dripped from those last few words, though mercifully, they had not been edged in steel.

"You're welcome," he said, hoping to tease her into a good mood.

She stepped in front of him, her hips swaying. Expression relaxed once more, she leaned against another column. "Let's get back on track," she said. "How long before you start trying to murder me again?"

Murder. A sharp pain lanced through his chest. That's what he would be doing to her, he thought, murdering her. Ashamed, he bent down and resumed his futile sifting through the rock and sand. "I do not know."

"Won't it piss off Cronie Wonie if you wait too long?"

"He did not give me a deadline."

"Maybe we could, like, discuss this again in a hundred years."

Lucien snorted, even as he realized she was teasing *him* into a good mood.

"That's not gonna work for you, then? You're all booked up?"

"Something like that," he muttered.

"What about tomorrow? You free?"

"I am booked for the next few weeks."

"And you can't squeeze in a fight with me?" She almost sounded eager.

For you, anything. "Sorry."

"I'm starting to think you aren't taking this killing business seriously."

"Oh, I am serious about it." Unfortunately. "Do not worry."

She sighed, mournful. "What about scheduling time to make out? Can you do that?"

An image sparkled inside his mind: Anya chained to his bed, legs parted, core glistening. His cock swelled. Again. "Sorry. Not that, either."

She shrugged as if she didn't care, but he saw hurt in her eyes. She stared down at her sandaled feet and kicked a rock. "Don't be surprised if I sneak up on you and take your head."

"Thank you for the warning."

"My pleasure. Shit!" she suddenly cried.

He stiffened, going for a weapon. "What is wrong?"

"I was looking at my feet."

Gradually he relaxed. "And that is bad?"

"That's horrible! The worst thing ever. I never look at my feet."

His gaze shifted to her toes, painted a wild shade of red. "I think they are adorable." He didn't give her time to respond. Cheeks heating, he said, "Perhaps I will make time in my schedule to sneak up on *you.*"

A slow grin lifted her lips, her expression tender. "You are so cute, thinking you have that kind of skill."

He had to press his mouth together to keep from returning the grin. The woman amused him as much as she aroused him.

"Maybe I'll look for those artifacts, too," she said, almost as an afterthought. "If I find them, I might lock you inside that cage. Then you'd *have* to be nice to me."

Before he could growl a response, she grinned again, gave him a finger wave and disappeared.

CHAPTER SEVEN

FOR THE NEXT WEEK, ANYA dogged Lucien's every step when she wasn't stealing to keep herself sane. Even when he was escorting souls. She hated when he visited hell. Hated the heat, the smells, the taunts and jeers that emerged from the dark yet fiery pit. Always Lucien tried to act unaffected by them, but she could see the unease in his eyes. That saddened her. He'd seen the worst the world had to offer over and over again, and had had to anesthetize himself to survive.

Now she wanted him to see the best; now she wanted him to feel.

She told herself she wanted those things because it would be entertaining to watch the prince of doom and gloom let some light into his life. She didn't look deeper than that because she was afraid of what lurked beneath the explanation.

She sighed, knowing she should have given up on Lucien days ago. Attacked him, at the very least, or drawn him away from the temple for a flash-chase. But she suspected he wouldn't raise a hand against her and knew he would refuse to follow her. So she remained invisible and stayed close. Besides, whatever he learned about those artifacts, she learned, too.

After she'd mentioned looking for them herself, she'd realized she did indeed want them. Once she had one of those babies in her hot little hands, she'd make him beg for it. Gods, his expression was going to be priceless. Especially when she turned him down and bargained with Cronus. Her life for an artifact. Talk about a win-win situation!

"Go away, Anya," Lucien whispered.

He couldn't see her, but she stuck her tongue out at him, anyway. Those were the only words he'd spoken to her all week. If he said them again, she planned to materialize and slap him across the face, then quickly disappear.

"I am serious."

He always knew when she arrived. Once he'd told her that he smelled her. She'd been pleased, because it meant he was aware of her. She was still pleased by it, but damn if it didn't ruin her element of surprise.

Right now, the warrior stood in the Temple of the All Gods, peering at the bare, cracked walls with savage intensity. He and the other Lords had come here every day, their determination awe-inspiring in the face of their failure to find anything.

No wonder I want him so badly.

Lingering at Lucien's side was foolish and dangerous. It only intensified her desire for him. Seeing his butterfly tattoo on a regular basis was causing all kinds of naughty fantasies to play through her mind. Like: spending hours licking it. Like: taking Lucien's cock into her mouth while caressing it. Like: finger painting it with chocolate sauce and having it for dessert.

He'd probably try to stab her if she suggested any of those things. She'd never met a man less sure of his appeal and more outraged when a woman tried to tell him of her desire. How could others not see how mouthwateringly sexy he was? How rugged? How he tempted feminine instincts on every level?

Lucien bent down and once again sifted through rock and

sand, looking for gods knew what. Sunlight stroked him lovingly, the bitch. *He's mine.*

"Go away, Anya," he repeated.

Grrr! She materialized. Rather than slap him, though, she sat on a boulder beside him. He was shirtless again, his skin slightly burned, cut up and bruised.

He didn't face her. "I said go away."

"Like I'm going to obey you. You aren't my daddy. Unless you want to be. 'Cause I've been a bad, naughty girl and I need a spanking."

A pained groan escaped him. "Anya. Please." Sweat trickled over his spine, illuminating a few of the scars scattered there.

She reached out to caress them, but froze when one of the warriors called out.

"Lucien. Your woman…" The speaker was Paris, she realized. His voice was strained, even more so than before. Not getting any out here, was he? Poor man. Without sex, Paris weakened. If he could have brought a woman with him to fulfill his needs, all would have been well in his world. But he couldn't sleep with the same woman twice. Promiscuity, the lecherous demon, wouldn't let him.

Anya knew the trials of a sex-curse and sympathized. While hers was the opposite of his, preventing her from ever going all the way, both curses dictated their actions and jacked with their free will. It sucked rotten eggs.

Nothing can bind me but that curse, she thought darkly. She'd been bespelled before she'd acquired the ability to escape confinement, so the curse had already been a part of her. There was no escaping it.

Her gaze returned to Lucien and her shoulders sagged. No, much as she might wish otherwise, there was no escaping it.

"Just stay where you are," Lucien shouted to Paris. "She is my responsibility."

His responsibility? She didn't know whether to be delighted or insulted. "Why not let your friends come over here and play with us?"

He glanced at her through slitted eyelids, a fast look/look-away motion. Still, the moment his gaze hit her, moisture flooded between her legs. Her stomach tingled and her skin ached for him. He was pure sex appeal, all sweaty and dirty and manly. Yum.

"What are you wearing?" he croaked.

"A maid's uniform. You know, to help you dust."

He cursed under his breath. "Just as before, my friends are beyond the stone," he told her, "and they will remain there, working. They do not need a distraction."

How many times would he tell her she was a distraction? She eyed the crumbling stone cupped in his palms and frowned. Maybe, if she proved useful, he'd see her as something more. "I remember this place in its prime. Before it was moved down to earth, we were taught here, the other deities and I. How to control our powers, how to act properly, blah, blah, blah."

Lucien couldn't hide the interest that colored his face. "I was never allowed inside," he admitted. "We went only where Zeus did, and he didn't choose to spend time here."

Eck. To be bound to that temperamental shithead would have been torture. "A pity the place is so damaged now. You might have liked it."

"What did it look like?" he asked, dropping the chunks and sifting through another handful. Each pebble he found he held up to the light, turned to study every side for markings then discarded over his shoulder.

"Towering statues circled the entire temple. Ivy rode some of the walls, and diamonds, emeralds, sapphires and rubies glistened from the floors. I'm sure old glory-seeking Cronus will spruce everything up when he and his brethren of assholes take over."

Lucien snorted. Even though she hated herself for it, she rejoiced in the sound. His amusement was like an aphrodisiac to her, and *she* had caused it.

"What else?"

"Let's see." She tapped her chin with a nail painted ice-blue. "Every doorway was flanked by two white columns. Pillars of strength, they were called."

"And how many rooms were there?"

She allowed her mind to return to the days she'd spent here. While she'd loved the beauty of the temple, she'd hated the beings inside it. How many times had the goddesses-in-training complained to the teacher, "Why does *she* get to study here? She's not one of us. She only causes trouble." How many times had the young gods jeered, "I don't know why she bothers to wear a robe. Everyone knows she spends more time out of it."

She pushed aside the remembered hurts. "There was the main altar room, of course, which you're now crouching in. There was a meeting hall where worshippers washed and gathered before sacrificing. Then the interior chamber and the priests' lodgings."

He nodded as though he was soaking in her every word. "Tell me more about this altar room."

Happy to oblige, she said, "If we traveled back in time, there'd be a white marble table in front of you. And there would be murals on the walls. Gods, those were cool. I need to redo one of my apartments and have the images painted—"

"Murals? What did the murals depict?" Lucien asked, cutting her off. He stood and pinned her with a hard stare, urgency radiating from him.

Wow. If she'd known she only needed to talk about

boring temples to elicit his full attention, she would have done it days ago.

"Well?" he insisted.

She shrugged, pretending a casualness she suddenly didn't feel. "Godly feats of strength, victories. Even a few defeats."

His eyes glinted. "And was the box here, Anya?"

"No. I'm sorry." She hated to disappoint him.

He scrubbed a hand down his face. She approached him, wanting to touch, but stopped halfway, unsure of his reaction. This close, she could see that even more dirt than she'd realized streaked his chest and arms and his pulse hammered wildly. Her mouth watered at the sight. His butterfly tattoo vibrated with…awareness? Was it alive?

"What thoughts tumble through your head?" he asked.

"Naughty ones."

His brown eye darkened and his blue eye swirled. Both fixed on her minuscule, black-and-white lacy uniform, pupils dilating. "You enjoy tormenting me, do you not?"

She pinched her fingers together and said, "Just a wee bit. But don't worry—I'm not singling you out or anything. It's just a little quirk of mine, tormenting the men who want to kill me."

A brilliant beam of light broke through a cloud—cloud? On this hot day? Had she accidentally summoned it? She didn't look up. Couldn't. That beam had struck his face, illuminating his scars and casting shadows under his eyes. In that moment, he appeared as evil and sinister as a man could be. He appeared otherworldly. Wicked.

Delicious.

Her heartbeat sped up and her nipples beaded into tight little knots. *Reach for me. Please.*

He didn't.

She had to tear her gaze from him. Wanting him like this was foolish. Not just because of her curse, but because he wouldn't do anything about it. *Nothing wrong with buttering him up, though, like you told him you were doing.*

Unless she fell for him in the process. *That* would be a problem. A big one. Already the intensity of her desire was staggering. Any more...

"Anya," he said, drawing her from her thoughts.

"What?" She didn't face him, but withdrew a strawberry lollipop from the link of her belt, unwrapped it and ran her tongue over the tip. A little moan of pleasure escaped her. Scrumptious. She'd discovered the lollipops years ago after one of her human friends had died in a car wreck. Ever since, they'd been her comfort food of choice.

Lucien was in her face a second later—she was beginning to hate when he did that!—and swiped the candy from her hand. Her eyes widened as he tossed it to the ground.

"Hey! That was uncalled for."

He was scowling. "Do not eat those things in front of me."

"Why?" She threw up her arms in confusion.

"Because," he replied mulishly.

The scent of flowers was growing stronger, wafting from him, twining around her and drawing tight. "If you want one for yourself, just freaking ask me next time."

"I don't."

"Then—"

"No more talking. I must work." He spun away from her and went back to his mound of sand.

But not before she saw the fire blazing in his eyes.

Almost afraid to hope, she studied him more closely. His shoulders were stiff and his back ramrod straight, as if he were fighting desire. For her?

A hotter, deeper arousal bloomed inside her. Maybe, like her, he didn't mean half of the things he said. Maybe he truly did yearn for her.

She couldn't ask him. He'd just deny it. But that begged the question of why. Why did he not want her to know? Why did he not want to want her? Obviously, he thought she was easy. Why not take what he assumed she'd given to a thousand others? And what would he do if he knew how laughable that idea really was?

"You're wasting your time in that sand," she said in an airy tone, finally deigning to help him so he would pay attention to her again. *Come over here and kiss me.*

"No more talking."

"Well, you are."

"Disappear."

"Make me." *Please. Want me like I want you. Don't let me be wrong about this.*

He didn't reply.

Frustration ate at her, and she plopped onto the nearest boulder with a huff. "I want those artifacts as much as you do," she grumbled, "and your cold-shoulder treatment isn't helping our cause."

That snagged his attention. He flashed to her, knocking her off the boulder and onto the ground. Air shot from her lungs as his heavy muscular weight suddenly restrained her.

Note to self—mention the artifacts more often. Short as her costume was, she was able to spread her legs and welcome him into the cradle of her body. Instant pleasure speared her, shooting from head to toe and lingering in between.

"Why do you want them?"

"Duh. Power." The power of having bargaining chips, but he didn't need to know that.

"I thought we had covered this," he said, his voice cracking. "You will have nothing to do with the artifacts."

"Then you should have killed me." Licking her lips, she stared up at him. As always, he stole her breath. "I've decided I want them really, really bad."

He uttered a low growl. "No. I think you want to die. You are provoking me on purpose, while I have been giving you time to enjoy the last days of your life."

"Well, aren't you sweet," she muttered. Still, she didn't try to push him off her. In fact, she wound her arms around his neck. "I'm just trying to survive, lover. And have a little fun while I'm at it."

His nostrils flared, as if he'd just remembered something unpleasant. A muscle ticked in his jaw, making his scars all the more prominent. Her mouth watered. She wanted to tongue them. "Aligning yourself with me will not save you."

Back to that, were they? Damn, tell one little lie and it would haunt you forever. "Why haven't you killed me, then? And don't give me that bullshit about letting me enjoy the last days of my life. You don't let other souls enjoy the last of their days."

A heavy pause. His expression darkened. "Perhaps I have spared you because you know something, something that can help me find the artifacts and thereby the box. Tell me."

"If I knew something, I would have gotten to them already, dumbass."

"Then you are no good to me." He pulled back slightly and raised his fist as if he meant to strike her.

Over the last week, she'd watched him do this many times. Knew he wasn't going to hit her but reach inside her with a ghostly hand and rip out her spirit, leaving her body a helpless shell.

She should kick herself for taunting him. *I just wanted time with him,* she inwardly whined. Really, it was all she could think about anymore. All that propelled her out of bed. Well, that and his kisses.

"I don't know where the artifacts are," she said quickly, "but I can teach you more about the temple. How's that?"

He nodded, as if he'd merely been waiting for her to say those words. "Go on."

Had he just manipulated her? Sneaky devil. And yet, knowing he'd done so only caused her arousal to intensify. Hardly anyone bested her anymore.

She kneaded his shoulders, scratching them a little. He didn't tell her to stop. His breathing became more erratic, shallow. Her gaze dipped, his bare chest entrancing her as his body heat enveloped her. *I could stay like this forever.*

"Anya," he moaned. As her fingers worked him, his eyes closed in surrender.

"What were we talking about?" she asked.

"The…temple," he said, and the words were pained. "Yes, the temple."

"I'll tell you a secret about myself and all the gods who have passed through its halls," she whispered.

"I am listening. Do not stop."

She deepened the touch, allowing her fingers to inch down his back. Toward his ass. "Most of our powers are dependent on a little something called action and reaction. People act, and we are free to react. To help. Or hurt, for that matter. It's why I couldn't help Maddox and Ashlyn until they'd done something to untie my hands, so to speak."

Lucien's eyelids cracked open. Pleasure was banked in the depths of brown and blue. "Must be a closely guarded secret, because I did not know." He paused. "Maddox and Ashlyn each had to sacrifice something to ensure your aid."

"Yes." She beamed up at him. "Now you're thinking like a god."

"So to learn what I wish to know, I, too, must offer a sacrifice." He nodded, then reached behind him to grab one of her hands. He pulled it forward and laid it on her chest, but he didn't pull back, didn't break the connection. No, he traced each of her fingers.

Warm tingles rushed through her blood.

He was hard. She could feel his massive erection probing between her legs. He wasn't the first man to lie on top of her, but he was certainly the biggest. The sexiest. And the most fascinating. Because of her curse, he was also the first man she'd ever really *wanted* there.

Finally, Themis's words made sense.

Anya had been running home, crying again after an encounter with an overly-handsie young god, and had run into the goddess. Themis had taken one look at her and nearly fallen to the ground in shock. Too preoccupied to determine why, Anya had hurried away. The next day, Themis had arrived on her doorstep.

"You seduced my husband," she'd heard the goddess of Justice shout to her mother.

Dysnomia had raised her chin and squared her shoulders. But she hadn't uttered a word in her own defense.

"Your daughter is the image of my husband. She is his offspring. Do you deny it?"

"No, I do not deny it."

Anya had been shocked to her core. She'd always wondered who her father was, and to learn the powerful prison guard Tartarus had sired her both delighted—no longer would she be called *minor*—and angered her. Why had he ignored her all these years?

"You knew he was mated," Themis cried, "yet you lay with him, anyway. For that, for bearing his bastard child, you will be punished. Justice will be mine."

Horror blanketed Dysnomia's pretty face, but she said, "I am who I was born to be."

"That does not excuse you. From this day forward, you will sicken every time you welcome a man into your body, and you will be unable to rise from bed for days. Never again will you steal a man's affections unscathed. So I have said, so it shall be done."

Whimpering, her mother fell to her knees.

"And you," Themis said, eyes narrowing on a trembling Anya, who peeked around the corner.

"No!" Dysnomia shouted, trying to rise. "Leave her alone. She is innocent."

The goddess continued mercilessly. "Innocent? I think not. She is your daughter—that is crime enough. You will one day desire a man, Anarchy, and he will desire you, as well. Nothing will matter except being together. You will not care who he is, what he is or who he belongs to. You'll take him. Just like your mother, you'll take him."

"And you'll die alone because you're mean and hateful," Anya spat at her, unable to imagine herself feeling that way about any of the leering gods, much less welcoming another woman's leftovers.

"You will not have the opportunity to follow in your mother's indiscriminate footsteps. To allow a man to penetrate your body is to bind yourself to him for all eternity. You will live for him and only him. His pleasure will be your pleasure. His pain yours. If he discards you and takes another lover, you will feel the agony of his loss but you will not be able to leave him. If he dies, you will never recover from the grief. Your mother's legacy ends today. So I have said, so it shall be done."

The words themselves had wrapped around her, nearly choking her. They'd seeped past her skin, past her bones and straight into her soul, a fiery brand she had never been able to deny. She'd walked around in a daze for weeks afterward, the dual shocks of learning her father was a mated man and coming to terms with her curse nearly more than she could bear.

As the shock wore away, she'd begun to hate her father for denying her existence, and all men for what they could do to her if she wasn't careful. And she'd been scared, so scared.

When her mother had sent her to combat lessons, hoping to help her protect herself now that so much was at stake, she'd taken them seriously. As her strength had increased, her hatred and fear ebbed. Not her determination to remain alone, however.

In all the days since she had been cursed, she had never been tempted to give a man that much power over her. Losing her freedom when the gods had jailed her in her father's prison had only strengthened that determination.

Until now.

Now she wanted to know the bliss of Lucien's most intimate touch. Inside her. Deep. Pumping. Grinding. She knew she would have wanted those things whether he was mated or not.

Just thinking about having him caused more of that wondrous moisture to pool between her legs, dampening the thin sheath of panties she wore. Her skin felt too tight for her body, and she couldn't stop her thighs from rubbing up and down his. *Freedom,* she reminded herself. There was nothing greater.

The humans she'd chosen to make out with over the years had never been allowed to actually penetrate her. Aias, the Captain of the Immortal Guard, she had kissed and made out with, as well. But when she called a halt to their heavy petting, he'd called her a tease and a whore—oxymoron-spouting bastard—and had pinned her down.

He'd scowled down at her and ripped at her clothes, his own pants. Fear had consumed her. She'd screamed at him, demanded he release her. He'd laughed. She hadn't been able to flash, hadn't yet had the ability since it had come with her father's one and only gift to her. She'd fought with every ounce of strength she possessed and ultimately managed to deliver the death blow, just as she'd been taught.

Anya had never regretted her actions. Not even when she'd been rotting in prison. No one took what belonged to her. No one.

"What are you thinking about?" Lucien asked, his voice husky with…arousal?

Why not tell him the truth? "You. Sex. Theft. Another man."

"A lover?" he asked, his voice dark now.

Jealous? "Something like that."

His eyes narrowed.

"Does the thought of me with another man fill you with rage, Flowers?"

"Hell, no," he barked, tearing from her embrace and standing.

A sense of loss slammed into her. Gingerly she rose. Brushed the dirt from her fishnets. *It's best this way,* she told herself. *You were too close to giving in to a man who may not even desire you. One who definitely wants to kill you.*

"Let us return to our previous conversation. Ashlyn had to sacrifice herself to save Maddox," Lucien said tightly. He strode back into what had once been the altar room, spinning and studying the open space. "What can *I* sacrifice?"

"Lucien," Strider called. "It's getting close to chow time."

"I just need a little more time," he replied. He didn't look away from her. "Anya? Sacrifice?"

"Are you asking if sacrifices were made here?" She'd lost the line of conversation, too troubled by her own unhappy thoughts. "Yes. So?"

"Blood sacrifices?"

"Yes." Where was he going with this? "When the temple was moved to earth, blood sacrifices were made."

"And what did the patrons who came to this temple sacrifice, exactly? What did they make bleed?"

Again she allowed her mind to travel back to those days. Even she had been worshipped by mortals then. Everyone ignored the gods these days, writing them off as the stuff of myth and legend. That didn't bother her as it did the others. She liked her anonymity.

"They sacrificed their family members," she finally answered, stomach knotting. Oh, how she'd hated that. Another reason she was glad the days of old were, well, old. "Mostly innocents were chosen. Virgins. They cut their throats and watched them bleed out."

Lucien paled. "That is what's expected here? What's needed?"

"Not always. Sometimes blood freely offered by the one in need is more of a sacrifice than killing someone else and would have done the trick, but no one wanted to consider that. They would have had to hurt themselves, and most people would rather chop up a loved one and call it a noble act."

Some of his color returned. He withdrew a dagger from his boot, the metal whistling as it slid along the leather.

She backed away, palms up and out. "What, you thinking of sacrificing me now?"

"You are neither a virgin nor a loved one," he muttered.

Teeth grinding, she stopped abruptly, feet planting into the ground. Bastard. He had no idea about the former, and like she really needed the reminder about the latter. Like he'd had to point that out again. "I'm getting a little tired of your insults, Flowers. I've helped you today. I helped you last week. I helped you a month ago."

He sighed with regret. "You are right. I'm sorry. That was uncalled for, and I will not say such a thing again."

"Yes, well." She hadn't expected him to apologize, and that

he'd done so threw her off her A game. "What are you—" Her words were cut off as he sliced his left wrist, then his right. Shocked, Anya rushed to him. "You're insane, Lucien. Absolutely insane." He wasn't going to die, she knew that. Still!

"We shall see." The wounds were large and gaping.

Her wrists throbbed in sympathy. She'd once stabbed him, sure, but right now, this moment, she couldn't bear to see him hurt. She grabbed his arm and tugged one of his wrists to her, hoping to stanch the crimson flow with her costume. Some of his blood dripped on her, then the ground.

The moment it touched the sand, Lucien bellowed a roar and dropped to his knees. Her concern doubled. "Lucien. What's wrong?" He was immortal and couldn't be killed by normal means, but that didn't stop her from worrying. He could have been cursed. He could have—

He roared again and clutched his stomach.

"Lucien. Tell me what the hell is wrong!"

His eyelids were squeezed shut; panting, he slowly opened them. Both of his irises were suddenly blue. Otherworldly, crystalline, churning like a storm. He stood to shaky legs and pulled from her grip as if in a trance, walking forward, toward the temple's only remaining wall.

"I can see it," he said.

Relief nearly felled her. He was having a vision. In the old days, when a sacrifice pleased the gods or even the temple itself, a reward was given. Anya thought perhaps the temple was pleased to be used again. "What do you see?" She had to force her arms to remain at her sides, so badly did she want to hold him.

"I might have found something," he called, ignoring her.

All four of the warriors ran to him, swooping around columns like avenging angels. They spotted her and gaped. Her French maid costume was naughty and for Lucien's eyes only. Still, she didn't flash away to change. She didn't want to miss a moment of this.

The men didn't speak to her, though Paris did lick his lips in anticipation, as if she were a feast that had been prepared just for him. She rolled her eyes. Would have flipped him off, but thought he might try to take her up on the "offer."

"Why are you bleeding?" Strider demanded, withdrawing a dagger. A feral scowl was directed at Anya. "And what the hell is she wearing?"

She flipped *him* off without any hesitation.

"The woman is not to be handled in any way," Lucien said flatly, still focused on the wall. "She is mine."

Mine, he'd said. Smiling, she gave each Lord a taunting pinkie wave. "You hear that? I'm his, so you can all suck dirt."

Lucien muttered, "And you had better keep your hands to yourself, Anya, or you will lose them."

"Please. Like your buddies could best me," she replied, unsure whether he heard or not. He gave no reaction.

As the Lords gathered around Lucien, she muscled right into their circle. And yeah, she pilfered a few daggers along the way. Gods, that felt good. She hadn't done enough of this lately, too consumed with Lucien. Stealing always soothed her riotous emotions, slowing her heartbeat and easing the seemingly constant ache in her stomach. The guys didn't realize what she'd done or they would have attacked her, she was sure. As it was, they let her through without comment.

What had Lucien found? What was he seeing?

Lucien splayed his arms, pushing everyone behind him and gazing at the wall once more.

"Lucien?" Strider said, clearly confused. Anya studied him out of the corner of her eye. He had blue eyes and blond hair, was tall and muscled, tanned. His features were roughly hewn, and he had a wicked sense of humor, which she normally preferred.

Why hadn't she been attracted to *him?*

"What do you see?" Paris asked. Eagerness and excitement hummed through the group.

"Waiting is fun," Gideon said, glaring.

"Do you recall what the two mortal researchers told us about Zeus and the artifacts?" Lucien asked.

A murmur of *yeses* arose.

"They were mostly correct. I'm looking at a mural that seems to be alive. The images are shifting, revealing detail after detail. After Zeus imprisoned the Titans, he commanded Hydra to hide and guard their treasured artifacts. Hydra split herself into four fearsome beings which scattered, each beast guarding one relic."

"Oh, man," Anya said. "If Hydra's the guard, you boys are in trouble. She's a whack job, for sure. Two heads on one snakelike body—make that eight heads on four bodies, if Lucien's vision is accurate—and all those heads suffer from constant PMS."

"Each serpent was to hide for eternity, never revealing her location again, even to the gods," Lucien continued.

Strider grunted. "How does this help us, then?"

Amateurs. "Do you see any symbols?" Anya prompted Lucien.

Pause. Frown. "Yes."

"Well, what are they? Zeus might not have wanted the other gods to know their location, but he would have made damn sure he could at least be pointed in the right direction if he so desired. In his glory days, when he stole whatever he wanted from whichever god he happened to want it from— it's the one thing I ever admired about him—he would hide them until the heat died down by using vision-symbols as treasure maps. He spelled them to change if the item was somehow moved."

Lucien didn't turn to her, but he did say, "You told us he told Cronus what had happened to them. You told us Cronus looked, but didn't find them."

"Hello. Does that mean Zeus told the truth? They're enemies, remember? Just tell me about the symbols already!"

Lucien pressed his gorgeous lips together, refusing to answer.

"Fine. Don't tell me. I'll just leave the area and give you a chance to tell your boys. I totally will *not* remain here, invisible and eavesdropping." She grinned at him, waiting.

He growled low in his throat.

"Seriously, you know I'll find out eventually so stop wasting time. Besides, I'll save you a lot of steps trying to figure it out on your own. You need my help. Again. Admit it."

"Fine. We need your help." He worried two fingers over his jaw, the picture of pique. "The first symbol has two lines edging down with a curved line weaving them together."

"South Africa," she said without hesitation.

"How do you know that?" Paris said, looking more strained than before. He'd sidled next to her and now pinched her butt.

She slapped his hand and stepped away. "I'm smarter than you," she told him smugly. "That's how I know."

Paris gripped her wrist almost desperately. What he meant to do with her she wasn't sure. He'd— Lucien moved between them, ripping them apart.

Lucien was snarling at the warrior.

"Fine." Paris sighed and backed away. "I get the message. No touchie." He stopped, looked down at his waist. "Shit! My blade is gone."

The other Lords looked from Lucien to her, from her to Lucien, as if needing direction.

"What?" she finally demanded. "You think I took it?"

"Mine is missing, too," Strider said with a grin, "but you can keep it. Think of me when you use it."

The grin surprised her, and she found herself smiling in return. Until Lucien snarled at him, too. She rolled her eyes, though she was secretly pleased.

"Get back to work, big boy," she said. "I know how you hate distractions."

Thankfully, the snarling ceased. "The second symbol," Lucien said, once again drawing everyone's attention to the wall, "is a single, jagged line."

"That's the Arctic. Ah," she added, placing her hand over her heart. "Those icy climes are bound to bring back memories of our first date. The one where you took a nice, refreshing dip and I watched from the glacier. Remember?" She didn't give him a chance to respond. "Maybe this is a sign we're meant to be BF's forever and ever. Is this a great moment for a huggsie, do you think?"

His lips pulled taut. "The third is a horizontal, curved line with a similar line growing out of it."

She'd take that for a no. "That's the States."

"The last is a straight line that curves at the bottom, almost like the end of a machete."

"Egypt," she said. Then she grinned and clapped her hands. "You know what this means, don't you? More traveling, and more treasure hunting! Where are we going first? Huh, huh, huh?"

"How do you know those locations?" Lucien asked, repeating Paris's question as he finally faced her. His eyes were still shrouded in that otherworldly blue.

"Maybe Zeus went around telling everyone about them and what they meant."

"How do you know?" he insisted.

Her mother had been Zeus's lover at the time and had over-heard a little state business, but that little gem wasn't something she liked to shout from the rooftops. "I told you. I'm smart."

"And how do *we* know we can trust you?" Paris asked, hands on his hips.

"Duh. You totally can't. But you need me, so I guess that plants you right between a rock and a very naughty hard place."

Lucien grabbed her arm and squeezed, forcing her to face him. "You are not going with us, Anya. Remove the thought from your mind now."

Oh, really? "Try and stop me. I dare you."

"You know I can. Stop you, that is."

She arched a brow, her confidence unshaken. "Do I? I'm still standing here, alive and well, aren't I?"

Was it her imagination, or did steam rise from his nostrils, smelling of hellsmoke? Just then, he was like her own personal demonic dragon. Sweet! She could practically see the wheels turning frantically in his head as he tried to calm himself down. He was beyond sexy when he was on edge. "Admit it. You wouldn't have known what the symbols meant without me. You need me."

"You could be lying," he said, once again echoing Paris's suspicions.

"Waste time researching, then. What do I care? I can find the Hydras while you sit at a computer. I'll gather the artifacts *and* locate the box, and I'll do it before you and your Testosterone Squad have even booked a flight."

All four warriors growled at her.

"What? Touchy subject?" she asked them, all innocence.

"We're splitting up," Lucien said, not looking away from Anya. "Paris, you and Gideon will travel to the States."

Paris glowered up at the sky. "Ah, man. Why am I stuck with Lies?"

"Biggest land mass, most people. It will be better to have two warriors searching there," he explained. "Strider, you will go to South Africa. Amun, to Egypt." He stared over at Anya. "I will head to the Arctic."

"You might want to wear a coat," Anya suggested helpfully.

Lucien's eyes narrowed. She barely resisted the urge to blow him a kiss.

"I'll ring Sabin's cell," Strider said, "and tell him what we've found. Who knows? Maybe he'll discover something more at the Roman temple."

"Do you know anything about that location, Anya?" Lucien asked.

"Only that it was called the Temple of the Unspoken Ones."

"Unspoken Ones? I've heard of them," Gideon said.

Which of course meant that he hadn't. Just thinking about the temple caused her to shudder. "Parents used to threaten their unruly children with banishment to that doomed place. Maybe because screams could always be heard echoing from the walls."

"Who are the Unspoken Ones?"

"I never saw them. I kept my distance. And as the name proclaims, they were rarely spoken about outside of the occasional parental threat."

Lucien sighed. "Call Sabin if you wish," he said to Strider, "but I plan to flash to Rome and tell him in person. I'll scout the temple while I'm there. My blood acted as a catalyst here. Perhaps it will there, as well."

Hope filled the air. They were closer to success than ever before, she knew.

"Where should we begin looking when we reach our destinations?" Paris asked. "Right now, all I know is that I'm supposed to go to the States. As you said, that's a big damn place. With lots of women," he added as an afterthought. His lips lifted in a slow smile, the strain on his face seeming to ease at just the prospect of fresh meat.

"Where should they look?" Lucien demanded of Anya.

Again, everyone turned to her.

They wanted her help, then they didn't, then they wanted it again. *What? I'm just a dumb, annoying minor goddess. Not needed. Not wanted. Not—*

"You can go with me," Lucien snapped.

Ah, such enthusiasm. Irritated, she ran her tongue over her teeth. Still, his demands and growls were better than all those weeks of implacable composure. Huh. Maybe she should push him a little more. "Sorry. What'd you say?" She cupped a hand over her ear. "I couldn't hear you."

"You can go with me," he repeated loudly. Darkly.

Now she crossed her arms over her chest. *Keep pushing like this, and he just might jump you.* Please, please, please. "Are you going to try to kill me?"

"You know I must, but I will give you fair warning before I do."

She hadn't wanted him to stop, anyway. "Fair enough." Could this day have gone any better? Soon she would be traveling alone with him, probably fighting with him. The prospect shouldn't have thrilled her, but it did. She wanted a chance to nurture the desire she'd seen in him earlier, dangerous though that was. "I accept."

"Where should we look?" Paris repeated.

"I don't have all the answers, you know." This kept up, and soon the men would only respect her for her mind. Ugh.

"Anya," Lucien warned.

"What? I don't! Just have Ashlyn follow any rumors about giant, ugly monsters. That'll probably be Hydra. Oh, and she likes water. So maybe follow rumors about giant ugly monsters spotted near water."

The men nodded, and she was once more forgotten as they chatted amongst themselves about what supplies they would need, when they would leave and blah, blah, blah.

Anya sidled up to Lucien and ran her fingertip down his sternum. "We're going to have fun, you and I."

He had been telling Strider what he knew of South Africa, but his words quickly died. Eyes blazing, he whipped to her. What he meant to say or do, she might never know. She blew him a kiss and disappeared.

CHAPTER EIGHT

As HE SHOPPED FOR PROVISIONS he would need for his upcoming trip—intermittently collecting eighteen souls and escorting them to their final resting place—Lucien did not feel Anya's burning gaze on him. Nor did he smell her enticing strawberry scent.

Where was she? What was she doing?

Who was she doing it with?

His hands balled, knuckles throbbing, the joints so stiff they felt brittle.

He missed her more than ever. He had gotten used to her presence; nothing felt right when she was gone. Besides, he worried about her. Had Cronus tired of Lucien's halfhearted attempts to slay her and taken it upon himself to destroy Anya?

Now his nails dug into his palms, drawing blood. *She is fine.* Cronus had been unable to kill her, which was why he'd given the task to Lucien. Anya was safe from the god king.

But time is ticking...

Lucien expected the bastard to arrive at any moment and punish him for his failure. Punishment was beginning to matter less and less, however.

He wanted to spend more time with her, and he was about to get his wish. Too bad they weren't heading for Hawaii. But Lucien had known Anya would follow him wherever he chose, so he'd picked the Arctic, the one place he'd thought—hoped—would cool his desire.

Because more than missing her, he desired her. Badly.

He was becoming obsessed with her. Lately all he could think about was stripping her. Licking between her legs, pleasuring her in every way imaginable and even some that weren't. Watching her face while she climaxed. Fisting her hair while she sucked his cock. Lately? Ha!

Even now, he trembled. Trembled like a damned mortal.

His long-neglected body practically sobbed for Anya each time she approached him. Forcing himself to walk away grew more and more difficult. And forcing himself to discourage her advances was even more so.

Stop thinking, finish shopping, he commanded himself as he stalked down the city's paved streets. He'd flashed from the island to Athens, and sunlight shone brightly. Last time he'd been here, all those centuries ago, dead bodies had littered the street and blood had flowed like crimson rivers.

He pushed the image to the back of his mind. The air was crisp and salty. He needed to enjoy this mild weather while he could. All too soon he'd feel the icy blast of the Arctic. With Anya.

Damn this! What would it take to exorcise her from his head completely?

Determined, Lucien made a mental checklist of everything he needed. A coat. Boots. Thermals. Thick socks. And gloves. He would have flashed to Buda and collected everything there, but the items he owned were meant for *manageable* winters. The Arctic was another story. He'd have to endure freezing winds and snow as far as the eye could see. Perhaps luck would be on his side and he would find Hydra quickly. He placed a call to Maddox and had him ask Torin to search any possible sightings.

What was Anya doing?

He didn't even try to stop the thoughts this time. Obviously, fighting did no good. Anya. In the Arctic. Alone with him.

Perhaps finding Hydra quickly would not be such a wonderful thing.

Last time he and Anya had been together in the cold, she'd pushed him into the icy water. The memory shouldn't have made him smile, but it did. Anya, standing on that glacier, waiting for him, then shoving him with all of her strength, had been a beautiful if macabre sight. Even his testicles had frozen.

She had laughed, a tinkling sound of genuine amusement. Heady and seductive. He wanted to hear it again.

Gods, he admired her courage and her tenacity. Anyone else would have cowered at having Death hunt them.

Where was she? he wondered again. Had she finally tired of him?

As he passed a corner shop, he slammed his fists into the wall. Stone abraded skin. Whether Anya was tired of him or not, he would soon have her to himself, away from the other warriors. Hopefully he would learn more from her. Hopefully he would prevent her from learning more from him.

Hopefully he would better do his duty.

His clipped steps slowed, and he forced himself to take in the sights. Emerald trees framed most of the buildings, stretching overhead and casting shadows. There were no cars on the streets—those were prohibited—so people had to walk to their destinations.

Merchants were out in force, selling everything from fruit and vegetables to flimsy scarves to doorknobs. None of which would keep him warm in the Arctic.

"You'll never find what you need here," Anya said, suddenly keeping pace beside him.

His blood instantly heated as he glanced around, making sure no one had witnessed her sudden appearance. The only people staring at her were men, and he didn't know if they were shocked or simply captivated.

She was lovelier than ever.

Her pale hair was knotted at the base of her neck in an intricate braid and a pink ribbon circled over her ears. She wore a fur-trimmed coat and knee-high boots with a matching trim of fur.

"Where have you been?" he asked, the question harsher than he'd meant it to be. Finally she was with him, and that should have been all that mattered. *She's where she belongs,* his mind added, and he frowned. *When she's by my side, I can keep her out of trouble.* Nothing more.

"Oh," she said, waving a hand through the air. "Here and there."

Had she been with another man? His jaw clenched. Best not to allow his mind to travel that route, so he changed the subject. "Why are you dressed like that?" He wore a black linen T-shirt and slacks, and he was sweating.

"'Cause we're going to Switzerland, silly, and it's cold there. You, my friend, are way underdressed."

"Anya, I—"

"There's only one hour's time difference," she said, cutting him off, "so this is the perfect time to go shopping in Zürich."

He sighed. "Why must we go to Zürich to shop?" *We.* Damn the thought! He needed to think of them separately. Never as a pair. Too dangerous.

"Because it's snowy and I look good in white. Race you there!"

She disappeared, leaving a trace of her strawberry scent. Bereft without her, Lucien scanned the crowd a second time. Several people had noticed her disappearance, he knew for a fact, because several jaws were dropped.

The citizens of Budapest knew he and the others were different, if not to what extent, and for the most part left them alone. Protected them, even. Perhaps because the warriors poured so much money into the community. Perhaps because the people were afraid of what would happen if they didn't.

Still. Since leaving ancient Greece and the destruction he'd caused, he had been very careful not to let mortals see his abilities. He did not want rumors of his presence circling. He did not want the human media chasing him and the others, and he certainly did not want more Hunters after him.

But despite all this, he did not try to explain what had happened to Anya. He, too, simply disappeared. Hopefully the witnesses would assume they'd imagined the entire episode. There was a compulsion inside him to be with Anya. He couldn't wait a second more. His heart had not slowed down since her arrival.

He felt more on edge with her than with anyone else in the world. He lost his legendary calm—not that he had erupted in her presence, thank the gods—and he had no business strengthening any ties between them when he had been ordered to kill her. And yet, he could not seem to help himself.

Her lighted trail did indeed lead to Zürich. He had been here a time or two collecting souls, but had never been able to linger or explore. The same was true with every country he had ever visited. Collect, escort to heaven or hell, and return home in time for midnight—and Maddox's curse—to arrive. That had been the way of his life for centuries. In the month since the curse had been broken, the warriors had been too busy researching Pandora's box for Lucien to do any traveling on his own. Not that he'd wanted to at that point. Hunters were in need of destruction, his friends in need of peace.

He only prayed he was not compelled to take another soul this day. He wanted this time with Anya, uninterrupted and unspoiled.

Fool. This could be a trap. She could mean to hurt you.

He found her standing on a polished wooden deck, sunlight streaming around her. Cold air swirled between them. Behind her was a breathtaking view of snowcapped mountains.

She was facing him, tendrils of hair wisping over her face as she splayed her arms wide. "What do you think?"

"Exquisite." And she was.

A gradual, almost tentative, definitely vulnerable smile lifted the corners of her lush lips. She stared at him and said, "I think so, too."

Did she mean him? Rather than entice or soothe or excite him as her words were probably supposed to do, they angered him. He wanted her more than he wanted to take his next breath, and she played his affections like a violin. His entire body tensed.

Here we go again, he thought. *Letting her pull your emotional strings. Letting her affect you.* "Let's get this over with," he said tightly.

Slowly she lost her smile. "Over with? You are such a mood ruiner. Well, I'm not going to let you spoil this for me. Have you eaten lunch?"

"No."

"Food first, then. Shopping later."

"Anya, I think—"

She strolled past him as if he wasn't speaking and sauntered through an opened archway that led into a spacious apartment—why not a mansion?—of vivid colors and luxuriant sensuality. Not knowing what else to do, he followed her.

"This is yours, I presume," he said. "I expected something bigger."

"I keep a home everywhere and this is all the space I need. More…intimate this way." In the center of the living room, there was a low wooden table piled high with food, and she eased onto one of the violet pillows in front of it. "I haven't been to this one in a while because of you-know-who."

"Cronus?"

She nodded and began heaping two plates high with—he sniffed, realizing it was chicken pot pie, freshly baked bread and steaming vegetables. Not the extravagant meal he would have expected a goddess to prefer.

"Sit," she said, not looking up at him. She spooned a bite into her mouth, eyes closing in absolute delight.

He did as commanded, chest aching at the domesticity of the scene and the raw enjoyment she took from such a simple action. He had never had a wife, never been with a single woman for more than a few months—the length of time he'd had with Mariah before she died—so had never experienced anything remotely domestic. Unless you counted Paris's feeble attempts at cooking, which Lucien most definitely did not.

Mariah. Dead. Thinking of her just then did not bring the usual surge of resentment, guilt and anger. Was he finally, at long last, healing? With every day that passed, he thought of her less and less. Which was as sad as it was freeing.

Death had not cared about her, even though Mariah had been Lucien's everything.

Would Death mourn the loss of Anya?

He suspected so. Even now, the demon was purring.

"You never told me the real reason Cronus wants you dead," he said.

Anya sipped a glass of dark, rich wine, peering at him over the rim. "Not true. I told you I have something he wants."

"Your body?" The words left his mouth before he could stop them.

"According to you, I give that to everyone." There was a trace of bitterness in her tone. "Are you going to eat or just watch me?"

Stomach suddenly grumbling, he bit into the pie. Succulent, perfectly prepared. "Did you make this?" He could not picture her slaving in a kitchen.

"Gods, no. I stole it."

The disgust on her pixie face was comical, and he found himself grinning. "Stole?"

"Yes." She stared at his lips, her blue eyes heating. "I like it when you smile."

He swallowed. "Cronus," he prompted, trying to halt whatever thoughts were rolling inside her head. "Why doesn't he seek you out and kill you himself? You are out in the open now. I'm sure he has been able to lock in your location."

"He's an inter-heavenly man of mystery. No one knows why he does the things he does."

"And you have no guess?"

"Well," she shrugged, "he's an idiot. There, that's my guess."

Lucien tensed, waiting for lightning to strike and thunder to boom. Several minutes ticked by before he was able to relax. "This *something* he wants. Tell me what it is. Please. And for gods' sake, Anya, give me a straight answer for once." If he knew, he could steal it from her, give it to Cronus and end this nightmare.

"For once?" She shook her fork at him. "I give you straight answers all the time."

"Again, then," he said on a sigh.

She stared at him for a long while, not speaking, not moving. Finally she said, "You want the truth, I'll tell you. But the information will cost you. We'll trade. A question for a question."

"Done. What do you have that Cronus wants?"

"I have a...a...damn it, Lucien. I have a key, okay. Happy now?"

"Yes. There. We have both answered one question."

"We both have no— Damn you! I did ask a question, didn't I? *Happy now?* Score one for you."

"You have a key," Lucien prompted. "A key to what?"

"That, I won't tell you." She popped another bite of chicken into her mouth, chewed, swallowed.

"What does it open?"

"I'm done answering your questions," she said flatly. "You don't play fair."

He didn't berate her sense of fairness, but continued the game. "Why don't you give it to him?"

"Because it's mine," she snapped. She dropped her fork, and it clanged against her plate. "Now hush it before I flash you to an alligator pit. You're ruining the meal I spent hours preparing."

"You just told me you didn't cook it."

"I lied."

"A key will matter little when you are dead," he pointed out, unwilling to close the topic. Too much was at stake.

"Fuck you, Death."

She only called him Death when she was mad, he realized. Otherwise, it was sweetcakes, baby doll and Flowers. And lover, his mind piped in. He preferred those. Except for Flowers, the names made him feel like a man. Not an immortal, not a cursed warrior. Not ugly. And not someone who would ultimately destroy her.

He frowned. "I can't believe you are willing to die for a mere key."

"It's not like any other key, and you don't have to kill me."

"I must."

"Whatever." She drained the rest of her wine. "I answered a few more of your questions, now answer a few for me."

"Very well." He speared a crisp green bean. "What would you like to know?"

She propped her elbows on the table and rested her chin

in her upraised palms. "Have you ever disobeyed a command from the gods?"

"No. But then, I was not ordered to do anything until the Titans won the heavens. The Greeks left us alone after bestowing Maddox's death-curse."

"Have you *tried* to disobey the Titans, at least?"

"Again, no. Not personally. But Aeron refused to kill those four women, and you have seen the results. Bloodlust has consumed him. He wants to kill everyone now. Even his friends. Maybe even himself. We had to lock him away, taking even more freedom than he lost when all of us were cursed with our demons. It's something we vowed never to do to each other."

"I understand," she said, suddenly seeming lost in thought. "Losing your freedom is a punishment worse than death."

"Yes." Lucien studied her, amazed by what he saw. He'd never seen this playful woman quite so serious. She must be recalling the time she'd spent locked away, perhaps tortured. His hands tightened into fists. "How long were you imprisoned?"

She shrugged. "Seemed like forever and I believe ancient scrolls say a hundred years, but it was more like two."

Clearly she meant to sound cavalier. She failed. "What did you do while locked away?"

"Think, pace, hurt. Talk to the man in the cell beside mine. He was a little cocky, but that was better than silence." She sighed. "Have you ever fought the demon of Death?"

His brow furrowed in confusion. Better confusion that fury at what she had suffered. "What do you mean? Fought it physically?"

"No. I know it can't leave your body unless you die or it's sucked out. I know it's trapped inside you and the two of you are one. But have you ever resisted its desire to take a soul?"

His entire body tensed. This was not a matter he usually discussed. Anya had revealed a part of her secret, however. He could do no less. "Yes."

"And?" Her focus intensified, her eyes like a laser beam on him. "What happened?"

None of the warriors knew he had once been in love; none knew he had watched his lover slowly wither away, her body rotting. "If I do not escort a soul, its physical body suffers untold agony. More than any person should ever have to suffer. More than Fate intended."

"Hit a nerve, did I? There's a muscle ticking under your eye." Rather than press him for more information, she ate the rest of the meal in silence.

As he watched her, the dark memories her questions had brought to the surface receded, replaced by desire. *Take her.* The words whispered across his mind. Maybe because every movement she made was more sensual than the last. *Make love to her.*

No. You are not a monster. Not anymore, at least. He could spend time with her, but nothing more.

When she finished eating, she stood. "Want to make out a little or just jump straight into the shopping?"

She had not removed the beige coat and looked toasty warm. More than that, she looked strippable. *He* wanted to be the one to warm her. "Shopping," he forced himself to say. But he did not stand.

She shrugged as if his answer hadn't mattered to her, and that irritated him. The irritation angered him. And the anger annoyed him. He should feel nothing.

"You can leave your weapons here," she said with a teasing grin. "Hunters never come up this way. Neutral territory and all."

"I do not remove my weapons. Ever."

Her gaze traveled the long length of him in a heated caress. "Not even to shower?"

His cock stirred as he imagined her in the shower with him, water raining over her naked body. "Not even."

"Why, Lucy. That's totally barbaric." She bit her lower lip and sauntered around the table, bending down to whisper in his ear, "But it's something I'd like to witness firsthand."

A fallen lock of her hair brushed his cheek, and he found his eyes closing in ecstasy. His blood suddenly caught fire, nearly raging out of control in seconds. Rather than kiss her as he so desperately wanted—stupid, dangerous…wonderful—he somehow found the will to rise and move away from her.

"You really know how to drag a party down."

"Anya."

"No. Not a word. Let's get out of here," she said, voice cracking slightly.

He was ashamed to realize his legs were shaking. He was so hard his cock actually hurt. One stroke, and he would come.

Anya didn't look back as she strolled to the front door. Opened it, left the apartment, expecting him to follow. He took a moment to breathe in and out, letting the cold air soothe him.

Every muscle in his body was clamped down, eager and needy for her. Only her. Even the demon seemed to ache for her, no longer purring but roaring hungrily.

Think of the artifacts, the box. Think of Hunters. Think of holding Anya's dead body in your arms.

That sobered him.

An angry whisper suddenly drifted past him. "I'm waiting, Death."

Cronus.

Lucien's blood chilled completely. Finally the god king

had returned. Why here? Why now? *Because your reprieve is over.* The king had not materialized. What was he doing?

"You have failed me, Death. Over and over again, you have failed me."

"I am sorry."

"Liar!"

The boom of the word nearly burst his eardrums.

"You will not suffer for it," the god added quietly, "but your friends will. I'll start with Paris, sending him to a place where no women reside. I will prevent him from leaving and I will laugh as he weakens. I will laugh when he is forced to turn to other men for strength. And when I'm through with him, I'll look to Reyes."

Fight him, as Anya does. "You would kill them, then? Set their demons free to roam the earth in a crazed frenzy? No mortal will bow before you once the demons are through wreaking their havoc."

"Zeus might not have been able to protect the people from your demons, but *I* can. Do you wish to hear what I'll do to Reyes?"

Fight! "You would prevent him from hurting himself, I'm sure. Perhaps flood him with pleasure he is no longer equipped to handle."

"Do you dare mock me?"

"No. Nor do I wish to do that with which you have charged me."

"I am aware of that, Death. I am also tired of waiting. Which of us do you think will emerge the victor and receive what he desires?"

"What if—" Lucien pressed his lips together. Should he do this? *Yes,* he decided a moment later. He should. There was no other way. "Anya has something you crave. What if I procure it for you?"

For several seconds, there was only crackling tension.

Then, more calmly, Cronus said, "I will allow you to try. If you fail in this, you *will* bring me her body. If you fail in that, I will not be so lenient. I will do everything I claimed and more. And I'll make you watch while I do it. Now go!"

A great gust of wind shoved Lucien forward. Cutting off a growl, he righted himself and followed the path Anya had taken. He found her in the lobby of the building, alive and well, though Cronus was nearby. He had to get that key from her. Right now, it was the only way he knew to save her. If he failed…

His stomach twisted into a painful knot. He would not fail.

He allowed his gaze to scan the building. There was a huge fireplace with a crackling blaze in the corner. Beside it, a desk was manned by two males staring at Anya in open approval. Lucien scowled. Unaware of the mortals, or perhaps uncaring, she tapped her foot impatiently and studied her bright pink nails.

They'd been red yesterday. Hadn't they? Perhaps they'd been blue. She changed them every day, nearly as often as she changed moods.

Lucien hissed at the men as he strode past them, unable to hold the noise back. He was too raw to care about consequences. Too raw to care that being possessive of a woman like Anya would bring nothing but heartache.

She's not yours, and she can never be yours. Even if nothing else mattered, stealing her precious key would ensure that.

He didn't speak as he passed her, but she kicked into motion beside him. He could feel her body heat and smell her strawberry scent—his two favorite things, he realized. His world would not be the same without them.

"What do you want to buy first?" she asked him, unaware of his thoughts and turmoil.

Lucien opened his mouth to ask about the key, but the words refused to form. Earlier, she had ended their conversation the moment it had been mentioned. He would have to soften her first, he supposed, and earn a bit of her trust.

"A coat would be nice," he said. Though sunlight poured from the sky, chill wind beat against him.

"Then a coat you shall have. I know the perfect place." She twined their fingers together and tugged him to the left.

Instinct demanded he pull away. He didn't. Instead he tightened his grip, wishing he could hold on to her and never let go. She gasped, threw a sweet smile over her shoulder. Death rubbed against the corridors of his mind, reaching for her, wanting to touch her, too.

She ushered him down an ice-covered road. Cars meandered by and people strolled along the snowy sidewalks, in and out of the cobbled shops. All around were those majestic mountains. The gods really had outdone themselves with this spectacular scenery.

This could have been heaven.

"In here." Anya tugged him into a shop named Machen Teegeback.

"Warm Muffins?" he translated, having mastered many languages over the years. "We just ate. And I thought we were shopping for a coat."

She chuckled. "This isn't a bakery, lover. It's an outlet." Inside were coats, gloves, hats and all the things he would need to stay warm. "Now, don't you worry. Anya will dress you just right."

With another delighted chuckle, she trekked through the store, throwing different colored coats at him. "This one will match your eyes. Well, one of them anyway." Pause. "This one will look great against your skin." Pause. "Mmm, this one has easy access to my new favorite place through the pockets."

Pause. "Oh, score! Look at this." She held up the masculine version of the coat *she* wore before tossing it at him. "We'll be twinkies while we're climbing glaciers."

Unless he found that key, she would not be traveling with him. Selfishly, he was disappointed at the thought. "I only need one coat. Which do you—"

With a furtive glance at the cashier, she stuffed a pair of large wool gloves inside her jacket.

He frowned, certain he was mistaken about what had just happened. "What do you think you are doing?"

"Stealing." There was such relish in her tone, it was like a sexual high.

A shiver trekked the length of his spine. "You were not teasing about the food, then. Are you short of funds?"

"Hardly. I'm loaded." She anchored her hands on her hips and pouted up at him. "Don't tell me the big bad demon is upset. 'Cause you shouldn't be. I'll pay them back another day, Sally Sunshine. Maybe."

"Return the gloves, Anya." *Is this the way to soften her?* His jaw clenched. No, it wasn't, but he refused to back down. "No."

"Very well. I will pay for them." Lucien dropped the coats Anya had thrown at him, gently clasped her arm with one hand and pinched the gloves with the other. His palm brushed the side of her breast. Gulping, burning up, he gathered one of every item he needed, strode to the register, and paid with the bills Paris had given him earlier.

As they walked to the door, Anya fumed at his side. "I have to do it, okay?"

Her intensity surprised him. "Why?"

"You have your compulsions and I have mine. I can either burn the place down or take a measly pair of gloves."

Understanding dawned. She had her own demon to fight,

a dark nature she wished to control. He knew how hard such a thing could be. "I am sorry I took them away from you."

A pause. A sniffed, "No problem."

Carrying their purchases, he exited the building and stood at the curb, waiting for her to join him. Cold air slapped at him, but he didn't pull the coat from its sack. His skin was still on fire from having Anya next to him.

He wanted her next to him again, and it had nothing to do with getting his hands on that key. A minute passed, and she did not exit. What was she doing? He turned and walked forward with every intention of reentering the shop.

The door flew open, however, and Anya emerged. Her lips curled in a smug grin. His skin heated another degree.

"I might have to dig through the ice as I search for this artifact. I need the proper tools," he said. "Where can I acquire them?"

"Ugh. Digging will *not* be fun."

"Fun is not the purpose of the trip."

"Killjoy." She reached into her jacket and withdrew a pair of black gloves. Using her teeth, she ripped off the tags. Then, staring him in the eye, she tugged the leather over her hands.

"You stole them?"

"That's what I like about you, sweetcakes. You're an observant kind of guy."

Lucien shook his head, his lips twitching. He marched forward, forcing her to follow or be left behind. "Tell me why you must steal to prevent yourself from burning a building. You hinted, I deduced, but I would like to hear firsthand."

She kept pace beside him. "Remember those wars Reyes mentioned that night at the club? Well, guess what? I did start them. When I first walked among mortals, I was insane with my need for disorder and my every movement seemed to spur them into fury. With each other, not me. Worse, I couldn't look at a torch without knocking it over. Sometimes I didn't even realize I'd done it until the flames were dancing at my feet and people were screaming. And those screams, oh, gods, those screams." She sighed dreamily. "They were so delicious to my ears. Like auditory ice cream. More and more, I wanted to hear them. *Needed* to hear them."

"Anarchy means to be without law. Perhaps, deep down, those screams represented the chaos your nature demands."

"Yes," she said, eyes widening.

"The demon inside me is Death. For the longest time, it craved the absence of life, no matter what I had to do to accommodate that desire."

"You really do understand." She shook her head, her expression a little shocked. A strand of hair fell, and she hooked it behind her ear. "One day I caught myself reaching out, about to cut a chandelier from a ceiling just to hear the glass shatter and the people shriek, when a woman walked by. She was wearing a ring and the diamond winked in the light, brighter than any chandelier. Gods, I wanted that diamond. I followed her and stole it. The moment I slipped it on my finger, this grinding need inside me just…quieted somehow. I've been stealing ever since."

He was silent a moment. "You may steal from me anytime." Sadly, he feared it was he who would soon be stealing from her. More than ever, he did not want to take her life. Like him, she could have become a living nightmare but she strove to be more. Better.

She tossed him a grin. "Thank you."

His chest started aching. *The key. Ask about the key.* "Have you spent much time in the Arctic?" he found himself asking instead.

"A little. Oh, this is going to be fun! Well, aside from the digging part." She clapped excitedly. "Just the two of us, snuggled up to keep warm, no worries about Hunters. I doubt any human could survive the cold for long. Now, come on. I don't want to walk anymore. It's a waste of time." In the next instant, she disappeared.

He followed with no hesitation—

Arriving in Greece. The island, his rented home. He dropped his bags, not sensing or seeing any of the other warriors. They were probably still gathering supplies.

Anya plopped on the cream-colored leather couch as if she hadn't a care. With a blissful sigh, she removed her stolen gloves, followed by her boots, revealing pretty white leggings. She tossed both aside. Next she removed her coat—revealing a white lace bra.

His eyes nearly popped out of his head. "*That* is what you have been wearing all day?"

She grinned wickedly. "Yes. Do you like?"

His cock swelled to life. Again. This time thicker, fuller. Harder, hotter. She was sexier now than when she'd worn the maid's uniform—and she'd nearly felled him then. Thank the gods he hadn't known what little she'd worn underneath. He might have killed everyone who looked at her, and then attacked her there in the snow.

He couldn't tear his gaze away from her. Her stomach was flat and the color of cream, her navel a sensual feast to his eyes. Her breasts were full and ripe, the pink nipples hazily visible and oh so hard. The leggings conformed to her body like a second skin.

"Well? Do you like?" she repeated, stretching out. Her feet were bare, the pretty nails glittering in the light. "You could have seen this and more earlier, but you were too busy being stubborn. Don't be stubborn this time."

"You are beautiful, Anya."

"Come over here and kiss me, then," she beseeched huskily.

"I can't," he croaked out.

"Why not?" She ran a fingertip down her stomach, around her navel. "It's not like I'm asking you to screw me. Just kiss and touch me a little. And FYI, you should know this is the last time I'm going to offer myself to you. Your continued rejection is screwing with my confidence."

A roar sounded in his head. Not touch her? Not kiss her? "Why not more than kissing and touching?"

"Because." She crossed her arms over her middle, smashing her breasts together.

Holy gods. "Answer me."

"Why should I? You rarely answer me." Again she ran a fingertip down the planes of her stomach.

His gaze followed the action. He swallowed a sudden lump in his throat. She would give herself to other men, but not him. The realization sunk in, and he ground his teeth together. Him, she would only allow to kiss her. He wasn't good enough for anything else.

He wanted to hate her for that, but he'd done this to himself. He'd purposefully carved himself so that women would not want him. And though she obviously found him lacking, he still sought to save her life. "We need to discuss something, Anya."

"What? The best way to move your tongue?"

"The key. Give me the key Cronus wants, and I'll do anything you want, kiss you however you want me to."

Color leached from her cheeks. "Hell, no. I don't want you that badly."

He'd known that, but hearing her say it cut deeply. "Giving up the key will save your life."

"Without the key, my life isn't worth living. Now, I don't want to talk about it anymore. I want to talk about us."

"There can be no us until you give me that key."

"The key is mine," she shouted, "and I will never give it up. Do you understand? Never! I would rather die."

"You *will* die if you don't. You are forcing my hand, Anya."

"What, you plan to steal it?"

He didn't answer.

"You'll regret it if you try."

Still no response.

"Forget the key! We were having fun and could be having more fun right now."

"Cronus came to me, threatened those I love. I am out of time, Anya. I am to bring him the key or you. I would rather bring the key."

The pulse in her neck fluttered riotously. "When did he come to you?"

"Before we went shopping," he admitted.

"That's why you went so easily. You thought to sweeten me up so I'd just hand the key over." She laughed bitterly. "Or maybe you thought I'd slip and tell you where it is and you'd steal it. So much for your lofty principles."

"Which is it to be? You or the key?"

"Me." She raised her chin. "I told you. I will not part with the key."

"Anya," he said, hating himself. Hating Cronus. Hating even the woman he was trying to save. She made him *feel*. Now, more than ever, emotions were his enemy. "This is your last warning."

"Lucien, I can't give it up." Tears filled her eyes. "I can't."

Those tears… "Why?"

"I just can't. I *won't*."

Then there was nothing more for him to say. *Do it. End it. It is time.* "Here is your warning. I will make this quick. Kill you first. Take your soul after." He flashed to her, was straddling her hips in the next instant, his daggers withdrawn and cradled in his hands, raised, ready to strike.

Those teary eyes went wide with shock.

"I am sorry," he said, and struck.

CHAPTER NINE

PARIS ROAMED THE PAVED STREETS of Athens as the sun shone bright and golden. The air was peaceful, serene, and the white-washed, Old-World sights riveting. Gentle waves from the sea only a short distance away added the perfect sound-track.

He should have been preparing for his upcoming trip to the States.

He wasn't.

He was looking for a woman, any woman, who would have him. But no matter what he did or said, the females of Greece weren't responding to him as the females of Budapest—hell, as the females everywhere else on earth—had.

He didn't understand it, either. His physical appearance had not changed. He was a handsome motherfucker. His demeanor had not changed. He was the most charming person he knew. *Nothing* about him had changed. Yet before traveling here, he'd had only to cast his gaze upon a woman to have her stripping, readying herself for his pleasure. Here, nothing. Nada.

Women of every age, size and color treated him like a leper.

Sadly, at this point, all he needed was five minutes and a pair of spread legs.

Without sex, he weakened. Became vulnerable and unable to defend himself from Hunters and their vicious attacks.

Had it been possible, he would have chosen one woman, married her and taken her with him everywhere, enjoying her and her alone. But apart from the obstacle of human women's mortality, the demon inside him would allow no such thing. Once he'd slept with a woman, he couldn't get hard for her again. No matter how much he wanted to be with her.

It was why he'd stopped trying for anything more than a single night. To stay alive, he would have to cheat on a wife constantly, and he refused to do such a thing.

Someone look at me, want me. If he couldn't find a female…the things he was forced to do sickened him.

Not rape, please not rape, but the demon had no gender preference. Paris did. Paris only wanted women. His stomach cramped as memories tried to fill his mind. Hated memories. He clenched his teeth in an effort to halt them.

Find a prostitute, Promiscuity suggested, needing sex as much as he did.

Tried. It's as if they're hiding from me. Paris actually preferred prostitutes. They both got something out of the deal, and his lover didn't leave with expectations of a repeat performance.

A brunette sauntered down the sidewalk across from him. *Female.* He scented her before he saw her, turning his head to draw in more of her sweet feminine fragrance. *She'll do.*

He was halfway to her before he realized he'd taken a single step. "Excuse me," he called when he reached her. Desperation laced his tone.

Her gaze slid to him. Appreciation curtained her features, but that was it. Nothing more. No trancelike desire. Up close, he could see strands of silver in her hair and the age lines around her eyes.

Didn't matter. His mouth watered for her.

"Yes," she said in heavily accented English, not slowing.

Usually they stopped, already desperate to touch him. What made these Greek females different? "Would you like to…" Shit. He couldn't ask her to sleep with him, not right away. She'd probably balk. "Would you like to have dinner with me?"

"No, thanks. I already ate." And with that, she picked up speed and walked away from him.

He ground to a stop, stunned, unnerved. Irritated. What the hell was going on?

The gods, perhaps? Were they interfering? He glared up at the heavens. Bastards. He wouldn't put it past them. But why would they even care? They wanted to find their artifacts, didn't they? He and the other warriors were the best chance they had.

"I've done nothing to you," he barked.

Even as he spoke, a dark thought slipped into place. Maddox—Violence—had noticed a change in himself—becoming more wild, more uncontrolled—just before he'd met Ashlyn, the love of his life. Lucien seemed to be experiencing a similar phenomenon with Anya, not that stoic Death would admit such a thing aloud.

Were Paris to mention it, he suspected the new Lucien might club him to death in a fit of temper—a temper he'd rarely ever shown before.

Dear gods. Am I next?

No. No, no, no. Since Paris couldn't stay with one woman, he prayed he'd never meet a woman he could fall in love with. In fact, if he encountered a beauty whose name started with *A*—first Ashlyn, then Anya—he was running like hell. No way. Not for him.

A blonde passed him, carrying two paper sacks from which

the scent of fresh-baked bread wafted. He leapt into motion, chasing after her. "Allow me to help you with those," he said. Gods, he sounded desperate.

"No, thanks." She didn't spare him a glance, but kept moving.

Again, he ground to a stop. Fuck! What the hell was he supposed to do? If he had to fly back to Buda, he would do it. Or track Lucien down and endure another dizzying flash so he could get there faster. Those artifacts and Pandora's box be damned. He would—

Another blonde passed him.

Another rejection followed.

Another brunette.

Another rejection.

An hour later, his body was hard and hot and—fuck—still weakening. His hands were trembling, and he could feel the need for sex fueling his every cell—which was why, when someone ran into him from behind, he stumbled forward, nearly falling flat on his face before he managed to right himself.

"I'm so sorry," a feminine voice said.

A shiver danced through him at the sound of her decadent timbre. He turned slowly, afraid if he moved too quickly she would run away from him like the others. Papers were scattered around her feet, he noticed first, and she was bent down trying to gather them.

"That'll teach me to read and walk at the same time," she muttered.

"I'm glad you were reading," he said, bending down to help her. "I'm glad we ran into each other."

Her lids raised, and her gaze met his. She gasped.

In awareness? *Please, please be awareness.*

She was plain, with hazel eyes, freckled skin, and wavy brown hair that fell past her shoulders. Her eyes were too big for her face, and her lips were so full they appeared bee-stung. But there was something mesmerizing about her. Something that compelled his gaze to linger, to drink her in and enjoy. A hidden sensuality, perhaps. A wicked flicker in those green and brown eyes.

The quiet, mousy ones were always the wildest.

"Your name doesn't start with an *A,* does it?" he asked, suddenly suspicious.

Her brow puckered in confusion, but she shook her head. "No. My name is Sienna. Not that you care and not that you really asked. Sorry. I didn't mean to just blurt it out."

"I care," he said huskily. He couldn't wait to strip her.

A rosy blush infused her cheeks, and she hastily returned her attention to the papers.

"You're…American?" he asked, handing her the papers he'd gathered.

"Yes. Vacationing here to work on my manuscript. Again, not that you asked. I can't place your accent, though."

"Hungarian," he said. Well, he'd lived in Budapest for enough centuries to claim the nationality. Quickly he changed the subject back to her. "So you are a writer?"

"Yes. Well, I hope to be. Wait, that's not right, either. I *am* a writer, but I'm not published yet." Stacking her bundle, she nibbled on her lush bottom lip. "I'm sorry I'm babbling. It's a habit of mine. Just tell me to shut up when you've heard enough from me."

"I'd love to hear more." Relief was swimming through him, as potent as the richest wine laced with ambrosia. Finally—a woman who didn't rush away from him as if he were poison.

Blushing again, she smoothed a lock of hair behind her ear.

He watched the action, his cock twitching in response. This woman's hands were exquisite, perhaps the most sensual body part he'd ever seen. Soft, delicate, with white-tipped, square nails. A thick silver chain was linked around her equally exquisite wrist. She wore three rings. Two were simple bands, again silver, and the third was a large iridescent opal.

Married?

He didn't like the thought, but wasn't going to let it sway him. He imagined those hands on his body and could have come.

He had to have her.

Could be Bait. The thought struck him out of habit, because it was something he worried about constantly. He studied her more closely. The freckles spread over her entire face, the lips nearly misshapen by their large size. Probably not Bait, he decided then. Bait was usually gorgeous. Like Ashlyn. Like Anya. Sienna wasn't gorgeous. Not even close. Still, he wasn't going to lower his guard.

Must have her. Now! the demon growled.

Soon…soon…

"You're just being nice," she said, breaking the silence that had encompassed them. She pushed to her feet, tucking her manuscript under her arm. She was very slim, almost flat-chested.

He stood, loving how small she was compared to him, how his big body dwarfed her. "Hell, no. I'm nice, but I'm not lying. I want to know everything about you."

"Really?" she asked hopefully.

"Swear."

Her clothes were unflattering, dark blue and bagging. He wondered if she wore sexy lingerie underneath. He'd like to see her in emerald-green lace.

"Would you, uh, like to get a coffee or something?" she asked.

"Yes." *Gods, yes.*

Slowly she grinned. "Where?"

That grin affected him soul-deep. He felt its radiance like

a punch in the gut. "Wherever you lead, I'll follow." He was already hard, but now he was invigorated. He'd charm and flatter her, then give her the best orgasm of her life. Afterward, they'd amicably part ways.

She'd have a night to remember, and his strength would be restored. For the rest of the day, at least. An even trade.

"Come on," he said. "We'll find something." *Soon.*

They meandered along the walkway, side by side. His awareness of her only grew. She smelled of soap and—he sniffed. Wildflowers. What were her most secret fantasies?

"There's a café just around the corner," she said.

"Perfect." A tremble racked him. Weakness or desire? He didn't know, didn't care. *Distract yourself.* "What's your manuscript about?"

"Oh." She waved a hand through the air. "You don't really want to know, and I'm embarrassed to say."

"A romance novel, then?"

Her eyes widened and she peered over at him. "How'd you know?"

"Lucky guess." He knew women, even if he couldn't get close to any one of them. While most loved all things romantic, they hid their romance novels as if they were something to be ashamed of. They couldn't know that *he* read them. He loved them, actually, and would have liked a happy ending for himself.

Until the impossible became possible—aka the Titans dressed in tutus and waved their magic wands while dancing and singing about love—he'd just have to make do.

Finally they rounded the corner and the outdoor café came into view. Circular tables and high-backed chairs were lined in front of a large glass window. One was vacant, so they quickly claimed it.

"How long have you been in Greece?" she asked, settling the papers and her purse in her lap.

"A little more than a week, but I've been working."

"Oh, that's terrible. You haven't had a chance to see the sights, have you?" She propped her elbows on the tabletop and peered over at him, expression rapt. "Are you here alone or with a group?"

Ignoring her question, he said, "I'm looking at the best sight right now." *All right, boy. That's getting a little cheesy, even for you. What, you gonna ask her to research the love scenes of her book next? Bring it down a notch.*

She blushed once more, though, a pretty pinkening of her freckled skin. His cock throbbed in reaction.

A waitress arrived and they placed their orders. He was surprised when his companion—what had she said her name was?—ordered straight, black coffee. He would have placed money on something sweet. He ordered a double espresso for himself.

When the drinks arrived a few minutes later, he returned his attention to Freckles. She became lovelier by the second, he realized. Underneath the freckles, her skin was a creamy shade of pearl, her eyes now more green than brown.

"Thank you for the coffee," she said, sipping. She reached over with her free hand to pat his fingers. At the instant of contact, warm, heady tingles raced up his arm—unexpected and as exquisite as she suddenly was.

She gasped. He fought a moan.

"My pleasure," he answered, arousal building…building… Was it too soon to make a move? Would she run?

"So, you never told me. What are you doing in Greece?" She pulled her hand away, but stared at his as if there were something wrong with it.

"I just felt like traveling," he lied. Wait. He'd mentioned something about work a bit ago. "For work. I'm a…model." It was a lie he'd used time and time again.

"Wow," she said, obviously distracted. Frowning, she reached out and touched his hand again.

Again, tingles rushed through him. And her, as well, it seemed. She gasped a second time and turned her hand over, studying it. Perhaps now was a good time to make his move, after all.

"I love the feel of your skin."

Shifting nervously, she looked away. "Thank you."

Slowly, so slowly, he claimed her hand and raised it to his mouth. He placed a soft kiss on the inside of her wrist. The warm tingles sparked between them, constant now, and so erotic he was willing to beg her to sleep with him.

When she didn't protest, he licked her pulse.

Gasping, she jerked. Not away from him, but in surprised...delight? He'd never had to wonder before, but couldn't quite read her expression. Couldn't release her, either. Touching her was like touching a live wire, pinning him in place, holding him captive with those electric jolts.

"I never do this," she said on a catch of breath. "I never have coffee with strange men or let them kiss me. Especially not male models."

"But I'm not kissing you."

"Oh. Well. I just meant—well, I just meant my wrist. You were kissing my wrist."

"I'd like to kiss you." He drank her in through the thick fan of his lashes. "Truly kiss you."

"Why? Don't get me wrong," she rushed out. "I'm glad. But why me?"

"You're a desirable woman."

"I am?"

"Oh, yes." His voice was husky with arousal. "Can't you feel the hum of my desire?"

"I—I—" She chewed on her lower lip again. A nervous habit?

It was endearing, but *he* wanted to chew on that lip.

"I don't know what to say," she said. She traced a fingertip over her mouth, as if she was imagining his tongue there, too.

"Say yes."

"But we're strangers."

"We don't have to be." Gods, he couldn't wait to taste her. All of her.

"We could, I don't know, go to my hotel room," she suggested shyly. "If you wanted to, that is. We can have a drink or something. I mean, more than coffee. But I'm not suggesting you have to have more if you don't want to. Oh, crap. I'm nervous! I'm sorry."

"Let's go somewhere new to both of us." He never entered a mortal's quarters. He'd made that mistake only once. And he couldn't take her to his temporary new home. That would place the other warriors in danger if Hunters were to follow. That left getting a hotel room himself. "Somewhere close."

"I—I—" she stammered again.

He pushed up, leaning toward her, and meshed his mouth over hers. She immediately opened without protest, and he swept his tongue inside for a hot, searing kiss. Her taste— better than he could have imagined. Mint and lemons, coffee and total passion. Already a lance of strength shot through him.

What would she taste like between her legs?

"O-okay," she breathed when he pulled away. Her nipples were hard. "Should we get a room?"

He'd trace his tongue around those nipples before sucking on them. He'd have her writhing while he pleasured her with his fingers first, then screaming while he filled her with his cock. He would spend hours enjoying her.

With a groan, he straightened and took her hand. She

didn't protest as he helped her to her feet. He tossed several bills on the table.

"This way," he said.

They held hands as they raced down the walkway, and Paris again wished he could flash like Lucien. He wasn't sure how much longer he could wait to have this woman. Of course, when the passion was over, she'd lose her appeal. But until then…

"Wait," she suddenly said.

He was panting, he realized, and almost shouted, "No." He tugged her into an alleyway. Desperate, so desperate. The area was filled with sunlight, but at least they'd have a modicum of privacy.

"Yes," he said, pushing her up against the wall. Her navy shirt had a slit up each side, each revealing a tiny patch of smooth skin.

"I don't even know your name." She didn't shove him away as he'd feared, but gaped at him with white-hot need in those hazel eyes as she wound her arms around his neck.

I'm back, he thought, muttering, "Paris. My name is Paris." Then he kissed the breath right out of her.

She moaned, and he swallowed the sound. Her legs parted. His erection pressed into the sweetest part of her, rubbing, mimicking sex. *He* moaned this time.

Perfection.

She kneaded his back, her nails scoring past the material of his shirt. All the while their tongues dueled. When he palmed her breast, the kiss deepened, spinning into a tide of wildness.

Need skin to skin contact. He tunneled a hand under her shirt—smooth skin, ah, so good—up the flatness of her stomach—she quivered—and palmed her breast again.

She wasn't wearing a bra, and he got a taste of the skin he craved. Sweet merciful heavens. Her breasts were small, but perfectly tipped. He gently pinched one nipple, rolling it between his greedy fingers, loving the feel. She arched her hips, stroking his cock.

"So sweet," he growled.

"Paris," she panted.

"I need to be inside you."

"I—I—I'm sorry."

He kissed a path down her cheek, along her jaw. She wouldn't regret giving herself to him. He'd take such good care of her. She'd remember him with a smile for the rest of her life. "Why?"

"For this," she said. She no longer sounded breathless or aroused. She sounded determined.

A sharp needlelike pain stabbed at his neck. He pulled back from her in confusion. Staggered. Felt a strange lethargy work through him, causing his knees to tremble. "What… why…" His voice was weak. Wrong.

Her face swam in front of him, but he could see that she wore an emotionless mask. Her freckles blurred together. He watched as she closed the top of her opal ring, shielding the sharp point inside.

"Evil has to be stamped out," she said flatly.

Bait after all, he thought, and then his world went black.

REYES SAT IN THE SHADOWED corner of an Italian strip club, thinking that one bar was the same as any other, no matter the country. He'd come to Rome to search for Pandora's box, but he was having trouble concentrating and had succeeded only in pissing off his team, rather than helping them.

They'd finally told him to leave, to calm himself down before coming back to the ruins of the Unspoken Ones.

So here he sat, cutting his arm under the table so no one could see what he was doing. Possessed by the spirit of Pain, he needed to feel the sharp sting of agony on a daily basis. Nothing else soothed him.

Especially now, when all he could think about was Danika.

Where was she? Was she okay? Did she hate him or did she spend her nights dreaming of him as he dreamed of her?

Her image flashed through his mind. Blond, tiny, angelic. Sensual, courageous, passionate. Well, he imagined she would be passionate. He hadn't even kissed her yet, much less touched her or stripped her.

But he wanted to. Gods, he wanted to.

He had to get her out of his mind—which was the reason he'd come here. But the four naked women on stage, beautiful as they were, did nothing for him. He wasn't even hard. Couldn't get hard anymore without thinking of Danika.

So badly he wanted to track her down, guard her…love her. He couldn't. Despite his temporary restraints, Aeron would kill her one day soon, fulfilling the Titans' command. And Reyes didn't want to become involved with her, knowing he'd lose her. For there would be no stopping Aeron—to stop him, Reyes would have to kill him or condemn his friend to a lifetime of torment.

Unfortunately, Reyes was not that selfish. Aeron was his brother in all but blood. A warrior who had stood by Reyes's side and at his back, slaying Hunters. They'd bled together. They'd saved each other. To forget that for a woman, a momentary pleasure…he bit the inside of his cheek.

The knife dug deep into his wrist, nicking a vein. He felt the warm rush of blood down his arm. The wound healed immediately, however, the tissues quickly weaving back together.

He sliced another groove, grimaced. Sighed in sweet relief.

"Lap dance?" one of the dancers asked him in Italian.

"No," he replied, harsher than he'd intended. Another sigh

escaped him, this one devoid of any hint of relief. He wasn't doing himself any good, staying here. He wasn't calming down, but was growing even moodier.

"Sure?" She cupped her lace-clad breasts. "I'll make you feel good."

Only once since being paired with the demon of Pain had he felt actual pleasure and that was while looking at Danika. The pain of that pleasure had been…addicting. Nothing else would do anymore, it seemed. "I'm sure. Leave me."

The stripper flounced away in a huff.

He scrubbed a hand over his face. Surely there was something he could do to help Danika. The thought of her vibrant life being snuffed out was nearly too much for him to bear. Too *painful,* even for him.

Perhaps he could petition the gods, ask them to rescind their command for Wrath—Aeron—to kill Danika.

Maybe, he thought, leaning back in his chair, feeling a measure of peace for the first time in weeks. He would need something to bargain with, something they coveted. He didn't know much about the Titans, who hadn't been in power very long. What did they want? And how could he procure it?

AERON CROUCHED IN THE corner of the cell, his body battered and bloodied from his many rages. The pain didn't bother him, though. No, it strengthened him.

Kill, kill, kill.

He had to escape this prison. *A prisoner inside my own home.* Bloodlust held him in a tight clasp, squeezing, squeezing…so much so that he saw the world in a haze of reds. He couldn't eat without imagining his knife slicing through Danika's neck—then her sister's, her mother's, her grandmother's. He couldn't breathe, sleep or move without imagining it. *Kill.*

For so long, he'd hoped and prayed he would lose this desire to kill. But every day, the urge grew stronger. His friends no longer visited him except to slip a tray of food into his cell; it was as if they'd written him out of their lives.

Kill, kill, kill. He needed out of this dungeon. Needed to destroy. Then the desire would leave him. He knew it. And oh, he could almost taste those deaths in his mouth. Yes, he needed out.

No more waiting. No more hoping for peace. He'd do what was necessary, what he'd been commanded.

He stared over at the bars. A plan began to take root in his mind. He grinned. Soon…

CHAPTER TEN

ANYA COULDN'T BELIEVE LUCIEN had just tried to kill her. Truly kill her, and not in jest. Yeah, she'd known he'd been commanded to do it. Yeah, he'd claimed he meant to see it through. And yeah, he'd even tried before.

But his previous attempts had been halfhearted. This hadn't. He'd meant to slay her. Permanently, no take-backs. If she hadn't flashed from the couch when she had, he would have cleaved her head from her body. And now he was hot on her trail, still determined to take her out.

Hurt and anger flooded her as she flashed from one location to another, each blurring together as she tried to lose him. Today she'd shopped with him and laughed with him. She'd told him about the key. For once he'd seemed to like—and enjoy!—her presence. More than that, he'd promised to take her to the Arctic with him.

And then he'd tried to kill her.

The heat of her anger intensified, and the sharpness of her hurt cut deep. How dare he! She'd been nothing but kind to him.

Well, she thought, eyes narrowing, that was going to change. *She* was now going to kill *him*. No more desiring him. No more kissing him and imagining him inside her. Seething, she flashed to her apartment in Switzerland and quickly changed into a tee and black stretch pants that wouldn't easily stain with Lucien's blood, reminding her for years to come of what she'd had to do to him. Flashed to two other places, gathering weapons.

Once she was armored in knives, throwing stars and a Taser, she flashed back to his home in the Cyclades. She wasn't just going to kill him, she was going to have fun electrocuting him before slicing him up like a Christmas ham.

He was gone. Still looking for her, she knew.

He would appear soon enough.

She stood in place, feet apart, hands at her sides. Waiting… eager…

He arrived a split second later. His gorgeously scarred features were devoid of emotion. Seeing him, she remembered something she wanted to do to him and grinned evilly. *Payback was going to be a bitch.*

"Anya."

Rather than attack him, she flashed to his room in Budapest. She gathered the chains he'd used on her, flashed to that glacier in Antarctica and wrapped them around her waist like a belt.

"Bastard," she said as cold wind cut into her skin. Lucien hadn't known that she was the one immortal no chains could hold, no prison could contain. Thanks to her father, who had gifted her with the All-Key, she could escape any place at any time. She could escape anything—except her curse.

I will not give it up.

To give the key away was to chart the course of your own downfall, as she well knew. Her father had known he would weaken when he gave it to her, but he had done it. To make up for his absence most of her life, to prove he really did love her.

To her horror, he'd quickly begun to crumble. Now, all these years later, he was a shell of his former self. He did not remember who he was, what he'd done throughout his lengthy life, or that he had a wife. He could barely take care of himself. And because Anya had left Themis rotting in prison, Anya's mother had to see to his needs.

Both were happy, though, Anya liked to think. Dysnomia, because she had a man who needed her and didn't revile her. Tartarus, because the prison and his bitch of a wife no longer bound him.

That didn't mean Anya would reduce her father's sacrifice to a bargaining tool in her war with Cronus, losing everything she had gained. If she gave the key away, she would be vulnerable again. Her powers, gone. Her memories, wiped out. Her ability to escape any chain, destroyed.

Damn Cronus, anyway. She wished like hell he'd never learned of the key, but figured he had seen Tartarus, who had been blessed with the key as a child, give it to her. They'd been locked in the same prison, after all, so it made sense. And if she hadn't used it to free her parents after Cronus locked them up, the god would have most likely forgotten about it. But she had, and here they were.

"Chaser and chasee," she muttered.

Mostly Cronus wanted the key out of her possession to prevent her from using it against him again. She'd tried to tell him that she didn't care about the other gods and wouldn't return to the prison. Like the distrustful deity he was, he hadn't believed her. And to be honest, he was smart not to. If he locked her parents up again, she'd simply return and bust them out.

A scowling Lucien appeared in front of her. "Anya?" She didn't miss a beat.

"Ready to have some fun?" She didn't give him time to answer. Weighed down with the chains, she flashed to a busy street in New York—fingers crossed he would be run over—then to a gay strip club in Italy—fingers crossed he would be groped—then to a zoo in Oklahoma—fingers crossed the elephant shit was ripe.

"Enjoy," she muttered with relish.

Anya flashed one final time, back to where she'd begun: his home in Greece. Lucien was still following her trail. Lightning-quick, she hid the chains under the bed and palmed her Taser.

When she straightened he was there, just in front of her. Her breath caught. He was still scowling, teeth bared and sharp, Death glowing in his eyes. He had a bleeding cut on his leg and he smelled like shit.

Her nose wrinkled. "Step in something?" she asked innocently.

"That, I did not mind." He took a menacing step toward her. "What I did mind was being hit by a cab, then landing on the lap of a naked man. With an erection, Anya. He had an erection."

She grinned. She just couldn't help herself.

"Now," he continued in that outraged tone, "you are going to tell me why you flashed to my room in Buda."

"No. I'm not." Grin widening, she lifted her arm and Tasered him.

His entire body shook, his expression frozen in outrage and anguish. Only when the last volt escaped did she drop the weapon. Hissing, he jerked the plugs from his nipples. Her aim had been dead on.

"Anya!" he growled.

Careful not to allow her expression to betray her, she whipped out two silver-tipped throwing stars and launched them at him. The whoosh was the only warning he had before the stars embedded in his heart.

He howled. "Again in the heart? Where is your originality?" He winced as he yanked them out, and his jaw set stubbornly as he tossed it to the ground. "This doesn't have to be messy, Anya."

"Hell, yes, it does." She threw another star.

He ducked, and the tiny blade sailed over his shoulder. Then he took another step toward her. Brave man. "Why can't you give Cronus the key?"

"Why couldn't you pick me rather than Cronus?" she ground out. "Why couldn't you pick me rather than your friends?"

Oh, gods. Had she truly said that? Whined like that? Heat spread over her entire face. Of course he'd picked his friends. She might wish otherwise—even the night Ashlyn sacrificed herself for Maddox, Anya had dreamed of Lucien being willing to do the same for her—but that was the way of the world. Lovers, whether they'd done the deed or not, came and went. Friends were forever.

Lucien paused. "For all I know, Anya, you will forget me tomorrow. Why should I risk all that I hold dear for a few days with you?"

Because I'm worthy, damn it! Foolishly, selfishly, she would have liked to hear that he'd go through anything for her, no matter how little or long they'd be together. Punishment. Hell. Torture. A combination of all three. "I could have helped you find those artifacts. I could have helped you fight Hydra. I could have helped you find that godsdamn box."

His shoulders sagged slightly. "I know."

Her hurt increased. He'd rather kill her than to 1) risk getting to know her more and perhaps watch her walk away one day and 2) obtain her aid for an item he desperately craved.

Growling low in her throat, she launched yet another star. He wasn't fast enough this time and it sliced into his already injured thigh.

"Damn it, Anya." He jerked it out and tossed it aside, even though he could have tossed it at her. "Calm down."

"Calm down? Are you serious?"

"Yes."

Shithead. "You wanna kill me, you're going to have to work for it."

"Very well." Eyes narrowing, he allowed his long legs to eat up the rest of the distance between them.

She flashed to the living room, but he was right behind her. She whipped around and jumped backward, placing a coffee table between them. He simply picked it up and tossed it aside. The glass shattered on impact, raining shards all over the room. The wooden legs splintered.

Why, why, why did the force of his determination and strength arouse her? Now of all times? She wouldn't let that arousal affect her, though. From the beginning, he'd done nothing but insult her, smash her hopes and ignore her feelings. He deserved whatever pain she dished out.

"If we are going to fight, it might as well be honorable," he said, and then he disappeared.

She wasn't given time to wonder where he'd gone.

He reappeared a moment later holding two swords. He threw one in her direction, and she caught it by the hilt. Heavy, but that wouldn't be a problem. She was much stronger than she looked.

"There's no fun in honor," she told him, waving the thick metal back and forth.

"Try it. You might be surprised."

"Seriously, though. You want to swordfight a *girl?*" She tried to put enough censure in her voice to shame him, even though she hummed with excitement. Could he beat her?

"You are hardly a typical girl, so yes. I want to fight you."

"I'll take that as a compliment, Flowers."

"It was meant as one."

Lucien was on her in the next heartbeat. She raised her

sword to parry and metal clinked against metal, the force of which caused her to stumble. He continued to surge forward, continued to push her backward, his thrusts quick and unceasing, but she managed to twist to the side, swing and slice into his shirt. Oopsie, flesh too.

Blood seeped through the cotton, soaking it to his stomach. The flow swiftly stanched, and the wound, she suspected, closed. Damn immortal warriors and their supernatural healing! Because they were designed for battle, they healed much quicker than even the gods.

"Luck," he said.

"Talent." *Clink.* She kicked a lily-filled vase at him, and it shattered against his chest. Droplets of crimson appeared, blending with the sweat that trickled from his temples.

"We shall see."

"Should we worry about visitors?" she asked, dodging as he lunged at her.

"This place was chosen for its isolation. More than that, we paid dearly to be ignored, no matter what was heard." He jumped backward, hunching to remove his stomach from her line of fire.

"Well, aren't you a Smartie McSmartpants." She went low, aiming for his ankles. Hobbling him would be amusing.

Unfortunately, he hopped out of the way. They began a dance of thrust, parry and retreat, moving throughout the entire home. *Clank.* Something fell to the ground and splintered. *Clank.* Another item followed suit.

Within fifteen minutes, the couch and love seat were destroyed, as was every knickknack and even the television. Curtains were ripped down, and holes were punched into the walls. Much longer, and the authorities *would* arrive. Anya was panting, growing tired, but she managed to cut Lucien on his upper arm, calf and again his stomach.

He'd managed to cut her not at all.

Oops. Take that back. The tip of his sword slashed across her left shoulder, causing the shirt to gape and reveal the lace of her favorite demi-bra. The skin above it stung.

"You cut me," she said, gaping at him.

"I am sorry." And he did sound apologetic.

She growled, a predator locking on the evening's meal. "Not yet, but you will be!" She withdrew a dagger and stabbed at his thigh.

Contact.

"Ouch!"

End this. There was only one sure way to do that. She spun on her heel as she chopped at him, forcing him to turn and backing him toward the bedroom. He was strong—stronger than her, she admitted, for she knew he had been pulling back every time his blade almost nicked her. Why he did that, she didn't know, since he'd finally gotten serious about killing her.

"I don't know why I hung around you so long," she said amid thrusts and parries. "I don't know why I helped you."

"That makes two of us." His straight, white teeth bared in another scowl.

"You know what? I'm sick of your poor-me routine. It's old, sweetcakes."

"There is no routine," he gritted out.

"Like hell." Spinning, she swung at him with her fist. Contact. "You have scars. So the hell what. That doesn't mean all women think you're ugly."

When she swung at him again, he batted her wrist away. "You cannot think me handsome, and so you cannot want me. Not really. You have even admitted it."

"People lie all the time, asshole. I believe I've mentioned that I personally do so on a regular basis."

He stilled, panting. His eyes widened with astonishment. And hope? "You lied about why you have stayed with me?"

"Wouldn't matter if I did. I hate your guts now." She dropped her sword and shoved him. "You were going to kill me."

He stumbled backward, finally past the threshold of the bedroom. He dropped his sword, too, and it clanked against the floor. "From the beginning, I meant to kill you. My intentions were never a secret."

"Yeah, but you weren't serious about it." When he made no move toward her, she pushed him again. Again, he stumbled. "Would you really have taken my soul?"

His knees hit the edge of the bed. "Yes. No. I don't know. You torment me like no other and I am constantly second-guessing my decisions about you."

She pushed again and his legs buckled. As his ass slapped against the mattress, she dove for his stomach, slamming her shoulder into him and knocking the breath from his lungs.

"Anya," he managed to gasp out.

"Nope. You don't get to talk anymore."

"You do not hate me," he said darkly. He had a hold of her wrists a second later and was jerking her on top of him, his mouth slamming into hers. His hot tongue thrust inside her mouth as surely as his sword had thrust at her body, only now his aim was deadlier.

Sweet lightning, she mused, a little dizzy. The man knew how to kiss, letting his tongue continue to invade her mouth with all kinds of electric heat. Her nipples hardened, and that damn moisture pooled between her legs. Every cell she possessed sparked to wild life.

You're not supposed to desire him anymore.

Well, he wasn't supposed to kiss me.

Grab the chains. Now!

As their tongues dueled, Anya forced herself into action.

But she grabbed on to Lucien rather than the chains, gripping his head so tightly her nails scoured his scalp. Such an embrace would have killed a human, but Lucien seemed to revel in it, his erection pulsing under her.

Just a few minutes of play, then *I'll lock him down.*

He just…he tasted so damn good. Better than she remembered. Man and dark fever, power and roses. His touch was exhilarating, his hands kneading her ass as he ground his swollen shaft between her legs. Much more, and she would come. Then ask for even more. Beg.

Gods, she hated her curse.

And she hated herself for even thinking about fulfilling it. *No way you* want *to be bound to this man, unable to love another, unable to kiss and touch or even dream about another.* So why did the possibility excite her? Why did she want to smile at the thought of spending eternity with Lucien? Her heart belonging to him, even if he tired of her?

Don't think about that now. She straddled Lucien's waist, pressing his cock closer…closer…hitting exactly where she needed. She gasped in ecstasy, her entire body rejoicing.

"Take off your clothes," he commanded. "I want to feel your skin."

Yes, yes. "No." Common sense spoke for her. Her desire for him wasn't going to change the night's ending: Lucien chained to the bed and at her mercy, to be punished for trying to take her head.

That doesn't mean you can't enjoy him for a little while longer and take off something. Her hands fisted on Lucien's chest. Obviously, he wasn't the only one who second-guessed himself.

"I want you, all right?" he said. "I can deny it no longer. Know that I am not going to try to kill you during the act. You have my word."

But there was shame and guilt in his voice.

"Fuck me now, kill me later, hmm," she said, not offended when she probably should have been. "Well, you can take off *your* clothes." Oh, to feast on his glorious body. "Mine have to stay on."

He stilled, stared up at her, passion receding from his face and leaving that blank mask she hated.

She almost sobbed. She wasn't ready for the make-out session to end.

"Why will you not strip for me?"

"Why are we talking? I thought I told you that you weren't allowed to do so anymore," she hedged, pressing closer and sliding her tongue back into his mouth. She didn't want to tell him the truth, but she didn't want to lie to him, either. Not about this. She would much rather enjoy him.

He returned her passion for a few minutes more, hands tracing over the curve of her spine. There was desperation in his kiss. A desperation that was reflected in her own, she was sure. She never wanted it to end, could have stayed in his arms forever. But he finally cupped her jaw and forced her to look at him.

Tension lined his mouth. "You led me to believe my scars did not bother you," he said softly.

"They don't," she replied just as softly.

"Anya. Of all the times to tell me the truth, this is it. Please."

"They don't!"

His eyes tapered, nearly shut, feathered lashes pointing at her like spikes. Suddenly there was an evil glint in both the blue and brown iris, as if the demon of Death had taken over. Lucien gripped her hips and moved her off him.

Confused, she perched at the edge of the bed.

"You want me, but you will not take off your clothing for

me," he said. Actually, he growled. "I do not think you really want me, after all."

"I do."

Staring at her, he unsnapped his jeans.

She pulled her gaze from his face, watching the movement of his fingers. Breath caught in her lungs. What was he doing? Stripping for her, as she'd requested? But why would he—

Unziiip.

Her jaw fell open as his erection sprang free. Huge, swollen, long, with a rounded tip already beaded with moisture. Her tongue nearly rolled out of her mouth. Was she drooling?

"You want me," he repeated flatly. "Well, now you're going to have to prove it."

"Wh-what?" So damn big.

"Prove it. Suck my cock."

At his uncharacteristically crude language, her gaze jerked back up to his face. Anger was banked there, as was self-deprecation. His cheeks were flushed with shame. Did he expect her to scoff and walk away? Did he think to teach her a lesson about playing with him?

"What's the problem? Do you not want me?" he mocked. "Can you not bring yourself to do more than kiss me?"

Oh, yes. He expected her to walk. She'd never performed this act before, considering it too humbling and too intimate in light of her curse. With Lucien, however, she was aroused by the thought. His pleasure would be a thing of beauty, she had no doubt.

"Was this to be my punishment for trying to kill you or was this just another attempt to soften me?" he demanded before she could respond. "Either way, we both know you never meant to take it any further. Your cruelty astounds me."

Cruel? When she ached for him? When part of her wanted

to finally forget her curse and spend an eternity in his arms? "I can keep myself alive, thank you very much. I don't need your help, and I've never needed to soften you. Didn't I admit that already? And FYI, you don't have any room to talk about cruel intentions."

"You are stalling," he said. "Do it. Suck me."

He thought he was being harsh, forcing her hand to make her leave. He should have known better. She never would have guessed it, but she truly *wanted* to do this. Had craved it, perhaps, from the very first.

Slowly, she crawled up his body until her mouth was level with his shaft. His breath caught, the room again going silent. "Anya, you—"

"I'm not doing this to prove anything," she told him raspily. "I'm doing this because I can't seem to stop myself. I must. Your taste…I have to know…can't be as good as I imagine." And with that, she took him into her mouth, fully, completely, sliding all the way down and feeling him hit the back of her throat. Odd, the sensation, but she liked it.

He groaned in pleasured agony, and the sound poured over her skin like a caress. His hands tangled in her hair. "Anya. Don't. I shouldn't have…Anya."

Up, down, up, she moved, the way she had seen in the naughty movies she sometimes watched.

"You don't…you don't… Ah, gods. Anya. Don't stop. Please, don't stop."

From commanding to begging. She reveled in her power, in the need emanating from him. Need that was filling *her* up, ratcheting her own pleasure up another notch. *Mine.*

Up and down she continued to move. Her tongue swirled all the while, stroking everything it touched. She cupped the heavy weight of his testicles. He arched into her movements, going deeper, his every muscle clenched tight. She could feel the passion-hum in his blood. Wanted more. Had to have more.

"Changed my mind. Anya, stop. Stop!"

Merciless, she continued her upward glide, flicking her tongue over the swollen head. Sucking. Scraping with her teeth. She treated his cock exactly as she treated her favorite lollipops. Only she liked the taste of him more. Such desire…oh, his desire.

He was hard for her, and only her.

"I'm going to— Anya!" He roared her name as the climax ripped through him, shooting hot seed into her mouth.

She swallowed every drop and even licked the last little bit away, instinctively knowing that would please him. As she sat up, he continued to spasm in pleasure, even though he was spent. His eyes were closed, his mouth open in wonderment. *I did this,* she thought with pride. Never had she felt more powerful and never had she seen a more erotic sight.

Her own need reaching a new level, she straddled him. She was so wet her panties were soaked.

His eyelids slowly opened and he peered up at her, his expression sated. "Anya. You did not have to do that."

"I wanted to," she said. "And I want *you.* Don't ever doubt that again."

Tenderness glowed on his face. "What are you keeping from me, then? Why can I not strip you?"

That tenderness… Vulnerability claimed her, for no one other than her mother and her father had ever looked at her like that. As if she were precious. As if she were a treasure. Anya's heart lurched in her chest.

Lucien reached up and caressed her cheek. A shiver traveled through her.

"Why, Anya? I've tried to resist you since the moment I

first smelled your strawberry scent," he said. "As you can feel, that has not worked out for me."

Even now, his shaft was growing, thickening with renewed desire. Her eyes widened, and she tried so very hard not to soften even more toward him. If what he said was true, he'd wanted her from the very beginning and had been fighting it. Every unkind word and action had been a means of keeping her at a distance.

He'd hinted at such a thing before. Now, with him underneath her...

She was suddenly conflicted and didn't know what to do with him. Shit. This really complicated things because the basis for her—forced, damn it—dislike and anger had been obliterated.

Still, he wouldn't stop trying to kill her. He couldn't. Unless he chose her over "all the things he held dear." How selfish of her to have asked that of him, when she had nothing to give in return.

"Anya."

"What?" She blinked, returning her focus to Lucien.

His lips twitched. "Concentrate."

"Oh, sorry. Did you say something?"

He arched his hips up, rubbing his erection against her clitoris. "I asked why you want to keep your clothes on. Are *you* scarred?"

Shiver bumps dotted her skin. "No." Not physically, at least.

"It will not bother me if you are. I swear. I will kiss them better," he said huskily.

Her stomach quivered. What a delicious man. She braced her palms flat on his chest, felt the wild drum of his heartbeat through his tattered shirt. She was going to tell him, she decided. After everything they'd been through, he deserved to know.

"I'm cursed," she finally admitted. If he reacted poorly, she might be able to loathe him in truth. Her obsession might wane.

His brow furrowed. "You, too, are possessed by a demon?"

"No. Mine's just a run-of-the-mill curse."

"Ah, yes. Reyes mentioned a curse, but could not figure out what it was."

"That's because only a select few know and they are currently in hiding to avoid being locked up by Cronus. Well, and the one who did it knows, but that frigid bitch is behind bars."

"Who cursed you and why?" There was anger in his tone, as if he meant to kill whoever it was. "Reyes said it might have been Themis."

Her stomach did that quiver thing again. "It was. My mother and Tartarus, Themis's husband, got it on and nine months later—hello, baby Anya. Themis didn't know until she saw me, for I am the female version of my dad, you could say."

"I remember Tartarus," Lucien said. "I used to bring him prisoners. He was an honorable man, even handsome, but I did not want to strip him."

"Lucien just made a funny." She grinned. She couldn't help herself. "When Themis realized what had happened, she kind of freaked out. I didn't understand the full consequences of her curse until days later when the numbness wore off. Gods, I wanted to cut off her head."

Lust flashed in Lucien's eyes, brief, gone in an instant, but undeniable. "I do not know why it turns me on to hear you talk like that."

She thought she knew why. He was Death. He saw weakness and human infirmity on a daily basis. She was a woman who gave as good as she got. She was strong. Determined. And that had to be a welcome change. At least, she hoped so—because that's who and what she was, and she wanted so badly for him to like her.

"Tell me about the curse." His gaze lowered to the waist of her pants and his fingers soon followed, tracing a line over the upper hem.

Sweet heaven. *Here goes.* "If ever I allow a man to penetrate me, I'll be tied to him forever. No other man will appeal to me."

Lucien's brow once again furrowed. "That—"

"Is terrible, to think of losing my free will to a man." Except with Lucien, the thought did not carry such a stigma. "I will never be able to leave him, no matter what he does to me. If he falls in love with another, all I can do is watch him, longing for him to no avail."

The more she spoke, the more he radiated sympathy. "For a long time, my will was bound to Death's. What he wanted to do, I did, unable to stop him."

"So you know how bad it can be, yes?"

"Yes. Which is why I would never force my will upon yours. Not in something like this." He licked his lips, leaving a glistening sheen she wanted to taste. "So you have never…"

"No," she gritted out with a single shake of her head.

He was still and silent for a long while, just looking at her. She didn't know what was rolling through his mind. His expression was once more blank, unreadable.

Finally he said, "I judged you harshly and for that, I am sorrier than I can ever say. Anya…" Whatever he meant to add, he must have changed his mind. There was a pause, then, "Have you ever climaxed?" The words were croaked.

What reaction she'd expected from him, she didn't know. She only knew that wasn't it. An apology? Amazing. "Only by myself," she admitted without shame. "I'm not sure if fingers count as penetration, so I've never allowed a man below the waist."

"Do you trust me not to penetrate you?"

"I—maybe." *Silly girl. Shouldn't trust him even a little.*

An intense fire suddenly banked the contours of Lucien's features. "Take off your clothes for me, Anya. I won't penetrate you in any way, I swear it. But I do want to touch you. Everywhere. I *have* to touch you."

He disappeared before she could reply. Losing her anchor, she crashed facefirst into the mattress with a yelp. She rolled to her back, scowling. That bas—

He reappeared on top of her. And he was naked.

She sucked in a breath, waiting for him to try to shove inside her as Aias had done. There was a storm of panic, but a moment passed and he did nothing. Gradually, the storm receded and she relaxed. As she did, she realized the feel of his weight was divine, the touch of his bare skin pure temptation.

"Let me," he said.

"I—I—" Her mouth watered. To be pleasured and not fear the consequences…

"Let me have you in every way that I can without actually penetrating," he said, nuzzling her neck. "Please. I want to taste you."

Of all the men she shouldn't trust, Lucien topped the list. But gods, she wanted his mouth on her. She wanted to at last experience a climax with a man. With *this* man. Only this man.

Decision made, she flashed to the side of the bed. She stripped as fast as she could, Lucien's gaze burning her, then she flashed beside him. He was lying on his back now, giving her a full view of him. Scars stretched from his face all the way down to his right leg.

The overhead light shone brightly, caressing his entire length. And there was a lot to caress. Velvet skin poured over hard steel. He had no chest hair and only the slightest sprinkling on his legs.

That black butterfly tattoo still mesmerized her and even seemed to pulse under her scrutiny, as if seeking her touch.

She reached out, grazing her fingertips over the edges as she'd longed to do since first seeing it. Heat seared her. Lucien must have felt it, too, because he arched into her stroke with a groan.

"I've wanted to do that for a long time," she admitted.

"And I've wanted you to do it."

Tracing the jagged black lines, she asked, "How did you get the scars?"

"I carved myself with a poisoned blade," he admitted with only the slightest hesitation, "and set myself on fire. When I healed, I did it again. And again."

Gods. The pain he must have endured… "Determined to die?"

"At first, perhaps. The woman I loved had died, and I was the one to escort her soul to the heavens."

He'd been in love? Anya hated the thought, but she liked the thought of his suffering even less. "I'm sorry for your loss."

He nodded in acknowledgment. "When I realized that I would live, I prayed for the scars to remain. Someone must have answered that prayer—who it could have been, I do not know—because they finally stopped healing."

Sounded like the kind of prayer her mother might answer, since physical imperfection defied the natural order of immortality. "Why would you pray for such a thing? I'm not complaining, I'm just curious."

"I wanted them to remain so that women would turn away from me and I would never again be in danger of falling in love. I wanted them so that I would always remember to do my job, never falter."

"I didn't turn away from you."

"No, you didn't."

"You faltered."

"Yes. I am glad."

So was she. Anya returned to her studies. His erection was huge. Thick and perfectly tipped, just like before. *Mine,* she thought.

"Come here," Lucien said, his voice heavy with arousal.

Last chance to resist.

Shaking, she crawled up his body, so hot, so needy. She was bare and wet and slid up his cock. Both of them sucked in a worshipful breath. Amazing! Oh, what other delicious things had she been missing?

"Closer," he said.

She leaned down. When her breasts were smashed against his hard chest, he melded their lips together in a white-hot kiss. He even rolled her over. Again she experienced a moment's panic that he meant to break his word, but he merely kissed a path to her pebbled nipples.

His hot tongue traced a circle around them, making her shiver. Then he blew a cool breath, hardening them further. *Then* he sucked them into his mouth, one at a time, lancing pleasure straight to her core. It was the most stimulation she'd experienced in...forever.

In minutes, she was writhing, tugging at his hair, arching her hips, needing more. "Lucien," she panted.

"I haven't pleasured a woman in a long, long time," he said, his voice broken. "Tell me if I do something wrong. Something you do not like."

"I like. I like, I swear!"

He trailed kisses down her stomach, getting closer and closer to the juncture between her thighs. "Lucien," she said again. *Stop him. No, don't let him stop. More. More! No, no more.* "Lucien." She squeezed her knees together.

"No penetration, not even with my tongue. I'm just going to lick you."

Oh, gods. Her legs fell open of their own accord, and there was nothing she could do to stop them. If she didn't come soon, she would die. Erupt into flames. Something, anything to end the torment.

Maybe that was the point of this encounter. Kill her with pleasure. But she couldn't make herself care.

He gripped her knees and spread them farther apart, pushing them up and making her as vulnerable as a woman could be. *If he tries to sink a finger inside of you, just flash.*

Leaving him might kill her, too, she decided.

Besides, she forgot her own advice the moment his tongue stroked her. The pleasure was so intense, she screamed. So startling, so real, so wondrous, she gripped his head and drew him back when he tried to pull away, most likely to ask if she enjoyed it. Nothing, in all the centuries of her existence, had ever felt so miraculous.

"More?" he asked.

"More. Please."

"You taste so good. So damned good. Can't get enough." He licked and he sucked and he tormented and he teased, and she loved it all. She arched against his face, letting him tongue her until she was sobbing with need.

She would have given Lucien anything he asked just then, but he never asked for anything more than her enjoyment. He gave and gave and gave, his mouth working her with nips and licks, and it was heaven, pure and right and so wondrous she would never be the same.

And then her entire body simply exploded.

Pleasure shot through her with the force of a bullet, grazing parts of her she hadn't known existed. Stars winked behind her eyes, and her spirit might even have left her body to soar through the heavens. How fitting that Death should be the one to spark such a sensation. She alternated between stiffening and relaxing in the most intense orgasm of her life, babbling incoherently, perhaps shouting Lucien's name.

When she collapsed against the mattress, he said, "Not done. Not even close," and then his tongue was expertly riding the waves of another orgasm, taking her over another incredible hurdle in a matter of seconds.

"Lucien, Lucien, Lucien." A benediction. In that moment, he was her savior. She was free. Blessedly free.

When the last of the tremors left her, she was boneless. Sated and resplendent. He could have sunk his fingers inside her, and she couldn't have stopped him. Wouldn't have cared. But he climbed up her body and rolled them over, propping her on top of him, keeping his word.

"Still not done?" she said, panting and gazing down at his glowing eyes. She had to put a stop to this soon, had to figure out what to do with him, for she was softening toward him. Wanting what could never be. Wanting what he could not give her and she could not give him. Yet she couldn't have moved upon threat of death.

"No," he said. "We're not done."

CHAPTER ELEVEN

SO MANY THOUGHTS WERE POURING through Lucien's mind. Anya wanted him. Truly wanted him. She'd sucked him, had drunk him dry. And had not seemed the least bit repulsed by his scars. No, she had seemed to glory in him.

He was still shocked. Death, too. The demon had yet to stop purring.

Lucien had not expected Anya to take him in her mouth. He had expected her to leave in a huff. He had expected her to be anything but a virgin. That this sexy, courageous, spirited woman had never been with a man...

He'd practically called her a whore, yet she was as pure as new-fallen snow. Guilt clawed at him. What a terrible curse to have hanging over one's head, especially for an independent woman like Anya. A goddess, no less, whose torment would not end in seventy to eighty years but would continue for an eternity.

How well he knew about eternal damnation.

How could Cronus order the death of such a precious woman? How could Lucien possibly kill her, even with dire consequences hanging over his friends' heads?

He couldn't, he realized. He'd never wanted to fall for a woman again, one he would one day have to cart to the hereafter. Yet here he was. Could have been perfect, Anya being an immortal like him, but she would not give up her key, whatever it was, and Cronus would not remove the death-command without it. Perfect, no. A nightmare, yes. But Lucien had fallen for her.

She understood him, amused him, even liked him. Certainly seemed to lust after him. She was everything he was not, and he was the better for it.

Perhaps it did not have to be a nightmare. If he were to steal the key from her… She would be angry, but he did not care. Anger was better than death.

Where did she keep it? He doubted she would let it out of her sight, but he hadn't seen anything resembling a key on her naked body. Could it be locked away in one of her many homes?

No telling when Cronus would next appear. Lucien would have to act quickly.

"Your turn again," Anya whispered in his ear. She rose over him like a sea siren in the ocean blue, pale hair tumbling down her shoulders in sensual disarray. Her skin was flushed and rosy with satisfaction, her lips red and swollen from his kisses.

He had never seen a more breathtaking sight, and all thoughts of the key vanished.

"You do not have to," he said, but he wanted her to do it. Desperately. He had neglected his body for so long, and the pleasure he found with her was so intense. "You took care of me earlier."

"That was earlier, and you're ready for round two. Besides, I like taking care of you." Her lips curled in a slow, wicked smile. "I can't seem to get enough of you."

"I cannot get enough of you, either." He caressed a lock of hair from her cheek. "Foolish me, for trying to push you away."

"Yes. Foolish. But don't worry. I'll punish you for that. I'll give you a tongue lashing you'll never forget." She rained little kisses down his cheek and neck, taking special care with his scars, licking and nibbling them.

What an amazing creature, he marveled. His cock was harder than ever before, pulsing with need. Rather than sate him, one taste had slain him. He was addicted to Anya. Her heat. Her softness. One taste made him want another and another and another.

He might never get enough of her.

In the past, it had been easier to go without sex than to risk any softer emotion, wondering if he would later have to watch his lover die. Right now, he *couldn't* go without.

Anya fascinated him, as well as Death. Her wit and tenacity gave her the courage to face him when anyone else would have run screaming. Not just because of his appearance, not just because he was possessed by a demon, not even just because he'd intended to kill her, but because of the insults he'd hurled.

Insults she had not deserved.

"I am sorry," he began, hands tangling in her hair. As he did so, he felt the first tug of Death. Heard a roar. Lucien blinked. The demon was being drawn to souls who needed him and was furious at the thought of leaving the bed. "I said it before, but I do not think I can say it enough."

"Why are you sorry?" The hot tip of Anya's tongue circled his navel.

Lucien tried to resist, tried to tune the demon out. "I was rude to you when you deserved only kindness." His testicles drew up and his cock twitched, seeking her. He bent his knees and planted his heels in the mattress. Her fingers curled around the base of his shaft, and he moaned. *Sweet fire.* He—

Felt another tug from Death, this one stronger, more intense. *He* nearly roared, and the sound would have blended with the demon's frenzied snarls. *We'll move quickly.* It was the first time he'd ever had to prompt the demon into action.

Stay.

She will be here when we return.

Hurry!

"I must go. Do not leave." He sat up and pressed a quick kiss to Anya's lips. "Please do not leave."

With that, he allowed his body to become mist and sink into the spirit world. Death seemed to be pacing the corridors of his mind, but flashed him to a small room. Blood coated the walls. Blood and other things he did not want to contemplate.

Two bodies lay on the floor, a man and a woman. The man, Lucien instantly knew thanks to his demon, had wrongly suspected the woman of cheating on him, had shot her and then turned the gun on himself.

Bastard, he thought, then stilled. Hadn't he basically accused Anya of the same? Scowling, Lucien pounded a ghostly hand into the man's body first and jerked the spirit out, not even trying to be gentle.

The spirit struggled against Lucien's hold. Screamed when he saw Lucien's eyes. Faster than he had ever moved before, Lucien flashed to hell and practically threw the spirit inside. He went back to the room and gathered the woman more gently.

She saw him and gasped. "Naked," she said, staring at him. "Am I in…heaven?"

Should have dressed first. "Not yet." Spirits often tried to talk to him, and he rarely replied. This time, his response was automatic. "Soon. The angels are much prettier than I." He escorted her skyward just as quickly, ready to return to his own piece of heaven.

He wasn't sure how long he had taken, but he flashed back to the home in Greece and materialized. Finally, Death quieted.

Anya was on her back, one hand massaging her breasts, one hand between her legs, two fingers pumping in and out.

She was moaning, pink and dewy.

Once again, Lucien was on fire, burning, burning, as he crawled on top of her, jealous that he was not the one inside her. At the first touch, he and the demon sighed in unison. This was where they belonged.

Anya's eyes popped open. She grinned sensuously. "I couldn't wait."

Lucien rolled them over, pinning himself underneath her. "I am glad. I liked the sight of you."

"Mmm, you're so strong," she praised. "So determined. Why can't I get enough of you?"

Her eyes met his for a split second, and he felt like the most beautiful man ever to walk the earth. There was so much passion and admiration in that crystalline gaze of hers.

"You amaze me," he told her, caressing her cheek. Tenderness flooded him. He'd eschewed gentler emotions for so long he didn't yet know how to handle them. But he was willing to try. For Anya.

"Just wait…" Sensuously she moved down his body. Her head bent and her lush lips opened over the rounded head of his shaft one more time. Down she pumped, again taking him all the way to the back of her throat.

This time, there was no guilt to cloud his passion. He hadn't shamed her into this; she truly desired him. And the knowledge made him dizzy, made him sizzle. He was scorched and blistered to his soul as he arched his back, seeking more of that moist heat.

"So hot," she praised. Her teeth scraped the head gently, heating him even more.

"Anya." He clawed at the covers.

One of her hands dabbled at his testicles, and the other

stretched up his chest to pluck at his nipple. All the while she continued to drive her mouth up and down. Soon he was writhing, mindless of anything but the pleasure.

It was nearly more than he could bear.

Surely he, Death, would die when he came this time. Surely he—

Somewhere in the back of his mind, he registered the slam of a door, the low baritone of a voice exclaiming at the destruction found in the living room.

Anya's heavenly mouth stopped moving. He nearly roared, nearly cursed, nearly hacked the entire bed to pieces. *Where is your calm?* He was panting, sweating. Aching. The demon was snapping ferociously again.

"Lucien," Anya said. She was breathless.

He struggled to control his body, his mind, drawing in shallow rasps of air as best he could. Blood screamed in his ears. Desire continued to beat hard fists through him. He needed to come. He needed to make Anya his woman, over and over again.

"Lucien," she repeated as the voice became louder.

"What the hell happened?" he heard Strider growl. Footsteps pounded.

"Defeat," he snarled. "Do not enter my bedroom. I need a moment."

"*We* need a moment," Anya called.

The footsteps ceased. "One minute, and I'm coming in."

Lucien tried to sit up just as cold steel clamped around his wrist. Brow puckered, he looked to the side. Frowned. Anya had locked him to the bed.

"Anya," he said. "A game?"

"No."

A pause. A muscle ticked below his eye. "Chains cannot hold me."

"These can." She hopped off the bed and rushed to the

closet, jerking a shirt and pair of pants from the hangers. "Sorry, sugar, but we aren't done talking and I can't let you leave until we are."

He tugged at the chain. It rattled, but didn't break. Dread coursed through him. He tried to flash, but failed. The reason she'd gone to his room in Buda became clear. She'd gathered *the* chains. "Let me go. Now."

She looked at him, a flitter of sadness in her eyes. "I don't have the key."

"It is in my pants. Those," he said, motioning to the closet floor with his free hand. In his preoccupation with Anya, he'd forgotten to leave the key in Buda with the chains, so had been carrying it around.

She picked them up. "These?"

"Yes."

She dug the small metal key out and held it in her flat palm. Tiny dark clouds formed around it, a contained gust of wind seeming to swirl just above it. In a blink, the clouds disappeared and the wind died. The key was gone. She brushed her empty hands together in triumph over a job well done.

"Anya!" he shouted. "What did you do? Where is the key?"

"Lucien?" Strider called, concerned.

"Not yet," he called back.

"Don't worry," Anya said. "You aren't helpless. That little key Cronie Wonie wants, well, it's the All-Key and it can unlock anything. Even those." She pointed to the chains.

"Prove it. Unlock me. Now!"

"Sorry, sweetcakes, but you need a little Lucien-time, and I'm nice enough to give it to you."

"Anya!" He was naked and undeniably aroused. If only a raging hard-on would go away because of a little anger. He wished, but no. "We had a truce."

"Which is why you're chained and not dead." Fully dressed

now, she approached the bed. His clothing bagged on her, but she had never been more beautiful.

He lunged for her, hoping to grab on to her wrist, but she danced out of his reach with a laugh. "You deserve this, and you know it. Take the punishment like a good boy."

"Anya," he said again, trying to sound composed. He didn't. If his voice had been a sword, she would have been hacked to pieces.

Staying out of striking distance, she pinched the edge of the comforter and tossed it over his erection. "There. Your modesty can be preserved."

Even then, he wanted her. Ribbons of hair streamed around her and she was staring at the blanket with longing, as if *she* wanted to be the one draped over him.

"Anya—"

"Get rid of Defeat, and I'll come back." With that, she disappeared.

His head fell against the pillow. "Damn this!" He slammed his unfettered hand into the headboard behind him.

Strider burst into the room, two blades upraised. "Ready or not," he said, "here I come." He glanced at the damaged chamber and then the chains. "What the hell happened? House is a mess, too."

"Put those away," Lucien said, motioning to the weapons with a tilt of his chin. "Anya and I had a little fight."

All hint of concern left Strider's harsh features. "And then you decided to play a game of bondage? I dig." He laughed. "I didn't think you were into that kind of thing."

"Shut up and get out of here. She won't come back until you do."

"Hell, no. I'm not leaving." Strider plopped onto the side of the bed. "One, I want to witness the fireworks. Two, I'm not leaving you helpless. We may not have been in touch these past few centuries, but that doesn't mean I don't have your back now. Just don't get any ideas. I don't swing that way."

Lucien kicked him in the chest, sending him to the ground. "Strider." He covered his face with his free hand. "Gods, this is humiliating." Had Reyes or Paris been the ones to find him, it would not have been so bad.

"You want popcorn or something?" Strider asked, darting to his feet with a grin.

"I want you to leave."

"Uh, no."

"I'm not helpless. And she won't hurt me. She could have already, but she didn't."

A pause. A sigh. "Fine." Strider strode from the room.

Lucien thought the warrior meant to leave the home completely, but Strider returned a few moments later holding a small black cell phone.

"This little baby has camera and e-mail capabilities." Wiggling his eyebrows, he snapped a few photos of Lucien on the bed, making sure to get the chains.

"Stop," Lucien growled.

"Uh, again, no. Now make love to the camera for me. Good, good. The angry sex look is perfect. Man, this is one for the scrapbook."

Lucien glared at him. "Some men fear my anger."

"Hate to break it to you, Death, but I don't think they will when they see you attached to a headboard, a blanket tented over your lap."

Heat infused Lucien's cheeks. "I will pay you back for this. You know that, don't you?"

Strider suddenly sobered. "Don't challenge me. You know I am Defeat's keeper, and I'll do anything—even kill my own mother if I had one—to win a challenge. I can't stop until I do."

Lucien threw a pillow at him. "Then put the camera away and leave."

Smiling again, Strider finally did as ordered. Well, one order at least. He stuffed the camera in his pocket. "So, hey. Have you seen Paris?"

"No. Why?"

"He took off earlier to do some shopping, and I haven't seen or heard from him since."

"He's probably with a woman. Or two. I wouldn't worry about him. Knowing him, he'll want to be at top strength before he joins the search, which means he might be a few days behind us. He has needed even more sex than usual lately."

"Apparently he's not the only one." Strider leered at him. "Gideon will be ticked if Paris left without him. Guess I'll have to let the boys work it out. I've got a plane to South Africa to catch. I'm eager to start looking for little Miss Hydra and whatever treasure she's hiding."

"Did you call Sabin?"

"Oh, yeah. He's excited as hell. Says they haven't had any luck at the Temple of the Unspoken Ones, even with several blood sacrifices, but he senses that something is there and doesn't want to leave."

"Good." Hopefully someone would find something sooner rather than later. "I have not had a chance to flash to him." His mind had been too consumed with Anya.

Strider's phone gave a loud beep. The warrior withdrew it and flipped it open, grinning. "Speaking of Sabin, I already e-mailed your picture to him and he just replied. He thinks you look real good like that. Says you should pose more often."

Lucien fell back, banging his head against the board. The chains clinked. "Get out of here. Anya and I have something to settle."

"Man, you are one lucky son of a bitch. I'd like to settle something with that delicious cupcake."

Lucien's eyes narrowed, rage sparking to life. "Do not talk about her like that."

Strider blinked in wonder, but left it alone. "I'll stay close until I know you're free. See you around, Death. Have fun." He strode out of the room, then out of the house, the door closing behind him with a snap.

"I am alone now," Lucien called.

No response.

"Anya."

Nothing.

He waited several more minutes, then called her name again. Still she did not respond. Damn this! Was she playing with him? Punishing him?

Or was something wrong with her?

A horrifying image suddenly popped in his head, so vivid he broke out in a sweat. Anya standing in the middle of her apartment in Switzerland, Cronus looming over her. They were locked in a heated debate.

Lucien's demon snarled, and Lucien began to suspect the image was indeed real. It was simply too detailed, down to the bead of sweat on her temple. What were the two saying? He couldn't hear, and panic speared him.

Had Cronus decided to kill her on his own, then? Lucien struggled more forcefully against the bonds, but the links never budged.

"Anya!"

CHAPTER TWELVE

"I WANT THE ALL-KEY, ANYA."

Tensing at the sudden intrusion, Anya faced her nemesis, her heart pounding inside her chest. Here he was, up close and personal. Cronus, the brand-new king of gods. A vile bastard. And the guy who'd ordered Lucien to hunt her down and slay her like an animal.

Hey, that'd make a great singles ad, she thought drily. *Powerful SWM with a penchant for ordering hits, looking for SWF to help rule the world. Interested? Stroke my ego and give me all you hold dear.*

"I want an eternity of peace," she replied, "but we don't always get what we want. Do we?"

His teeth clinked together.

Anya had come here to change her clothing, which she'd done a few minutes ago, going from baggy to sexy in minutes. Thank the—not the gods, that was for sure—Cronus hadn't materialized then. She didn't want any man but Lucien seeing her naked.

Lucien.

She'd been so preoccupied with thoughts of him that she hadn't realized Cronus had made an appearance in her Zürich apartment until he'd spoken. That wasn't like her. Usually she knew. Usually she sensed and ran.

She could have flashed just then, but she didn't. Suddenly

she wanted to hear what the big dumb-dumb had to say. Did he mean to complain about Lucien?

"The key," Cronus snapped. "Give it to me."

"We've covered this before, bossie baby. My answer hasn't changed."

He circled around her, facing her, glaring at her, so close his thick silver beard tickled her chin. His long white robe brushed her legs and his ambrosia scent wafted around her. Power radiated from him.

The Greeks had been powerful, too. Zeus with his lightning and Hera with her penchant for jealous revenge. But this being had mowed them down as if they were insignificant flies and would love to do the same to her.

Unexpectedly, he straightened. His expression cleared. "I have seen your interactions with Death."

"So?" she said, trying not to reveal an ounce of trepidation. Which interactions had he witnessed? The idea that he might have watched the two of them in Lucien's bedroom revolted her. "What of it?"

"You like him."

"Again, so? I like a lot of men." *Please don't hear the lie in my voice.*

"Willingly give me the All-Key, and I will bind him to your side. He will be yours to command for all eternity."

Oh, that was tempting. Cronus probably had no idea just how great a gift he was offering. Finally, she would be on equal footing with a man. To have Lucien for as long as she wanted him, to simply ask him to do something and know he would comply. But she'd spent centuries fighting to prevent such a fate herself. She couldn't wish it on another, especially a man as proud as Lucien. Plus, he was already bound by his demon. *Plus,* he'd only just been released from Maddox's death-curse. Taking even more of his freedom would be criminal.

"Nope. Sorry. I'd be tired of him within a week. Right now his attempts to kill me are amusing, and I'm enjoying toying with his affections, but…" She shrugged as if she were already tired of it. "Why don't you just *take* the key from me?" She batted her lashes at him innocently. "Why don't *you* kill me for it?"

His scowl returned. "You would like that, wouldn't you?"

"Maybe a wee bit." With the taunt, she heard her father's voice in her head as clearly as if he'd spoken the words yesterday, though too many years to count had passed. *Men will try to kill you for what I am about to give you, because they'll wrongly think it's the way to win it from you.*

Kill me. For what? I don't understand. She'd shaken her head. *Never mind, just don't give me whatever it is. I don't want any more men after me. Just let me go.*

And risk your being found and imprisoned again? No. Soon you will realize the key's reward is worth its hazards. You will never be bound again. You will be able to travel anywhere you desire with only a thought. You will be free. Always.

Key? Father—

Listen to me. If they can kill you, they can snatch it, but he who strikes the death blow will be rendered powerless for the rest of his life. Because of that, many will leave you alone. Some, though, will forget the consequences in their lust to control the key's powers.

Are you listening? he'd chided, shaking her. *Be vigilant. It has to be given freely for the recipient to remain strong. But then you, the giver, will be the one rendered powerless. For the key is alive, part of you, and absorbs pieces of you that will be transferred should you pass it on to another. Understand now?*

No!

Once you take it, never let it go. It is yours, my gift to you. Proof of my love.

Teary-eyed, she had opened her mouth to ask if *he* would be rendered powerless by giving the mysterious key to her, but he'd already taken matters into his own hands, so to speak. He'd already begun to weaken.

"I'm not going to use it against you," she told Cronus now. "Well, not again."

"As you said, we have covered this. You will."

"Only for my parents. Which means, only if you capture them again."

"I am unwilling to take your word. You are a known liar."

There was no denying that. Not without lying. "Look, we both know you want Lucien to kill me, making him power-less while you keep your strength. The key will be up for grabs, but he'll be too weak to make a play for it, leaving the field wide open for you. I could tell him. He might tell you to go fuck yourself then."

"You do not believe that or you would have told him already."

Maybe. Maybe not. She suspected she hadn't told Lucien not because of what he'd do to Cronus but because of what he'd do to her. Like walk away from her for good. Besides that, would he even have believed her? He probably would have thought she'd made the whole thing up to keep him at bay.

"We both know it will not stop him from obeying me," Cronus said. "He loves his warriors too much to watch them suffer, even if the price of their freedom is his own."

"So why hasn't he obeyed you already, huh?"

"You have bewitched him."

She should be so lucky. She sighed, the sound part exas-peration, part remembered pleasure. Lucien… Even now he was in bed. Naked. Did he still want her?

His desire had been a thing of beauty, and she'd been eager

to see it through to the end. To taste him again. She, too, probably would have climaxed again, for just the thought of sucking him to another orgasm made her tremble.

Trying to distract herself, she flipped her hair over one shoulder and eyed Cronus. Time to get his mind off Lucien. "Having the key might—*might*—fortify Tartarus and make it the stronghold it once was, locking the Greeks inside forevermore so that they don't escape like you did. But where is the fun in that? Where's the adventure?"

"I lost my sense of adventure long ago." He waved a dismissive hand through the air. "I will not be overthrown again. I will not have the Greeks escaping, and I will not have you aiding them. To ensure my continued reign, I need the key."

"Listen, you're not the only one with problems. I'm hunted on a daily basis, remember? Giving up the key means losing my strength, my abilities, my memories—perhaps even my freedom. If I'm ever locked away again, I won't be able to escape."

"I have offered you my protection in the past. You have always turned me down."

"And I will continue to do so." He could change his mind. He could demand further payment from her to continue protecting her. He could forget about her.

"Tell me what you want, then, and it is yours. Things do not have to end badly for you."

"There's nothing I want." Things were perfect for her right now. No one could bind her, and no one could kill her without severe consequences. She had a kind-of boyfriend who rocked her world, even if they couldn't seal the deal. Why give any of that up?

Besides, anything she wanted she could procure on her own. And she *did* have a plan for getting Cronus off her trail. Those artifacts the Lords were searching for. Cronus wanted them back. They were a source of his power, and as she well knew, Cronus loved him some power.

Once she had them—and used them to find Pandora's box—she'd trade them for that vow of protection. Even from him. For herself, for Lucien. Best of all, she'd still have the key.

She studied her nails. "Mind if I take off now? This conversation is boring and I have places to go, yada, yada, yada."

Cronus's eyes narrowed. "One day in the near future I will know what it takes to humble you. I will know what it takes to crush you. And when I do, you will wish you had given the key to me this day."

He disappeared in a melodramatic flash of blinding blue light. Anya stumbled forward, knees suddenly going weak. She scrubbed a hand down her face, feeling the first tremors of anxiety. Antagonizing the king of gods had not been smart, but it was not in her nature to cower or obey.

I will know what it takes to crush you, he'd said, and she believed him. All Cronus had to do was threaten to destroy Lucien, and she feared she would give him anything. Maybe even the key. She couldn't let Cronus know how much Lucien was coming to mean to her, that her days and nights were filled with thoughts of him.

Cronus had to suspect, at least a little, she realized. Why else offer her Lucien's eternal affections?

Shit, she thought. She'd have to do something to throw the big cheese off. Would ignoring Lucien, painful as it sounded, do the trick? Or would Cronus see the longing on her face, the torment in her eyes? Hell, would she even be able to stay away from Lucien? She hadn't managed the feat yet.

Wouldn't be wise to keep her distance, she decided. She would find the artifacts faster working *with* him rather than against him. Relief and need trembled through her. *I get to be with him again.*

Yeah, you get to be with him, but you can't let Cronus see how much you care.

She frowned, relief fading. Did that mean there could be no more physical pleasure?

The answer proved grim. Kissing would be fine because she'd kissed others. But anything else would merely prove how special Lucien was to her. Her shoulders sagged. *I'll have to be my usual flippant self and keep things light.* No more touching, no more skin-to-skin contact.

"Fucking Cronus," she grumbled to cover her sudden tears.

LUCIEN HAD WORKED HIMSELF into a fit of rage.

It had happened only once before, a prolonged fury that lasted several days after Mariah's death, and he'd vowed never to let it happen again. The destruction had been too great. But as he'd watched Anya with Cronus, he'd been unable to stop himself from slipping into the dark throes of fury.

Now red glowed behind his eyes; a cold sweat slicked his skin. Death roared like a banshee inside his mind. His breath was so hot it was like fire as it pushed from his nose. He was more demon than man, darkness clouding his every thought.

He'd already hacked the bed to bits, freeing the chain from the headboard but not from himself. After that, he'd blazed a path of destruction through the entire house. Because the chain was still attached to his wrist, he couldn't dematerialize. Didn't matter, though. He was too busy seething. Too busy imagining death and blood and killing. Had one of the other warriors walked into the room just then, he would have attacked. Would have been unable to stop himself. And wouldn't have cared.

Cronus could have killed Anya, and there would have been no way for Lucien to aid her. He hadn't been able to help

Mariah, and the guilt had tormented him ever since. Anya, though… He roared, loud and long.

"Uh, you wanna explain this?" a woman asked when he quieted.

Hearing the voice, he wheeled around with a snarl. He saw the outline of a lithe female form. Pale hair. Delicate shoulders. He clutched a sword in his hand. *Kill, kill, kill.*

Scowling, he stomped toward her.

She backed away. "Lucien?"

Lifting the sword high above his head, he gave it a menacing twirl. *KILL.* The tip flew down, aiming for the woman's neck. She must have moved because the sword hit the floor rather than flesh. He hissed.

A moment later, something tapped his shoulder from behind.

He swung around. A fist connected with his nose. His head whipped to the side, and warm liquid rushed down his lips and chin.

"You better calm down, Death, or you're going to make me mad."

He lifted the sword again, but it was knocked from his grip. With another roar, he leapt forward, grabbing the woman. He shook her, meaning to snap her in half.

"Lucien," she said, and this time there was a calming, hypnotic quality to her voice. "Lucien. Seriously. I'm not a rag doll. Calm down. Tell me what's wrong."

Finally a sense of awareness slithered into his mind and man raced ahead of demon. His captive's skin was hot—he recognized that heat. She smelled like strawberries and cream—he recognized that fragrance.

"Tell sweet little Anya what's going on in that fat head of yours," she cooed. Soft hands caressed his cheeks. "Pretty please, with a cherry on top of me."

Anya.

The name echoed in his mind, cracking the red haze and allowing light inside. He blinked his eyes and a perfect pixie came into focus. A snowfall of hair. Bright blue eyes. Pink cheeks.

"Anya?"

"Right here, lover."

Dear gods. He glanced around the room, saw the destruction and the blood. His blood. He'd cut his hands, he recalled, when he'd punched the walls. Regret slammed into him.

Not again.

"Did I hurt you?" He returned his attention to the woman in his arms, studying her intently. Her skin was rosy soft, not bruised, and her eyes were gleaming. She wore a tight black T-shirt and equally tight black pants, neither of which were ripped. Glittery black heels encased her feet, open at the toes and showcasing black-painted toenails.

"Did I hurt you?" he repeated.

"Would you care?" she asked, head tilting to the side. "I mean, you've wanted to in the past."

He pressed his lips together. He could not let her know how much he was coming to admire her. How much he was coming to *need* her. *I think your tongue on her clitoris told her plenty.* Only when he'd stolen that key from her and her life was safe would he admit to such feelings.

"Never mind," she said airily. "The answer wouldn't matter anyway." She turned her back on him, strode to the couch he'd hacked to bits and settled on the tattered arm. "Really, what was that about? I've never seen a more demonic display. Your eyes were red." She shuddered. "Freaky stuff, and not in a good way."

"I told you once not to make me angry." Gods, he couldn't believe he had journeyed so far toward the dark side of his nature. He was always so careful. The thought of Anya hurt, however... He had to cut off another roar.

He would never have been able to kill her, Lucien at last admitted. Not even in the beginning. It was disgusting, really, how protective he felt of her. He was as bad as Maddox. "What do you want from me, Anya? Why did you come back?"

"First, to do this." She was *tsking* under her tongue as she stood and sauntered to him. She gripped his chained wrist and drew it into a muted beam of moonlight streaming in from the window. With her other hand, she waved it over the metal.

A bright amber radiance glowed from between her fingers. He felt warmth, felt the chain snap open and heard it fall to the floor.

"The All-Key?" he asked, shocked.

"Yes." She dropped her arm. "You going to tell me what made you so angry?"

"I saw you talking with Cronus."

"What! You saw? How?"

"I do not know how, just that I saw you, in my mind. What did he say?"

She blinked at him. "He wanted the key."

That damned key! "Tell me why it is a light that comes from *inside* you." He'd expected metal.

"No. What I will tell you is that if you kill me, the key will drain your powers. There. Now you know. That's why Cronus wants you to do his dirty work. And before you say anything, I never planned to tell you because one, I had no intention of dying and two, you would have thought I was lying to keep you away. But now you know. You can't say I didn't warn you."

He wasn't going to kill her, so the warning mattered little. "How is Cronus going to take the key from you if it is inside you?"

"You already know that part. You kill me, you weaken, *he* swoops in and takes it from my poor dead body."

"So you have to die for someone else to possess it?"

"No. I could willingly give it."

"Then give it to him, woman!"

"I give it to him, *I* weaken. Permanently. Worse, I won't be able to flash. Get it now?"

Oh, yes. Suddenly he *did* get it, and he almost vomited. He couldn't steal the key from her without killing her and she couldn't give it to Cronus without deteriorating, therefore Lucien had nothing to trade the god in exchange for Anya's life. *What in hell was he going to do?*

Unaware of his inner turmoil, Anya glanced around the room. "While throwing your tantrum, did you destroy our supplies for the Arctic?"

"Yes."

"I can't believe I once thought you were too controlled. Seriously, learn some self-discipline, for gods' sake. You should be embarrassed."

"I am."

"Good."

Think about the key later, when you are alone and not consumed by the scents of strawberries and destruction. "Before you left, you said you wanted to discuss something with me. What?"

"I forgot."

He doubted she had—Anya forgot nothing—but he allowed the lie without comment. "Did you return to spend a few more hours in bed?"

Her cheeks colored prettily. "I'm here to get my stuff because I'm ready to start looking for those artifacts. I'm bored, after all, and it sounds deliciously dangerous, trekking through snow in search of an ancient relic."

There was something in her eyes—too bright a gleam, maybe. A forced casualness, perhaps. Again, she was not speaking true. "You left me for Strider to find naked and chained to a bed," he said to lighten her mood. Perhaps then she would tell him the truth. "Have I thanked you for that?"

"No, you haven't." She grinned slowly, her amusement genuine this time. "Did he likie?"

"He must have. He took a picture." Mortification heated Lucien from the collarbone up as he remembered.

Anya laughed outright, and the sound of that laughter was magical. His skin tingled, and he felt as if he'd just conquered the entire world.

"What did you wish to discuss?" he asked gently. "Tell me true."

Her smile faded. "I wanted to tell you…I wanted to say…I'm not sure I like your attitude."

"I am not sure I know what you mean."

"Just, I don't know. Don't be so ooey-gooey nice to me. It's nauseating."

"Nauseating?"

"You an echo now? Yeah. Nauseating. Jeez."

He crossed his arms over his chest and peered down at her, confused. "Why are you acting like this? After the way you begged me to keep licking you?"

Her breath hitched, and she backed away from him. Just a step, but he didn't like it. "I realized that was a mistake, that's all," she said.

What was going on here? "Do you no longer trust me?"

"No."

"Why? I could have entered you then, and we both know it. But I didn't. And I think we both know you were close to asking me for more."

Her eyes glowered up at him. "I was toying with you. Faking it."

He, too, glowered. "I'll believe a lot of things about you, *sweetcakes,* but that isn't one of them. Not anymore."

"That's the saddest thing I've ever heard." She brushed a piece of lint off her shoulder.

"Do not make me prove my words."

"Fuck you." Another brush of her shoulder. Her hand was shaking, he noticed.

"You would like that, would you not? If I fucked you?"

Giving up her casual facade, she slapped him, palm dragging against his cheek. "One, you shouldn't talk like that. And two, don't make me state the obvious. I…I…felt sorry for you, obviously." The last was croaked. Tears even sprang into her eyes.

A muscle ticked in his jaw. He could feel the urge to hurt building inside of him again. Hot, hungry, begging for a chance to render more damage. To destroy. He'd have liked to tell himself that Anya was lying about this—he had felt her pleasure, her joy in his touch—but old insecurities died hard.

She was beautiful and could have her pick of equally beautiful men. Perhaps she'd wanted him earlier for the novelty of lying with an ugly man, didn't want him now that she'd done so, and thought this was the best way to cut him loose.

"I'm not going to try to kill you again, so you can cease trying to soften me," he told her.

"How nice for me," she muttered, looking away. There was a guilty flush to her skin.

"Just know that if you hit me again, I *will* hit you back," he lied. He would never be able to hurt her, and he knew it.

"A girl can hope," she said silkily, changing tactics.

His anger sizzled another degree. "Stay here or go home, but I'm going to purchase more supplies and I want to do it alone."

Her shoulders squared, and her chin lifted. "I'm going with you, so there."

"No. You are not." He shook his head. "I am done with you right now."

She ran her tongue over her lips. "Whatever. I know someone. He lives in Greenland, and he has everything we'll need. We'll pop into his place, borrow what we want and make our way into the Arctic."

He. The word pounded through Lucien's mind, stirring up a storm of jealousy. "Who is *he?* And why did you not pop us to him earlier rather than dragging me to Switzerland?"

"He's my friend, and I didn't take you to him because I wanted you to see my—I wanted to shop with you and thought we had plenty of time," she said, kicking at a shard of glass on the floor. "Damn it! I'm looking at my feet again."

"Well, stop." She'd thought they had plenty of time, which meant she didn't think so anymore. Why? "Did Cronus threaten you?" The moment the words left him, Anya's behavior began to make sense.

She turned away from him, her back stiff. "As if I care about that bastard's threats."

Oh, yes. Cronus had indeed threatened her. "What did he say to you?"

"Stop, just stop. Cronus said nothing important. Besides, what's between me and another guy isn't really any of your business, is it? Now, do you want to visit William or not?"

"Not. I don't want anyone knowing what we're looking for. Tell me what Cronus said to you."

"William won't even know we're there. Promise. And damn it, Cronus said nothing."

"You mean to steal from this William?"

"Yes. So are you ready or not?" she asked coolly.

He studied her. The woman in front of him wasn't the woman he'd kissed and tasted earlier. She was harder, more distant. He didn't like it, but did not know how to change her back.

Lucien wished he had the strength to challenge the god

king here and now. He wished he had the strength to walk away from Anya for good. She was tying him in knots. But despite what he'd claimed a few minutes ago, he did not want to be alone. Did not want to be without her.

As if sensing his capitulation, she swung around and gave him a pinky wave. She was pale, her eyes sad, but her lips were smiling. "See you there, Flowers."

Lucien didn't follow right away. He gathered his daggers and his Glock, checked the chamber, saw that it was loaded. No telling who this mysterious William was. To be honest, though, his identity didn't really matter. Lucien already hated him.

Maybe, while in Greenland, Death would be summoned to take the bastard's soul.

A warrior could hope, anyway.

And then, right on cue, Death *did* summon him. Unfortunately, it was to the States, so neither of them were happy. Lucien sighed. He quickly strapped on all his weapons and dematerialized. Anya and her mystery man would have to wait.

How long can I keep this up? Anya wondered darkly. The hurt on Lucien's face when she'd claimed to have felt sorry for him had nearly undone her.

She'd actually felt like crying. Still did. Taking a page from Cronus's book, she'd determined his weakness and had exploited it. *If you can't resist him, you have to make him resist you.*

Rather than pop into William's home, she flashed to his porch and waited for Lucien. Ice-cold wind instantly slapped her mostly-bare skin. A hard shiver racked her. *Shoulda changed, dummy.* But she'd been eager to escape Lucien, if only for a moment, before he discovered her lies for what they were.

A minute passed, and then another. Lucien remained—frustratingly—absent. If she stood out here any longer, her lips would turn blue, damn it, and that wasn't a good shade for her. Where was he? She couldn't follow his energy like he followed hers, and that really sucked. Had she pushed him too far? Had he decided not to come? To go out on his own?

He had. Oh, he had. Why, that wretched beast!

Well, what did you expect? You were cruel to him.

I had to be.

Before her libido could work up a retort, Lucien finally appeared. He landed behind her. She didn't see him; she *felt* him. Quick as a snap, her entire body relaxed. *Don't look, don't look.* A peek at those mismatched eyes, and she might very well throw herself in his arms, sobbing an apology.

Remaining in place was one of the hardest things she'd ever done. After the way she'd treated him, he might be glad for her restraint, though.

"What took you so long?" she asked, doing her best to keep the censure from her tone.

"I do have responsibilities, Anya." His neutral voice mirrored hers.

Still upset with her, was he? It was for the best, but oh, how she wished otherwise. "So Death did a little phoning home?" Despite her breeziness, she experienced a wave of compassion. "How many souls did you have to take this time?"

"Twelve."

She hated that he'd gone alone. Numb as he tried to make himself when shepherding souls, she wasn't fooled. He probably had stress lines around his eyes and mouth. *Don't look!* Unable to stop herself, she reached back and squeezed his hand. He didn't pull away, but brought her hand to his lips.

A warm tingle rushed through her, and she melted. How, after everything, could he still treat her tenderly? Gods, she wanted to kick her own ass. He deserved so much better than she could ever give him. Even if it were safe for her to drop the aloof act, at best she would be a lover who couldn't even go all the way.

Just get this over with. "I decided we should talk to William first. Don't worry, he won't spill your secrets." Gulping, she knocked on the towering, arched double doors before Lucien could protest. Curving red-and-black serpents were etched over their entire surface. A moment passed. Another. No answer. She knocked again, harder this time.

"This is a nice home," Lucien remarked. At least he didn't yell at her for making him meet William.

"Yes." The house wound in a half circle around a snow-covered lawn. There were points on the roof that stretched all the way to the night sky. "Willie would have it no other way, the egotistical ass."

A porch light flipped on, chasing away the shadows. One of the doors was pulled open, and William's dark, beautiful head peeked around it.

"Anya?"

She heard Lucien utter a low, menacing growl as the half-clad warrior stepped outside and gathered her into his arms for a hug. "Hiya, angel," she said. "Can we come in? It's freaking freezing out here."

"Wear more clothing next time," Lucien snapped behind her.

William remained in place and flicked him a curious glance, then arched a dark, questioning brow at Anya.

"My flavor of the week," she explained, hating herself. Lucien was so much more than that, but she couldn't risk admitting it aloud. "You're looking good, sugar." And he was. He was tall and ungodly handsome with mystic symbols tattooed on his bare chest.

More than that, he radiated sex. Raw, down-and-dirty,

nothing-held-back sex—which was what had gotten him sentenced to eternity in Tartarus. He'd pleasured Hera and a few thousand others, and when Hera learned about those thousand others…heads had rolled.

Right now, William's pants were unsnapped as if he'd hastily tugged them on. Obviously, he'd been doing more than just radiating.

"I'm looking good? *Good?*" William laughed. "I've never looked better, and I know it. Get in here and warm up." He moved out of the way.

She sailed past him, Lucien close at her heels. "Lucy, this is Willie. He's a sexual deviant and spent a little time in the cell next to mine before some sucker paid his bond and set him free. A woman, no doubt. The moment William left, he forgot about me and failed to post my bond." ·

"There was no bond for you."

"Excuses, excuses. You always did look out for number one. Willie, this is Lucy. He's mine."

When she realized what she'd just said, she groaned. That little confession had slipped from her without permission. Stomach knotting, she swung around to assess Lucien's reaction. His features were blank, and he was staring at William.

"I am Lucien, not Lucy."

"I'm William, but you can call me Sexy. Everyone does."

Other than that, the two men didn't acknowledge each other in any way.

"O-kay. This is *awkward,*" she sang, acting as if she hadn't a care. "Someone say something. Please."

"Have you ever been Anya's—what did she call it—flavor of the week?" Lucien asked.

William snorted. "I wish. And it wasn't from lack of trying on my part."

Lucien looked to her for verification, and she shrugged. She should have draped herself over William but couldn't bring herself to touch anyone but Lucien that intimately. "He's not my type, all right." She added drily, "He's never tried to kill me."

Lucien glared at her.

"Is that what it takes?" William laughed. "If so, I'll—"

"You will not touch her," Lucien snapped.

Anya blinked in surprise. Two voices had emerged from Lucien's lips. Both had been dangerous; both had been lethal. Had she just heard his demon? She shivered in arousal. This man was hard enough to resist when he was swinging a sword at her. When he acted possessive, it was downright foreplay.

Her legs started shaking, for gods' sake.

"So what are you doing here?" William asked.

"William," a woman suddenly called, drawing everyone's attention.

"We're still waiting," another whined.

Anya leveled a grin at the sexpot. "Two at once now?"

He shrugged sheepishly. "I couldn't decide which one I wanted, so I settled on both."

"How magnanimous of you." Her gaze slid up the stairway behind him and latched on to the two robe-clad women on the landing. They were peering down, hair in complete disarray, skin rosy. *If only that were me, beckoning Lucien.* "Well, don't keep them waiting."

"Make yourself at home," William told her. He moved to kiss her cheek but quickly backed away when Lucien snarled. "See you in the morning, Annie Love."

"Love?" Lucien spat.

William's backward stride increased in speed and he held up his hands, but he was grinning. "Teasing. I was only teasing."

"We need to borrow some stuff," Anya called, grabbing his attention. "That's why we're here. Not that I don't love to visit, of course."

"I'm amazed you didn't just steal everything you needed."

"I would have," she said, pointing her thumb in Lucien's direction, "but the big guy frowns on theft for some reason."

"I do not. Not anymore," Lucien said. "You need it."

"He'll have to get used to it if he's going to hang with you. Later." William turned to the stairs and bounded up, two steps at a time.

"Oh, Willie. Side note here," she called, halting him. "I'm kinda being hunted by the gods and—" for Lucien's benefit, she paused for dramatic effect "—the demon of Death. By coming here, I might have brought war and chaos to your doorstep. You okay with that?"

"Totally. What's a visit from Anya without a little chaos?" He wound his arms around the women and patted their asses. "We'll talk more in the morning, 'kay?"

The women giggled. Ugh. Giggling. That disgusted Anya. She might talk like a sorority girl, but she would never lower herself to giggling like one. And then the trio disappeared around the corner, and she forgot all about them.

"Well, you heard the man," she said, turning to Lucien. "We get to make ourselves at home. Let's start grabbing what we need."

Lucien crowded her with his big body, closing all distance between them and pushing her against the wall. He was glaring at her so intensely that she lost her air of forced ease. "What?"

"The only thing we're going to do is finish what we started."

CHAPTER THIRTEEN

HE WAS GOING TO MARK HER.

The moment Lucien had seen William the Handsome put his hands on Anya, an all-consuming need had rushed through him: mark her so that every man who looked at her knew she belonged to someone else.

The need was stronger than his rage had ever been. The need was more potent than even his desire to have this woman in his bed. Everything inside him, even the demon, screamed *mine*.

A word she, too, had used to describe him. Had they been alone when she'd said it, he would have thrown her onto the nearest bed and demanded she repeat the word over and over again.

Nothing like this had ever happened to him. Not even with Mariah had he acted this volatile. He'd loved her, but his emotions toward her had been peaceful. Tender. What he felt for Anya was tender, yes, but it was also as uncontrollable as a midnight tempest.

Yet as wild as Lucien felt, his demon had never been calmer. Somehow, Anya had soothed the beast. Hearing her voice, smelling her sweetness…even now Death purred for her.

"F-finish?" she gasped. She flattened her palms against his chest. Not pushing, but not welcoming, either. Her eyes were wide, heated. "What do you mean?"

"You know what I mean." Overhead he could hear those two females giggling. Could hear William uttering a mock growl. "You left me hard, and now you're going to take care of it."

Her eyes widened farther, black lashes so long they cast those pretty shadows on her cheeks. "But I thought we weren't going there anymore. I told you I didn't want you. And I thought you didn't want me because I…because I…you know." She looked away from him, over his shoulder. "Was sorry for you and all."

"You thought wrong." He wouldn't penetrate her—he couldn't take her freedom, no matter how angry he was with her—but he was going to have her in every other way. "We can do it here, or we can do it in my chambers in Budapest. The choice is yours."

"But…but…" Still she struggled. "What brought this on? William?"

"Choose," he barked. He slapped his hands on the wall behind her, beside her temples, the vibrations knocking the two portraits above her together.

She shivered and licked her lips.

He got in her face, placing them nose to nose. Their breath mingled, and he drew hers into his lungs. She still smelled of strawberries and cream, though he hadn't seen her with a lollipop. Her gaze snapped back to his, blazing with heat.

"Lucien."

She hadn't called him sweetcakes or angel or even the newest, Lucy. That was a step in the right direction. He suspected she picked a foolish endearment for everyone she wanted kept at a distance.

There would be no distance between them. Not anymore.

"Choose, Anya." If she didn't want him, she would simply have flashed away. Besides, there was lust and excitement in her expression, and they fueled both emotions in him. "I do not care what your reasons are for wanting me. I don't care that I should not want you."

She gulped. "But...but...we shouldn't do this."

"Why?"

"Because."

"Not good enough. We are going to do this. Choose."

"But I don't want to?"

He knew she'd meant the words as a statement of fact, yet they had not emerged as such. "Why?" he asked again.

Biting her lips now, she lowered her gaze to his mouth. His cock twitched in reaction. He could deduce what she was imagining. Another stroke of his tongue on her clitoris and a gentle tug from his teeth.

"Bad things will happen if we do," she whispered.

"Like what?" The only bad thing he could think of was going another day without having this woman naked and under him.

An eternity passed. "I don't want to talk about it."

"You're right. Now isn't the time for talking. Here or Buda?"

Another lick of her pink tongue. Next time that tongue left her mouth, it was going to be inside his own, he decided. No exceptions.

She swallowed. Whispered, "Here" and threw herself into his arms. Her lips meshed against his.

Yes. Gods, yes. Finally. As their tongues dueled, her taste filling his mouth, he felt weightless. Then his feet hit solid ground. He opened his eyes and found himself inside a spacious bedroom. A crystal chandelier hung overhead, dripping teardrops of muted light. The walls were covered in murals of flowers and vines, each a multihued feast to his gaze.

The bed was huge, with black silk sheets he couldn't wait

to press Anya against. There were wooden chests and even a tranquil stone waterfall in the far corner. A beautiful place, to be sure, but he was suddenly tempted to flash Anya somewhere else. Somewhere the handsome William had never set foot in.

Anchoring his hands under Anya's ass, Lucien hefted her up. Her legs immediately hooked around his waist, placing the new center of his universe in close proximity to his cock. He rocked against her, the action as necessary as breathing.

Moaning, she bit down on his bottom lip. He felt a shiver move through her. "More," she gasped out.

He did it again.

Again she bit down and shivered.

Lucien gripped the hem of her shirt and jerked it over her head. That incredible hair tumbled down her bare shoulders. She wore a bra of ice-blue glitter, and the sight of it mesmerized him.

The tops of her breasts pushed upward, beckoning. Lovely, so lovely. Yet they weren't what claimed his attention. Knives were strapped to every inch of visible skin. Some were twined with the bra's straps. Some were simply taped. With what, he didn't know. He only knew he liked it. A lot.

Took him a while, but he finally dropped the last to the floor.

He unhooked her legs from him and set her down. She cried out in protest, wobbled. He kissed her neck. Pleasure lit her lovely face as her head fell back, and she palmed her breasts in invitation. He dropped to his knees, snagging his fingers on the waist of her pants.

He had to know if her panties matched her bra.

In seconds, the tight little pants were at her ankles and he saw that knives and throwing stars were strapped to her legs. "I knew you were armed; I just did not know how much." She braced a hand on his shoulder and stepped out of the pants as he disarmed her.

"You like?" she asked when he finished.

The panties were tiny, a barely-there strap of glittery blue material, a perfect match. He gulped. "I like." His voice was hoarse, broken.

"Your turn," she said, a nervous edge to the words.

Nervous? Anya? Slowly he stood. As he peered down at her, he saw a proud, beautiful woman who radiated vulnerability, joy and affection. And yet she had once told him that he didn't matter. He had told her the very same thing. He hadn't meant it, and he was beginning to believe she hadn't, either.

He knew who to blame and vowed Cronus would pay.

Not allowing himself to spoil the moment with those dark thoughts, Lucien pushed them to the back of his mind and caressed a fingertip along the curve of Anya's delicate jaw. *I will take care of this woman. I will find a way to steal the All-Key without harming either of us or I will hide her from Cronus. Then I will spend my days making her happy.*

"You are so beautiful," he told her.

"Thank you. Strip."

Gods, he wanted to be inside her—*had* to be inside, soon, now, always—but refused to steal her freedom, forcing her to stay with him. He dropped his arm before his fingers could lengthen into claws. While researching all possible ways to steal the All-Key without adverse side effects, he would have to find a way to break Anya's curse, as well.

"Well?" she prompted.

He reached back, gripped his shirt and pulled it over his head. Before he'd gotten it all the way off, her hands were on his chest, removing his own weapons. "I think you had me out-armed." She tossed them to the floor, metal clinking against metal. When the last knife was gone, her fingers splayed over him, caressing his nipples, his tattoo.

His stomach tightened and his cock jerked. Heat was spreading through him faster than he could flash. He loved when she touched him. Made him feel like a god, all-powerful, unstoppable. Desired.

"You're so strong," she praised. "I love that you suffered and survived. Does that make me a bad girl?"

He cupped her cheeks. "Nothing could make you bad."

"Not even this…" She unfastened his pants and worked them over his hips, tossing his blades aside along the way.

When he was completely bare, Anya stared at his butter-fly tattoo, tracing her fingers over the jagged edges, oohing and ahhing. The skin rose under her touch, heating.

She gasped in delight. "Alive?"

"I had not thought so until now. That is where the demon entered me, as you know, but it has never done that before."

"He must like me."

"He does."

"Good boy," she whispered, kissing the butterfly. Once again, it rose to meet her, tingling where she touched.

Lucien wasn't sure why the gods had chosen butterflies as the external mark of the demon. The Butterfly Effect, perhaps. A reminder that the single flap of a wing—or in the warriors' case, a single foolish decision—could alter the entire fabric of reality. Whatever the rationale, he'd always hated the brand. Why not a weapon or a demon horn? Some-thing that said, well, I Am Man.

Lucien had enough insecurities.

Anya dropped to her knees and pressed a soft kiss to his naval, right at the bottom tip of a wing. Then her hot tongue flicked out, tracing the edge. Electric jolts speared his veins, his organs, even his bones.

Rumbling grunts of satisfaction, he let his head fall back. He was stroking the top of her head, urging her on, when he should have been pulling her to her feet.

"How many women have worshiped this magnificent body?" she whispered. A second later, her nails scored his thigh.

They didn't retract, either.

"Not many," he admitted. Mariah had been fascinated by him, but she'd also been terrified.

He hadn't blamed her for that terror. He had met her only a century or two after his possession, when he'd only just gained control over the demon; he'd still been a bit feral. Yet he'd also been a handsome man, well able to provide a woman pleasure.

She'd taken one look at him and decided he was "the one." He had done the same, for she had represented the gentle nurturing he had always craved. They had fallen into bed right away; she had been a widow and happy to have a warrior to attend her needs and protect her.

But even while she craved his protection—looters, mercenaries and plague had been rampant back then—she had feared that very aspect of him, afraid he would use his strength against her. He'd always been on guard, careful of his every action and word. With Anya, there was freedom to simply let go, for she seemed to bask in his might and revel in his underlying violence.

"I'm going to pretend I'm the first," she said. Her gaze lifted and met his in a heated clash. "Okay?"

"You are in every way that matters."

She smiled with wicked pleasure. "How long has it been for you, Lucien? Since you were last with a woman?"

"Thousands of years," he admitted without shame.

Now her eyes widened. "Surely you jest."

He shook his head. "No, no jest."

"But…why did you willingly deny yourself? You aren't cursed in that way. Don't get me wrong, I'm not complaining. I think I like you even more, knowing you have been without, just as I have."

"I like that, too."

"Why, though, did you deny your body's needs?"

"I am Death, Anya. A better question is why allow myself to make love to a woman when I will, perhaps, be called to take her soul one day?"

"Why make love to me, then?" she asked softly.

He tangled his fingers into her hair, marveling that each strand was like a ribbon of silk. "You, I cannot resist."

She leaned into his touch and kissed his palm. "I can't resist you, either, and I'm glad."

"As am I," he said. Anya had been worth the wait. No other woman equaled her in any way.

"I think we're both done waiting." Never pulling her gaze from him, she rose like the moon in the sky and backed up to the bed. When her legs hit the edge of the mattress, she eased down. She scooted back, sexy bra and panties glistening in the muted light.

Once in the center of the bed, she stopped and braced her weight on her elbows.

Her legs parted…parted…parted…revealing the very heart of her. His heart stopped before slamming into a hard, erratic beat as he drank in her beauty. She was perfect sun-and-cream with a navel he wanted to tongue. Her stomach was flat, her thighs lithe.

Trembling, Lucien approached the bed. He hadn't— He stilled abruptly, frowned. Cursed. Death screamed.

"What's wrong?" Anya asked, frowning, too.

"Souls. I hate that this keeps happening at such moments." He had trouble speaking past the demon's ranting inside his head.

"Lucien—"

"Do not move. *Please.*" He disappeared, letting his spirit be pulled in whatever direction was needed. There were two souls in China in need of transport, their bodies destroyed by poison.

One was bound for heaven, one for hell. One, of course, was happy to go with him. The other fought and screamed. Lucien hated leaving Anya and nearly beat the uncooperative spirit to an ethereal pulp. Death raged all the while. Finally, job done, they were able to return.

Seeing Anya, Lucien sighed contentedly. Death calmed.

She wasn't fingering herself this time, but had waited for him. Through the bra, he could see that her nipples were beaded. Her legs were still parted, and he could see the moisture dampening the panties.

When she spotted him, she grinned slowly. "I didn't want to finish without you."

"I am glad." He crawled onto the bed.

Anya stopped him with a foot on his stomach before he could lie on top of her. "I think we need to set a few ground rules."

"No rules." He lifted her foot and kissed the arch.

She fell backward, gasping. "Keep that up, and I'll happily look at my feet."

He licked.

"One. One rule, then." His tongue flicked out again, darting over her big toe. Goose bumps broke over her skin. "Oh, gods," she cried. "No one has ever done that. Who would have thought such a thing would be pleasurable? Oh, yes."

A wave of possessiveness swam through him. The passion on her face would haunt him for the rest of his days, for it was pure and undiluted, uninhibited. "What rule? I have already agreed not to penetrate you."

"Not that," she said, hips arching. "Lick again."

He did.

She moaned.

"What rule?"

"Oh, yeah. My rule." She removed her bra and tossed it aside. It landed on top of the pile of knives. Her nipples were pink little berries made for his tongue. Kneading her breasts, she gasped out, "Neither of us leave this bed until both of us are satisfied. *That's* my rule."

Of all the things he had expected her to say, that was not even close. His stomach clenched with something he refused to name. "I agree. If you agree to a rule from me."

"What?" she asked suspiciously.

"Here, in this bed, there will be no fighting." He sucked her toe into his mouth, twirling his tongue. "Only ecstasy."

She gripped the sheets. "Agreed. Agreed, agreed, agreed!"

There was a bellow of lust in his head as he tore the panties off her and finally crawled on top of her. His cock was hot but her feminine core was hotter as he slid against it, careful not to enter.

She didn't shy away, but let him glide against her. "I've never been this close to a man."

"Me, either."

A soft, raspy chuckle escaped her. "Why do I trust you? You, I should run from at every opportunity."

She paled when she realized what she'd said and he frowned. "What is wrong?"

Determination fell over her features as she stared up at him. "Nothing's wrong. I *don't* trust you. That's what I meant to say. 'Cause I mean, really. Let's be honest. You mean nothing to me but a good time. And why the hell have you stopped? I didn't give you permission to stop."

She'd spoken loudly, cruelly, practically sneering the

words. What was she doing? He might have believed her yes- terday, even an hour ago, but not now. Not while she was under him, naked, her body wet with desire for him.

She had not slept with William, had not let the handsome man touch her in any sexual way. She came to Lucien for her needs and trusted him not to take more than she could give. So, yes. He knew she did not mean what she'd said.

Cronus, he thought again, gnashing his teeth. But Lucien didn't challenge her. Not now. She *did* trust him, and he would trust that she did not mean to hurt him, that she believed she was helping him by acting that way.

Leaning down, silent, he cupped her chin and angled her head for a kiss. A deep, probing kiss. At first, she did not respond. She even tried to pry away. Then her tongue tenta- tively met his, gently, sweetly. She moaned. Her fingers fisted in his hair.

As he tasted her strawberry flavor, a sense of urgency bloomed. *Mark.* He released her jaw and palmed her breast. *Mine.*

Mark her. Yes, yes. *She's mine.* He placed his lips at the center of her throat and sucked. Sucked and sucked. She writhed and writhed, her hands remaining in his hair, holding him captive. She uttered a breathless series of pants, and he felt her nipple pearl against his palm.

When he finally lifted his head, he saw that there was a bruise on her neck, already blue. Satisfaction thrummed through him. "I did not spend enough time with your breasts last time we were together."

"No." Her nails scraped over his head, and he knew she was as hot and hungry as he was, already lost in passion. No longer did she try to rebuff him.

"Allow me to remedy that." Lowering again, he sampled one strawberry nipple, then the other.

"Lucien," she gasped.

"I love when you say my name."

"More, Lucien. Please, more."

Sucking on those nipples, rolling them over his tongue, he slid a hand down the sensuous contours of her body. Her legs spread as wide as she could get them.

She gasped when his fingertip found her clitoris. "No…no entering…but maybe…"

"I know. No sinking them inside, as deep as I can get them. No touching you all the way to your soul. No becoming one being rather than two. No feeling your inner walls spasm around me."

She gripped his shoulders, nails sharp. Her head thrashed from side to side as if she were imagining all that he said. Her eyelids squeezed together, and her white teeth tortured her bottom lip.

Sweet heaven, she was so wet she drenched his hand.

"I hate my curse," she croaked.

"I hate it, too. I hate my own curse. But if it is what brought me to you, I will gladly bear both for eternity." He rubbed her, circling quickly, then slowing when she was close to climax, letting her calm, then quickening again.

Only when she was out of her mind, screaming with the force of her need, shouting his name, begging, pleading, desperate, did he give her release. Her body jerked. Her hands dug into him with so much force his bones would have snapped if he'd been human.

All the while, Lucien watched her face. The way her lips parted and her breath turned shallow. The way sublime pleasure and ultimate satisfaction blanketed her expression. The way her eyelids popped open with wonder, as if she could see stars around her.

When she stilled, he laid his head on her breast, listening

to her racing heartbeat. Her skin was slick with sweat and passion. He was ready to explode, but he didn't want to ruin this moment.

She flipped him to his back, however, and smiled down at him. "Now I'll show you how bad I can be." She reached between her legs and wet her hand with her own juices, and then she gripped his shaft.

Up and down she pumped, a smooth glide that drove him wild. Reaching back, he gripped the headboard and tried to hold himself steady. He had been aroused so many times over the past week, his body was practically weeping with relief as she worked him.

Her fingers slid over the head of his penis with each upward slide, squeezing and teasing. "Anya," he panted.

"Mmm, I see what you mean about the name thing." As she spoke, her other hand pulled at his testicles. "I like it. Say mine again."

"Anya, I'm going to…going to…"

"Do it. Come for me. I want to see."

His hips lifted. "Don't stop. Don't stop."

"I won't. Give me," she purred. Her hand went so far down on his shaft, he couldn't hold the pleasure back a moment more.

He tensed, hot seed shooting from his shaft and onto the ropes of his stomach. He roared and roared and roared. "Anya!"

"More." Her hand continued to ride him. "Everything. Every drop."

His muscles were tensing, relaxing, tensing, relaxing. His hips were as far off the bed as possible, his heels digging into the mattress. He would have thought it impossible, but he spurted again, his mind shooting into a winking black hole that sucked him under with wave after wave of pleasure.

"Good, so good," she praised.

Finally spent, he collapsed. She cleaned him off with a towel before crawling up his body and settling into his side. He wound his arms around her, holding her captive. *Ask her about the key.*

No. Not now.

A lifetime is more important than a single moment.

True. He opened his mouth to demand she tell him about the key, but the words refused to form as she snuggled closer, closed her eyes and sighed contentedly.

No, nothing is more important than this moment. A short while later he fell asleep with a smile on his face.

NOT EVEN A DAY HAS PASSED, and I've already fallen into bed with him, Anya thought, burrowing deeper into Lucien's body while he slept.

She'd tried to resist, tried to keep him at a distance. But he'd just been so damned passionate, possessive and irresistible. His jealousy toward William… Gods, she could have had an orgasm just watching Lucien struggle with it.

She'd tried to pretend Lucien meant nothing to her, saying horrible things she'd had to rip out of her mouth just in case Cronus the Voyeur had been watching, but she'd been unable to walk away when Lucien told her to choose her place of pleasure.

After what had happened in this bed, she no longer knew what to do about Cronus or how to throw him off the scent of her true desire for Lucien. There'd be no denying it now. Part of her was glad. She couldn't hurt Lucien again, she just couldn't. Over the past week he had somehow become important to her—someone to cherish.

Lucien stirred in her arms, grumbling, before he bolted upright and frowned.

She frowned back. "What's wrong?"

"I'm being summoned," he said groggily.

He didn't wait for her response; he simply disappeared. Panic infused her as half an hour dragged by and he failed to return. Had souls summoned him or had Cronus? Should she go looking for him? Where the hell should she even start—

Suddenly Lucien appeared, healthy and whole, and curled beside her. His delicious heat surrounded her as he closed his eyes and sighed. "Foolish souls," he muttered. He didn't sound groggy anymore; he sounded sorrowful. A bit upset. "Why do they fight?"

Relieved, she relaxed against him and traced hearts all over his chest. The few times she'd watched him do his escort duties, he had finished in minutes. She'd wanted to know what had taken him so long tonight, and now she could guess. There'd been a lot of dead people. "Give me a little warning next time, and I'll go with you."

He opened his eyes to study her. "Why would you want to visit hell?"

So you won't have to bear the burden alone, she thought, but said only, "Could be fun."

"Not fun, I promise you." He traced a path up and down her arm, and she saw a cut healing on his wrist.

Had one of the spirits injured him? If so, they were lucky they were already dead. "Just take me. Okay? Please, please, please with a cherry on top of me. I want to go."

His palm settled over her breast, and he kissed the mark he'd left on her neck. "Take you. Mmm, I like the sound of that." His cock swelled and pressed against her clitoris.

Moaning, she opened her legs. "That's not what I meant, but I like where your head's at. Literally."

He chuckled and proceeded to "take her" over the edge of satisfaction. Only later did she realize he had never answered her.

CHAPTER FOURTEEN

PARIS SLOWLY CRACKED OPEN his eyelids. They were heavy, as if boulders held them down. His mouth was dry and stale, as if something had died inside it, and his skin was itchy. His ankles and wrists were encased in something cold and heavy.

What the hell was wrong with him? Where was he? He didn't remember agreeing to play bondage games with… whatever her name was.

"Good. You're finally awake."

He recognized that sweetly innocent voice, yet couldn't match it to a face. He frowned. White lights pulsed in front of him, and he blinked against them as his eyes watered. Last thing he remembered, he'd been kissing a woman. Her warm hazel gaze and brown hair finally flashed across his consciousness. Freckles, a plain face.

He'd been kissing this woman—what was her name?—and then he'd blacked out. Right?

"Paris," she said, her voice laced with steel now. Suddenly she was crouching in front of him.

The plain face he'd just envisioned was here in the flesh. He scrubbed a shaky hand over his own face, trying to orient himself further. Chains rattled, pulling at his arm. Had she… surely not. She didn't have the strength to take him down.

Hunters must have attacked them.

"Did they lock us up?" His voice was craggy. There was

a thick fog in his mind, and he was having trouble fighting past it. He'd been without sex for a while, which explained his weakness and the fact that he'd been overpowered.

"I locked *you* up," she said with a sigh.

She had what now? Despite the brain-fog, he gave her his full attention. Her hair was pulled back in a severe twist. Her freckles were covered with makeup, and her eyes were enlarged by thick glasses.

He was rock hard for her in that instant. "Why would you do something like that?"

"Can't you guess?" She reached out and tilted his head to the side, studying his neck. She traced a fingertip over a sore spot. Puncture wound, he realized, the answer to her question slipping into place.

"You're my enemy." Even as his blood froze, his every cell leapt at her touch, greedy for more. But she didn't appear the least bit aroused by him. She was all business, plain and simple.

"Yes. The wound isn't healing," she said with a frown. "I didn't mean to jab you with the needle quite so forcefully. For that, I'm sorry."

She was sorry? Please. Their kiss replayed in his mind. Her hot little tongue in his mouth…her breasts in his hands, small but sensitive…a sharp pain. His eyes narrowed on her. "You tricked me. Played me like a piano."

Again, "Yes."

"Why? And don't tell me you're Bait. You're not pretty enough." He said it just to be cruel.

Her cheeks darkened to a rosy red, taking her from plain to the pretty he'd just denied in seconds. "No, I'm not Bait. Or rather, I wouldn't have been to any warrior but you. But then, you don't care who you screw, do you, Promiscuity?" Every word dripped with disgust.

His gaze roved over her. "Obviously not."

The color in her cheeks deepened, and his cock hardened another inch. *Down boy.*

"Aren't you afraid I'll hurt you?" he asked silkily.

"No." She arched a dark brow. "You haven't the strength. I made sure of that."

Don't antagonize her, idiot. Seduce her, get your strength back and blow this place. He forced his expression to soften, to glaze with passion. Sadly, he didn't have to force the passion. "You enjoyed yourself while you were in my arms. Admit it. I know women, and I know passion. You were on fire for me."

"Shut up," she snapped.

Emotion. Excellent. "Want to give me a go before your friends show up?"

She gnashed her teeth and straightened, widening the distance between them. Without her in his face, claiming his attention, he was able to study the room. Or rather, prison. Dirt floor, barred walls.

He snorted in disgust—a disgust reserved all for himself. He'd known better. He'd known to be careful, yet he'd been careless and stupid. He'd practically handed himself to the Hunters with a bow and a thank-you card. How the other warriors would laugh at him when they found out.

"So you're a Hunter, are you?"

"If by Hunter you mean a defender of all that is good and right and just, then yes." Refusing to look at him, she removed her watch and showed him the tattoo of Infinity etched there. "I've been fascinated with demons and their evil crimes my entire life—was always buying books about them, attending meetings and seminars. These men approached me about a year ago, asked me to join them. I said yes and I've never regretted it."

The symbol should have sickened him; it always had

before. This time, his tongue ached to trace the hated image. "And what do you hope to do with me?" he asked. He wasn't panicked. Yet. Hundreds of years ago, he'd been cornered by Hunters. He'd managed to escape with only a few wounds.

This time would be no different; he'd make sure of it.

"We're going to experiment on you. Observe you. Use you as bait to capture more demons. And then, we're going to draw out your demon when we find Pandora's box, killing you and trapping the monster inside." Once again, she was matter-of-fact, as if they were discussing what to eat for dinner.

His brow quirked. "That it?"

"For now."

"You might as well kill me, then, sweetheart. My friends won't surrender themselves to save little old me." No, they'd kill everyone in this building.

"We'll see about that, won't we?" she said, defensive.

Stop antagonizing her. He needed to romance her, this enemy—by whatever means necessary. Once he climaxed inside her, he would have the strength to kill anyone who got in his path. Even her. Bitch.

Why couldn't he have been given the spirit of Violence, like Maddox? He wouldn't have had to rely on anything except anger to gain strength. Fucking demon of Promiscuity. It was nothing but a nuisance.

A few times, in desperation, the demon had forced him to turn to—*don't think of that. Not now, not when you need to be aroused.* "Love," he said, using his huskiest tone. "I'm sorry if I hurt your feelings a moment ago. I was angry and lashing out at you." He made sure to soften his expression again, to let his eyelids drift to half-mast, to let his lips relax as if preparing for a kiss.

She smoothed a hand over her mousy hair and looked down at her white tennis shoes. "That's fine. I understand. You are a slave to your evil nature."

She'd only been a Hunter for a year, she'd said. She was a baby, naive. Any other Hunter would have realized what he was doing and left him. Would have cursed at him, slapped him, not radiated a sense of vulnerability.

"I think you're lovely," he said. Unfortunately, that was the truth.

"You're lying."

"No. I was lying earlier, when I called you plain. The moment I saw you, I wanted you. I imagined your naked body on my bed, your head thrown back, your hands, oh, your hands—" His gaze sought them. Yes. They were as smooth and perfect as he remembered. "Your hands seeking the moist heat between your legs, unable to wait for me to join you."

As he spoke, he projected the images into her head. That was the only benefit to the demon. It could ride the undercurrents of his voice and enter a human's mind, showing the listener exactly what Paris described.

Most times, he hated to use the gift. The guilt afterward... He made people desire what they normally wouldn't desire, just as the demon did to him. But this woman was a Hunter, and she didn't deserve his concern.

"Don't—don't talk like that," she whispered. A tremor racked her.

"When you're close to orgasm, I'll lick you. Right between your legs. You'll scream my name."

Her breathing became choppy; her nipples hardened underneath her shirt—a white shirt that did nothing to hide the lace of her bra. An unexpected bit of femininity, considering she was dressed like a sexually repressed ice maiden. Why?

On her legs she wore unflattering black slacks that bagged, and her tennis shoes were clunky and mannish.

"I'm going to pound inside you all the way to the hilt, and then I'm going to flip over and you're going to ride me."

"Don't say things like that," she scolded breathlessly. She pulled at the collar of her shirt. "You're evil, and…and…"

"A man who craves your touch." He was a lot of things, but he wasn't evil. He didn't kill indiscriminately, didn't rape. He and his friends poured money into Buda, fortifying the economy, supplying food to the needy. That counted for something, right?

Hunters were the evil ones, viewing the world in black and white to justify their relentless pursuit of "Utopia," mowing over any human who got in their way.

Her breath hitched.

"I'm picturing you naked even now," he forced himself to continue. "Your skin is flushed, your nipples hard, moisture dripping between your legs."

Gasping, she shut her eyes. "S-stop. Please."

"You're aching for a man's touch, aren't you, sweetheart?" *What the hell was her name?*

He never remembered names. He could fuck a woman only once, so there was never any need. Besides, he didn't want to call out the wrong name in the midst of passion. Women tended to take offense at that. "Come here. Let me give you what you need."

"This isn't right," she breathed, but she stepped closer to him.

There was limited slack on his chains, so he couldn't reach out. He'd have to convince her to do all the work. "I'm hard for you. My cock is hungry for you. Only you."

Goose bumps broke over her skin.

With her face softened with arousal, she was almost beautiful. Her lashes were long, the longest he'd ever seen, and feathered like a peacock's tail. "Feel your breasts for me. They want to be touched."

Tentatively she reached up and did as he'd commanded. Another gasp escaped her. "Oh, my."

"Good. That's good."

"I—I—"

Don't give her time to think. But watching her was destroying his concentration. "Unbutton your pants and reach underneath them for me. Under your panties, too. Touch your clitoris. Spread your moisture around."

She started to do as commanded, but froze with her hand poised at her flat belly. "I can't. I shouldn't."

"You can. You should. You want to, you know you do. It will feel so good."

"No, I…" She shook her head, horror sprinkling into her eyes, as if she were seconds away from fighting past his hold on her mind.

Confusion and shock rocked him. She should not be able to fight him. "Your clit is crying for your touch…sweet. But if you don't want to touch yourself, come over here and I'll lick you. I'll lick you until you scream."

She was walking toward him before he'd gotten the last word out. He breathed a sigh of relief. Almost…there… "Just a little more, sweetheart. Just a little closer."

Just before she reached him, however, and just before he could nuzzle her pants down and sink his tongue inside her hot sheath—where he would refuse to give her an orgasm until she rode him—she froze again.

"You keep calling me *sweet* and *sweetheart.*"

"That's because you are sweet. I can't reach you like this," he said, trying not to whine. "Just a little closer," he repeated. "I need you so badly."

"What's my name?" She no longer sounded quite so breathless.

His jaw clenched and panic infused him. "What does a name matter? You want me, and I want you."

She frowned and backed away from him. "You don't even know my name, and yet you're willing to sleep with me?"

"I would not be sleeping."

"They told me not to trust you. They told me not to get close."

His panic increased, hope slipping away. "Sweet, let's—"

"Shut up!" Scowling, she massaged her temples. "I don't know how you did that to me, reduced me to *that,* and right now I don't care. But don't you ever—ever!—do it again or I won't wait to find the box before I kill you."

She stomped away, opened the barred door and slammed it shut behind her, locking him inside. Alone.

To grow weaker. Fuck.

MADDOX CARRIED A TRAY of food to the dungeon. He hated that Aeron had to be locked away like this, but like the other warriors, he had no alternate solution. Aeron had once been the strongest-willed among them. Fierce but loyal, by turns as rigorously controlled as Lucien and as volatile as Maddox used to be.

Maddox chuckled, remembering. They'd enjoyed sparring, he and Aeron, and had spent many hours honing their skills together. When Maddox lost control of his demon, it had been Aeron who helped bring him down. Now Aeron was merely a shell of his former self. Wild, savage, hate-filled.

If Aeron were set free, he would kill four innocent women, just as the gods had commanded. And if he killed those women, he would never recover from this bloodlust. From the beginning, Aeron had known that taking innocent lives would push him over the brink.

Maddox knew how that felt.

He had killed Pandora seconds after the demon of Violence entered his body. And he had spent untold centuries paying for it, killed every night the very way he had killed her— stabbed in the stomach six hellish times. Only, unlike poor Pandora, *he* always awakened the next morning knowing he had to die again.

But Ashlyn had saved him in more ways than one, giving him a reason to finally live. Now his precious woman carried his child.

As always, the thought caused his heart to swell and faint sickness to churn inside his stomach. What kind of father would he be? Already he loved the baby, knew he would protect it even if he were killed and had to fight his way from hell to do so.

He wanted the same sense of family for Aeron. Love, absolution. Freedom. Yet, the man truly was consumed by bloodlust. He couldn't be trusted around the warriors, his friends and brothers, much less a human female. So how he would find a woman to tame him, Maddox didn't know.

His head canted to the side as he descended the steps to the dungeon. There was no rattle of claws against the bars. For the first time in weeks, no curses echoed off the walls. It was eerily quiet. He set the tray on the floor and rushed forward.

When he reached Aeron's cell, Maddox experienced a wave of undiluted fear. The gaping bars had been pried apart. Aeron was gone.

ACTING AS GUARD, REYES PACED the moss-laden perimeter of the too-quiet, sinister-looking Roman temple as his friends searched for clues about the Unspoken Ones. Since Lucien and the others knew where to begin looking for the artifacts,

Sabin's crew was now hunting for information about the Titans. Their weaknesses. Their enemies.

Though the temple had been buried beneath the sea, blood still stained the remaining walls—walls composed of human bones. So far, the warriors had found nothing. Not even cutting themselves and dripping fresh blood onto the altar had worked. Reyes wondered for the hundredth time just what had occurred in this temple during its golden age. Sometimes he would swear he heard screams whistling on the breeze.

Lucien had appeared a short while ago, looking more relaxed and sated than Reyes had ever seen him. He'd even looked happy. What had brought on the change? Reyes was jealous, whatever it was. Jealous and glad for him. Yet even Lucien's sickeningly happy blood hadn't produced results. There had been no vision, no clue. And Reyes was tired of all this futility, of the helplessness and failure.

This morning, news of the temples had blasted from television stations all over the world. He wasn't sure why they were no longer hidden. He only knew humans would be arriving soon—Hunters, tourists, treasure-seekers and researchers alike. Time was more precious than ever.

"Damn this," Reyes growled. He needed pain, he decided, or he'd shatter and kill someone. A mortal, a warrior. Didn't matter. "I'll be nearby," he told Sabin as he stalked past him. "Shout if you need me."

Sabin didn't try to stop him. By now, he knew better.

Reyes had a dagger unsheathed by the time he reached the temple's surrounding forest. He leaned against the nearest tree, one with red leaves that made the branches look like they were bleeding, and began carving X's in his arm. With the sharp slices and release of blood, real blood, some of his anger drained.

If Danika could see you now...

He snorted. She already hated him. To see him like this would hardly deepen an emotion that was already boundless.

In his pocket, his cell phone buzzed and he uttered a frustrated sigh. Sabin had supplied him with it a few weeks ago. Reyes wasn't sure he liked it—sometimes a man needed to be free of everything, even contact with others—but he'd kept it. Just in case something happened.

With a growl, he dug it out and flipped it open. "What?"

"Aeron has escaped," Maddox said without preamble.

Everything inside of Reyes screamed in denial. In protest. In rage and more of that damned helplessness. He'd known this day would come. He just hadn't expected it to come this soon. *Should have swallowed your love for him and chained him.* "How long?"

"Last time I saw him was twelve hours ago."

As Wrath, Aeron would be able to find Danika no matter where she was hiding. He would sniff her out and use his wings to reach her quickly. "I'll find him," Reyes said.

Before he could disconnect, Maddox added, "Torin had me place some kind of tracking dye in Aeron's meals, just in case. He'll e-mail the coordinates you need to your phone. I called you first, wanted you to know because…you know. Just bring our friend back. Alive."

Reyes didn't answer. He couldn't. If he failed in this, Danika would die.

If she wasn't already dead.

CHAPTER FIFTEEN

"NICE HICKEY," WILLIAM SAID at breakfast the next morning when he spied Anya's neck.

I do not blush, I do not blush. And yet, her cheeks heated. Damn Lucien and his wondrous mouth. And speaking of Lucien's wondrous mouth, he'd used it to pry information about the All-Key out of her this morning.

She knew he was looking for a way to take it from her without destroying either of them so he could get the god king off her back. He'd begun sucking on her nipples right after he'd questioned her and she hadn't wanted him to stop. She'd ended up telling him the key was bonded to her, body and soul, as much a part of her as his demon was a part of him. That's why the giver weakened; they were giving away a part of themselves. She had seen disappointment light Lucien's eyes and it had stirred something tender inside her. He of all people would understand the danger of losing a vital part of yourself.

She sighed. Right now, she, Lucien and William were sitting at a small round table; eggs, bacon and pancakes were spread over its surface. The air was syrupy-sweet and salty crisp, the food itself perfectly prepared.

After dressing in a decadent white cashmere body suit, she'd flashed to her favorite diner in Atlanta, ordered the feast and flashed back. And yes, she'd pretended to cook it herself. Warriors that they were, the men had yet to praise her efforts, which was completely unacceptable. They thought she'd slaved over every dish and yet they hadn't even said thank-you. Bastards.

She sat between them. Lucien kept a stern eye on William, growling whenever the sexpot reached in her direction. His possessiveness was just too cute. No wonder she had spent the entire night in his arms, unable to force herself to leave him. He made her feel desired. Well, that, and also safe. She'd never spent an entire night with a man before and hadn't known there'd be an endearing—and addicting—sense of security on top of the intense physical pleasure.

"I have told you to keep your hands—" Lucien's words trailed off, and she felt his body go rigid.

Anya turned to him. Both of his eyes had gone blue. She grabbed on to his arm. Time for the two of them to collect souls, it seemed.

"I must go," he said.

"You're taking me. Remember?"

He shook his head. "You will stay here."

"Don't make me go invisible on you and follow without permission."

"Like before." A resigned statement. "I have not been able to figure out how you did that."

She shrugged. "I'm Anarchy, remember? I don't obey the laws of nature—or anything else."

"What are you guys talking about?" William asked.

She ignored him. One, because she knew William would hate it and quite possibly throw an amusing fit, and two, because she knew Lucien would disappear the moment she turned her attention from him. "Leave me behind, and I'll sit in Willie's lap the entire time you're gone."

William grinned, curiosity forgotten. "Leave her behind, my man. I'll take extra special care of her."

Lucien bared his teeth in a fierce scowl, but he twined his fingers with Anya's. "Fine. Let's go."

He dematerialized, taking Anya with him. They entered the spirit world, everything becoming a collage of bright colors and lights. Lucien floated quickly to a badly burned, still-smoking shop in…Shanghai, she realized, glancing at the surrounding buildings of red and white, with pointed tops and sloped roofs. She could almost smell the foods being sold at the street market.

There were several bodies lying on a charred floor. Never loosening his hold on her, Lucien went to the first, the closest, and dipped his hand into the man's chest. A gasping spirit emerged, flailing against Death's hold.

The three of them were poised at the gates of hell in the next instant. The heat nearly melted the skin from her bones. She shuddered. The shouts, the tormented cries. Was this where she would go if Cronus had his way and she died? Just the thought of it sickened her.

"He purposely set the fire," Lucien said through clenched teeth.

This isn't about you right now. This is about Lucien. She released his hand and moved behind him, winding her arms around his waist and offering comfort, reminding him that he wasn't alone. His muscles were tense, but slowly they relaxed.

Two large boulders drew apart, opening a wide chasm. Multiple pairs of scaly arms reached up, and Lucien tossed the flailing spirit at them. Evil laughter erupted, followed closely by beleaguered screams.

Many times during any given day, Lucien witnessed this terrible scene. Anya kissed his ear, drawing his attention from the flames. "Lots of people die. Every minute. Every hour. Why don't you have to escort all of them?"

"Some remain to wander Earth, some are reborn and get

the chance to start anew. Some, I think, are escorted by angels."

Ah. She should have known. She'd run into a few angels herself over the years. Beautiful creatures, if a bit haughty. "The souls escorted by you are the luckiest. Ready for the others?"

Lucien nodded, and he appeared less strained.

The other two humans must have been good little boys because they got to go to heaven. As always, the pearly gates made Anya gape. They sparkled with jewels and mesmerized with their hum of power. Beyond them, a cherubic choir rejoiced, their voices soothing, somehow delighting each of the senses. Wow.

I want to come here if ever I die.

When have you ever been good?

I'm good. Sometimes.

"Thank you, Anya. For coming with me. For comforting me."

"My pleasure." She and Lucien popped back into William's kitchen. The sexpot was still sitting at the table, but Anya's gaze snagged on her lover. Lucien was watching her, heat in his eyes. Heat and awe and appreciation.

"And where did you guys go?" William asked.

"Nowhere." She concentrated on William, Lucien's stare making her squirm in her seat. "So where are your women this morning?"

"Sleeping. Vamps need their beauty rest."

Lucien's eyes widened. He must not have encountered one before.

"Vamps as in vampires or vamps as in conquests?" She looked William up and down, but he wasn't marked. Granted, his legs were covered by black silk pants. "I'm guessing conquests. You don't look like you've been nibbled on—at least, not by anyone with fangs."

"Oh, I've been bitten, just not anywhere you can see. Unlike you," he added with a smiling glance at her neck.

Lucien had been in the process of drinking his juice, which he promptly choked on. Grinning, Anya pounded on his back. "I think you shocked him."

"Not possible," William said, studying Lucien. "We could hear the two of you going at it like rabbits. Stunned the hell out of me, but I have to say, making this little minor goddess beg for it was a nice touch."

"Thank you," Lucien said when his coughs subsided. But there was warning in his tone.

"I'm *not* minor, you dirty man-whore!"

Winking, William propped his elbows on the tabletop. "So what's going on? You know I love for you to visit, Anya, but why are you here and why are you being chased by the demon of Death?"

She opened her mouth to answer, but Lucien placed a restraining hand on her arm. When she glanced at him, he shook his head.

"I'm not going to tell any secrets, Flowers."

"Oh, secrets. Tell." William clapped.

She wanted to, she wouldn't deny that. She never kept anyone's secret. Where was the fun in that? Still, she remained quiet. For Lucien, anything. By this point, she wasn't surprised that even her naughty side wanted to impress him.

"We simply need to borrow some items from you," Lucien said.

"Like?"

"Actually," Anya said, "we'd like you to be our tour guide through the Arctic circle."

"Anya," Lucien warned.

"Well, *I* would. He lives so close he spends a lot of time

there. He knows the lay of the land. And that's not really giving away our secret, now is it?"

"Why do you want to enter the Arctic?" William shuddered. "It's colder than a witch's—unmentionables. And I should know!"

"I'm on vacation and feel like touring a few glaciers," she replied flippantly.

"You hate ice. You spend most of your time in Hawaii."

"We'll be fine without a guide," Lucien interjected. "Clothing, blankets and snowshoes should do."

"I'm not taking you into the Arctic," William said with a shake of his head. "I just got back from a trip there and I need some serious R and R."

Lucien shrugged as if he didn't care one way or the other. "Then we are agreed. Anya and I will go alone."

"The hell we will." Anya slapped her hand against the tabletop, rattling the dishes. "Willie will guide us wherever we want to go and he'll do it with a smile on his face. It will save time and he'll be a good soldier to have with us if a fight breaks out with you-know-who. Hydra," she added dramatically.

"You want to fight *Hydra?*" William paled. "I'm not going near that bitch. I lost sight of her a few years ago and that's the way I prefer it."

"Never thought I'd meet a woman you wouldn't screw." Anya forked a square of pancake. She lifted it to her mouth, saying, "For that matter, I never though *you'd* meet a woman you wouldn't screw. And speaking of that, where exactly *did* you come across Hydra? And how'd you escape alive?"

"I saw her twice, both times in a different location out there in the ice. And I escaped alive only because she couldn't bear to mar my gorgeous mug, but it was a close call," William muttered.

"This is good," Lucien said with a nod of his head.

She knew he was referring to the Hydra sightings, though he probably wished William hadn't been quite so successful in escaping, and couldn't contain her own excitement. But she wasn't done with the questions, either. "Why do you go out there, anyway?" she asked. "You've never said."

"It's close enough to my home that immortals try to hide there for a sneak attack. At first I wasn't sure if they'd come for Hydra or me—we both have our share of enemies—and after a while I just stopped caring. Anyone sneaks out there, I go after them."

"Who are your enemies?" Anya wondered aloud.

"I, uh, have a little problem with desiring mated ladies," William said, "and their spouses would like nothing more than my demise."

"You will stay away from Anya," Lucien growled.

What a sweet, sweet man, she thought, grinning and patting his hand. Lucien reached under the table and gripped her knee in an iron-hold, a command for her to hush. She didn't. "Last time I'll ask you nicely to take us," she told William.

Rolling his eyes, he pushed his empty plate away, leaned back in his chair and crossed his arms over his chest. He'd braided the hunks of hair at his temples. Now they were hooked behind his ears, colorful beads clicking together every time he moved. "Sorry, but my answer is no."

"Well, then." Anya, too, leaned back in her chair. She'd always admired this room. Vaulted ceilings, a granite island counter, modern appliances, baskets of fruit hanging from wall hooks. Would William destroy it in a fit of rage when she finished with him? "Maybe now's a good time to tell you that I have your book."

William froze, the patent stillness of a predator coming

over him. "You don't. You can't. I saw it this morning before I came down to eat." There was violence in his gaze.

Lucien picked her up and placed her in his lap. She snuggled her head into the crook of his neck. Protection wasn't something she needed, but she appreciated the gesture. "Think again," she said.

"Anya," William snapped. "You don't have it. *I* have it. *I saw it this morning.*"

"Watch your tone," Lucien snapped back.

"You saw a fake," she explained.

"You're lying." The warrior leaned toward her, pupils swallowing his irises.

Immediately Lucien was on his feet, shoving her behind him. *Be still my little heart.*

"I told you to watch your tone."

William thrust from the table, his chair skidding backward and slamming into the island. *Smack.* "If it's gone…" On a cloud of red fury, he stalked from the kitchen.

"Damn. He actually walked away without destroying the room. Come on. We don't want to miss this." Anya twined her fingers with Lucien's, gasping at the electric jolt she felt on contact.

Now she knew what those naughty fingers could do to her…

Trembling, she pulled him along after William, following the same path the warrior had taken. The hallway was well-lit with flickering gold bulbs. Wisps of colorful lace covered the lamps, which splattered rainbow hues throughout. The vampiresses' doing? Trying to domesticate the warrior?

There were no pictures or weapons on the walls as there usually were. She'd bet, oh, ten million American dollars on William having removed them last night after sating his vampires. He was well acquainted with Anya's penchant for theft—but too late to save his precious book. Silly man had had one of his witches cast a spell over the book's locked case a long time ago. A spell she had broken with her key.

"What is this book you mentioned?" Lucien asked, keeping pace at her side. "And did you really steal it?"

"A book of ancient prophecies decreed by the gods. And yes. I took it. William should have been a smart boy and studied it a few times over the centuries, but nooo, he was afraid he'd do more harm to his fate than good." She rounded a corner. Stairs loomed ahead. Damn, but this place was huge. She wasn't used to walking it; usually she just flashed.

"See, one of the prophecies is about William. Written around the time he went to prison, if memory serves. Something about a woman. Of course, there's always a woman. Anyway, his prophecy is encrypted, like a riddle, and somewhere in the book is the key to decoding it and saving himself."

"Anya! How could you fucking dare?" William shouted. His angry bellow echoed off the walls.

"I guess he found the fake."

"Will he try to hurt you?"

She grinned. "Not while I have *his precious*." She said the last in an evil demon voice.

Lucien just shook his head.

They turned another corner and were suddenly in the study. William was holding the fake she'd had made. First time she'd visited him here, she'd tried to pick a fight with him, had *needed* to fight. One of her mortal companions had died and her need for disorder had been high. William had been too sated to oblige her, falsely claiming he was more a lover than a fighter. He'd offered to sex her, though. She'd spent some time tossing and shattering glass instead.

Then she'd spotted the book in its tantalizing case.

Blood-red rubies were embedded on its cover and spine. They'd called to her, a siren's song. Knowing what the book meant to him had made the stealing of it all the sweeter, she was ashamed to admit. She didn't suppose it would console him to know, though, that she was now a wee bit ashamed.

"The cover appears to be the same, but the pages are blank," he growled.

She splayed her arms wide. "Sorry. I couldn't help myself."

"Someone should have put you down a long time ago."

"Like that would have done any good," she muttered.

"Why do I like you? Why do I always allow you back? You and your fucking All-Key are a menace. Give me back the book, Anya!"

"How does everyone know about this key, yet I had never heard of it?" Lucien complained, tossing up his hands.

"Why don't you just take the key from her?" William suggested to Lucien with an evil grin.

"Shut up, Willie!" She stomped her foot and pushed a hand through her hair. "He already knows."

"Everything?"

"Yes." *Well, kind of.*

William grinned. "Liar. So, Lucy," he said, tossing the empty book to the ground and slapping his hands together. "Did you know that if she gives you the key, she'll be giving you her memories? You'll know everything about her. Her every sin, every crime, every man she's ever touched. Even better, you'll know where she is every second of every day. She'll never be able to hide from you."

Lucien flicked her a guarded glance. "True?"

Reluctantly she nodded. "All part of the All-Key's charm."

"Who gave you this key?" Lucien asked her. "Why would anyone place such a burden on you?"

William took it upon himself to answer for her. "Her daddy

dearest gave it to her when the gods finally decided on her punishment for murdering the captain of their guard. She was to be made an immortal sex slave. Fitting, don't you think? Tartarus knew of her curse, however, and knew what that would do to her. So he stepped in to play savior for once in his negligent life.

"Why do you think the immortal prison eventually fell? How do you think the Titans eventually escaped? Without the key he'd housed inside himself, both Tartarus the man and Tartarus the prison were weakened. Eventually, both crumbled altogether."

True, all true. When she'd accepted the key inside herself, she'd been given some of her father's memories and had found herself attuned to his whereabouts. Even now, she had only to think of him and she knew where he was.

That's how she'd known Cronus had imprisoned him.

She'd gone back to Olympus, a place she'd sworn never to visit again. Out of guilt, yes, for all her father had given up for her. Out of love, too, because through his memories, she'd learned that Tartarus hadn't known about her existence until Themis uncovered the truth. After that, he'd wanted to be a part of her life but hadn't known how to go about it without further devastating the wife he'd betrayed or humiliating the lover who was already suffering for the night of foolishness they'd shared.

When Aias attacked her, Tartarus had wanted to cut out his own heart for not being there. And when she'd been in prison, he'd viewed himself as her protector, giving her extra blankets, food—until her sentence came in, and he'd had to choose between her life and his own.

Pushing the memories to the back of her mind, she focused on Lucien. His expression was still blank, unreadable in a way she despised. What thoughts were tumbling through his mind?

William clapped his hands again, as if satisfied with a job well done. "You want a guide? You've got a guide. Afterward, I get my book."

She nodded, not proud of herself as she should have been.

"Then come on, you two. Let's get packed up. I'm eager to get started so we can get this over with." William strode from the room, whistling under his breath.

A deceptive calmness, Anya knew. Nerves on edge, she gave Lucien's shoulder a little punch. "Anything you want to say to me?"

A gleam of hopelessness appeared in his mismatched eyes. "No matter how long or hard I research, I will not find a way to take the key from you without harming you, will I?"

She gulped. "No."

"And if Cronus does gain possession of it, you will never be able to hide from him."

"Right," she said, looking at her feet. Damn it, she had to stop that! She peered up at Lucien through the thick shield of her lashes. Uncertainty swam through her as she closed the distance between them. "Does this change things between us? Make you want to give up on us?"

The hands that had delivered her such pleasure last night locked on her jaw and angled her head up. "Understand. I am here. I am yours. I'm not giving up."

Oh, this man… Their lips gently met, soft, so soft, a mere brush, but she wasn't content with that. She might never be content with anything less than, well, everything this warrior had to offer.

"Harder," she commanded.

Tongues thrust together, twining, rolling, as they drank each other in. He now knew beyond any doubt that he could not use the key to bargain with Cronus, but he still wanted her. He could not break her curse, but he still wanted her. She was overjoyed and relieved, and fell a little deeper under his spell. *He's mine.*

If another woman ever—ever!—thought to take him from her, Anya knew herself well enough to know she would kill the bitch. Coldheartedly. Painfully. She couldn't imagine her life without him now. Didn't think she'd even really lived until the moment she'd first seen him. *Yes, he's mine.* Her hand tangled in his silky hair and she rocked against his erection. *Mine.*

Even as the thought formed, a booming laugh rang out.

Everything inside Anya suddenly lurched. Her nervous system kicked into high gear, her heart pounding erratically. Sweat beaded on her palms. She didn't rip herself away from Lucien, but she did end the kiss and stare up at him, wide-eyed. *No. Not now.*

He'd stiffened. His eyes were narrowed, she saw, with glints of the rage she'd encountered only that once in Greece. She'd never seen anyone so fierce. He looked as if he could happily kill everyone around him. Except her. His arms were still gentle around her waist.

"Cronus," he said tightly. No body, just that awful voice.

Mouth dry, she nodded. "What do you want, oh, Great One?"

The god laughed again. "Right now I will settle for letting you know that I've discovered the best way to bring you to heel, Anarchy."

A tremor worked through Lucien's body. "My king, she is—"

"Silence, Death. Once again you have failed to do your job, and I am done waiting. Slay her. Here, this instant."

Lucien's gaze fell back to Anya. His muscles were like stone. Heat stopped radiating from him, ice-cold determination taking its place.

She didn't want to die, but she didn't want Lucien to be punished on her account, either. If she'd just stayed away from him, none of this would have happened. Yeah, none of it. Not the kissing, the touching, the…loving?

No, she couldn't love him. Love would destroy her, caging her as surely as if she were in prison again. *Just give Cronus the key.*

I can't. She would lose everything. Her independence, her powers, her memories. She might even forget her own curse, sleep with someone and inadvertently bind herself to that man for eternity. Gods, what was she going to do?

"I cannot hurt her," Lucien said with a proud tilt of his chin. His voice, however, was tortured.

"I thought not. It is hard for me to believe the Greeks once relied upon you for protection." Tense pause. "Hear me. You shall weaken with every day that passes in which I do not have that key."

"What?" Anya gasped out.

"At first, I thought the warrior's love for his friends would spur him to act. Now I know. All along, it was you, Anya, who needed prompting."

Anya floundered for the proper response, horror raining through her. "Cronus—"

"I've seen the way you are with him. He isn't just a toy to you as you pretended, but someone who matters. And now you will have to choose what matters most—him or the key." Cronus laughed, as if victory were already in his grasp. "Can you hear the clock ticking? I can."

And then there was only silence.

Cronus had gone, she knew that, for the slight hum of power that always accompanied his visits had faded. Her breathing became choppy, and she was barely able to draw enough air into her lungs. Lose Lucien? No!

"Do not say a word," Lucien growled. He refused to look at her. "Finding those artifacts is more important than ever. They are a source of his power and we can use them. We will gather supplies as planned and head out."

"But—"

He stalked away, leaving her alone in the study.

Oh, gods. What the hell was she going to do?

CHAPTER SIXTEEN

WHAT THE HELL WAS HE going to do?

He loved Anya. Lucien admitted that now. Knew it with a soul-deep intensity that could not be denied any longer. He loved her. He hadn't been able to kill her, and he could not abide the thought of her being bound to Cronus, the god king able to find her at every turn. Nor could he abide the thought of her being weak and powerless. Not when she had come to mean more to him than his own life.

She enjoyed stealing, often lied, could kill without remorse, had a bounty on her head, could not make love, and yet he cherished her more than he'd ever cherished Mariah. He hadn't thought such a thing possible. But Anya was the other half of him, the better half. She made him feel whole, complete, like a man rather than a demon. An attractive man, no less.

She gave him something to live for, wiped away his pain, his past, and—when she kissed him—his insecurities. Her sense of humor delighted him, her actions intrigued him. Merely being in her presence gave him more pleasure than sleeping with another woman ever had.

He knew of only one way to save her now. Find an artifact as quickly as possible and pray Cronus wanted it more than the key. He would gladly trade the artifact for Anya's life, Pandora's box be damned.

There was no way Lucien would allow Anya to give up that key now, that much he knew. She would lose her powers, her memories, the freedom she so valued. Her life? Without her ability to flash, she would be vulnerable to all kinds of attack. She would be helpless. Trapped. If a man decided to bind her by penetrating her, she would not be able to disappear or fight her way free.

With a roar, Lucien slammed his fist into the wall of the bedroom he'd occupied last night. A bedroom he'd shared with Anya. Beautiful, sparkling, fiery Anya. The wall cracked; blood trickled from the broken skin on his hand.

Anya was the one woman who saw past his scars to the man inside. In her presence he felt as if he could conquer the entire world, and he did not want that feeling to end. Holding her in his arms had been the greatest experience of his life. Nothing else compared. Nothing else came close.

Lucien scrubbed his throbbing hand down his face. Throbbing? Yes. It hadn't healed instantly, but remained cut. Dark blue and purple bruises were forming over his knuckles.

You shall weaken, Cronus had warned.

He laughed darkly. No matter what he did, what path he chose, he *would* weaken.

"We'll find it," Anya said softly.

He whipped around. She leaned against the doorframe, a vision in white. Thick white fur coat, skin-tight white pants. White fur boots that climbed up her glorious legs. Pale hair spilled over her shoulders and down her chest. His heart skipped a beat.

She was holding a bundle of white clothing. "You already knew that Cronus approached me yesterday. Well, you were right. He threatened me and that's why I was so mean to you. I didn't want him to know that I was...that I..." She gulped.

"I love you, Anya," he admitted gruffly. "I love you, and I can't—won't—hurt you. Understand?"

Her mouth dropped open and the clothes fell from her arms. "Lucien. I—I—"

"You do not have to say it back. I've come to know you, Anya. You are wild and free and the thought of loving a man terrifies you."

She gazed down at her feet. For the first time, she did not berate herself for it. He was pleased. He wanted her to be comfortable doing anything with him, even that.

"I feel for you what I've never felt for another," she said quietly, "and I'm happiest when I'm with you. Why else would I have hung around when you were doing everything in your power to get rid of me? But love..." She swallowed again, shook her head. "I've spent my entire life trying to keep men at a distance. Somehow you worked your way under my skin, but I *can't* love you." The last was said on a tortured breath.

"I know." She would feel obligated to give up her freedom if she admitted that she loved him. He would not ask it of her. Not now.

"I've been on my own for a long time," she said on a desperate laugh, "and you and I both know just how long I have left. I can't place myself in someone else's keeping."

"I know," he said again.

"I just...I know I don't want you hurt. I...I need time to think."

According to Cronus, Lucien did not have much time. *Soon. The clock is ticking.* Lucien would search for Hydra for however long he had. If he failed to find her, if he failed to win the artifact, he would not fight his fate, he realized then. Had already accepted it, to be honest. He couldn't hurt Anya and couldn't allow Cronus to have the key. If he had to die to ensure her safety, then he would die.

He loved Anya enough to willingly give his life for hers. Without hesitation, without reservation.

He had not been able to give his life for Mariah, but he had wanted to. Had wished for it all these long centuries. Until now. Now he was glad he'd survived. He lived and died for *Anya*. He would regret the past no more; he would not spend another millennium craving something he could not have.

He would enjoy Anya for as long as they could be together.

"Why do I feel so guilty?" Anya whispered, and there was shame in the undercurrents of her voice. "Like I should give Cronus the key?"

There was only one answer: she did indeed love him. His heart swelled with joy and pride. And that was enough for him, knowing she loved him, even if she could not say the words. "You will not give it to him. Promise me. Promise me you will never give it away."

Tears filled her eyes. Minutes passed in silence.

"Promise me, Anya. Give me that peace of mind."

Her lashes were black and spiky, creating a shadow-fan under her ice-blue eyes. Or perhaps, in her anguish, bruises had formed there. Finally she said, "I promise." Then she laughed without humor. "Great. Now I feel even guiltier."

He reached out and sifted strands of her silky hair between his fingers. "You should not feel that way."

"Then how should I feel?" She sniffled.

"Come here," he said, giving the locks a gentle tug.

As she inched forward, her watery gaze landed on his hand. She gripped his wrist, turning over his palm, and frowned. "You're hurt."

"A tiny scratch, nothing more."

She lifted it to her lips and placed a soft kiss directly on the wound. "My poor baby. I don't like to see you hurting."

Electric jolts shot up his arm, hot and hungry. *Oh, yes, he loved this woman.* He traced the shadows with his fingertip, and then their gazes locked. "I would gladly be hacked to pieces to be so ministered to."

"Do you think he can do it? Do you think you'll weaken?" she whispered brokenly, though they both already knew the answer. "You're so strong. You're so vital."

"I will be fine," he lied.

"Maybe I should, I don't know, talk to Cronus or something."

Adamant, he shook his head. "You will not do that, either. He could make things worse."

Sadness couched every beautiful plane and hollow of her face; she remained silent.

"I told you. We will find the artifact."

"You guys coming?" William called, his irritation clear.

"In a minute!" Anya shouted without looking away from Lucien. "You need to get dressed. We can't have you turning into a popsicle, now can we?"

"Not again." He spent the next heartbeat of time memorizing her face, drinking her in and branding her essence onto his every cell. She caressed his cheek all the while, clearly not wanting to leave the room, either.

"I put your gear on the floor," she said.

He chuckled. "I know. I saw you drop everything." He kissed her softly. "I'll see you downstairs."

"Flowers, I—"

"Say no more, sweetheart. We'll find a way to make this work."

A tear finally spilled over, racing down her cheek. "Sweetheart. You called me sweetheart." Without giving him a chance to reply, she disappeared.

But he didn't think she left right away, because he could

still smell strawberries, could still feel her gaze burning into him. Then the skin above his heart tingled, as if she'd just traced an X.

A SULKING WILLIAM HAD refused to allow Lucien to flash him. Instead, the man had a helicopter take them to the coast of Greenland, where mountain met ice and many a human had died, forgotten and alone. The flying deathtrap could not go any farther, and Lucien was glad. He wanted out. The air was so cold, the engine kept sputtering, threatening to freeze.

He could have flashed before plummeting to the ground, so the thought of crashing didn't bother him. The fact that he was not in control bothered him. The fact that his stomach was in his throat bothered him. The fact that Anya's last memories of him might be of him hunched over and vomiting bothered him.

He nearly kissed the snow-covered land when he finally exited.

Three ATVs were already waiting for them, along with backpacks of food and water. William had seen to everything, not that Lucien trusted him. Lucien remained on guard, staying between the warrior and Anya at all times.

They climbed onto the vehicles, and he traded his lack of control for a sense of bleak isolation. An ocean of snow surrounded him. Beautiful, lovely to the extreme, but deadly. Was this how the demon had felt inside Pandora's box? Only instead of vast white there'd been nothing but eternal darkness?

"We can flash this stuff to where we need it," Anya grumbled with a glance at the backpack behind her. Heated breath caused mist to curtain her face. "I don't see why we need to haul its weight around and let it slap us in the ass every time we hit a bump."

"I agree," Lucien said.

"Well, I don't," William griped. "And obviously, you need me, so it's my way or no way."

She flipped him off. Lucien grinned at her show of spirit. Much better than the broken woman who'd left him in the bedroom.

The wind was glacial, so sharp and biting it cut past the thermal bodysuit he wore and all the way to the bone. Already he could feel his blood crystallizing, as if someone were blowing ice directly inside his veins.

"We need to climb to the highest peak," he told William. He'd checked his voice mail before leaving the house and, not surprisingly, he'd missed Torin's call while he and Anya… played. The warrior had left a message, saying he and Ashlyn had researched the area but had found no recent documented sightings of Hydra or any other beast. Too few people traveled up here, it seemed. The best place to look, Torin had advised, was the region's most dangerous area. The less traffic, the more appealing a spot it would be to a creature trying to hide.

"That's the one, then," William said, pointing straight ahead. "And don't try to flash, leaving me behind. You won't reach the top without me since I've left little presents for my…uninvited guests along the way." He paused, tilted his head. "In fact, just get flashing out of your mind, period. Maybe I should have told you earlier, but, well, you irritate me. I can't be flashed anywhere."

"What makes you so sure you cannot be flashed?" Lucien asked.

"Just trust me. Attempting to flash me hurts everyone involved. I made the mistake of rocking Hera's world, so Zeus made sure no goddess would ever be able to flash me to safety. Jealous husbands are dumb. Then Hera found out I was also rocking other goddesses' worlds, and next thing I know, I'm keeping Anya company in the slammer. Some women are more trouble than they're worth." William anchored a helmet on his head and motioned for them to do the same.

Lucien grabbed Anya's and looked it over carefully before he allowed her to do so. She gave him a secret smile before she pulled it on. His nostrils, lungs and chest stung as he donned his own. The crackle of Anya's breathing suddenly filled his ears. There was a headset built into the side, he realized, so they could communicate while they moved. Human technology could be a blessing.

"This is fun," Anya said.

It was as though she was purring straight into his ear, and his blood finally heated, melting the ice.

William cranked up his ATV and started forward. Lucien and Anya followed just a few feet behind.

"Maybe now is a good time to tell you that a group of men entered the circle about…oh, three days ago," William said into the headset. "Doubt they were looking for me."

Lucien didn't have to see his face to know the warrior was grinning with relish. "How do you know?"

"They're human. I don't mess with human women."

"Could it be Hunters?" Anya asked. Through the mask, Lucien could see her eyes blazing with curiosity.

"Most likely," Lucien said. How had they known to venture here, though? Before meeting their demise at the temple, the Hunters had complained about their lack of success.

Perhaps Cronus was somehow feeding them information as the warriors learned it, he speculated. His eyes narrowed in fury. That made sense—and did not bode well for the warriors.

"Where are they now?" he asked.

"Maybe dead." William shrugged. "Maybe on the mountain."

"I thought you monitored this place for jealous husbands," Anya said. "You should know."

"Maybe they disabled my cameras."

Maybe, maybe, maybe.

Anya leaned down—Lucien reached for her, but she maintained her balance—grabbed a handful of ice and threw it at the warrior, nailing him in the back. "Your attitude sucks. This is hardly the way to get your book back."

William continued to motor along without retaliating, almost as if he felt he deserved the chastisement. Snow and ice whipped from the chains and tires of the man's vehicle, blustering around them and making their visibility hazy. His posture was stiff, predatory, as if he expected to be attacked at any moment.

Something was terribly wrong with this situation. What, Lucien could only guess. Sadly, none of his guesses were optimistic.

TIME PASSED SLOWLY considering the sense of urgency pounding through her. Urgency and pain. Anya's ass hurt like hell. The heavy bag strapped to her four-wheeler did indeed slap at her as she'd suspected it would. Gods, she hated this. Hated not knowing the best course of action, hated not being able to read an entire situation. All she knew was that Lucien was the best thing to ever happen to her, William was clearly hiding something and she was miserable.

And if…*when* Lucien began growing weak—*because of me,* she thought guiltily—he would not be able to fight Hydra, even if they found her, placing him in greater danger. So many ifs. But Anya couldn't abide the thought of Lucien being hurt. He loved her. He'd admitted it without shame, without hesitation, and he'd meant it. Tenderness and joy had infused his confession, warming her body and soul. He loved the woman she was, not the woman he wanted her to be.

They had to find Hydra; they just had to. She'd once thought to use the artifacts to bargain for her own life. Now she knew she couldn't do that to Lucien. Instead, she was going to use them to bargain for *his* life.

Cronus would still hunt her, of course, because he would never stop desiring the key. Unless she killed him, which wasn't a bad idea. She might give it a shot, she thought, pursing her lips. After all, who better to murder a king than Anarchy?

Lucien would be pissed if he knew what she was thinking. He wouldn't want her to place herself at risk, no matter that she did so for him. For *them.* But she'd rather deal with his anger than watch him die slowly and painfully.

This is beginning to sound like love.

She shut down the thought before it could spread and deepen. If she admitted that she loved him, she wouldn't be able to resist making love to him. Already she was close to giving in. No matter the consequences. If she gave in, however, and he *did* die, she would be consumed with eternal grief and bound to a dead man. Not even the All-Key could break that tie.

Her stomach lurched with nausea. Her body numbed. No. No, no, no. Never. *He's not going to die. Don't think like that. You're going to do everything in your power to save him.* Besides, she suspected she'd be consumed with eternal grief anyway.

She wanted to reach out and take his hand. She wanted to jump off her ATV and onto his and snuggle in his lap. Wanted to feel his arms around her, holding her close. She didn't. Now was not the time. The stakes were too high.

Later, she promised herself.

As they continued through the snow, she found no hint of human invasion. No footprints or tire tracks. Perhaps the Hunters had already turned back. A girl could hope, anyway. She didn't want them near Lucien.

"Trip wires up ahead," William suddenly warned. "Follow me and don't deviate."

She and Lucien slowed down, getting behind the warrior in a straight line. Anya had the middle and Lucien claimed the rear. Her protector.

"How do you know?" she asked.

"I put them there," he muttered. "A man has to protect himself when immortals are always trying to sneak up on him."

Maybe the Hunters hadn't turned back. Maybe they'd been killed. "Any other little gems you've got waiting out here?"

"Oh, yeah," he said, but he didn't elaborate.

"Like what?" Lucien asked.

Anya could hear the tension in his voice. *He's worried for me, the sweetie.* Again she wanted to jump on him.

"Bombs, poison berries, ice caves," William said. "You know, all the B-movie stuff."

"Nice," Anya said. But her smile at the thought of all that mischief faded as a new thought occurred to her. *What if the Hunters laid a trap for us?*

CHAPTER SEVENTEEN

THEY RAN INTO THE HUNTERS three days later in the middle of the mountain.

Lucien should have been happy about that. There was nothing he liked more than killing those delusional zealots. Well, except for Anya. He liked her more than a good fight. But this time, he wasn't happy. Wasn't excited on any level.

He was weak and only growing weaker.

At the moment, he wasn't sure he could fight a mouse and win, much less a determined Hunter.

He'd known this would happen, but he hadn't expected it so quickly. If the days hadn't been so treacherous and the nights so cold, maybe his strength would have lasted longer. But they'd had to abandon their vehicles yesterday, the incline simply too steep. Now they relied on ice spikes, climbing for hours at a time and resting only when absolutely necessary. They ate one meal a day. They didn't really need more. Canned soup, barely heated. Anya could have flashed, but he suspected she didn't want to leave him.

Every night he, Anya and William stopped and set up camp, Anya conjured a fire and the three of them huddled together in a tent for warmth. He never slept, but stayed awake guarding Anya, cherishing every moment they were together. With mortality creeping up on him, he didn't want to miss a single second. He loved holding her close, her strawberry scent enveloping him.

Both William—bad—and Anya—good—seemed to be thriving, yet he could barely carry his pack anymore. He shivered constantly and had even fallen on his face a few times.

Like now.

Anya's arms suddenly banded around him, holding him steady. "Everything's going to be fine once we get to the top," she said. "You'll see."

Mortification rocked him. He was so weak, he could no longer flash. The demon had tried to pull him into the spirit world a few times, but had been unsuccessful and was constantly clamoring in his head, clawing at the doors of his consciousness, making him crazed.

Death couldn't leave him and travel to the souls on its own, because man and spirit were bonded and could not survive apart. Well, Death could survive, but not happily and not without dire consequences, as Lucien had tried to tell Cronus.

The tip of Lucien's boot hit a block of ice, and he stumbled again. Anya's grip tightened and he was able to right himself. Damn this! Cronus had not exaggerated. At this rate, Lucien would be dead in a week.

"Maybe we should leave him here and continue alone," William suggested.

"No!" he and Anya shouted in unison. He didn't want Anya to go on without him. He still didn't trust William.

"You're slowing us down, Death," William said flatly. "I'm ready to get home to my bloodsuckers and my book."

Death, the warrior had said. Neither he nor Anya had told William that Lucien was possessed by the spirit of Death—only that it was pursuing Anya. Who had told him, then?

"Just leave him alone," Anya snapped. She stopped, forcing William to do the same. Glaring, she launched into a tirade about the warrior needing a curling iron shoved up his ass and flipped to its highest setting.

Lucien suspected she did it to give him a moment to rest. Trying to find his breath, he braced a hand against the icy wall of the mountain ledge. What he hated most about his weakness was his inability to protect his woman. He—

Saw footprints, he realized with a frown.

His entire body tensed. "Anya, be quiet."

She whipped around to face him, surprise darkening her eyes. He hadn't spoken to her like that in days. He had been nothing but gentle with her, treating her as he would a precious treasure. That's what she was. But her safety came before her feelings.

"You did not just tell me to—"

"Hunters," he said, motioning to the ground. He withdrew a dagger from his waist.

Both she and William crowded around him, staring down.

"The prints stop at this wall." Anya frowned and pressed at the ice. "There aren't any prints leading away. Weird. Impossible, even."

"They shouldn't have gotten this far," William said with a frown of his own.

Lucien withdrew another dagger, this one from his boot. He almost dropped it, it seemed so heavy.

"There has to be a door that leads inside," Anya muttered, bending down and feeling for grooves with her gloved hands.

He loved that she didn't run from danger but thought to rush into the midst of it. Yet that scared him, too. This woman was meant to be pampered. Worshipped. Protected. She shouldn't have had to fight for anything; whatever she wanted should have been given to her willingly.

"Found it!" Grinning, she pressed against a crystal rock in the middle of the left side and the ice wall slid open, revealing a darkened doorway.

"How is that possible without my knowledge?" William

was shaking his head. "I knew people were journeying into the circle, but I watched them die. Didn't I? Either way, how could they have made a fucking camp for themselves?" Silver, three-pronged blades slithered from his coat sleeves and he clutched them angrily. "I don't know how many there are, but I'm going to kill them all. Their intentions are not pure; they could have been paid to take me out."

"Your ferocity is a little late," Anya said. "You have to admit that coming out here was a good idea, and you wouldn't have done it without me stealing your book. You can thank me with roses."

William snorted. "What the hell ever."

She turned a concerned gaze to Lucien. "Why don't you wait here, Flowers, and make sure no one else sneaks inside? We'll be back in a little while and—"

He growled low in his throat, his embarrassment intensifying. That she had so little faith in his ability… No. He knew that wasn't true. She was worried for him. Saw his weakness and didn't want him hurt further.

He knew he was feeble, but he wanted her to realize that he would never allow anything to happen to her. No matter the condition of his body.

He would just have to show her.

"I am going in," he said firmly.

"Lucien, you're—"

"Fine. I am fine." He ripped the white cap from his head and tossed it to the ground. He wanted nothing to impede his hearing or his sight. "We will go in with William in the lead," he said, taking charge, "you in the middle and me in the rear." That way she would have a shield in front and behind.

For a moment, it looked like she would argue. Then she pressed her lips together and nodded. "Fine."

"Do you have a gun?" he asked her.

"Only a few daggers." Three of which she already gripped, he noticed proudly. He hadn't seen her grab them.

"Good. That's good."

"Let's go," William said, impatient. "The more time we spend out here, the more time we give them to prepare." He brushed past them and entered the blackened mouth of the cave, determination in every line of his body.

Anya pressed a quick kiss on Lucien's mouth and started forward. He was right on her heels. His eyes quickly adjusted, and he saw the icy walls had been painted with mud to cause the gloomy effect. There wasn't a drip of water, it was simply too cold, and any liquid would turn to ice before it hit bottom, but he did hear the frigid whistle of wind.

Wind? His ears perked. No, not wind, he decided a moment later. The chatter of voices.

"—no closer to finding it and we've been searching for days," a male voice proclaimed.

"The old man said it was here."

Old man…the mythologist?

"We're close. I feel it." Another voice. This one sounded harsher, more determined.

"We'll die out here if we stay much longer." Yet another voice.

So. There were at least three Hunters.

"We can't give up." A fourth, and so far the angriest of the bunch. "The demons must be destroyed. Look at what they did to the people in Budapest. That plague killed hundreds, including many of our own."

"Have the others learned anything from the prisoner?"

Prisoner? He frowned. Who did they have? A Lord? Or other humans?

"Not a damn thing."

The voices were getting closer. Louder. The darkness was

giving way to light as the mud thinned. His grip tightened on the daggers.

"Damn it!" someone cried. "What if this Hydra is only a myth? What if the stupid relic doesn't exist? What if there's nothing out here and we came all the way to this godforsaken place for no reason?"

"Don't talk like that."

William stopped at a corner and held up his hand. Anya stopped, too, and Lucien nearly skated into her, his boots slipping on the ice and his coordination off. She reached back and quietly slapped her hands over his hips, blades pressing into him without cutting, keeping him upright and in place.

His cheeks heated with more embarrassment. And, not surprisingly, arousal. Whenever she touched him, wherever they were, whatever danger was near, he felt those electric tingles. He felt warm. He felt alive.

"The Cage of Compulsion is here," yet another voice said. "It has to be."

The Cage of Compulsion. The words echoed in his mind, followed quickly by another: *enslave.* At the ruins, the human mythologist had told him of a cage that could enslave whoever was imprisoned inside it.

Anya flicked him an excited glance over her shoulder. *We're close!* she mouthed.

He nodded and looked to William, who was scowling.

"If the mythologists can be believed, we can't get to the box without all four artifacts," one of the Hunters said. "That means we don't leave the circle until we have that damn cage."

William held up one finger.

Lucien wasn't sure if that meant "hold" or "attack on three." He'd only ever fought alongside his fellow warriors, and they'd been together so long they usually sensed each other's intentions.

When the immortal raised a second finger, Lucien had his answer. Apparently William did not like when humans invaded his "territory." Lucien drew in a deep breath, barely managing to refrain from jerking Anya behind him. She would resent him if he held her back. More than that, she could defend herself against, well, anyone. She'd proven that many times over.

The soldier in him—hell, the demon in him—recognized her skill, both reveling proudly. The lover in him could not help but continue to fear.

Three.

William lurched forward, blades raised. Anya was right behind him. Lucien's knees almost gave out as he surged after her. She could take care of herself, yes, but he was still her man and would do what he could.

A deafening roar resounded from William, and the Hunters jumped to their feet. In the center, ice cracked. There was a shout, a scream of terror and outrage at being discovered. Eight humans altogether, Lucien counted as they rushed forward.

William quickly stabbed three, one after the other, the action fluid, a lethal dance, his blades slicing forward, back and to the side with grace. Anya dispatched two, flashing to one, slicing his throat, then flashing to another before the human ever realized what was happening.

A bullet whizzed past Lucien's shoulder, close enough to graze his skin. Space was limited, and Lucien blocked the only exit. As two ran to him, gasping "Demon" and clearly intending to plow him down and escape, he spun and stabbed, spun and stabbed. Both Hunters collapsed to the ground, red pooling around them.

Someone managed to squeeze off another shot, and this one did more than graze. This one lodged in his stomach. Despite the pain, he didn't fall. He stood his ground. For Anya.

A fire blazed in the room's center, crackling and emitting delicious heat. One of the Hunters grabbed a scorching log and swung it at her. She jumped out of the way, but not before a flame sizzled over her coat, burning fabric and probably blistering her delicate skin.

She cried out in fury.

A red haze fell over Lucien, one word filling his mind: *Kill.* He lurched forward, no longer feeling the pain in his stomach. *Kill. Kill!* He had the man's neck in his hands in the next instant, not caring that the human was slapping him or that the flames were licking his clothing, his flesh.

He twisted with all of his might.

Bones snapped, and the man stilled. The crackling stick fell from the Hunter's suddenly limp hand, though the fire still licked at Lucien. He wanted to kill the man all over again. He even dropped the body and stabbed his dagger into the man's heart, again and again.

"Mine," he snarled. "Do not touch what is mine."

More. Kill more. He turned to the Hunters left standing— only to see that there were no Hunters left standing. They were dead, all of them. Lucien was panting as his sights slid to William, who was covered in blood and bending over one of the bodies, searching it. *Kill, kill, kill.*

"Lucien, you're on fire!"

Anya's voice penetrated his mind, shattering the death-craze, and he settled. She was all right. Unharmed. Alive. He drew in a calming breath as soft hands settled over his shoulders, patting him down. "I'm here, baby. I'm here."

His knees buckled, weakness suddenly slamming into him again. He hit the ground and cold seeped into him.

"You're going to be okay, lover," she continued to coo. "You're going to be okay. Say it. Tell me you're going to be okay."

"Okay." He felt the burn all the way inside him. He'd felt this way before, when he'd torched himself out of grief for Mariah. He had cried then; he smiled now. Anya was with him. Black winked in and out of his vision, the red haze completely gone.

"Lucien."

Anya. His sweet Anya. He realized he didn't have to fear his temper around her. He could let go completely with her. Being near her always managed to soothe the demon and his own dark thoughts in ways nothing and no one else ever had.

"Close your eyes, baby. I'll take care of everything."

His eyelids obeyed of their own accord. *Stay awake. Don't leave Anya alone with William.*

"Sleep."

Once again, he couldn't help but obey.

ANYA GAZED AT LUCIEN as he slept.

"He may not even live out the rest of the night," William said with an unconcerned shrug, never pausing as he searched the Hunters' bodies. What he was looking for, Anya didn't know.

She nearly flashed to him and stabbed him. Only the need to be near Lucien held her in place and saved William's life. "Don't talk like that. He's going to be fine."

"What's wrong with him, anyway? Isn't he supposed to be immortal? Every time I look at him, he's weaker."

"Fucking Cronus cursed him." *I deserve a slow and painful death for allowing things to reach this point. Me, not Lucien.* She hated seeing him like this.

"Why?"

"The god king is a bastard. That's why."

William looked from her to the sleeping Lucien, from Lucien to her. "Well, if I were you I'd go to the Big Guy and beg. Otherwise, your man is going to eat dirt for eternity."

"I told you not to talk like that," she snapped. She stared down at Lucien, remembering the way he'd jumped to her defense. All because she'd been burned. A burn that hadn't even reached her skin. Her heart skipped a beat. He'd erupted for her, and she was letting him suffer for it.

His breathing was labored, his skin charred. *What kind of woman am I?* Despicable, that's what. Not worthy of this man and his precious love. But even so, she couldn't live without him.

She loved him.

There. She'd finally admitted it. He was everything to her, and she couldn't imagine a single moment without him. Didn't *want* to imagine a moment without him. He was joy and he was passion. He was complex and honorable, sweet and tender, and the part of her that had always been missing.

She would have given Cronus the key then and there, but knew she would lose Lucien if she did so. She would not remember him, and she *needed* the memory of him. He was more a part of her than the key.

She was going to make love with him. Willingly. Without hesitation. Her eyes widened with the realization. Yes. That's exactly what she'd do. Maybe bonding with him would give him some of *her* strength, melding them body and spirit. Even the slightest chance overshadowed her fear of her curse.

Right now Lucien was unconscious, covered in blood and bruises and that blackened skin. One of the Hunters had managed to cut him across the forearm and shoot him in the stomach and neither wound was healing. Both were dripping blood all over the ice.

"I'm going to take him back to your house," she told William. "The search for Hydra will have to wait until his wounds are tended."

"Hell, no." The warrior jerked upright and scowled over at her. "You're not welcome at my house anymore."

"Well, you're going to have to find a way to flash there and drag me out because I'm going with or without your permission."

"I'll retaliate!"

"Don't forget who has your book, and that I wouldn't mind tossing it in a nice toasty fire," she warned, lying next to Lucien. She wound her arms around him, holding him as close as possible.

"Like I'd forget," William grumbled. "Fine. Go to my house. The vamps'll take one look at his wounds and make a meal of him. Or maybe I'll find Hydra while you're gone. Maybe I'll bribe her to eat you and spit out your bones."

"Just for that, I'm ripping ten pages out of the book before I give it back." Anya flashed the still-sleeping Lucien into the warm bedroom they'd shared only a few days ago, rolled him to his back and began cutting the clothes from his injured body.

CHAPTER EIGHTEEN

PARIS STARED AT THE PADDED white wall, his vision blurry, his mind foggy. He knew he'd been stripped and strapped to another table. He knew he hadn't had sex in days. But he didn't even have the strength to lift his head anymore. He'd been poked and prodded, and the Hunters had even sent in a blonde to arouse him so they could watch how the demon operated, but he hadn't been able to get hard for her.

This had happened only once before.

Long ago, immediately after his possession, he'd reached this point of desperation. He'd reached this point of weakness. Too feral for any mortal woman to approach, he'd been forced to accept the first person willing to fuck him.

He'd vowed never to let such a thing happen again.

He didn't want a male Hunter giving him strength. All he could think about was the brunette with the freckles. Sienna. He'd finally remembered her name and it was now branded into his every cell. If he couldn't have her, he just wanted to die. Somehow, some way, and for reasons he didn't understand—or perhaps didn't *want* to understand—she'd entranced the demon.

No other would do.

Why? Little Sienna had lied to him and betrayed him, drugged him and locked him up, but still he wanted to fuck her. Wanted her wet for him and only him. Wanted his name roaring past her lips and pleasure consuming her face.

Afterwards, he wanted the demon to enslave her, to make her so mad with lust for him that she would do anything he asked. Follow him wherever he went. Even beg him for another touch. He would deny her, of course, unable to take her again. And so she would suffer with her desires. He would laugh.

He might even fuck another woman in front of her.

Just the thought made him grin. Paris wanted her to suffer as he was suffering. He'd never wanted or hated a woman more, and both were only growing with every moment he spent inside this padded room.

All he had to do to make his dream a reality was convince the Hunters to send her to him. How, though? The answer seemed just out of his reach.

"What should we do with him now?" someone asked.

Paris closed his eyes, the lids so heavy he could no longer hold them up. There had been a parade of doctors in the room, but he was past the point of caring who came and went.

"At this rate, he'll be dead in a few days. Then he's no good to us, and the demon will escape him, terrorizing the world. *That* mistake was made once already. We can't allow it to happen again. No telling what catastrophes Promiscuity would cause. Rapes, the breakup of every marriage in the world, a rise in STDs and teen pregnancies."

"If nothing more, we have to keep him alive until we figure out how to contain that demon."

A pause. Then a sigh. "Sienna's the only one he's ever even spoken to and the only person he's remotely responded to."

Sienna's image flashed inside his mind. Mousy hair, plain features. Pale, freckled skin. A body so thin she barely had breasts. His cock twitched, though, showing the first sign of life in days. Delicate hands…soft lips…all over his body.

"Did you see that?" one of the men remarked. *"Sienna."*

His cock moved again.

"Go get her. Now."

"Are you sure? She's—"

"Get her."

Footsteps suddenly reverberated. There was the slide of a door.

Were they going to bring Sienna to him? Have her suck him off or welcome him into her body? Either way... He almost smiled. He hadn't had to say a thing. They were simply giving him what he'd wanted, gift-wrapped with a bow on top. Perhaps he'd used his gift of projection to touch their minds and just didn't know it. Perhaps his desire for her was *that* strong.

Would she actually do it or would she refuse?

No, she wouldn't refuse, he thought, excitement pushing past his fatigue. He wouldn't let her. Whatever he had to do, whatever he had to say, she would be his.

Afterward, he would escape—and he would take her with him. Until this, he'd never been one for revenge. He loved women. They were his life's blood. For Sienna, however, he was going to make an exception. He would... Darkness shrouded over his mind, cutting off his thoughts.

He must have fallen asleep, because the next thing he knew, warm fingertips were moving over his chest, bringing an electric tingle that jolted through him.

"Hello, Paris," he heard, and the words alone offered more pleasure, more strength, than he'd experienced in days.

How much time had passed, he didn't know. He only knew that when he pried his eyes open, Sienna was hovering over him, hazel eyes unsure. She'd taken off her glasses. The room was dimmed, not bright like it usually was, surrounding her in shadows.

But he could see that she was dressed exactly as she'd been before: baggy, bland clothing and hair pulled into a severe twist. She exuded a vulnerability he wanted to exploit as she jerked her hand away from him.

She wrung her fingers together in apparent nervousness.

"Come to pleasure me, did you?" he sneered before he could stop himself.

Her cheeks pinkened, and she looked away. "If you'd rather have someone else, I can leave."

"You'll do," he said, and breath hitched in her throat. He hoped his words hurt her. He hoped she hurt for a long, long time. "You realize this makes you their whore, right? Screwing a man for your friends, for a cause, for money even, since I'm sure you're on their payroll." *Shut up! Don't push her away.*

Her lips thinned as she eyed him again and whatever she saw on his face made her already fair skin pale. Once more, she lowered her gaze. This time, however, she began to back away. "I wouldn't have come if I wasn't attracted to you."

"A Hunter attracted to a Lord. How sad for you."

There was a heavy pause.

Just shut the hell up, man. Before you make her leave. You need her body, not her anger—not yet. "I'm sorry," he forced himself to say. "Sienna."

Shock parted her lips and she gasped, gaze flicking to him, staying. "You know my name."

"Of course. Like you, I'm attracted. Despite everything." Sadly, that was not a lie. Stupid demon.

She was shaking as she changed her direction and approached him. There was true desire in her hazel eyes, just as there had been the first time he'd seen her. Paris could feel his dick hardening, rising for her. Still a little vindictive, he tried to stop it. The situation was dangerous, but he wanted to make her work for it.

She reached his bed, stopped and licked her lips.

"Unchain me," he croaked out.

"I was told not to," she replied softly.

"Are they watching?"

She shook her head. "I asked them to turn off the cameras, and they agreed."

So naive she was, he found himself thinking again. He nearly rolled his eyes. No way would Hunters have willingly denied themselves the opportunity to observe the likes of him in action. They were watching. He didn't like the thought of them seeing Sienna pleasure him, but he would deal.

"Unchain me, then. They'll never know."

"I…can't."

Well, it had been worth a try. "So what are you waiting for, Sienna? Let's finish what we started at the café."

REYES HADN'T NEEDED AERON'S location e-mailed to him. The bodies left a trail. Death and destruction accompanied Wrath everywhere he traveled and that saddened Reyes, because he knew if Aeron had been in his right mind, he would have been disgusted with himself.

As I am with myself.

For years Reyes had hovered near moral collapse, hating himself for the things he had to do to appease his demon. Killing innocents, torturing, destroying entire cities. This was the worst, though, following his friend, a man he loved like a brother. A man who had once helped him learn to control the monster inside him. Because… Reyes swallowed bile. Because he'd decided to kill the obsessed warrior.

I'm more demon than man, that I could contemplate this act, he thought darkly, but didn't change his mind. He'd known it would come to this, choosing between Aeron and Danika. He'd always thought he'd choose his friend. Now, when the decision was upon him, he knew that for the lie it was.

He couldn't abide the thought of Danika being hurt. She

was the only thing in the world that gave him pleasure, though she'd never even touched him. He didn't deserve her; she probably wouldn't want him, anyway, but he was going to save her.

Hurry. Find her, get to her.

How? he almost screamed. Reyes was in the States, New York City to be exact, and Aeron's signal was beeping from his phone as if the warrior were flying overhead. But Reyes didn't see or hear him. No flap of wings, no animalistic roar.

All day, news stations had run somber stories of unexplained and violent deaths, of bodies ravaged by claws and teeth that didn't belong to a human. Now Reyes stood on a crowded street, cars honking behind him, people milling along the sidewalk beside him.

Had Aeron already found her? Was he finally sleeping, relaxed and at ease after a month of constant bloodlust?

Reyes barely resisted the urge to grab a mortal and shake, demand, roar.

A body suddenly fell from the night sky, plopping on the ground in front of him. A man. A human. Bloody. Dead. Several people gasped. Some screamed. Muscles tensing, Reyes lifted his gaze skyward. Finally, he caught sight of Aeron, who was grinning down at him tauntingly, wings flapping furiously toward one particular building.

Reyes locked his eyes on his friend—his target—and leapt into motion.

DO I HAVE WHAT IT TAKES to kill?

Danika Ford stared at herself in the dented and chipped bathroom mirror. She'd once considered herself an artist, a painter of—mostly—beautiful things. Everything she'd looked at had been fodder for her art. People: the turn of a wrist, the elegant slope of a back. Animals: fluidity and grace. Flowers: delicate petals and sensual colors.

Now she considered herself a fighter. A survivor.

A—she gulped—killer.

She had to be.

Just over a month ago, she'd been kidnapped while on vacation in Budapest and held hostage by six hulking giants who'd wanted to kill her. They hadn't, though. They hadn't even hurt her, actually, but she'd never felt so helpless, so out of control and desperate. And she refused to feel that way again.

Ever.

Those giants were after her once more; she knew it. Which was why she changed her location every few days. No matter where she was staying, though, she found someone to train her in hand-to-hand combat. She also trained with knives, with guns, with anything she could get her hands on.

Today her newest instructor had knocked her on her ass and told her she lacked the killer instinct required to survive in a life-or-death situation.

Several hot tears rolled down her cheeks now, and she slammed her fist into the glass. It shook but didn't break. *Am I so feeble?* Maybe her instructor was right. And he didn't even know the half of it. One of her kidnappers, Reyes, still plagued her dreams. She didn't want to hurt him, dark, sensual man that he was. She wanted to kiss him, to finally know his taste, to finally feel his strong arms around her.

Every night she dreamed of him.

"I'm a sick woman."

She stomped to her tiny rented bedroom, fell onto the mattress and picked up her disposable cell. Once she'd lived in a nice, average middle-class apartment, content, comfortable. Now she moved from shacks to motels to cardboard boxes to cars, poor and terrified, constantly looking over her shoulder.

Needing some reassurance, peace, *something,* she dialed her mother's own disposable cell number. Her entire family was in hiding—the four women separated to make the men's search more difficult—but they left their new numbers with friends and made sure to talk every day.

Her mom answered on the third ring, a sobbing rasp that instantly raised bile to the top of Danika's throat. "What's wrong?" she rushed out.

"It's your grandmother…she's…she's…oh, God, baby."

She was dead. Her grandmother was dead. "Murdered?" she managed to get out.

"I don't know. I can't find her, haven't heard from her. She seems to have disappeared for good. I've been so worried about you." Her mother sobbed, hiccupped.

Had Danika been standing, she would have collapsed. Rage skittered through her, even shuttered over her eyes. Rage and a strange kind of numbness, like she was standing in the middle of a dream and only needed to wake up. Wake up so that everything would be okay.

"You have to hide, baby. Please. I can't lose you, too."

Glass shattered in another room.

Danika gasped, snapping out of that numbing rage, her heart missing a beat and squeezing painfully.

"What's wrong?" her mom demanded.

"I think they found me," she whispered on a trembling breath. "Hide, Mom. Wherever you are, run and hide. I love you." Fighting terror-induced paralysis, she dropped the phone and stood to stiff legs. Oh, God. Her grandmother was most likely dead, and now she had been found. Weaponless. *You knew better. Think, think!* Legs shaking, stomach churning, she raced back into the bathroom and reached for the razor she kept on the sink.

Through the open door she could see a tall, muscled man stalk through the hallway, his wings scraping against the walls like fingers over a chalkboard. She nearly collapsed. Aeron. Aeron had found her. She remembered him well. His violent tattoos, his piercing gaze. If Reyes haunted her dreams, Aeron embodied her nightmares. He wasn't human, could fly like the dragons of myth, and was as fierce and deadly as any warrior of legend.

He paused in front of the bathroom doorway, sniffed the air. Blood spattered his face and stained his hands. Her grandmother's?

Do something! Danika shocked herself by lunging for him, razor swinging for his throat. *No killer instinct?* She slashed at his jugular. If she failed to kill him, he would be free to attack her mother and sister—and that she wouldn't allow. *Contact.* Fresh blood instantly poured from the wound.

He didn't go down. He didn't fucking go down!

He turned toward her, grasping his neck and growling. His eyes blazed with red fire, and his teeth were elongated and snapping at her.

She held up the now-dripping razor. "Want some more? Bastard!" she screamed. "Come and get it!"

"Kill," he roared. He grabbed her hair, jerking her forward.

Her nose smacked into his chest. A scream bubbled in her throat, but she quickly cut it off. *First rule of combat: stay calm.*

She allowed her legs to slacken and he lost his hold on her hair, several strands ripping free. She rolled to her back, curled her body and slammed her feet up and into his stomach. He stumbled backward with a hiss and smacked into the coffee table. Wood and glass shattered. He fell.

Always go for the throat, her instructor said in her mind. *Best way to render them helpless.* Eyes slitted, Danika climbed to her knees, closed the distance between them and punched him in the throat—right where she'd cut him—opening the wound further.

Rage built inside her to a desperate degree, and she punched him again.

He growled at her with those teeth so sharp they gleamed. "Kill. Kill, kill, kill."

"Fuck you." Punch. Dear God. She could see the outline of something under his face. Something…dangerous, evil. A skeleton, a demon. It snarled at her, a bony mask of hate and darkness.

"Kill."

She tried to punch him again, but he grabbed her hand and squeezed. That was it, just a simple squeeze, yet she felt some of the bones snap. A cry of pain escaped her.

And then, from the corner of her eye, she saw Reyes burst through the front door and rush into the room. He was a blur of dark hair, dark skin and dark, furious eyes. His daggers were raised and he was panting, sweating.

"Reyes!" she shouted as Aeron stood, driving her to her back as he continued to squeeze her hand. Part of her wanted to sag in relief. Part of her wanted to run from him, too.

You can't rely on him. He helped kidnap you.

He saw her and froze. "Danika." He gasped her name with such reverence she was nearly felled.

Think of your mother. Your sister. She arched up and kicked Aeron in the jaw. Finally he released her hand. God, the pain. Her fingers were limp; she couldn't move them, the joints already swollen as though she'd stuffed golf balls under her skin.

Aeron backhanded her, and she flew to the side, entire body vibrating in pain. Her teeth rattled together; her mind blinked in and out of focus. Reyes howled and attacked. The two men grappled to the floor in a tangled heap beside her. Aeron slashed with claws and teeth, Reyes with his daggers. They roared and they cursed and they snarled.

Blinking in an effort to orient herself, Danika pushed to her feet. Swayed, almost vomited.

"Run," Reyes shouted to her.

She stumbled forward, only managing to pick up speed when she reached the outside hallway. Why Reyes was helping her, she didn't know. Would he die in there?

Tears burned her eyes as she ran.

CHAPTER NINETEEN

THE PARTS OF LUCIEN'S SKIN not charred were tinted blue or painted red. And though he'd been burned like the marshmallow in the middle of a s'more, he was shivering from cold.

Concerned, Anya commanded a fire to start in the hearth. Instantly the flames leapt over the logs, crackling. Waves of heat wafted through the spacious room, yet Lucien's shivering only seemed to increase. *Don't panic. Stay calm.*

She'd never felt so helpless. Not in prison, and not with a determined Aias on top of her.

She quickly stripped, removed her spiked boots and climbed onto Lucien's battered body, running her hands over him to heat him. When she encountered the bullet wound, her throat constricted. She'd known it was there, had simply hoped it would have healed by now. Because of Cronus and *her,* it hadn't.

After hopping up, grabbing her shirt and ripping it in two, she climbed back onto the bed and bound Lucien's side. "Come on, Flowers. Warm up for me."

He didn't respond.

He was a block of blackened ice. Just being near him, her nipples hardened like rocks and goose bumps broke out over her skin. And for once those weren't symptoms of arousal. She pulled the covers around them to hold the heat captive, then spent the next hour simply talking to him in an effort to distract and soothe them both.

"You need to get well. Life would be totally boring without you. And baby, bad things happen when I get bored. Did I ever tell you about the time I dressed up like a teenager and attended high school for a few months? I'd been bored out of my mind for decades and when the idea hit me, I just decided to go for it. Food fights, catfights, turning on the sprinkler system at prom."

She paused, hoping for a response. Nothing.

"I wasn't naughty all the time, though," she continued. "You would have been proud. This dumb jock got a cute little nerd who worshipped the ground he walked on pregnant, then called her a slut, a whore, a skank—you know, all the names promiscuous men like to call women. Anyway, I'd once vowed never to put a curse upon another person. They suck, as you and I both know. But I cursed him with a raging hard-on, I just couldn't help myself. Nothing he did made it go away."

Lucien's body finally began to relax, his shivering easing, and he uttered a…chuckle?

Taking heart, she rushed on. "Once I attended a masked ball and dressed as the devil. Doesn't sound like a big deal, but the year was eighteen-nineteen and I created quite a stir, let me tell you. When I asked Baron something-or-other to sell me his soul, he tried to stab me with a butter knife."

Lucien moaned. "Anya."

Oh, thank gods. "It's going to be okay, baby. I'm here, I'm here." She kissed his clammy temple.

His eyelids cracked open. "Anya?"

"Right here, love." She kissed his jaw, continuing to run her hands over him. Now, however, her sole purpose was not to warm him. She needed to awaken his desire because she needed his cooperation for what she was about to do.

"Where are we?" He gazed around the room, his eyes glassy.

She didn't want him thinking. Not about their surroundings, not about what had happened in the cave and not about the future. He was too honorable and if lucid enough he might push her away. He would rather she keep her freedom than bind herself to him, even though it might give him the strength he needed.

"I love you," she whispered straight into his ear, her warm breath caressing. "I love you so much. And that I almost lost you…I can't bear it."

"Gods, Anya. I never thought to hear you say those words." His arms enfolded her in a hug, pulling her as close as he could get her. When her head rubbed against his decimated skin, he hissed.

"I'm sorry." She eased to the side. "So sorry."

"Say it again."

She knew what he wanted. "I love you, Lucien, and I want to be with you. In every way imaginable." She rose on her elbow and stared down at him. "Do you understand what I'm telling you?"

Weak though he still was, his shaft swelled against her thigh, long and thick and proud. He understood. "Anya…"

She meshed their lips together, not giving him time to protest. Her tongue stroked his, soaking in his masculinity. "Mmm," she moaned. She encircled his cock with strong fingers, stroking that too.

He groaned.

"Hurt?"

"Feels so good." He gripped her ass and pulled her on top of him again, some of her energy already seeping into him. The heady scent of roses enveloped the room. Then, suddenly, he stopped. His fingers became vises on her hips. "No, Anya. We can't do this."

"We can. We will." She strummed her fingers over the head of his penis, and he jolted at the sensation. "One way or another, I'm going to have you inside of me. Tonight."

Teeth bared, he arched into her touch. "Can't. Wrong for you."

"I'll decide what's right and wrong for me." She bit his earlobe and tugged. "Don't make me beg for you. Don't make me beg to feel you sliding inside of me, deep and hard and hot. Please don't—"

"Anya!" he roared. His hand tangled in her hair, and he jerked her down for another scorching kiss. "Don't beg. Don't stop."

Their tongues battled, their teeth scraped together, and she rubbed herself against him, for the first time in her life completely unconcerned by the thought of being penetrated. She wanted it. Desperately.

Need pounded through her. Need for this man and no other. It was a dark hunger inside her, carnal and savage, almost chaotic, definitely delicious. "I want to be with you forever."

"Yes, yes. Yes!" In between words, he nipped fiercely at her lips. "We won't go all the way."

He tried to sit up, but she pushed him down. "Yes, we *are* going all the way. Now let me do all the work, lover. You just concentrate on regaining your strength."

His eyes blazed up at her. "All I can think about is you. I need your nipple in my mouth."

"And so you shall have it." She rose up and offered him what he wanted. He sucked on it, flicking his hot tongue over the turgid tip. She felt the draw of his suction between her legs, felt moisture pool there like liquid fire.

"Let me taste you." His fingers glided between her legs, and she quivered. "Right here."

Clitoris throbbing for more attention, she climbed the rest of the way up and straddled his head. His tongue licked her, and she arched into his face. Every nerve ending in her body rejoiced. Every drop of blood in her veins sang.

"Lean forward, sweetheart. I want to finger you, too, but I won't. I—"

"You *will*."

He paused, squeezed her tightly. "Tell me again that you're sure. There's no going back after this."

"I'm sure," she said as she obeyed his command, wanting what he wanted. Her ass was lifted, her elbows braced on the headboard, and Lucien sank a finger all the way inside her. She didn't feel the curse kick in at all, but she nearly came. She did cry out. Having a man be part of her, even in such a small way, while having his mouth suck at her, was the most erotic sensation she'd ever encountered. "Oh, gods."

"Like?"

"*Love.*"

"More?"

"Oh, please."

Another finger joined the first, stretching her. His tongue never stopped working her clit. The decadence. The magnificence. Her hips were writhing of their own accord. She couldn't have stopped them upon threat of death. He'd pleasured her before, but this, oh, this…

"Lucien, Lucien," she chanted. Her head fell back, hair tickling her back. "Love you. So much."

"Can you take me? All of me?"

"Yes. Please." She gasped in bliss. Lightning shivers danced through her.

"I have to be inside you." His voice was rough, scratchy. "To the hilt." He pulled from her and tugged her down.

She mourned the loss of his naughty fingers until the tip of his erection found the opening of her sheath. He gripped her, holding her steady. She stared down at him, her hair a pale curtain around them.

"You are mine," he said, peering up at her, gazes locking together. He caressed her cheek.

"Always."

"I love you."

"I love you so much." He looked so beautiful to her. Still cut and bruised from battle, still a little weak but fueled by desire. For her.

"Sure you want this?"

"More than anything." And she did. She belonged to this man, now and forever.

"Mine," he said again, and surged all the way inside her.

A white light erupted between them, powerful, nearly blinding in its intensity. Anya cried out as her curse was unleashed, a sound that blended with Lucien's roar. She felt as if part of her soul had been ripped from deep inside and replaced with…a part of Lucien's?

Yes, yes. Lucien. Dark, savage. Wonderful, amazing. Purring inside her mind. There was a sharp ache between her legs, too, gone as quickly as it arrived, and then he was buried deep, so deep, and she was riding him. Slowly at first, savoring every new sensation. Then faster…faster…

"Good?" he managed to croak.

"Don't stop. Don't stop!"

"Never."

She twined their hands and pinned them over his head, leaning down and taking his breath, making him more a part of her. Making him every part of her. Sex was so much more than she'd ever imagined—and gods, had she imagined—because it was with Lucien.

I'm glad I waited. So glad.

Giving herself to him was not a curse, it was a blessing.

"Worth the wait," she told him, then delved her tongue into his mouth.

Their tongues battled in sync with their lower bodies. Pumping, pounding, sliding. The pleasure was building inside her, intense and combustible. He was so big, so thick and hard. So hers.

Almost there. So good, so good. The piece of heaven on earth she'd always craved. Filled completely, no longer empty. Part of something far greater than herself as he rocked inside her. "Lucien," she screamed, suddenly climaxing.

Everything inside her shattered, the most intense orgasm of her life ripping through her. She shuddered, her muscles clenching deliciously and locking down on his cock.

And as her inner walls milked him, he came, spurting inside her hotly. "Anya," he roared. "My Anya." He raised his hips, slamming as high and deep as he could possibly go.

Another climax immediately caught fire and raged through her, making her mindless for seconds, an eternity, drenching her in satisfaction, triumph and joy. Lucien was hers, truly hers, and she was his.

They were bonded, and she was glad.

As her spasms faded, she collapsed on top of him, a single thought registering in her mind: his skin was no longer black and blue, but tan and healthy.

She was grinning as she fell asleep.

LUCIEN DOZED ON AND OFF for several hours, a sleeping, sated Anya never far from his side, even when Death called him into the spirit realm. Lucien took Anya with him, cuddled in his arms. She hadn't awakened, though she'd managed to remain on her feet with him as her anchor. He thought perhaps she was truly relaxed for the first time in thousands of years, no longer worried about being attacked, captured or raped, and was finally catching up on her sleep.

Right now they were back in bed and one of his hands

cupped her breast, the other draped over her stomach. For the first time in his life, he was utterly content, at peace. He wanted to stay here forever. *Hold* her forever. To protect her, however, he could do neither.

He planned to contact the other warriors, tell them about Anya and instruct them to care for her if he failed to find the Cage of Compulsion in time. How he hated the word. *Failed.* It meant Cronus still had power over him. Meant he would die. Something he was prepared and willing to do, though he did not want Anya grieving eternally for him.

"We have to go back to the mountain," he said, the words echoing through the room.

Lucien's chest constricted as Anya moaned and her eyelids slowly opened. "Not yet," she grumbled, her voice sleep-rich and sexy.

"We must. No telling what William is doing up there. You have his book. He might be looking for a way to hurt you."

Rumpled and groggy, she inched up, silky hair tumbling down her bare shoulders. Gods, he loved her. For her sake, he should have pushed her away. He should not have penetrated that tight, hot sheath. But he could not make himself regret it. She'd given herself to him freely, completely.

"You're right, no telling what he's doing." Anya stretched like a contented cat. Buried under the thick covers as they were, their skin was slicked with sweat and she slid against him. "How do you feel?" she asked huskily.

"Better. The bullet popped out and the hole closed." He caressed her cheek. "Thank you for the gifts of your love and your body."

"Oh, anytime."

"Are you sorry?" What if she had bound herself to his demon, as well? Gods. The thought horrified him.

"Hell, no!" She rolled onto her stomach, folded her arms

and rested her cheek on her wrist. She peered over at him, more love than he'd ever seen in the blue depths of her eyes. "I'm, like, crazy-happy. That was absolutely, utterly, unbelievably, I'm-king-of-the-world amazing. But I know what you're thinking, and you can stop. Your demon can't get enough of me, and I have a thing for bad boys. Sure we don't have time for one more round? We could have a three-way. You, me and the demon."

What had he ever done to deserve her? "I am sure."

Pouting, she lumbered out of bed to dress. "Well, for future reference we need to get it on at least twice a day."

"No. That, I will not agree to. We must get it on four times a day."

That earned a soft chuckle from her.

Enchanted, he sat up. "Have you ever seen the Cage of Compulsion?"

As she tugged on her pants—surely it was a crime to cover such beautiful legs—she said, "No, but if I'm remembering my history lessons correctly, Cronus had Hephaistos the blacksmith make it for him because he had heard rumors of a coming insurrection and hoped to force battle plans and truths out of the beings he placed inside."

Lucien frowned as he considered her words. "Such an item hardly seems likely to aid a search for Pandora's box."

"Well, whoever is locked inside it is compelled to obey the command of its owner. I can only assume we're supposed to trap someone inside it and command them to tell us something. Maybe Hydra herself."

He pondered that for a moment, his frown deepening. "If you were locked inside and the owner commanded you to kill yourself…"

"First of all, no one can lock me inside of anything because of my…" She paled, guilt filling her eyes.

He didn't want her feeling guilty about keeping the key. "Anya."

"Yes," she added with much less enthusiasm. "Without the key, yes, I would be forced to kill myself, unable to stop the action."

His hands fisted on the covers. He didn't like the sound of this cage. He liked the idea of Cronus regaining possession of it even less. What else could he use to bargain for Anya's life, though?

Anya smiled at him, a little sad, as if she sensed his turmoil. Yes, she could, he realized a moment later, because *he* could suddenly feel *her* inner fear that he was not as healthy-looking as he'd appeared last night.

The bonding must allow them to sense each other's emotions. He even thought, if he tried, he would be able to read her mind.

"Up and at 'em, sexy," she said with false cheer, just before flashing away.

He tensed. "Anya?" Where had she gone? And *why* had she gone? "Anya!"

Just as he was gearing up to track her down, she reappeared. She was holding a bundle of clothing, which she threw at him. "I know where William keeps his weapons. Want a few?"

Lucien relaxed and nodded.

She blinked at him in surprise. "Really? We'll be stealing."

The corners of his mouth edged into a smile. "I have found that I do not mind that so much."

"Right on, Flowers!" She gave him another grin, all hint of sadness gone, and he once more felt as though he'd conquered the world. "I must say, your miseducation is coming along nicely."

"That's because my tutor is a strong and courageous

woman and I will do anything to please her." He quickly dressed and stood next to her, hating even the smallest distance. "She is everything to me, and her happiness is my happiness."

Expression suddenly serious, Anya rose on her tiptoes and pressed a soft kiss to his lips. "Don't worry, lover. Everything really will be okay."

Such assurance frightened him, because he knew it meant she was planning something. Something guaranteed to save him. Something foolish and reckless, like giving up the All-Key. She would weaken, like him. She would lose her powers, becoming vulnerable, trapped. He almost allowed himself to try to sweep into her mind, divine her thoughts, but stopped. She had willingly bound herself to him, and he would not betray her for it. Would not try to control her as the curse had intended.

"Anya," he said, grabbing hold of her shoulders and shaking. "You promised me you would never—"

"Let's go get those weapons," she interjected with another of those too-bright smiles. She disappeared a moment later, leaving him with nothing but air.

CHAPTER TWENTY

ANYA SHOWED LUCIEN WHERE William kept his weapons and together they liberated a machete, a hatchet and several bejeweled daggers. All while she kept up a steady chatter so that he wasn't given a chance to mention the All-Key again. When they finished, she materialized in the very cave she'd left the warrior in, Lucien hot on her heels.

Though she was dressed in her thermals and her coat, icecold air instantly assaulted her. Damn, she'd acclimated to the warmth; her body was no longer prepared for the chill. She shivered, her gaze locking on Lucien. His color was better, and he could stand without toppling over now, but there were shadows under his eyes and stress lines around his mouth.

He still wasn't operating at full strength, and that worried her. What's more, he thought he was going to die. Earlier, she'd *heard* the thought echo in his mind. She'd nearly burst into tears like a pitiful human.

"The cave is empty," Lucien said, his shock clear.

Not only was it empty, it was clean, as if no one had ever been there. As if fighting and death had not taken place. Dread curled through her, blending with her already-raw emotions. "Where do you think William is?"

"Either heading home or on his way to the top."

"Let's see if he's at the top, shall we?" She withdrew the mask she'd stuffed in her pocket and tugged it over her face, then flashed to the crest of the mountain, momentarily stunned by the abrupt change in temperature and light. The cave had been cold, but this…this was misery. Ice and frost formed in her nose and lungs; her blood turned to slush. Wind whipped, cutting like tiny knives. There was only the barest trace of golden moonlight, painting the rugged peaks with an ethereal hue.

Lucien…had not arrived yet, she realized.

She frowned, looking all around. She saw no sign of William, either. Just as she was about to flash herself back to the cave, Lucien finally appeared. He was wearing his mask, but she could feel the intensified fatigue radiating from him.

Shit. "No more flashing for you," she told him firmly. It was draining what little energy she'd managed to give him.

"I'll do whatever needs to be done," he replied, his tone just as firm as hers.

"Damn it, Lucien!" He was more important to her than anything else in the world. She would have offered Cronus the All-Key right then, anything to save her man, but she didn't trust the bastard. Once the king had the key, he could kill Lucien just to spite her for making him wait.

She had to be careful about how she went about this.

Her new plan was simple: find the cage, then somehow hide both it and Lucien. Lucien wanted it, and so he would get it. It was that simple. She wouldn't give the cage to Cronus in trade. Not when he could use it to find the box and hurt Lucien. No, she would trade the key instead, just like the old jerkoff wanted. There was no other way.

It was only a matter of time.

She rubbed her stomach to ward off the sudden ache.

"I still do not see William," Lucien said, dragging her from her thoughts.

"I'm here," a voice growled.

Anya turned and saw a silver spike clutched by a gloved hand slap over a ledge and embed at the top. William hefted himself up. His entire face was covered by a white mask, blending him into the snow. Except for his eyes. They seemed to glow brightly, a blue as deep as the ocean.

"A little help," he snapped.

Lucien crouched and gripped his wrist. Maybe it was bad of her, but she'd rather William fall than put Lucien *at risk* for falling. Anya moved behind her lover and latched on to his waist, holding him steady. Together they dragged William's muscled body over the edge.

The warrior stood, shaking snow from his shoulders. He even hunched over, trying to suck air into his lungs. "Been years since I've had to do that."

"You should look into flashing," she offered helpfully.

Still crouched, he reached up and flipped her off.

She chuckled.

Lucien snorted.

"I'm surprised you didn't head home," she said.

"And give you more reason to burn my book or tear out the pages?" William straightened and his glowing gaze slid over the vast expanse of snow. There was nothing but blanket after blanket of white as swirls whisked on the breeze, like glitter in the fickle haze of the moon. Then his attention turned to Lucien. "You're looking well, considering your recent injuries."

"Where could a monster hide in *this?*" Lucien asked, ignoring the compliment.

"She could be a chameleon," Anya suggested. "She could be the color of snow and we could be standing on her right now."

Everyone looked down. A few minutes passed, and nothing happened. There was a collective sigh of disappointment.

William focused on her, opened his mouth, closed it. Seeing the weapon strapped to her back and peeking over her shoulder samurai-style, he frowned. "Nice sword," he said drily.

"Thanks."

"It's one of my favorites."

"If you're nice, I'll give it back to you in a year or two."

"You're so good to me."

"I know. Now, I believe we were talking about Hydra."

William paused, studied the land again. "Well. Where to now?"

"This way," Lucien said, motioning them forward.

Anya stifled a groan but kicked into motion. "Don't tell me we've got miles of hiking to do. I might just sink into a fit of the vapors."

"Stay on alert," Lucien said, and the three of them inched along for several hours.

At first, she felt like a piece of ice bobbing in a glass of soda. Then her entire body went numb. That should have made things easier, but it didn't. Moving her arms and legs was like moving thousand-pound logs.

"Remind me why I like you," William said, breaking the silence. "Remind me why I welcome you into my home time and time again, even knowing trouble's going to follow you. 'Cause right now, I can't remember."

"You welcome her because she brings excitement and passion everywhere she goes," Lucien answered.

Ah. She melted inside, sudden warmth combating the numbness. Grinning up at him, she patted his shoulder. He was holding up well. He hadn't stumbled once, even though his legs felt like lead weights to him and Death was clamoring inside his head, demanding to collect souls, but wanting to stay with her.

Being able to read him so easily was wicked-cool, she decided. And knowing his sweet little evil demon purred for her, liked her even, was wondrous. Two bad boys for the price of one. Couldn't get any better than that. Still, she hated that Lucien was suffering. *Soon*, she vowed. *Soon that would end.*

He reached over and squeezed her hand, as if sensing her plan to contact Cronus. Okay. Maybe this reading each other thing wasn't so cool, after all. What would she do if he tried to stop her?

"Anyone know what Hydra is like?" she asked to distract him. "Good fighter?"

"She is unbeatable, and every time you cut off her head another will grow in its place." William sighed, a little dejected. "Do you really think you can beat such a creature, Anya? You're strong, but not *that* strong."

One of the spikes in Lucien's boot hit an icy rock that refused to break, and he stumbled. Weakened as he was becoming again, a moment passed before he was able to right himself. Anya didn't want William to think Lucien was less a warrior, so she forced her hands to remain at her sides rather than reaching out to help.

"What's wrong with you now?" William asked Lucien. "Anya wear you out or something?"

She slapped William's arm. "Don't talk about him like that. *He* wore *me* out."

"Ow," Willie complained. "That hurt. You're stronger than you think and pack one hell of a punch."

"Hush, you big baby. I thought I wasn't *that* strong."

"Well?" he prompted Lucien, not hushing. He did it just to spite her, she knew. "What's wrong with you?"

Lucien shrugged. "If the enemy assumes I am weakened, he will underestimate me."

William thought about that for several seconds, then nodded. "True. But I don't see any enemies around."

"Time will tell," Lucien said.

Anya experienced a wave of pride. *That's my boy.*

Another cold burst of wind cut through them. "What did you do with the Hunters' bodies?" Lucien asked William.

"I took care of them," was the staunch reply. "That's all that matters."

Anya had enjoyed fighting and killing them. They'd hoped to hurt and ultimately kill Lucien, and anyone who meant Lucien harm was now her enemy, as well. She would kill without hesitation. Without remorse. Without mercy.

"Why would you bother?" Ice chunks splattered from the toe of Lucien's boot and stuck to his leg.

There was a slight hesitation as William lifted his mask and scrubbed the sheen of ice from his lips. Mist puffed around his face. "If someone found them, humans would flood these mountains in droves to investigate their murder."

"Smart," Anya said. "Gods, where the hell is Hydra? I don't even see footprints and I'm starting to feel seriously PO'd, like I picked the wrong place and she's moved out of the Arctic. That would make me a big dummy and severely damage my street cred."

Lucien lifted his mask, lifted hers and pressed a quick kiss on her lips, decided that wasn't enough and gave her a second kiss, lingering over her mouth and tracing the seam with his tongue. His sensual fragrance filled her nose, drugging her with passion. "You are not a dummy."

"Yuck." William pretended to gag. "That's disgusting." Then he gaped at her. "You're bonded, aren't you? You gave in to your curse. For him. *Why?*"

"Love isn't disgusting, and that's all I'm saying about that." With regret, she pulled away from Lucien, righted her mask and slapped William's arm. "Just wait until it's your turn. I hope your soul mate drives you insane and wants nothing to do with you."

"I could be so lucky."

"We'll see," she said cryptically.

William ground to a halt, eyes practically glowing through the clear lenses shielding them from cold. "What do you know? Have you heard something? What have you heard, Anya?"

Wasn't nice to tease him like this, she thought with an inward smile. He avoided love because of the prophecy that hung over his head. He'd never told her exactly what the prophecy was and she hadn't had the patience to try to decode that cryptic book of ancient rhymes and ominous warnings.

"I haven't heard anything," she admitted. A week ago she would have lied and told him she knew something. She would have had him begging for the information, and that would have delighted her.

Lucien must be having a negative affect on her. Next she'd probably stop stealing. A grin curled the corners of her mouth. She'd probably be too busy having sex to bother with stealing, so that was a fair trade.

"You suck." William sighed and pushed back into motion.

Though she was tired and only growing more so, Anya managed to keep pace beside him. Soon she was stumbling over every block of ice in her path. "How much longer are we going to look?" she moaned. "Not that I want to give up or anything. I don't. I won't. I'm just wondering."

Lucien wrapped his arm around her, offering comfort, warmth and love. Her feet ached, she was bitterly cold, and yes, part of her wanted this night to be over with so she could be alone with him, pleasuring his body and—after the loving—thinking about how best to handle Cronus. But when

Lucien was near her like this, none of the bad stuff mattered. Only finding that stupid cage mattered.

Suddenly William planted his feet into the ground. Anya only realized what he'd done when she glanced to the side and he was no longer there. She and Lucien shared a measured look before backtracking.

"What the hell is that?" William gasped out. He'd paled.

"Where?" She studied the surrounding area, noting that it appeared to be an exact replica of every other mile they'd trudged. "I don't see anything."

"There," Lucien said, excitement in the undercurrents of his voice. He pointed.

She followed the line of his finger. At first, she saw only ribbons of dancing snow. Then, as amber moonlight glinted against the white flakes, she noticed the shimmery outline of an arched...doorway? Somehow the air was thicker there, like clear, rippling water.

Whooping, she threw her arms around Lucien. "This is it. This has to be it! Where do you think it leads?"

"Perhaps it is nothing," Lucien said.

William's head fell back and he stared up at the starless sky. Praying? "Maybe we should turn back."

"Hell, no," Anya said, releasing Lucien and stepping forward. "Lead the way or step aside, Willie. We're going through that thing."

CHAPTER TWENTY-ONE

PARIS HAD BEEN SHOCKED when Sienna actually stripped. That's all it had taken to fill his cock with blood and lust: the sight of her naked body. She was too thin, as he'd suspected, her breasts small. But they were tipped with the prettiest nipples he'd ever seen. Pink, ripe, made for sucking.

He'd been shocked further when she'd climbed onto the table and straddled him. Shocked still when she'd slid down his swollen shaft without preamble, without any type of foreplay, her hot sheath swallowing him whole.

And yet, a woman had never been so wet or ready for what he offered. As she'd pumped her way up and down his shaft, he'd roared and roared and roared. He'd hated his chains because he hadn't been able to plump her breasts. He'd hated his chains because he hadn't been able to rub her clit.

Most of all, he'd hated his chains because he hadn't been able to pull that plain little face down for a bruising, punishing kiss of teeth and tongue.

Didn't matter, though, he now thought darkly. He'd be able to punish her soon enough.

She'd gotten off quickly, exploding with a fury that surprised him. So had he. In a matter of minutes, an orgasm had rocked him to the core—right along with a healthy dose of humiliation. He'd never come so quickly. *Shouldn't care,* he'd told himself, because what none of his human captors could know was that, with every stroke of Sienna's inner walls, he'd felt his strength returning. Felt himself grow stronger and stronger and stronger.

Right now she was collapsed on his chest, panting and sated, silent, body slicked with sweat. *Do it. It's time.* Eyes narrowed, he gave a mighty jolt. The chains around his wrists and ankles broke, freeing him. After all his unsuccessful struggling, he was amazed by how easy it was.

At the *clink,* Sienna bolted upright. Her hair had come undone and fell all around her face in a wild tangle of browns. Her eyes were big and vulnerable, her skin flushed a rosy pink. Before she could jump off him, he grabbed her by the waist and hopped off the table, holding her under his arm like a sack of potatoes.

An alarm instantly screeched to life.

Yeah, the Hunters had been watching. He bent down and snapped up Sienna's shirt. He shoved it over her head. "Dress."

"Paris," she gasped, struggling against his hold. "Don't do this. Please." She no longer sounded like the unemotional traitor who'd drugged him. She sounded like a woman who'd just had the best orgasm of her life and was scared for the life of her lover.

What a good little actress she was.

"You better keep your mouth shut, woman." He didn't bother with clothes for himself as he strode to the cell doorway. "I *will* hurt you. Quite happily, too."

"If you try to escape, they might forget about unleashing your demon and kill you!"

"It's not like you really care, and they're welcome to try." He hoped they did. He couldn't hurt Sienna—yet—but he needed to hurt *someone* and release some of the tension inside him. Who better than a Hunter?

Some kind of dry spray rained from the ceiling, filling the cell with mist. It didn't affect him, just caused his eyes to tear a little, but Sienna began gagging. "How do I open the door?"

She rattled off some kind of code. He punched the numbers into the small, glowing box on the wall and the door slid open. Lights suddenly popped on, drowning the shadows.

Paris maintained a tight hold on his bundle as he stepped into the hallway. Red velvet walls surrounded him; naked white statues towered from marble daises.

A cathedral? Seriously?

There was no time to ponder his location. A flood of Hunters raced toward him, each firing a gun. *Pop. Whiz.* No longer willing to keep him alive, were they? They were using silencers, he realized. Probably concerned with the noise level, which meant they were afraid to draw a crowd—which meant they were in a well-populated area.

The demon inside him snapped and snarled in rage, quickly and easily propelling him out of the line of fire. Sienna bounced at his side. Once, she gasped. But that was it, the only noise she made. Better, she stopped fighting him.

Barreling forward, he kicked two Hunters in the stomach and sent them sailing into a sculpture of the Virgin Mary. The sculpture wavered on her perch, and one of the Hunters dropped his semi-automatic. Paris snatched it with his free hand and began shooting, continuing to move forward at a rapid pace.

He turned a corner, found more Hunters and kept firing. More shots were aimed at him, but he dodged. Only three managed to graze him. When he ran out of bullets, he tossed the gun aside and grabbed another. They lined the halls—as did dead bodies. He flew around another corner, and Sienna's breasts brushed his skin. He felt...no, surely not. He'd just had her. He could *not* get hard again. Not by her. But blood began to fill and harden his cock.

Never, in thousands of years, had he desired the same woman twice. He wasn't even sure what would happen if he gave in to the urge. Would the demon inside him go crazy? Would *he* go crazy?

"Which way?" he demanded of Sienna when he came to a fork in the hall.

"Left," she gasped out.

"If you are lying…"

"I'm not."

He turned left and leapt into a full sprint. A towering double doorway loomed ahead, three Hunters racing from it. They raised their guns at him, their expressions intent. He tried to fire, but he had used the last bullet.

He ducked and dove, shouting, "Hang on," to Sienna.

She did, winding her legs around his waist. He hit the ground and she bounced, and together they rolled into the Hunters, knocking them down like pins in the path of a bowling ball.

While they were down, he swiped up another gun and shot them in the skulls. Blood and brains splattered. Sienna whimpered, but didn't speak. Paris experienced a twinge of guilt that she'd witnessed his most violent side, but quickly tamped it out. Her opinion of him no longer mattered.

He shoved through the doors and found himself outside. The warm night air was sweet, innocent. Looking around, he realized that he was still in Greece and that he had indeed been inside a cathedral. Humans stood on the steps, gaping at his blood-stained nudity and muttering about the commotion.

In the distance, he could hear the wail of a siren.

Steps swift, he made his way to the side of the building and into a darkened ally. Sienna moaned, and it was a pain-filled sound. His gaze sought her. She was limp as a doll.

"Look at me."

She turned her head slowly, and he saw that her eyes were pooled with unshed tears, her features bright with anguish. He felt something warm run down his hip and frowned.

When he was certain they were alone, he set her down and looked her over. She'd managed to work her arms through the shirt and the material hung to her thighs.

His chest constricted. She was bleeding profusely, the shirt already plastered to her stomach in a wide crimson circle.

She'd been shot.

"Sienna," he said, upset in a way he didn't understand. He shouldn't care. He'd meant to punish her. Had wanted to hurt her.

"Paris," she gasped. "I should…have…killed you."

As if the words had sucked the last of her strength, her head lolled to the side. He wrapped his arms around her and pulled her into his embrace. Only a heartbeat later, she died.

LUCIEN GRABBED ANYA'S ARM and stopped her just before she crossed through that thick, dappled patch of air. She glanced at him curiously, and he shook his head.

"You first," he told William, just in case they were stepping into some sort of trap.

At first, the warrior gave no reaction. But then his eyes narrowed, and he shrugged. "Very well. I'll go first." Without another word, William walked past them into the glistening shimmer.

He disappeared as if he'd never been on the mountain.

Dear gods. It *was* a doorway. Lucien experienced a moment of joy. They might find the Cage of Compulsion after all. With the thought, his joy was tempered by apprehension. To win the cage, they might have to fight the mighty Hydra. He'd expected to do so, but the possibility had never been so real.

"After me," Lucien told Anya and stepped forward before she could protest. "Be ready to fight." He gripped a dagger in each hand, a little shaky and a lot weak, though he refused to succumb to either.

Whatever he'd expected the shimmers to feel like, they didn't. They were dry and as light as air. There was no moment of suspension, no dizziness. One minute he was surrounded by snow and ice, the next he was in paradise.

Warm air beat around him, heating him, melting the frost and making him sweat.

"Wow," Anya gasped behind him. She stepped up beside him, gripping the sword she'd stolen from William. "This is, like, amazing. Who would have thought a place like this was actually up in these mountains?"

William was—where? Lucien looked around the tropical island. There were lush emerald trees and blooming flowers of every color. The aroma of coconuts and pineapples scented the air, almost drugging. Definitely lulling. Beguiling. His brow wrinkled in confusion as his muscles relaxed of their own accord.

You were doing something. What? The answer—*William,* he suddenly remembered. The grass climbed up to Lucien's knees. He kept searching, fighting past the languor still beating through him. There! William leaned against a giant silver boulder at the far left.

He'd removed his coat, hat and gloves. He wasn't holding a weapon, but had his arms crossed over his chest. Determination gleamed on his face, though he did his best to appear nonchalant.

Lucien removed his own mask and coat and dropped them, not wanting the bulk to hinder him. With Cronus's curse looming over his head, he was slow enough.

Anya stripped down to a skin-tight white shirt and shorts

that stopped just below the curve of her ass. Despite his condition, he was instantly hard for her.

"This is where we need to honeymoon," she said. Laughing, she skipped forward and danced through the flowers, their soft petals caressing her skin as *he* wanted to do. "I don't see any sign of our monster. Do you? And do you care? This is the best I've ever felt!"

"No, I do not see her." Watching her, Lucien felt his lips curl into a grin. *She's captivating,* he thought. *She's mine.* And if they managed to win the cage, he might just get to live and keep her.

Suddenly she stopped, gasped and pointed. "Lucien, look look look!" she said excitedly. "The Cage of Compulsion."

He gazed across a crystal lake stretching before her. Sure enough, there was indeed an ordinary-looking cage perched on a boulder on the other side. Rather unspectacular for a godly relic, Lucien couldn't help but think. But those polished bars were tall enough to house a human and wide enough that the human could lie down and not touch the other side. Who was he supposed to lock in there, to learn about Pandora's box? he wondered. Anya had thought Hydra.

"It's not as glamorous as I'd anticipated," Anya remarked, echoing Lucien's thoughts.

"No."

"Hydra should *thank* us for taking it."

Hydra. He should be worried about her. Shouldn't he? "Be careful," Lucien said, trying to force his body to prepare for war. "The monster could be near."

Unconcerned, William stepped forward, plucking strands of tall grass along the way. "You vowed to give me back the book if I brought you here," he said to Anya. "And as you can see, I brought you."

"Yes, I did and yes, you did. As soon as we return, you'll have your book. You have my word."

A wave of dizziness worked its way through Lucien. He drew in a deep breath, but that only increased the dizziness. By the time he thought to cease breathing it was too late. He was nearly incapacitated. What was wrong with him?

"I'm sorry," Lucien heard William say, and then a sword was slicing through Lucien's middle, cutting through skin, organs and even bone, every point of contact burning as the warrior twisted, slicing deeper. "I had hoped it would not come to this."

Had he been his normal self, Lucien would have seen the blow coming and flashed. He would have healed. As it was, he couldn't move. Didn't care to move. He felt what little energy he possessed draining. Then his knees gave out, and he crumpled to the ground. Did William wield some sort of power?

Anya.

He heard her scream, a bloodcurdling cry of rage and fury, hate and fear. Suddenly he cared.

"You bastard!"

"Cronus came to me while you were packing, Anya," William shouted. "He threatened to kill me if I didn't kill the pair of you once the cage was found. I did not want to do this, but you forced my hand. I'm sorry. I am. You have to believe—"

"*I'll* fucking kill you, you traitor!"

The sword was pulled out of Lucien and black cobwebs wove through his vision, giving him limited eyesight. But he was able to see Anya with that sword in hand, a dark storm blanketing her lovely face. He saw William square off with her, determined, resolved.

They would battle to the death.

"No," he ground out. He couldn't let that happen. Couldn't let her fight the warrior. "No!"

"Rest, baby, and heal," she choked out. Relief pulsed from her, wrapping around him. She'd thought he was already dead. "I'll punish William for you."

"I do not want to hurt you," William began.

I once said that to her, Lucien mused dizzily.

"According to Cronus, you have to. Isn't that right? Still looking out for number one, I see. But I'm not worried. A dead man can't hurt anyone." She licked her lips, as if already tasting William's death. "You should have told me what Cronus wanted you to do." Like a predator, she circled him. "We could have thought of something to stop him."

"If there were a way to stop him, you would have done it by now."

"How could you do this? How, damn you? I love him."

"I know. And I truly am sorry."

Lucien tried to push to his feet, even as his body bled out, continuing to drain more and more of his strength. *You are a warrior. Act like one. For Anya.* Drawing on a reservoir he hadn't known he possessed—Anya's, he realized—he at last managed to stand.

No one noticed him. Anya raised her sword.

William raised his, as well.

A deafening screech sounded from the water, and Anya turned, distracted. That's when William lunged forward, swinging for her head.

Clang.

Anya met his weapon with her own and the two began a lethal dance of attack and retreat, swords always slicing toward each other. All the while a two-headed monster rose from the lake, half woman, half snake. Smaller serpents slithered over her head, hissing, jaws snapping. Each of them, including Hydra herself, possessed long, sharp teeth that resembled minidaggers.

Clutching his stomach in one hand and gripping one of his own daggers in the other, Lucien stumbled forward to battle the beast.

CHAPTER TWENTY-TWO

ANYA FOUGHT WILLIAM WITH all of the rage inside her. How dare he attack Lucien! How dare he hurt the man she loved! When she'd seen Lucien fall, when she'd seen the blood soaking his stomach, a part of her had seized and died.

I can't live without him. I won't *live without him.*

"You can't beat us both," William panted.

"Watch me." She ducked and swung, the tip of her sword slicing into his thigh.

He howled as his skin split and blood drenched his pants.

"Besides," she said. She let him back her into a boulder then jumped to the top of it without turning. With barely a pause, she leapt down for momentum, twisting in the air to change their positions. When she hit the ground, she was momentarily jostled and he swung at her, but she managed to parry and back *him* into the boulder, trapping him.

Another of those horrible roars sounded.

She wanted to look, but couldn't. William was an expert fighter and would take advantage of any distraction. Again. *Trust Lucien. He, too, is a warrior.* Yes, he was a warrior to his very soul. Her warrior. He was Death; he could defeat Hydra, no matter how weak or hurt he was. *Please let him defeat her.*

"Anya," William panted, trying to slap the sword from her hand.

She easily dodged, his motions slower than before. Good. He was tiring. Would probably do something stupid any moment. Like now—he swung low, and she was able to jump on the blade and kick his palm. His fingers opened and the weapon clanged to the ground.

She grinned slowly, her blade poised at his throat. "You shouldn't have fucked with me." From the corner of her eye, she saw Lucien approach the monster, his dagger raised. One of Hydra's heads snapped down to bite him, but he bounded out of the way, slicing as he fell.

One of Hydra's heads rolled to the ground.

The monster hissed and stretched and another head quickly grew from the gaping, bloody hole. Worse, the one on the ground had not died. It attempted to spin toward Lucien and bite his calf.

"Let's leave, you and me," William whizzed, twisting to the side and lunging for Anya's leg. "Before we become a meal."

She turned—*end it, end it*—and withdrew another dagger from her boot. She tossed it, even as her sword swung.

William was in the process of reclaiming his sword when the sharp tip slammed into his shoulder, knocking him backward. She didn't slow, but continued to turn...turn...and stabbed him in the stomach just as he'd done to Lucien.

Shock blanketed his face. He looked down and gasped out a pained breath. "You...won."

"Always." Growling, she shoved harder, pushing the sword out his back and into the boulder, pinning the warrior in place.

"Anya," he moaned, features glazing with agony.

"Hope you realize how lucky you are. I'm not going to chop off your head or cut out your heart. Not today. You'll recover from this wound, and I'll come for you again and again until I think you've suffered enough. *Then* I'll kill you."

She turned from him then, already racing toward Hydra to help Lucien. She felt no relief that William was defeated—she'd truly liked him until now. But Lucien was in danger, and he was all that mattered.

Along the way, she withdrew the last dagger from her boot. She saw that Lucien was holding his middle, blood still seeping from the wound. He'd managed to destroy one rolling head and cut off another—which was now rolling to attack him. Already another had grown in its place and was slapping at him. And yet he was still standing. Still fighting. She'd never seen a more powerful sight. Weak? No, the man was unbelievably strong.

She would have fallen and stayed put had she been injured like that. If she hadn't already been in love with him, she would have given him her heart in that moment. With his dying breath he would protect and defend. *Dying*. No. Oh, no.

Heart racing, she approached his side and hacked at the rolling snake head. "How do we kill it?"

"Go for the eye." Lucien swung at Hydra as she swatted him with her tail. He tumbled to the ground, but lurched back to his feet. "That's the only way I've found to destroy the heads."

Anya jumped on top of the rolling head, the tiny snake hairs biting at her thighs. Each chomp stung like the fires of hell, but she didn't back down. She sank her blade into one of the eye sockets. Instantly, the head jerked and the tiny snakes stiffened before going limp.

Blood rushed down her legs as she stood. Hydra batted at Lucien, her long neck swiping his legs out from under him. His body hit the ground again, shoving air from his lungs, and he moaned.

"Lucien!" She flashed to his side and crouched down.

"I'm fine," he said, pushing to his feet. He wobbled.

Distracted as Anya was, Hydra managed to dig her teeth into Anya's arm. She screamed, the pain almost blinding. Black stars winked over her vision and fire burned her blood. Poison? Snake venom?

Stay strong. But her legs were trembling, giving out, unable to hold her weight. And then Lucien was there, right beside her, stabbing the head in the eye. The creature screeched, an unholy sound that scratched at her eardrums, before falling to the ground, dead.

Just as before, another head quickly took its place.

Anya wavered, desperate to steady herself. Lethargy beat through her with tough fists.

"Stay awake, sweetheart," Lucien breathed in her ear, warming her, strengthening her. "I have an idea, but I can't do it without you. I need you to cut off her head and cauterize it when I've distracted her. Can you do that?"

"Lucien— Yes. Yes, I can do it." *For Lucien, anything.* Anya straightened her back and squared her shoulders. Her vision slowly cleared with every measured breath she forced in and out of her lungs, and she saw that both of Lucien's eyes were blue. He kissed her, and then his body dematerialized, shimmered. Returned.

He frowned. "I'm not strong enough to take my body. I have to go in spirit."

His body collapsed, unconscious, but connected to him as she was Anya saw his spirit pull from it. He floated to the creature—who could no longer see him in spirit form and evidently decided his motionless body was already dead, freeing her to concentrate all of her menace on Anya. Anya forced herself to march forward.

That bitch is mine.

CHAPTER TWENTY-THREE

LUCIEN SETTLED HIS SPIRIT ON the creature's back. She paid him no attention, was focused solely on Anya—who was splattered with blood, cut and bruised, and looked like an Amazon warrior willing to do anything to win the battle.

He reached into Hydra's body with a ghostly hand and grabbed on to her spirit. She roared, making him cringe. Would have made his ears bleed if he'd been in corporeal form. In a panic, she lunged at Anya, but he jerked on her spirit again, holding her in place.

Since her body was alive, he knew what he was doing hurt her. She screeched again, but remained in place as if tethered. Anya leapt, higher and higher, and quickly cut off one of the creature's heads. As it tumbled to the ground, as Hydra screamed, flames erupted in the center of Anya's hand. She slammed that fire into the wound just as another head formed.

Orange-gold flames melted the skin, sizzled it, destroyed it, and cauterized the wound. Hydra spasmed and jerked in rage. Furious now, she used the last of her strength to chomp at Anya. Lucien kept a firm grip as his woman twisted out of the way and swung her sword yet again.

Contact.

The second head fell. Anya produced another fire and burned the wound, even as two of the snakes bit her arm. She cringed, but maintained the flames. Roaring, the creature went limp and collapsed into the water. The sound of that final roar continued to echo until finally, blessedly fading.

He hovered there for a moment, awed. They'd done it. They'd won!

Anya fell to the ground, panting but grinning. Lucien floated to the ground himself and tried to enter his body— but it was as if a shield separated the spirit from the corporeal. He frowned. Tried again. Failed again.

Why could he not enter?

You're too weak. The thought slammed into his mind. He was weak, yes, but he should be able to enter. If he couldn't… Scowling now, he tried one last time to slip into his body. Nothing.

He could only hover there, powerless. He glanced over at Anya. In the circle of grass beside his body, she dropped to her knees.

"Get back here," she said, glancing up at his spirit. She gave him a tired grin. "I'll doctor your wounds."

He tried again. He did. He *had* to touch her at least once more, this woman who'd given him more happiness in a few weeks than he'd experienced in thousands of years. But he remained exactly as he was.

"Lucien," she barked, and there was worry in the undertones. "This isn't funny. Get back into your body!"

"I can't."

A moment passed before she gave any kind of reaction. Violently she shook her head. Her features gleamed with panic and disbelief. "You can."

"Anya…" It was best this way. He'd known it days ago, knew it now. His body would die and there would be nothing Cronus could hold over her head. She would be free, the key hers and hers alone.

"Don't give up," she said, once again shaking her head. A sob bubbled from her throat. "Keep trying."

"Anya."

"You're not going to die. Do you hear me?" Her eyes filled with tears as she stared up at him. "You're not going to die," she uttered brokenly. "I won't let you. Help me, William!" she shouted, her anger at the man clearly forgotten, but the warrior had passed out. She began to pound at Lucien's chest, trying to force his heart into motion.

"Anya. Please." Seeing her like this tore him up. He floated to her and attempted to push a hand through her hair, but the only thing he felt was the warmth of the air. "I love you."

Even as he spoke, Death roared with far more fury and pain than Hydra had. Lucien suddenly felt as though he were burning, his insides kindling to a thirsty fire. He, too, began to roar. The pain, too much. He was being ripped in half.

Gods. Man and demon were separating, he realized. Pulling apart.

"Lucien. What's wrong?" Anya shouted, pausing her ministrations to his physical form. "You're going to be okay. I'm going to give Cronus the All-Key. You're going to be okay," she repeated.

He wanted to respond, wanted to tell her to stay away from Cronus, but the burning increased and the words melted in his throat. If he and Death divided completely, Lucien would die in truth. Just as Baden had. Wouldn't he?

"I'll take care of everything." Anya disappeared. Before he could panic, she returned to that patch of bloody grass beside his body. Her eyes were luminous pools. "Tell me what's happening to you. Let me help."

Fighting the pain, trying to hold on to Death, he reached out again. Once more his fingers ghosted through. Tears were pouring from her now, and the sight broke him. "I love you," he finally managed to work out.

"Cronus," she screamed.

"Stop." He doubled over. Any moment now, Death would be completely free. Funny, he'd spent so many years wishing for a life without the demon, yet now they both were trying to cling to each other with what little strength they had left.

"Cronus!"

Lucien opened his mouth to speak again, but no sound emerged. His last tie with Death broke, and he knew nothing more.

ANYA THREW UP THE MOMENT Lucien's spirit disappeared. When her stomach was completely emptied, she screamed for Cronus again. "I'm ready to bargain. Do you hear me? I'm ready."

As always, he appeared in a blinding flash of light. She blinked against it and pushed to shaky legs. Lucien's spirit was still gone. Gone! Oh, gods. She'd seen the skeletal image of Death rip from him, howling—oh, gods, the howling—before it, too, disappeared. *Please, don't let me be too late.*

She closed her eyes and tried to reverse time, but failed. She'd done it once before, for Maddox and Ashlyn. Why couldn't she do so now? Why?

"I'm listening," Cronus said, and she felt him gliding toward her, his white robe brushing the thick grass.

She peered up at him, vision blurred through her tears. "The key is yours. Willingly given if you'll swear to bring Lucien back to life and leave us both alone."

"I want the cage, as well. Where did you hide it?"

Fighting the sense of urgency running rampant inside of her, the sense of loss and panic, she shook her head. "You can't have it. That belongs to Lucien. You only get the key."

"Do you want your lover to live?"

"If he dies, you will *never* get the key!" Tears falling freely, she scooped her hands under Lucien's head and lifted. She placed a soft kiss on his lips. *I love you. I'll make everything all better.* Please, please, please, let this make everything better.

"Much longer, and even I will not be able to bring him back," Cronus said cruelly. "As weak as he was, it took considerable effort to twine him and the demon together again to sustain Lucien's life a bit longer. Without the key, I will gladly pull them apart again."

Though she experienced a surge of hope that Lucien truly could be saved, her narrowed eyes flicked up at the god. "I will not cave on this. You may have the key. The cage belongs to Lucien. You once gave me a choice, Lucien or the key. Now I'm giving you the same choice. That is fair. That is just. And I will not budge on this."

He met her piercing stare with a scowl. What tumbled through his mind, she didn't know. Then he nodded, as though he sensed the absoluteness of her determination. Or perhaps he'd known all along that's how it would be, and had only hoped for more. "Very well."

"A deal is reached then. Lucien's life for the key." She was taking a terrible gamble, trusting a being she hated, who probably hated her. "If after this you take the cage from us, immortals far and wide will know of your dishonor. The Lords of the Underworld will turn against you and do all that they can to free the Greeks. There will be a war at a time when you seek only reverence. I know you consider yourself untouchable and stronger than mere immortal warriors, but know what? You were defeated once. You can be defeated again."

Cronus was silent as he raised his arms high in the air. A

second later, they were inside Lucien's room in Budapest. Lucien lay on the bed. She could see the rise and fall of his tattooed chest. He was naked, and his wounds were gone. His skin was healthy and tanned, and she could sense the demon nestled safely inside him.

Cronus stood beside the bed.

Without a word, Anya flashed to where her mother and father were in hiding, an island near Anya's Hawaiian home. Dysnomia was standing in front of the cage, frowning down at it.

"Sorry, Mom, but you don't need to watch it for me after all."

Pretty Dysnomia gasped at the intrusion, her dark hair swaying at her shoulders. She smiled when she realized it was Anya. "Hello, darling."

"I know what you're thinking. Two visits in one day when I swore to stay away from you to keep the Titans off your trail. But you're still safe, so don't worry, okay?" Anya kissed her soft cheek. "Tell Dad I said hi and that I'll visit again soon. Promise," she said and, grasping the artifact, flashed back to Lucien.

Cronus stood exactly where she'd left him.

She placed the Cage of Compulsion against the far wall. Anya had to admit, she was surprised when Cronus merely raised an eyebrow rather than attempting to take it.

"I have kept my end of the bargain," he told her.

Now she would keep hers. Suddenly nervous, Anya kissed the sleeping Lucien and flashed herself inside the cage. "I'm ready," she said, gripping the bars.

The god blinked in surprise and confusion. "You want to be locked away? Without the All-Key, you will not be able to escape and anyone who steps inside this room will be able to command you to their will."

"I know." But this way, if she lost her memory of Lucien when the key left her body, she wouldn't be able to run from him, hurting them both because of the bond between them. He would have time to win her heart again. "I love him."

Cronus stroked his beard in puzzlement. "Astounding. And unexpected from one such as you."

She let the "one such as you" slide. Loving Lucien was the best thing she'd ever done, and she'd do *anything* for him. "Let's get this over with." She gulped, pushed out a breath, then uttered the necessary words. "I, Anya, known across the ages as Anarchy, freely give Cronus, king of gods, the All-Key. I do this willingly and with no reservations."

Humming with anticipation, Cronus reached inside her with a ghostly hand, just as she had seen Lucien do to the dead all those many times. Her chest burned…burned…. A sharp ache erupted as he pulled his hand back, and then a bright amber light was pulsing in his palm. Anya's knees gave out and she collapsed. Closing his eyes, Cronus placed that light over his heart.

His smile of satisfaction was the last thing Anya saw before her entire world went black.

"LET ME OUT!"

Lucien had never felt so helpless. He simply didn't know what to do. Anya had been locked in the Cage of Compulsion for four days. Despite their bond, she had no idea who he was. She possessed only the memories of her time *before* accepting the key inside her body. Constantly she demanded he release her. But he didn't. He couldn't. She would leave; she might even try to kill him.

She'd threatened it often enough. And he could still sense her emotions, so he knew that she meant it. She, too, could still sense his emotions and asked him daily why he loved her.

Always she asked with confusion, as if they were strangers and he should view her with revulsion. Certainly she seemed to view *him* with revulsion.

Like a chained, hungry animal, he paced the length of his bedroom. She'd given up the All-Key for him. He hated that she'd done so and wanted to spank her and hug her at the same time. She'd lost her memories, but at least she hadn't lost her strength. He liked to think it was because of their bond. She'd once given him strength and now he was returning the favor.

If only he could make her remember him.

"Let me out of here!" she shouted at him. "You have no right to keep me. How did you move me from Tartarus without my knowledge?"

He stopped and stared over at her, his chest tightening. He hated what she'd given up for him, yes, but more than that, he hated to see her suffering. "Anya. We are bonded. Why do you not remember me?"

"Bastard." She reached through the bars and scratched his chest, drawing blood. "Come near me and feel pain. You got me? The captain was bigger than you and I killed him without blinking."

He sank to the floor in front of the bars, the last few days playing through his mind. When he'd woken up in his bedroom, alive, once again merged with Death, he had been overjoyed. Then he had seen Anya sleeping in the cage. *Then* she'd woken up and looked at him as though he were a stranger. Cursing at him. Hating him.

Would nothing go right?

It seemed a pall had settled over all the warriors. He'd learned that Paris had returned from Greece a broken shell of a man. Paris refused to talk about it, though, so no one knew what had happened. The warrior would soon be leaving for the States to join Gideon as planned, but Lucien couldn't help feeling guilty that *he* was the one who'd told the others not to worry about Paris. With the delay, that haunted look, something had clearly gone wrong.

Aeron and Reyes were in the States themselves, though no one had spoken with either and didn't know what was happening with them. Which, in turn, meant no one knew what had happened to Danika and her family. Lucien sighed. The other warriors were still searching for signs of the other Hydras. So far, no luck.

Lucien should be out there, searching with them. At the very least, he should be helping Paris recover from whatever had happened to him. That's the way things had always been. Something happened, and Lucien fixed it as best he could. But he couldn't leave Anya. Wouldn't. She was his life.

Unfortunately, he could not seem to fix her, either.

She remembered neither Maddox nor Ashlyn, though the couple visited her every day to thank her for what she'd done for them. She would listen, seem to soften for a heartbeat, but still her memories did not return. He'd even given her the lollipops she loved to no avail. What more could he do?

"I love you," he told her.

"Well, I hate you. Let me go!" The bars rattled as she shook them.

He dropped his head into his waiting hands. "You are not going to remember me, no matter what I do. Are you?"

"Go fuck yourself." She slammed her fist through the bars and into the back of his skull. "I will not be your slave. Do you hear me! I'm no one's slave."

With a heavy heart—and wanting to die all over again—he stood and unlocked the door.

At first, she simply stood there, looking at him. "Why are you so sad? Why are you freeing me?"

"I cannot bear to see you imprisoned."

"Why?" Not waiting for his answer, shaking her head and keeping as wide a berth as possible between them, she stalked from the cage and turned narrowed eyes on him. "What's wrong with me? Why do I hurt at the thought of leaving?"

Tears ran down his cheeks, and he scrubbed them away. He didn't dare hope. Not yet. "I am your mate."

"I have no mate." She marched toward him, fury in her crystalline eyes. Along the way, she swiped one of the daggers he'd set on the nightstand. "You're going to pay for locking me up."

Seeing her like that, a memory clicked into place. She'd once stood before him exactly like this, telling him about the cage. Whoever was inside had to do exactly as the owner commanded.

Even kill yourself? he'd asked.

Yes, she'd answered.

It was so simple, really. Scowling, she lunged at him. Careful not to hurt her, hopeful for the first time in days, he knocked the blade from her hand and grabbed her, flashing into the cage, then flashing himself out before she knew what was going on.

She screamed at him as he locked the door. "I'll kill you for this! What kind of sadistic mind game are you playing?" Her gaze snagged on his tattoo, which was pulsing black and red. She blinked as though mesmerized, lost some of her fury. "Pretty."

Maybe she was remembering. Hope intensifying, he gripped the bars and stared at her. "Sit down, Anya."

She fell on her ass and glared at him, resentment back in her eyes. It was working. She opened her mouth to yell, but he said, "Be silent, Anya."

Her lips pressed together. The resentment became utter fury. If this failed…

"Remember me, Anya. Remember our time together. I command you to remember."

Her eyelids squeezed shut, and she gasped. Her features contorted, as if in pain. She fell to her back and curled into a ball, clutching at her temples.

"Anya!" he shouted, concerned, swinging open the door and crouching beside her.

A long while passed as she writhed, moaned and cursed, clawing at her head. He held her, muttering soothing words, hating himself. *What have I done to her?* The woman had given up everything for him.

Finally, though, she stilled. A fine glaze of sweat slicked her skin. Shadows had formed half-moons under her eyes.

"I'm so sorry, sweetheart. I'll let you go, but don't expect me to forget you. We're bonded. I'll be on your trail, doing everything in my power to win and romance you. So prepare to see a lot of me. I love you too much to let you go."

"Like I'd ever allow you to let me go. You're mine. I love you, too, Flowers." Her dark lashes swept up, her eyes suddenly shining with love. "Gods, I'm so glad that you're alive."

Such astounding happiness skipped through him, he was shaking as he crushed her against his chest. "Anya, sweet Anya."

"I love you so much," she said.

He buried his head in her neck, inhaling her strawberry scent. "Thank the gods, Anya. I was dying inside every time you looked at me as if I were a stranger."

She kissed and nipped at his face, her hands tangling into his hair. "I thought I'd lost you."

"You gave up everything for me."

"Well, that's because you're the most important thing in my life."

He squeezed her tightly and flashed onto the bed with her still in his arms. Somehow, some way, he would find a way to restore her powers. Maybe putting her back inside the cage and commanding her to regain them would work. If not... "I'll spend the rest of my life making it up to you."

Grinning, she wound her legs around his waist. "That was always my plan. Now, catch me up on what's been happening."

He, too, grinned. Never, in all of his life, had he been so happy. He told her what he knew about his friends. "William escaped the mountain and has healed. He followed us here and wants his book. I have not allowed him inside the fortress, but he calls me every day."

Her eyes narrowed. "Oh, I'll give him the book, as promised. Later. I might rip out a few pages first, but accidents happen."

"He has apologized countless times and his sorrow seems genuine. Mostly, I just want him gone, and he won't leave until he speaks with you."

"Later. Right now, you're going to make love to me."

Lucien's grin widened as he slowly stripped her, savoring the sight of her luscious curves and creamy skin. "You're going to wed me, yes?"

"Oh, yes."

"Good. I know the perfect spot for our honeymoon."

"The paradise where you almost died?" Her hands worked desperately at his clothing.

"No. Paradise is right here." He slid two fingers deep inside her.

Moaning, she arched her hips into him. "Then where?"

"There are three more artifacts to find. Most of the warriors are out searching for them. Except for Reyes, who went in search of Aeron and Danika." In and out he pumped. "Are you up for another treasure hunt?"

"Always." She rolled him over and impaled herself on his shaft. Both of them groaned at the heady pleasure. "But I've already found the only treasure I'll ever need. And speaking of treasures, what are we going to do with the cage?"

"Keep it. Now that you remember me, there are a few things I'd like to do to you inside it."

"Mmm, me like. And maybe later we can try and help my dad regain *his* memory. He and my mom deserve a little happiness after all they've endured."

"A noble idea."

"Enough talking. I believe you had some plans for me…."

He was grinning happily as he worked them both over the edge.

* * * * *

In July 2008,
Gena Showalter continues
The Lords of the Underworld
with...

THE DARKEST PLEASURE

The story of Reyes,
Keeper of Pain.

Turn the page
for your sneak preview!

DANIKA FORD HAD BEEN COLD for so long that the blazing-hot blanket draped over her shocked her out of the death-sleep. Her eyelids popped open, and a gasp shoved past her lips. Remnants of her nightmare refused to fade, however, preventing her from seeing what surrounded her. She saw only a darkness slashed with crimson, the night bleeding from lethal wounds. She heard swords clanking, demons laughing evilly, and the whoosh of heads as they rolled.

Death, death, her every breath proclaimed.

Calm down, just calm down. This isn't real. You know better.

The dreams were not premonitions of the future, for they never came true. Until Reyes and his friends had entered her life, that is.

Most of Danika's dreams were turbulent—screams and fatality infused in every macabre scene. All her life, that's how it had been. Used to be, she would awaken from those painful nights and paint what she'd seen in an attempt to suck the madness from her subconscious—and keep it out.

On the opposite side of the spectrum, her dreams were sometimes utter serenity. Angels, their wings spread in white-feathered glory, would float through the bright azure skies. Their beauty always amazed her, and she would awaken smiling and full of verve rather than sweating and trembling.

Like now.

"I'm here, angel, I'm here."

That deep, rich voice belonged in her nightmares *and* those angelic glimpses, both heaven and hell rolled into one mesmerizing seduction. As she lay there, the nightmare quieted and the darkness faded, light pushing its way into her mind.

A bedroom came into view, but it wasn't the one she remembered falling asleep in. Weapons adorned the walls, from throwing stars to swords to daggers. Even axes. There was a polished vanity, but no chair. The owner didn't sit there? Didn't study his reflection to brush his hair?

His? *How do you know this room belongs to a man?*

In and out she breathed, the familiar scent of sandalwood and pine filling her nose. Oh, she knew. A man, definitely, and one in particular. The knowledge rocked her. *Maybe you're wrong.*

The bed was swathed in black cotton; Danika was draped by a half-clothed man. He possessed skin of chocolate and honey, taut muscle and ripped sinew. No hair marred his chest, but there was a menacing butterfly tattoo that stretched from one shoulder to the other and up his neck. *Menacing butterfly*—two words that could be used together to describe only one man.

Reyes.

"Oh, God." She bolted upright, dislodging him. Panting, she scrambled to the edge of the mattress, never turning her back to him.

Slowly Reyes sat up.

Their eyes met in a heated clash, his as dark as his skin. Turbulent. His lips pulled in a tight frown. Three wounds were healing, one scabbed on his shoulder, one on his sternum and one on his stomach.

"Where am I?" she asked, the words a mere whisper.

"My home."

"In Budapest?"

"Yes."

Her eyelids narrowed. "How did I get here? How did you find me?"

He looked away, hiding his gaze under his lashes. "You know I am not human. Don't you?"

Knowledge she wished she didn't possess and a conversation it was best not to pursue. *Why, yes, Reyes, I do know you're a demon. Your greatest enemy told me and now I'm here to destroy you.* "You came for me," she said, changing the subject. Part of her had hoped for just such a thing; part of her had feared it.

"Yes," he repeated.

"Why?" Without the heat of his gaze holding her captive, she was able to scan her own body. She was still clothed, thank God. Her sweater had been removed, but her white T-shirt was still stained with grease and now blood, her jeans ripped from her struggle with her assailant.

Suddenly the bed bounced, and her eyes jerked back to Reyes. He had propped his back against the headboard, widening the distance between them. That should have pleased her. Yes, it should have.

"I have a feeling I will always come for you." His angry voice whipped through the silence, his accusing expression laying the blame at her feet.

Once again her eyelids narrowed to tiny slits. "Let me guess. You'll always come for me because you like hurting me. Well, why didn't you kill me while I slept? I wouldn't have been able to fight. You could have cut my throat, quick, easy. That *is* what you ultimately plan to do, isn't it? Or have you changed your mind?"

A muscle ticked in his jaw. He remained silent.

"Have you captured the rest of my family?"

Again, no reply. Only that increasingly erratic tick.

"Answer me, damn you!" She slammed her fist into the mattress. The panicked action offered no relief from the sudden horror blooming in her chest. "Do you know where they are? If they're alive?"

Finally he deigned to speak again. "I have done nothing to them. You have my word."

"Liar!" She'd sprung across the bed before she even realized what she was doing, slapping his face, pounding her fists into his wounds to cause maximum pain. "You know something. You have to know something."

His eyes closed and a blissful smile lifted the corners of his lips.

Her fury intensified. "You think this is funny? Well, what about this?" Seething, not knowing where the desire to do this came from, she launched forward and sank her teeth into his neck, incisors digging so deep she immediately tasted blood.

He moaned. His hands tangled in her hair, not jerking her away but urging her closer. She offered no resistance; she couldn't. Embers of her anger and helplessness were twisting, breaking apart and realigning into something infinitely sweeter. The heat of him…so good, so damn good. He burned her soul-deep, flames licking at her, consuming her. She liked it, liked hurting him, liked having her mouth on him, and the knowledge shamed her.

"Stop, Danika. You have to stop."

No, she didn't want to stop. She wanted—*what the hell are you doing? Nibbling on the enemy?*

Her jaw went slack. Gasping for breath, she jolted backward. His arms fell to his sides, his features hard, tight. She wiped her mouth with the back of a shaky wrist.

Monster, she reminded herself. *He's a monster.*

Horror—at her feelings, her actions, and his—washed through her. Must have coasted over her expression, too, because he said, "Do not touch me again, and I will not touch you."

A violent tremor overtook her, and she crossed her arms over her middle. She'd wanted to hurt him, had *liked* it even. *Seriously, what the hell is wrong with me?* "Go to hell."

He sighed. "Didn't we once have this very conversation? I'm already there…"

Lords of the Underworld
Glossary of Characters and Terms

Aeron—Keeper of Wrath

All-Seeing Eye—Godly artifact with the power to see into heaven and hell

Amun—Keeper of Secrets

Anya—(Minor) Goddess of Anarchy

Ashlyn Darrow—Human female with supernatural ability

Baden—Keeper of Distrust (deceased)

Cage of Compulsion—Godly artifact with the power to enslave anyone trapped inside

Cameo—Keeper of Misery; only female warrior

Cloak of Invisibility—Godly artifact with the power to shield its wearer from prying eyes

Cronus—King of the Titans

Danika Ford—Human female, target of the Titans

Dean Stefano—Hunter; right-hand man of Galen

dimOuniak—Pandora's box

Dr. Frederick McIntosh—Vice President of the World Institute of Parapsychology

Dysnomia—Greek, Goddess of Lawlessness

Galen—Keeper of Hope

Gideon—Keeper of Lies

Gilly—Human female, friend of Danika

Ginger Ford—Sister of Danika

Greeks—Former rulers of Olympus, now imprisoned in Tartarus

Hera—Queen of the Greeks

Hunters—Mortal enemies of the Lords of the Underworld

Hydra—Multiheaded serpent with poisonous fangs

Kane—Keeper of Disaster

Legion—Demon minion, friend of Aeron

Lords of the Underworld—Exiled warriors to the Greek gods; now house demons inside them

Lucien—Keeper of Death; leader of the Budapest warriors

Maddox—Keeper of Violence

Mallory Ford—Grandmother of Danika

Pandora—Immortal warrior, once guardian of *dimOuniak* (deceased)

Paring Rod—Godly artifact, power unknown

Paris—Keeper of Promiscuity

Reyes—Keeper of Pain

Sabin—Keeper of Doubt; leader of the Greek warriors

Sienna Blackstone—Female Hunter

Strider—Keeper of Defeat

Tartarus—Greek, God of Confinement; also the immortal prison on Mount Olympus

Themis—Titan, Goddess of Justice

Tinka Ford—Mother of Danika

Titans—Current rulers of Olympus

Torin—Keeper of Disease

William—Immortal, friend of Anya

Zeus—King of the Greeks

REQUEST YOUR
FREE BOOKS!

2 FREE NOVELS
FROM THE ROMANCE/SUSPENSE
COLLECTION PLUS 2 FREE GIFTS!

YES! Please send me 2 FREE novels from the Romance/Suspense Collection and my 2 FREE gifts (gifts are worth about $10). After receiving them, if I don't wish to receive any more books, I can return the shipping statement marked "cancel." If I don't cancel, I will receive 4 brand-new novels every month and be billed just $5.49 per book in the U.S. or $5.99 per book in Canada, plus 25¢ shipping and handling per book plus applicable taxes, if any*. That's a savings of at least 20% off the cover price! I understand that accepting the 2 free books and gifts places me under no obligation to buy anything. I can always return a shipment and cancel at any time. Even if I never buy another book from the Reader Service, the two free books and gifts are mine to keep forever.

185 MDN EF5Y 385 MDN EF6C

Name _____ (PLEASE PRINT) _____

Address _____ Apt. # _____

City _____ State/Prov. _____ Zip/Postal Code _____

Signature (if under 18, a parent or guardian must sign) _____

Mail to **The Reader Service:**
IN U.S.A.: P.O. Box 1867, Buffalo, NY 14240-1867
IN CANADA: P.O. Box 609, Fort Erie, Ontario L2A 5X3

Not valid to current subscribers to the Romance Collection,
the Suspense Collection or the Romance/Suspense Collection.

Want to try two free books from another line?
Call 1-800-873-8635 or visit www.morefreebooks.com.

* Terms and prices subject to change without notice. N.Y. residents add applicable sales tax. Canadian residents will be charged applicable provincial taxes and GST. Offer not valid in Quebec. This offer is limited to one order per household. All orders subject to approval. Credit or debit balances in a customer's account(s) may be offset by any other outstanding balance owed by or to the customer. Please allow 4 to 6 weeks for delivery. Offer available while quantities last.

Your Privacy: Harlequin is committed to protecting your privacy. Our Privacy Policy is available online at www.eHarlequin.com or upon request from the Reader Service. From time to time we make our lists of customers available to reputable third parties who may have a product or service of interest to you. If you would prefer we not share your name and address, please check here. ☐

BOB08R